ETERNITY

'Bear goes beyond the petty accelerations of the future which inspire lesser SF writers, and takes huge, intuitive and intelligent leaps . . . The mystery of an Isaac Asimov space saga together with the plausibility of Arthur C. Clarke. Bear is the face of science fiction for the nineties' *Fear Magazine*

ETERNITY

Greg Bear

First published in Legend 1990

9 10

© by Greg Bear

The right of Greg Bear to be identified as the author
of this work has been asserted by him in accordance
with the Copyright, Designs and Patents Act, 1988

First published in Great Britain by Victor Gollancz Ltd 1989

Legend Books
Random House, 20 Vauxhall Bridge Road, London SW1V 2SA

Random House Australia (Pty) Limited
20 Alfred Street, Milsons Point, Sydney,
New South Wales 2061, Australia

Random House New Zealand Limited
18 Poland Road, Glenfield
Auckland 10, New Zealand

Random House South Africa (Pty) Limited
PO Box 337, Bergvlei, South Africa

Random House UK Limited Reg. No. 954009

A CIP catalogue record for this book
is available from the British Library

Papers used by Random House UK Limited
are natural, recyclable products made from wood grown in
sustainable forests. The manufacturing processes conform to
the environmental regulations of the country of origin

ISBN 0 09 970630 X

Printed and bound in Great Britain by
Cox & Wyman Ltd, Reading, Berkshire

For David McClintock;
friend, fellow admirer of Olaf Stapledon,
and above all, *bookseller*.

Only when space is rolled up like a piece of leather
will there be an end to suffering, apart from knowing
God.

– **Śvetāśvatara Upaniṣad**, VI 20

ETERNITY

In the end, there is cruelty and death alone over the land. Not in a single ray of light or grain of sand will you find solace, for all is dark, and the cold gaze of God's indifferent, heavy-lidded eyes falls on all with equal disdain. Only in your inner strength is there salvation; you must live just as a tree must live, or the cockroaches and fleas that flourish in the land and ruin of Earth. And so you live, and feel the sting of knowing you live. You eat whatever comes to hand, and if what you eat was once a brother or sister, so be it; God does not care. Nobody cares. You whore, and if you whore with man or woman, nobody cares; for when all are hungry, all are whores, even those who use the whores. And disease flourishes when all are whores, for germs must live, and spread across the land and ruin of Earth.

Some say we will climb back to the sky on our own. Some say we all should have died; should have died, for penance. But that was not to be. For by time's freak and history's whim, the angels come from the Stone, to march over the land and offer what solace the land cannot; to push back the clouds and smoke and let sun pass through, to sow our crops and harvest our food, then to pass the plows on to us. You marvel at this, and do not curse the angels in the madness of your guilt; for they are a glory like a dream, and you do not truly believe.

They minister to your disease, and in time you join them to minister unto others. Medicine becomes religion; help the sole commandment; healing the greatest gift to God on can imagine.

They bring miracles from out of the Stone. They stay among us, but are not for us, and a few grumble, but the few are ignored as the chaff is ignored. What the few grumble about is division and dissatisfaction, for we are never happy. And never content, and never satisfied. But the angels do not listen.

And then from the Bible Lands and points east, from the Lands of the Book and out of the People of the Book comes rebellion. For their lands have not been scorched and they can still find strength in the soil, and they are ingenious and know the Law of Tree and Flea. Because they are Chosen of God, they fight these angels who are not angels, but devils to them; they fight and they are subdued by miracles and made pacific. And the People of the Book sleep the sleep of the pacific, building and working but not fighting. So it is in the land where humankind first opened its eyes.

And then in the land sunk in evil at the tip of the Heart of Darkness, like white dregs in a black bottle, from this land comes speakers of Afrikaans and English in their fine uniforms, driving ahead of them their slave armies, to despoil all the untouched Southern Lands of the Earth. They fight and they are subdued by miracles and made pacific, in their way. And they sleep the sleep of the pacific, building and working and not fighting. So it is at the bottom of the amphora of Africa.

Light and learning begin again above the soil, for strength returns to the soil, and to the flesh. All this we owe to the angels. And if they are only men, only our own children come back clothed in light, what is that to our gladness and gratitude?

They lift us from the Law of Tree and Flea, and make us human again.

– **Gershom Raphael**,
The Book of the Death, Sura 4, Book 1.

1

Recovered Earth, Independent Territory of New Zealand, A.D. 2046

The New Murchison Station cemetery held only thirty graves. Flat grassland surrounded the fenced-in plot, and around and through the grassland a narrow runoff creek curled protectively, its low washing whisper steady above the cool dry wind. The wind made the blades of grass hiss and shiver. Snow-ribboned mountains shawled in gray cloud glowered over the plain. The sun was an hour above the Two Thumb Range to the east, its light bright but not warm. Despite the wind, Garry Lanier was sweating.

He helped shoulder the coffin through the leaning white picket fence to the new-dug grave, marked by a casually lumpy mound of black earth, his face a mask to hide the effort and the sharp twinges of pain.

Six friends served as pallbearers. The coffin was only a finely shaped and precisely planed pine box, but Lawrence Heineman had weighed a good ninety kilos when he died. The widow, Lenore Carrolson, followed two steps behind, face lifted, puzzled eyes staring at something just above the end of the coffin. Her once gray-blond hair was now silver-white.

Larry had looked much younger than Lenore, who seemed frail and phantasmal now in her ninetieth year. He had been given a new body after his heart attack, thirty-four years before; it was not age or disease that had killed him, but a rockfall at a campsite in the mountains twenty kilometers away.

They laid him in the earth and the pallbearers pulled

away the thick black ropes. The coffin leaned and creaked in the dirt. Lanier imagined Heineman was finding his grave an uneasy bed, and then dismissed this artless fancy; it was not good to reshape death.

A priest of the New Church of Rome spoke Latin over the grave. Lanier was the first to drop a spade of damp-smelling dirt into the hole. Ashes to ashes. *The ground is wet here. The coffin will rot.*

Lanier rubbed his shoulder as he stood with Karen, his wife of almost four decades. Her eyes darted around the faces of their distant neighbors, searching for something to ease her own sense of displacement. Lanier tried to look at the mourners with her eyes and found only sadness and a nervous humility. He touched her elbow but she was having none of his reassurances. Karen felt as if she didn't belong. She loved Lenore Carrolson like a mother, and yet they hadn't talked in two years.

Up there, in the sky, among the orbiting precincts, the Hexamon conducted its business, yet had sent no representative from those august heavenly bodies; and indeed, considering how Larry had come to feel about the Hexamon, that gesture would have been inappropriate.

How things had changed . . .

Divisions. Separations. Disasters. Not all the work they had done in the Recovery could wipe away these differences. They had had such expectations for the Recovery. Karen still had high hopes, still worked on her various projects. Those around her did not share many of her hopes.

She was still of the Faith, believing in the future, in the Hexamon's efforts.

Lanier had lost the Faith twenty years ago.

Now they laid a significant part of their past in the damp Earth, with no hope of a second resurrection. Heineman had not expected to die by accident, but he had chosen this death nonetheless. Lanier had made a similar choice. Someday, he knew, the earth would

2

absorb him, too, and that still seemed proper, though not without its terror. He would die. No second chances. He – and Heineman, and Lenore – had accepted the opportunities offered by the Hexamon up to a certain point, and then had demurred.

Karen had not demurred. If it had been her under the rock slide, rather than Larry, she would not be dead now; stored in her implant, she would await her due resurrection, in a body newly grown for her on one of the precincts, and brought to Earth. She would soon be as young or younger than she was now. And as the years passed, she would not grow any older than she wished, nor would her body change in any but accepted ways. That set her apart from these people. It set her apart from her husband.

Like Karen, their daughter Andia had carried an implant, and Lanier had not protested, something that had shamed him a little at the time; but watching her grow and change had been an extraordinary enough experience, and he realised he was far readier to accept his death than this beautiful child's. He had not overruled Karen's plans, and the Hexamon had come down to bless the child of one of their faithful servants, to give his own daughter a gift he did not himself accept because it was not (could not be) made available to all the Old Natives of Earth.

Then, irony had stepped in and left a permanent mark on their lives. Twenty years ago, Andia's airplane had crashed in the eastern Pacific and she had never been found. Their daughter's chances for a return to life lay in the silt at the bottom of some vast deep, a tiny marble, untraceable even with Hexamon technology.

The tears in his eyes were not for Larry. He wiped them and drew his face into stiff formality to greet the priest, a pious young hypocrite Lanier had never liked. 'Good wine comes in strange glass,' Larry had once said.

He came into a wisdom I envy.

In the first flush of wonder, working with the Hex-

3

amon, all had been dazzled; Heineman had after all accepted his second body gladly enough, and Lenore had accepted youth treatments to keep up with her husband. She had later dropped the treatments, but now she seemed no more than a well-preserved seventy . . .

Most Old Natives did not have access to implants; even the Terrestrial Hexamon could not supply everybody on Earth with the necessary devices; and if they could have, Earth cultures were not ready for even proximate immortality.

Lanier had resisted implants, yet accepted Hexamon medicine; he did not know to this day whether or not that had been hypocrisy. Such medicine had been made available to most but not all Old Natives, scattered around a ruined Earth; the Hexamon had stretched its resources to accomplish that much.

He had rationalised that to do the work he was doing, he needed to be healthy and fit, and to be healthy and fit while doing that work – going into the deadlands, living amidst death and disease and radiation – he needed the privilege of the Hexamon's medicine.

Lanier could read Karen's reaction. Such a waste. All these people, dropping out, giving up. She thought they were behaving irresponsibly. Perhaps they were, but they – like himself, and like Karen – had given much of their lives to the Recovery and to the Faith. They had earned their beliefs, however irresponsible in her eyes.

The debt they all owed to the orbiting precincts was incalculable. But love and loyalty could not be earned by indebtedness.

Lanier followed the mourners to the tiny church a few hundred meters away. Karen stayed behind, near the graves. She was weeping, but he could not go to comfort her.

He shook his head once, sharply, and glanced up at the sky.

No one had thought it would ever be this way.

He still could hardly believe it himself.

In the single-story meeting room of the church, while three younger women set out sandwiches and punch, Lanier waited for his wife to join the wake. Groups of two or three gathered in the room, ill at ease, to step forward as one and pay their respects to the widow, who took it all with a distant smile.

She lost her first family in the Death, he remembered. She and Larry, after their retirement from the Recovery ten years ago, had behaved like youngsters, hiking around South Island, taking up various hobbies, occasionally going to Australia for extended walka-bouts, once even sailing to Borneo. They had been or had seemed carefree, and Lanier envied them that.

'Your wife takes this hard,' a red-faced young man named Fremont said, approaching Lanier alone. Fre-mont ran the reopened Irishman Creek Station; his half-wild merinos sometimes spread all the way to Twizel, and he was not considered the best of citizens. His station mark was an encircled kea, odd for a man who made is living from sheep, still, he had once been reputed to say, 'I'm no less independent than my sheep. I go where I will, and so do they.'

'We all loved him,' Lanier said. Why he should sud-denly open up to this red-faced half-stranger, he did not know, but with his eye on the door, waiting for Karen, his mouth said, 'He was a smart man. Simple, though. He knew his limits. I . . .'

Fremont cocked a bushy eyebrow.

'We were on the Stone together,' Lanier said.

'So I've heard. You were all confused with the angels.'

Lanier shook his head. 'He hated that.'

'He did good work here and all over,' Fremont said. *Everybody's decent at a funeral.* Karen came in through the door. Fremont, who could not have been more than thirty-five, glanced in her direction and then turned back to Lanier, speculation in his eyes. Lanier compared himself with this young and vigorous man: his own

5

hair was solid gray, hands large and brown and gnarled, body slightly bent.

Karen seemed no older than Fremont.

2

Terrestrial Hexamon, Earth Orbit, Axis Euclid

'Let's *talk*,' Suli Ram Kikura suggested, turning off her collar pictor and folding up in a chair behind Olmy. He stood by her apartment window – a real window, looking through the Axis Euclid's interior wall at the cylindrical space that had once surrounded the Way's central singularity. Now it revealed swimming aeronauts with gauzy, bat-like wings, floating amusement parks, citizens tracting on causeways formed by faint purple fields – and a small arc of darkness to the left, near-Earth space visible beyond the interior wall.

The colors and activity reminded him of a French painting from the early twentieth century, a park scene suddenly bereft of gravity, strolling couples and children of orthodox Naderites scattered crazily every which way. The view changed constantly as the axis's body rotated around the hollow at its center, a streaming display of Hexamon life and society, of which Olmy no longer seemed a part.

'I'm listening,' he said, though he did not look at her.

'You haven't visited Tapi in months.' Tapi was their son, created from their mixed mysteries in Euclid's city memory. Such conception had only returned to favor the past ten years; before that, when orthodox Naderites had dominated Euclid's precinct government, natural births and *ex utero* births had been the order of the day, and the hell with centuries of Hexamon tradition. Hence, the children playing in the Flaw Park beyond Ram Kikura's window.

Olmy blinked, guilty about avoiding his son. The

point was always quickly reached with Suli Ram Kikura. 'He's doing fine.'

'He needs us both. A partial on demand is no replacement for a father. He's up for his incorporation tests in a few months and he needs – '

'Yes, yes.' Olmy almost wished they had never had Tapi. The weight of responsibility now, with his researches also heavy on him, was too much. He simply did not have time.

'I don't know whether to be mad at you or not,' she said. 'You're facing something difficult. I suppose a few years ago I could have guessed what it is . . .' Her voice was rich and even, well-controlled, but she could not hide concern mixed with irritation at his quiet obtuseness. 'I value you enough to ask what's bothering you.'

Value. They had been primary lovers for more decades than he cared to count. (*seventy-four years*, his implant memory stores reminded him, unbidden), and they had lived through – and taken part in – some of the Hexamon's most turbulent and spectacular history. He had never seriously courted any woman but Ram Kikura; he had always known that wherever he went, whomever else he established a brief liaison with, he would always return to her. She was his match – a homorph, neither Naderite nor Geshel in her politics, lifelong advocate, one-time senior corprep for Earth in the Nexus, champion of the unfortunate, the ignored and the ignorant. With no other would he have made a Tapi.

'I've been studying. That's all.'

'Yes, but you won't tell me what you've been studying. Whatever it is, it's changing you.'

'I'm just looking ahead.'

'You don't know something I'm not privy to, do you? Coming out of retirement? The trip to Earth – '.

He said nothing and she pulled back, lips tightly pressed together. 'All right. Something secret. Something to do with the re-opening.'

'Nobody seriously plans that,' Olmy said, an edge

8

of petulance in his voice unseemly in a man over five centuries old. Only Ram Kikura could get through his armor and provoke such a response.

'Not even Korzenowski agrees with you.'

'With me? I've never said I support re-opening.'

'It is *absurd*,' she said. Now they had both probed beneath armor. 'Whatever our problems, or shortages, to abandon the Earth – '

'That's even less likely,' he said softly.

'– And re-open the Way. . . . That goes against everything we've worked for the past forty years.'

'I've never said I wanted it,' he reiterated.

Her look of scorn was a shock to him. Never had their distance been so great that either could have felt intellectual contempt for the other. Their relationship had always been a mix of passion and dignity, even in the years of their worst dispute . . . which this showed signs of equaling or surpassing, though he refused to admit disagreement.

'Nobody *wants* it, but it sure would be exciting, wouldn't it? To be gainfully employed again, to have a mission, to return to our youth and years of greatest power. To open commerce with the Talsit again. Such wonders in store!'

Olmy lifted one shoulder slightly, a bare admission that there was some truth in what she said.

'Our job here isn't finished. We have our entire history to reclaim. Surely that's labor enough.'

'I've never known our kind to be moderate,' Olmy said.

'You feel the call of duty, don't you? You're preparing for what you *think* will happen.' Suli Ram Kikura uncurled and stood, taking him by the arm more in anger than affection. 'Have we never truly thought alike? Has our love always been just an attraction of opposites? You opposed me on the Old Natives' rights to individuality–'

'Anything else would have damaged the Recovery.' Her bringing the subject up after thirty-eight years, and his quick response, showed clearly that the embers of that dispute had not died.

'We agreed to differ,' she said, facing him.

As Earth's advocate in the years after the Sundering and in the early stages of the Recovery, Ram Kikura had opposed Hexamon efforts to use Talsit and other mental therapies on Old Natives. She had cited contemporary Terrestrial law and taken the issue to the Hexamon courts, arguing that Old Natives had the right to avoid mental health checkups and corrective therapy.

Eventually, her court challenge had been denied under special Recovery Act legislation.

That had been resolved thirty-eight years before. Now, approximately forty percent of Earth's survivors received one or another kind of therapy. The campaign to administer treatment had been masterful. Sometimes it had overstepped its bounds, but it had worked. Mental illness and dysfunction were virtually eradicated.

Ram Kikura had gone on to other issues, other problems. They had stayed lovers, but their relationship had been strained from that point on.

The umbilicus between them was very tough. Disagreements alone – even this – would not cut it. Ram Kikura could not, and in any event would not cry or show the weaknesses of an Old Native, and Olmy had given up those abilities centuries ago. Her face was sufficiently evocative without tears; he could read the special character of a Hexamon citizen there, emotions withheld but somehow communicated, sadness and loss foremost.

'You've changed during the past four years,' she said. 'I can't define it . . . but whatever you're doing, however you're preparing, it diminishes the part of you that I love.'

His eyes narrowed.

'You won't talk about it. Not even with me.'

He shook his head slowly, feeling just another degree of withering inside, another degree of withdrawal.

'Where is *my* Olmy?' Ram Kikura asked softly. 'What have you done with him?'

'Ser Olmy! Your return is most welcome. How was your journey?' President Kies Farren Siliom stood on a broad transparent platform, the wide orb of the Earth coming into view beneath him as Axis Euclid rotated. Five hundred square meters of stressed and ion-anchored glass and two layers of traction field lay between the president's conference chamber and open space; he seemed to stand on a stretch of open nothingness.

Farren Siliom's dress – white African cotton pants and a tufted black sleeveless shirt of Thistledown altered linen – emphasised his responsibility for two worlds: Recovered Earth, the Eastern hemishphere of which rolled into morning beneath their feet, and the orbiting bodies: Axis Euclid and Thoreau and the asteroid starship Thistledown.

Olmy stood to one side of the apparent void in the outer shell of the precinct. The Earth passed out of view. He picted formal greetings to Farren Siliom, then said aloud, 'My trip was smooth, Ser President.'

He had waited patiently for three days to be admitted, using the time for the awkward visit to Suli Ram Kikura. Countless times before, he had waited on presiding ministers and lesser officials, fully aware, as centuries passed, that he had developed the old soldier's attitude of superiority over his masters, of respectful condescension to the hierarchy.

'And your son?'

'I haven't seen him in some time, Ser President. I understand he is doing well.'

'A whole crop of children coming up for their incorporation exams soon,' Farren Siliom said. 'They'll be needing bodies and occupations, all of them, if they pass as easily as I'm sure your son will. More strain on limited resources.'

'Yes, Ser.'

I've invited two of my associates to attend part of

your briefing,' the president said, hands folded behind his back.

Two assigned ghosts – projected partial personalities, acting with temporary independence from their originals – appeared a few meters to one side of the president. Olmy recognised one of them, the leader of the neo-Geshels in Axis Euclid, Tobert Tomson Tikk, one of Euclid's thirty senators in the Nexus. Olmy had investigated Tikk at the start of his mission, though he had not met with the senator personally. The image of Tikk's partial looked slightly more handsome and muscled than his original, an ostentation gaining favor among the more radical Nexus politicians.

The presence of projected partials was both old and new. For thirty years after the Sundering, the separation of Thistledown from the Way, orthodox Naderites had controlled the Hexamon and such technological displays had been relegated to situations of extreme necessity. Now the use of partials was commonplace; a neo-Geshel such as Tikk would not be averse to casually scattering his image and personality patterns about the Hexamon.

'Ser Olmy is acquainted with Senator Tikk. I don't believe you've met Senator Ras Mishiney, senator for the territory of Greater Australia and New Zealand. He's in Melbourne at this moment.'

'Pardon the time delay, Ser Olmy,' Mishiney said.

'No fear,' Olmy said. The audience was purely a formality, since most of Olmy's report was contained on record in detailed picts and graphics; but even so, he had not expected Farren Siliom to invite witnesses. It was a wise leader who knew when to admit his adversary – or adversaries – into high functions; Olmy knew little about Mishiney.

'Let me apologise again for disturbing your well-deserved retirement.' Earthlight flooded the president. As the precinct rotated, the Earth again seemed to pass below them. 'You've served this office for centuries. I thought it best to rely on someone with your experience and perspective. What we're dealing with here, of course, are largely historical problems and trends . . .'

'Problems of cultures, perhaps,' Tikk interposed. Olmy thought it brash for a partial to interrupt the president; but then, that was neo-Geshel style.

'I assume these honorables know the task you set for me,' Olmy said, nodding at the ghosts. *But not the whole task.*

The president picted assent. The moon slipped beneath them, a tiny bright platinum crescent. They all stood near the center of the platform now, the partials' images flickering slightly to indicate their nature. 'I hope this assignment was less strenuous than the ones you're famous for.'

'Not strenuous at all, Ser President. I've been afraid of losing touch with the details of the Hexamon–' *or indeed the human race*, he thought, '–living so calmly and peacefully.'

The president smiled. Even for Olmy, it was hard to imagine an old warhorse like himself living a life of studious leisure.

'I sent Ser Olmy on a mission around the Recovered Earth to provide an independent view of our relations. This seemed necessary in light of the four recent assassination attempts on Hexamon officials and Terrestrial leaders. We in the Hexamon are not used to such . . . extreme attitudes.

'They might be the last vestiges of Earth's political past, or they might indicate breaking strains we are not aware of – reflections of our own "belt-tightening" in the orbiting precincts.

'I asked him to bring me an overview on how the Recovery was proceeding. Some believe it is finished, and so our Hexamon has designated the Earth itself "Recovered," past tense, job accomplished. I am not convinced. How much time and effort will be necessary to truly bring the Earth back to health?'

'The recovery goes as well as could be expected, Ser President.' Olmy consciously altered his speaking and picting style. 'As the senator from Australia and New Zealand is aware, even the Hexamon's vast technologies cannot make up for a lack of resources, not when you wish to accomplish such a transformation in mere decades. There is a natural time required for Earth's wounds to heal, and we cannot accelerate that by much. I estimate that about half the task has been accomplished, if we say that full recovery is a return to economic conditions comparable to those preceding the Death.'

'Doesn't that depend on how ambitious we are on Earth?' Ras Mishiney asked. 'If we wish to bring Terrestrials to a level comparable with the precincts or Thistledown . . .' He did not finish his sentence; it was hardly necessary.

'That could take a century or more,' Olmy said. 'There's no universal agreement that Old Natives want such rapid advancement. Some would doubtless openly resist it.'

'How stable are our relations with Earth just now?' the president asked him.

'They could be much improved, Ser. There are still areas of strong, overt political resistance, Southern Africa and Malaysia among them.'

Ras Mishiney smiled ironically. Southern Africa's attempted invasion of Australia was still a sore memory, one of the greatest crises in the four decades of the Recovery.

'But the resistance is strictly political, not military, and it's not very organised. Southern Africa is subdued after the Voortrekker defeats, and Malaysia's activities are unorganised. They do not seem worrisome at the moment.'

'Our little "sanity plagues" have done their job?'

Olmy was taken aback. The use of psychobiologicals on Earth was supposed to be highly confidential; only a few of the most trusted Old Natives knew of them. Was Ras Mishiney one such? Did Farren Siliom trust Tikk so much that he could mention them casually?

14

'Yes, Ser.'

'Yet you've had qualms about these mass treatments?'

'I've always recognised their necessity.'

'No doubts whatsoever?'

Olmy felt as if he were being toyed with. It was not a sensation he enjoyed. 'If you're referring to the opposition of Earth's former advocate, Suli Ram Kikura . . . we do not necessarily share political beliefs even when we share beds, Ser President.'

'These are past matters now. Forgive my interruption. Please continue, Ser Olmy.'

'There's still a strong undercurrent of tension between most Old Natives and the ruling parties of the orbiting bodies.'

'That's a painful puzzle to me,' Farren Siliom said.

'I'm not sure it can be surmounted. They resent us in so many ways. We robbed them of their youth–'

'We pulled them up from the Death!' the president said sharply. Ras Mishiney's assigned ghost gave a faint smile.

'We've prevented them from growing and recovering on their own, Ser. The Terrestrial Hexamon that built and launched Thistledown rose from just such misery, independently; some Old Natives feel perhaps we've helped too much, and imposed our ways upon them.'

Farren Siliom picted grudging agreement. Olmy had noticed a hardening of attitude against Old Natives among Hexamon administrators in the orbiting bodies the past decade. And the Old Natives, being what they were – many still rough and uneducated, still shocked by the Death, without the political and managerial sophistication earned through centuries of experience in the Way – had grown to resent the firm but gentle hand of their powerful descendants.

'The Terrestrial Senate is quiet and cooperative,' Olmy said, avoiding Ras Mishiney's eyes. 'The worst dissatisfactions, outside those already mentioned, seemed to be in China and Southeast Asia.'

'Where science and technology first rose after the

15

Death, in our own history . . . willful and strong peoples. How resentful are the Old Natives overall?'

'Certainly not to the point of worldwide activism, Ser President. Consider it a prejudice, not a rage.'

'What about Gerald Brooks in England?'

'I met with him, Ser. He is not a threat.'

'He worries me. He has quite a following in Europe.'

'At most two thousand in a recovered population of ten million. He's vocal but not powerful. He feels deep gratitude for what the Hexamon has done for the Earth . . . he merely resents those of your administrators who treat terrestrials like children.' *Far too many of that kind*, he thought.

'Resents *my* administrators.' The president paced on the platform. Olmy watched this with a deep, ironic humor. Politicians had certainly changed since the days of his youth – even since the Sundering. Formal deportment seemed an art of the past. 'And the religious movements?'

'As strong as ever.'

'Mm.' Farren Siliom shook his head, seeming to relish bad news to fuel a smoldering irritation.

'There are at least thirty-two religious groups which do not accept your administrators as temporal or spiritual rulers–'

'We don't expect them to accept us as *spiritual* rulers,' Farren Siliom said.

'Some officials have tried several times to impose the rule of the Good Man on Old Natives,' Olmy reminded him. 'Even on the honorable Nader's contemporaries . . .' How long ago had it been since a fanatic orthodox Naderite corprep had recommended using an illegal psychobiological to convert the faithless to Star, Fate and Pneuma? Fifteen years? Olmy and Ram Kikura had helped suppress that notion before it had even reached a secret Nexus session, but Olmy had almost converted overnight to her radical views.

'We've dealt with these miscreants,' Farren Siliom said.

'Perhaps not harshly enough. Many are still in positions of influence and continue their campaigns. At any rate, none of these movements advocate open rebellion.'

'Civil disobedience?'

'That is a protected right in the Hexamon,' Olmy said.

'Used very seldom the past few decades,' Farren Siliom countered. 'And what about the Renewed Enterprisers?'

'Not a threat.'

'No?' The president seemed almost disappointed.

'No. Their reverence for the Hexamon is genuine, whatever their other beliefs. Besides, their leader died three weeks ago in the old territory of Nevada.'

'A natural death, Ser President,' Tikk said. 'That's an important distinction. She refused offers of extension or downloading to implants—'

'Refused them,' Olmy said, 'because they were not offered to her followers.'

'We do not have the resources to give every citizen of the Terrestrial Hexamon immortality,' Farren Siliom said. 'And they would not be socially prepared, at any rate.'

'True,' Olmy acknowledged. 'At any rate . . . they never opposed Hexamon plans beyond their immediate territory.'

'Did you meet with Senator Kanazawa in Hawaii?' Ras Mishiney asked with a hint of distaste. Olmy suddenly understood why the senator was attending. Ras Mishiney was heart and soul in the camp of the orbiting bodies.

'No,' Olmy answered. 'I wasn't aware he had been anything but cooperative with the Hexamon.'

'He's gathered a lot of power to himself in the past few years. Particularly in the Pacific Rim.'

'He's a competent politician and administrator,' Farren Siliom said, reining in the senator with a glance. 'It isn't our duty to keep power forever. We're doctors

17

and teachers, not tyrants. Is there anything else of significance, Ser Olmy?'

There was, but Olmy knew it would not be discussed before these partials.

'No, sir. The details are all on record.'

'Gentlemen,' the president said, raising his arms and opening his hands to them. 'Have you any final questions for Ser Olmy?'

'Just one,' Tikk's partial said. 'How do you stand on the re-opening of the Way?'

Olmy smiled. 'My views on that issue are not important, Ser Tikk.'

'My original is most curious about the views of those who remember the Way vividly.' Tikk had not been born until after the Sundering; he was one of the youngest neo-Geshels on Axis Euclid.

'Ser Olmy has a right to keep his opinions to himself,' Farren Siliom said.

Tikk's partial apologised without any deep sincerity.

'Thank you, Ser President,' Mishiney's partial said. 'I appreciate your cooperation with Earth's parliament. I look forward to studying your complete records, Ser Olmy.'

The ghosts faded, leaving them alone above the dark fathomless void, now empty of both Earth and Moon. Olmy looked down and spotted a glimmer of light amidst the stars: *Thisteldown*, he thought, and his implants quickly provided a calculation that confirmed his guess.

'One last question, Ser Olmy, and then this meeting is completed. The neo-Geshels . . . if they manage to get the Hexamon to re-open the Way, do we have the resources to continue the Earth's support at present levels?'

'No, Ser President. Successful re-opening would cause long delays at the very least in major rehabilitation projects.'

'We're already strapped for resources, aren't we? More than the Hexamon is willing to admit. And yet, there are Terrestrials – Mishiney among them – who believe that in the long run, re-opening would benefit us all.' The president shook his head and picted a symbol of judgment and a symbol of extreme foolishness: a man sharpening a ridiculously long sword. The pict symbol no longer had a connection with war, *per se*, but its subtext was still a little surprising to Olmy. *War with whom?*

'We must learn to adapt and live under the present circumstances. I believe that deeply,' Farren Siliom said. 'But my influence is not boundless. So many of our people have become so very homesick! Can you imagine that? Even I. I was one of the firebrands who supported Rosen Gardner and demanded a return to Earth, to what we thought of as our true home – but no one alive in the Way had ever been to Earth! How sophisticated we think we are, yet how irrational and protean our deepest emotions and motivations. Perhaps a better grade of Talsit would help, no?'

Olmy smiled noncommittally.

The president's shoulders slumped. With an effort, he squared them again. 'We should learn to live without these luxuries. The Good Man never availed himself of Talsit.' He walked to the edge of the platform, as if to avoid the abyss beneath their feet. Earth was coming into view again. 'Have the neo-Geshels carried their activities to Earth? Beyond people like Mishiney?'

'No. They seem content to ignore the Earth, Ser President.'

'The least I'd expect from such *visionaries*. That's a political wellspring they'll regret overlooking. Surely they can't believe the Earth will have no say in such a decision! And on Thistledown?'

'They're still openly campaigning. I found no sign of subversive activities.'

'Such a delicate balance a man in my position holds, trying to play so many factions against each other. I know my tenure in this office is limited. I'm not good at hiding my beliefs, and they are not the easiest beliefs

19

to hold these days. I've fought the notion of re-opening for three years now. It will not die. But I can't help believing that no good will come of it. "You can't go home again." Especially if you can never decide where home is. We're in a delicate time. Shortages, weariness. I see the inevitability, someday, of re-opening. . . . But not now! Not until we have finished our tasks on Earth.' Farren Siliom regarded Olmy with an expression near pleading. 'I'm as curious as Senator Tikk, I'm afraid. What *are* your opinions about the Way?'

Olmy shook his head slightly. 'I'm resigned to living without it, Ser President.'

'Yet you won't be able to renew your body parts soon . . . or are the shortages already acute?'

'They are,' Olmy admitted.

'You'll resign yourself to city memory willingly?'

'Or death,' Olmy said. 'But that won't be for years.'

'Do you miss the challenges, the opportunities?'

'I try not to worry about the past,' Olmy said. He was being less than candid, but he had learned long before when to be open, and when not.

'You've been an enigma for all your centuries of service, Ser Olmy. So the records tell me. I won't press you. But in your brief . . . considerations of the problem, have you thought of what might happen to us, should we re-open the Way?'

Olmy did not answer for a moment. The president seemed to know more about his recent activities than Olmy found comfortable. 'The Way could be reoccupied by Jarts, Ser.'

'Indeed. Our eager neo-Geshels tend to overlook that problem. I can't. I'm not unaware of your researches. I believe you show extreme foresight.'

'Ser?'

'Your researches in city memory and the Thistledown libraries. I have my own active rogues, Ser Olmy. You seem to be accessing information with a direct bearing on re-opening, and you've been studying for years, at some personal cost, I imagine.' Farren Siliom regarded him shrewdly, then turned back to the railing, knocking it lightly with the knuckles of one hand. 'Officially, I'm releasing you from any further duties. Unofficially, I urge you to coninue your studies.'

Olmy picted assent.

'Thank you for your work. Should you have any further thoughts, by all means let me know. Your opinions are valued, whether or not you think we need them.'

Olmy left the platform. The Earth had rotated into view again, perpetual responsibility, unfamiliar home, sign of pain and triumph, failure and regrowth.

3

Gaia, Island of Rhodos, Greater Alexandreian Oikoumenē, Year of Alexandros 2331–2342

Rhita Berenikē Vaskayza grew wild on the shores near the ancient port of Lindos until she was seven years old. Her father and mother let the sun and sea have their way with her, teaching her only what she was curious to know – which was a great deal.

She was a brown, bare-limbed wild thing, wide-eyed and elusive among the brown and white and faded gold battlements and columns and steps of the abandoned akropolis. From the bright expanse of the porch of the sanctuary of Athēnē Lindia, palms pressed against the crumbling walls, she stared down the cliffs into the azure unending sea, counting the steady, gentle march of waves against the rocks.

Sometimes she crept through the wooden door into the shed that housed the giant statue of Athēnē, rising thick-limbed and serene in the shadows, looking decidedly Asiatic, with her radiant brass crown (once gold) and her man-high stone shield. Few Lindians came up here; many thought it was haunted by the centuries-dead ghosts of Persian defenders, massacred when the Oikoumenē regained control of the island. Sometimes there were tourists from Aigyptos or the mainland, but not often. The Middle Sea was not a place for tourists any more.

The farmers and shepherds of Lindos saw her as Artemis and believed she brought them luck. In the village, her world seemed full of welcoming smiles from familiar faces.

On her seventh birthday, Berenikē, her mother, took her from Lindos to Rhodos. She did not remember much about the island's biggest city besides the imposing bronze Neos Kolossos, re-cast and erected four centuries ago, and now missing all of one arm and half of another.

Her mother, with red-brown hair, as wide-eyed as her daughter, led her through the town to the white-washed brick and stone and plaster home of the first-level Akademeia didaskalos – the master of children's education. Rhita stood alone before the didaskalos in the warm sunny examination chamber, barefoot in a plain white shift, and answered his simple but telling questions. This was little more than formality, considering that her grandmother had founded the Akademeia Hypateia, but it was an important formality.

Later that day, her mother told her she had been accepted into the first school, her lessons to begin at age nine. Then Berenikē took Rhita back to Lindos, and life went on much as before but with more books and more lessons to prepare her and less time to run with wind and water.

They did not visit the sophē on that journey; she had been ill. Some said she was dying, but she recovered two months later. This all meant very little to young Rhita, who knew almost nothing about her grandmother, having met her only twice, in infancy and at age five.

The summer before she began her formal schooling, her grandmother called upon her to return to Rhodos, and to spend some time with her. The sophē was reclusive. Many Rhodians thought she was a goddess. Her origins and the stories that had grown up around her supported their beliefs. Rhita had no fixed opinions. What the Lindians said and what her father and mother told her were confusingly far apart on some points and close on others.

Rhita's mother was almost frantically thrilled by this privilege, which Patrikia had accorded to none of her other grandchildren. Her father, Rhamōn, accepted it with the calm, self-assured air he had in those days, before the sophē's death and the factional fighting at the Akademeia. Together, they took her to Rhodos by horse cart, driving along the same cobbled and oiled road they had followed two summers before.

Patrikia's house stood on a rocky promontory overlooking the Great Naval Harbor. It was a small gypsum-plaster and stone dwelling, in late Persian style, with four rooms and a separate study on the low cliff above the beach. As they walked up the path through the vegetable garden, Rhita looked over a brick wall at the ancient Fortress of Kamybsēs across the harbor, rising like a huge stone cup from the end of a broad mole. The fortress had been abandoned for seventy years, but was now being refurbished by the Oikoumenē. Workmen clambered along its thick crumbling walls, tiny as mice. The Neos Kolossos guarded the harbor entrance a hundred arms beyond the fortress, still armless, standing with more dignity withal on its own massive block of brick and stone, surrounded by water.

'Is she a witch?' Rhita asked Rhamōn softly at the front door.

'Hsss,' Berenikē warned, crossing Rhita's lips with her finger.

'She's not a witch,' Rhamōn said, smiling. 'She's my mother.'

Rhita thought it would be nice for a servant to open the door, but the sophē had no servants. Patrikia Vaskayza herself stood smiling in the doorway, a white-haired brown-skinned dried stick of a woman with shrewd, deep-seeing eyes wreathed in leathery wrinkles. Even in the heat of summer, the wind blew cool on the hill, and Patrikia wore a floor-length black robe.

She touched Rhita's cheek with a dry finger tip, and Rhita thought, *She's made of wood.* But the sophē's palm was soft and warmly sweet-scented. From behind her back, she brought out a garland of flowers and looped them around Rhita's neck. 'An old tradition from Hawaii,' she explained.

Berenikē stood with head bowed, hands pressed firmly to her sides. Rhita saw her mother's awe and vaguely disapproved; the sophē was very old and very skinny, to be sure, but not frightening. At least not yet. Rhita tugged at the flowers around her neck and glanced at Rhamōn, who gave her a reassuring smile.

'We'll have lunch,' Patrikia said, her voice husky and almost as deep as a man's.

She walked slowly ahead of them into the kitchen, measuring each step precisely, slipper-shod feet scuffing the rough black tile floor. Her hands touched a chair back, as if she were greeting a friend, then tapped the rim of an old black iron basin, and finally smoothed along the edge of a bleached wooden table laden with fruit and cheese. 'After my son and daughter-in-law – sweet people that they are, but they intrude – after they go home, we can *really* talk.' The sophē glanced sharply at Rhita, and despite herself, the girl nodded agreement, conspiring.

They spent much of the next few weeks together, Patrikia telling her tales, many of which Rhita had already heard from her father. Patrikia's Earth was not the Gaia Rhita had grown up on; history had gone differently there.

On a warm hazy day when the wind was still and the sea seemed lost in glazed sleep, her grandmother walked slowly ahead of her in a nearby orange grove, a basket of fruit slung over one arm. 'In California, there used to be orange groves all over, beautiful big oranges, much bigger than these.' Patrikia lifted a reddish, plum-sized fruit in her thin, strong fingers. 'The groves had almost disappeared by the time I was your age. Too many people wanted to live there. Not enough room for the groves.'

'Is California here, or there, Grandmother?' Rhita asked.

'There. On Earth,' Patrikia said. 'There's no such name here.' She paused, staring up at the sky reflectively. 'I don't know what's happening where California would be in this world . . . I suppose it's part of Nea Karkhēdōn's western desert.'

'Full of red men with bows and arrows,' Rhita suggested.

'Maybe so. Maybe so.'

After eating alone together in the kitchen, Rhita listened quietly to the sophē in the welcome cool of the summer's evening, an old oil lamp glowing and smoking sweetly on a wicker table between them, supplementing the twilight as they shared glasses of warm tea. 'Your great-grandmother, my mother, comes to visit me now and then . . .'

'Isn't she in the other world, Grandmother?'

Patrikia smiled and nodded, her face a mass of wrinkles in the golden-orange light. 'That doesn't stop her. She comes when I sleep, and she says you're a very bright girl, a wonderful child, and she's proud to share her name with you.' Patrikia leaned forward. 'Your great-grandfather's proud of you, too. But don't let us get you down, dear. You've time enough to play and dream and grow up before your day comes.'

'What day, Grandmother?'

Patrikia smiled enigmatically and nodded at the horizon. Aphroditē dazzled and shimmered over the sea like a hole in a dark silk lamp shade.

Rhita returned to Patrikia's house two years later, no longer a wild child made polite by the presence of an impossibly old grandmother, but a studious, well-groomed young girl intent on becoming a woman. Patrikia had not changed. To Rhita, she seemed like a preserved fruit or an Aigyptian mummy that might survive forever.

Their talk this time was more about history. Rhita

26

knew quite a bit about Gaia's history – and not precisely as the Oikoumenē wanted it taught. The Akademeia Hypateia used the distance between Rhodos and Alexandreia to some advantage. Decades before, the Imperial Hypsēlotēs Kleopatra the Twenty-first had given the sophē far more discretion as to curriculum than the royal advisors found pleasing.

At eleven, Rhita was already aware of politics. But she was proving even more adept at numbers and the sciences.

In the long evenings on the porch, watching the death of days along purple and gray and red horizons, Patrikia told Rhita about Earth, and how it had almost killed itself. And she told Rhita about the Stone that had come from the stars, hollow like a gourd or some exotic mineral, built by Earth's children from a future time. Rhita puzzled over the subtle geometries that allowed such an enormous object to be whipped back through time into another closely similar universe. But her head seemed filled with sunlit bees when Patrikia described the corridor, the Way, that Earth's children had attached to the Stone . . .

She slept restlessly and dreamed of this artificial place shaped like a never-ending water-pipe, with holes leaking onto an infinity of worlds . . .

As they gardened, weeding and killing insects, planting barricades of garlic around tender young flowers, Patrikia told Rhita the story of her arrival on Gaia. She had been young then, sixty years ago, when she had been given the chance to seek a gate in the Way that might take her to an Earth free of nuclear war, where Patrikia's family might still live.

Instead, she had miscalculated and come to Gaia.

'I became an inventor at first,' she said. 'I invented things I knew from Earth. I gave them the bikyklos. Farm tools. Things I remembered.' She waved her hands as if to dismiss them. 'That lasted only a few years. Soon, I was working for the Mouseion, and people began to believe my stories. Some treated me as if I were more than human, which,' she shook her head firmly, 'I am *not*. I will die, my dear, probably very soon . . .'

Within five years of her arrival on Gaia, Patrikia had been called to the palace to meet with Ptolemaios Thirty-Five Nikephoros. The old ruler of the Oikoumenē had questioned her closely, examined the devices she had brought with her and managed to keep safe, and proclaimed her a true prodigy. 'He said I was obviously not a goddess, and not a demon, and attached me to the court. Those were hard times. I made the mistake of describing Earth's weapons to them, and they wanted me to help them build bigger bombs. I refused. Nikephoros threatened to imprison me – he was feeling quite pressed by Libyan desert armies then. He wanted to wipe them all out with one blow. I told him again and again what the bombs had done to Earth, but he didn't listen. I went to prison in Alexandreia for a month, and then he released me, sent me to Rhodos, and told me to start an akademeia there. He died five years later, but the Hypateion was well established. I dealt with his son well enough . . . a nice boy, rather weak. And then his granddaughter . . . first her mother, of course, a strong, willful woman, but brilliant, but then the Imperial Hypsēlotēs herself as she came of age . . .'

'Do you like it here?' Rhita asked, adjusting her broad straw sun-hat. Patrikia pushed her wizened lips out and shook her head ruefully, admitting and denying nothing.

'This is my world, and it is not my world,' she said. 'I would still go home, given a chance.'

'Could you?'

Patrikia nodded at the bright sky. 'Perhaps. But not likely. Once, another gate opened on Gaia, and with the queen's support, I spent years searching for it. But it was like a marsh ghost. It vanished, reappeared somewhere else, vanished again. And now it has been gone for nineteen years.'

'Would it take you to Earth, if you found it?'

'No,' the sophē said. 'It would probably take me back into the Way. From there, however, I might be able to go *home*.'

Rhita felt sad, hearing the old woman's soft voice fade on the last word, her face deep in shadow under her hat, feline black eyes closing, opening halfway, infinitely tired. The sophē shuddered and looked appraisingly at her young granddaughter. 'Would you like to learn some interesting geometries?'

Rhita brightened. 'Yes!'

She lay half-asleep on her cot in the bare whitewashed room, listening to waves from a distant storm breaking just a few dozen arms away, great poundings of Poseidon's fists on the rocks, coinciding in her dreams with the slow thump of the hooves of a huge horse. Moon filled a near corner with cold light. Rhita opened her eyes to slits, feeling a presence in the room with her. A shadow crossed the moonlight, carrying something. The girl stirred on her leather bed, still not fully awake, her body lost in comfort.

The shadow came closer. It was Patrikia.

Rhita's eyes closed and then opened slightly again. She was certainly not afraid of the sophē, but why was she in her room at this late hour of the night? Patrikia grasped her granddaughter's hand in her own dry, strong fingers and placed it on something metallic, hard and smooth, unfamiliar yet pleasant to touch. Rhita murmured an incoherent question.

'This will know you, recognise you,' Patrikia whispered. 'By your touch, you make it yours, years from now when you mature. My child, listen to its messages. It tells you where, and when. I am too old now. Find the way home for me.'

The shadow passed from her room, and the moonlight faded. The room filled with darkness. Rhita closed her eyes and soon it was morning.

On this new morning, Patrikia began teaching Rhita

two languages that did not exist on Gaia, *English* and *Spanish*.

The sophē died, attended only by her three surviving sons, in the bare room where five years before her granddaughter had slept and dreamed of horses. Now a young woman, beginning her third-level studies at the Hypateion, Rhita hardly knew what emotions she felt. She was of middle height but gawky, her face bluntly, boyishly attractive, her figure slight; her hair was reddish brown, and her brows arched quizzically over green eyes, her father's eyes in her mother's face. *What part of her was Patrikia? What did she carry of the sophē?*

Her father was a slow, careful man, but his grief and worry were evident as he led the stade-long funeral procession across the sun-beaten carved stone roadway to the Merchant's Harbor, taking the sophē's frail body to the boat that would carry it out to sea. His two brothers followed, Rhita's uncles, teachers of language in the Hypateion; after them came the entire faculty of the four schools, dressed in gray and white. Rhita walked a step to one side and behind her father, saying to herself, *I do what she wanted me to.*

Rhita studied physics and mathematics. That was what she carried of the sophē.

Her talents.

One year after the funeral, as spring greened the orchards and the vineyards and olive groves came into flower, Rhita's father took her to a secret cave a dozen stadia northwest of Lindos, not far from where she had been born. He refused to answer her questions. She was a grown woman now, or thought she was. She had already taken a lover, and she objected to being ordered about, being led mysteriously to places she knew and cared nothing about. But her father insisted, and she did not enjoy defying him.

The caves were blocked by thick, narrow steel vault

doors. ancient with rust but with hinges well-oiled. Overhead, a flight of Oikoumenē jet gullcraft maneuvered, probably from desert aerodromoi in Kilikia or Ioudaia, leaving five nail-scratches of white against the soft blue sky.

Her father opened the vault doors with a ponderous key and nine twists of a combination dial hidden in a locked recess. He preceded her into the cool darkness, past casks of wine and olive oil and dry stores of food hermetically sealed in steel drums, through a second door into a tiny rear tunnel. Only when the gloom became impenetrable did Rhamōn press a black button and turn on a light.

They stood in a low, wide cavern, the air sweet with the smell of the dry rock. In the yellow glare of the single light bulb, her father advanced behind his looming shadow to a rough-hewn, stout wooden cabinet and pulled out a deep drawer. The wood's groan sounded heavy and sad between the hard walls. Within the drawer were several fine wooden boxes, one as large as a traveling case. He withdrew that one first and carried it to where she stood, kneeling before her and unlocking the lid.

Within, surrounded by a cushion of velvet molded for something at least three times its size, was an object barely as wide as her two palms spread together. It resembled a pair of handlebars from one of the sophē's *bikykloi*, although much thicker, with a curved saddle pointing away from the juncture.

'These are yours now, your responsibility,' he said, lifting his hands as if refusing to touch the box any more. 'She was saving them for you. You were the only one she thought could take up her work. Her task. None of her sons were up to the job. She thought we were suited for administration, not adventure. I never argued with her . . . these things scare me.' He stood and backed away, his shadow swinging off the box and its contents. The sculpted-looking thing within gleamed white and pearl.

'What is it?' she asked.

'It is one of the Objects,' he answered. 'She called it a "clavicle." '

The sophē had brought three Objects with her from the Way in her wonderful journey to this world. Their powers had never been explained to Rhita; Patrikia had simply told her what some of them did, not how. Her father brought forward the other boxes, laying them on the dry floor of the cave, opening them. 'This was her teukhos,' he said, indicating a flat metal and glass pad a little larger than her hand. He reverently touched four small shiny cubes nestled next to the pad. 'These were her personal library. There are hundreds of books in these cubes. Some have become part of the Hypateion's sacred doctrine. Some have to do with *Earth*. They're in languages that don't exist here, mostly. I suppose she taught you some of them.' His tone was not resentful, merely resigned; perhaps even relieved. Better his daughter than him. He opened the third box. 'This kept her alive while she came here. It gave her air to breath. All of these are yours.'

Bending over the largest box, she reached for the saddle-shaped Object. Even before her finger brushed the surface, she understood that this was the key that opened gates from within the Way. It was warm and friendly, not unfamiliar; she knew it, and it knew her.

Rhita closed her eyes and saw Gaia, the entire world, as if marked on an incredibly detailed globe. The globe spun before her and expanded, drawing her down to the steppes of Nordic Rhus, Mongoleia and Chin Ch'ing, lands beyond the power of the Alexandreian Oikoumenē. There, in a shallow swale, above a trickling, muddy stream, glowed a brilliant red three-dimensional cross.

She opened her eyes, terrified and pale, and stared down at the clavicle. It was three times its former size now, filling the molded velvet cushion.

'What's happening?' her father asked.

She shook her head. 'I don't want these things.' She

ran to the cave opening and into the sunshine. Her father trailed after, slightly hunched, almost obsequious, calling out, 'They are yours, my daughter. No one else can use them.'

She outran him and hid in a cleft between two weathered boulders, wiping tears from her eyes. She suddenly hated her grandmother. 'How could you do this to me?' Rhita asked. 'You were crazy.' She pulled her knees up to her chin, bracing her sandaled feet against the rough dry rock. 'Crazy old woman.'

She remembered the shadow in the darkness when she was a girl and kicked out against the stone until her heel was bruised. The months Rhita had spent almost alone with her, listening to her stories, thinking of that fabulous world . . . she had never imagined that it actually existed, as real as Rhodos or the sea. Patrikia's world had always been as far away as dreams, and as unlikely.

But Grandmother had never lied, never even stretched the truth, about anything else they had discussed. She had always been perfectly straightforward, treating her as an adult, explaining carefully, answering her questions with none of the dissembling adults often hid behind.

Why should she have lied about the Way?

As dusk softened the outlines of the tree branches overhead, visible through the cleft, Rhita emerged from the rocks and walked slowly down the slope to the cave. There, her father waited, sitting beside the vault door, a long green stick held in both hands across his knees. She didn't even consider the possibility he might hit her; Rhamōn had never physically punished her. The stick was just something to fiddle with and contemplate.

Gentle, careful Father, she thought. Life was complicated for him. The politics of succession at the Akademeia was getting nasty. He didn't need any more grief.

He stood, threw the stick away and wiped his hands on his pants, staring at the ground. She went to him and hugged him fiercely. They they returned to the cave, gathered up the Objects in their cases and, fully burdened, carried them down the hill to the whitewashed house where Rhita had been born.

4

Terrestrial Hexamon, Axis Euclid

The journey into Axis Euclid city memory was brief. Olmy chose a downline link and dropped a complete copy of himself into the matrix buffer to await entry into the central crèche. His body appeared to sleep; in fact, a partial in his three implants was processing data on recorded Talsit ambassador interviews, searching for behavioral oddities that could give him clues to true Talsit psychology. He knew he had no time for rest; he could feel it as well as think it, an itch, a compulsion, a restless impatience difficult to control.

If he felt a personal kinship to any male beside Korzenowski, it was Tapi, his son. He had known many children in the city memory crèche, sometimes as a tutor, sometimes as a judge; few were as high in quality as Tapi, and Olmy was convinced his opinion was objective. In less than five years of city memory education, the youngster was progressing to a level of sophistication rare in the crèche. Olmy doubted the boy would have any difficulty earning an incarnation; still, the exams were not easy.

He had resented Ram Kikura's motherly suggestion that he visit Tapi; and yet, without her making the suggestion, he might have sacrificed such a luxury to his work . . .

Fatherhood was not a simple proposition.

They had applied to create Tapi seven years ago, two years after Olmy's official retirement. At that time, the conflicts between the orbiting bodies and Old Natives on Earth had not seemed particularly strong or destructive; the Recovery had seemed on track, and both had felt there would be time to create and nurture a child. They had planned the boy's mentality in close cooperation, deciding against the orthodox Naderite fashions of less structured creation as well as physical childbirth. Ram Kikura, with a feminine sensibility that had struck Olmy with its strength and conviction, had said, 'A mother and father are not made by a few hours of pain and awareness of bad physical design . . .'

They had referred to the great philosophical treatises on mentality, and used classic design templates for non-parental aspects that Olmy (actually, Olmy's tracer) had found uncatalogued in Thistledown's third chamber library. Working in city memory for eight days (almost a year in accelerated time) they and their partials had combined the parental mysteries, selected large blocks of parental memory for endowment at certain growth stages, and overlaid the templates with great care to create the mentality they would call Tapi. The name came from Tapi Salinger, a twenty-second-century novelist they both admired.

Some conceived in city memory had as many as six parents. Tapi was biparental, with a predisposition toward masculinity. He had been born, achieving active status, six years before, both parents in attendance, one of only thirty children quickened in city memory that year. His body image at that time had been a six year old boy, Polynesian in appearance – Polynesians and Ethiopic blacks had been considered the most beautiful of the human races in Ram Kikura's youth – and extremely puckish in behaviour. Indeed, Ram Kikura had begun to call her son Robin instead of Tapi, but as he had matured and sobered (though never losing the spark of Robin Goodfellow), Tai prevailed. For the first year of their son's life, Ram Kikura and Olmy stayed in constant personal attendance, leaving city memory only for pressing duties, which were few. They had established several fantasy living spaces, allowing Tapi to grow in several simulated eras almost simultaneously.

The wonder of city memory was the flexibility of mental reality. With most of the resources of Hexamon libraries a part of the memory matrix, construction of simulated environments was a matter of a few moments' effort. The wisdm of historic time – as documents and as perceived by the Hexamon's greatest scholars and artists – was available to Tapi, and he had thrived on it.

Then difficulties had arisen, not with Tapi but with the Hexamon itself. The political winds had shifted and some had even hinted at re-opening the Way. The neo-Geshel party had grown in strength, countering the best prognostications of the Naderite political advisers. Olmy had felt the cold draft of history compelling him to prepare . . .

And as the next few years passed, he spent less and less time in person with Tapi, leaving the duty of fatherhood to permanently downloaded partials. Ram Kikura had also found less time, but still maintained close contact with Tapi. Tapi had never shown resentment, nor had his growth slowed, but Olmy often felt the pangs of regret.

The downline buffer was given access and Olmy's original was loaded directly into the city memory crèche. Tapi waited for him, his self-designed image now that of a young man, a good approximation of what a natural son of his parents might have looked like – Olmy's build and unaltered eyes and lips, Ram Kikura's nose and high cheekbones, a handsome young male with the few stylish flaws that were the hallmark of intelligent body-design. They embraced, an electric concatenation of physical and mental mergings that in an earlier time might have been considered embarrassingly intimate for father and son, but which was the norm in city memory. Olmy measured his son's progress from that embrace, and Tapi was given a healthy dose of parental approval.

Picts and speech were unnecessary in city memory, but resorted to nonetheless; direct mind-to-mind communication was laborious and time-consuming, used only when precise communication was necessary.

'I appreciate your coming, Father,' Tapi said. 'Your partials were growing tired of me.'

'I doubt that,' Olmy said.

'I kept testing them to see if they matched you.'

'Did they?'

'Yes, but I irritated them . . .'

'You should always be polite to a partial. They carry tales, you know.'

'You haven't accessed their memories?'

'Not yet. I wanted to see you fresh.'

Tapi projected a haze of body plans for Olmy's approval. The young man's body would be self-contained, but without the reliance on Talsit parts and other maintenance items in short supply. His design would not be able to exist so long without maintenance and nutrition, but for these times it was a better design than Olmy's. It was certainly more practical. 'What do you think?'

'It's very good. You've earned council approval?'

'Provisional.'

'You'll get it. Elegant adaptation,' Olmy said, and meant it. He almost wished he could apply for reincarnation and try it out. Still, he had lived with Talsit parts for so long . . .

'Do you think they'll re-open the Way?'

Olmy gave him the mental equivalent of a grimace. 'Don't race ahead,' he said. 'I haven't got more than a few memory hours, and I don't want to spend them discussing politics. I want my son to teach me all he's learned.'

Tapi's enthusiasm was electric. 'Wonderful things, Father! Did you ever study Mersauvin structures?'

Olmy had, but only briefly, finding them tedious. He didn't tell his son this.

'I've made the most remarkable correlations,' Tapi continued. 'At first I thought they were tedious abstractions, but then I plugged them into analysis of synthetic situation and found the mot *incredible* judgments. They allow the most complex predictive modeling. They act as self-adapting algorithms for social scaling and planning . . . they even model individual interactions!'

Tapi moved them into a private buffer. 'I decorated this myself,' he said. 'Nobody's seen fit to overwrite yet. I think that's a compliment from my crèche mates . . .'

It certainly was. Private buffer decors in the crèche were usually as vulnerable and fleeting as ice in a fire. The decor, to Olmy's view an exhausting array of mental tests and demonstrated algorithms, was far more complex and accomplished than anything he could have done.

'I took some liberties with my formal lessons,' Tapi continued. 'I applied the Mersauvin structures to external events.'

'Oh? What did you learn?'

Tapi displayed a jagged and discontinuous curve. 'Many breaks. The Hexamon is under severe strain. We're not a happy society any more. We were once, I think; in the Way. I compared the present dissatisfaction with psychological profiles of nostalgia for previous stages of life in natural-born homomorphs. The small mimics the large. The algorithms show that the Hexamon wants to return to the Way. My teachers haven't graded me very well on this, I'm afraid. They say the results lack rigor.'

'What you're saying is, we all want to go back to the womb. No?'

Tapi agreed with smiling reluctance. 'I wouldn't put it so baldly.'

Olmy studied the jagged curve with a combination of pride and the familiar sinking feeling. 'I think it's very good. That's not a simple parental compliment, either.'

'You think it will predict?'

'Within limits.'

'I . . . may be acting foolishly, but I thought there

was strong predictive value here, too. So I've made my decision on primary vocation. I'm training for Hexamon defense.'

Olmy regarded the boy's image with more pride, and an even stronger sensation of sorrow. 'Like father, like son.'

'I've studied your history, Father. It's admirable. But there are ways I think I can improve on the pattern.' Tapi's image burst into an enthusiasm of colors and then reshaped itself, dressed in defense force black. 'I will try to aim for higher office toward the latter stages of my career. Within one or two centuries of active duty, normal time. I wonder why you never made the move toward leadership roles.'

'If you've studied your father closely enough, you'll know.'

'The old ways. Old disciplines. Once a soldier, always a soldier. The best and highest expression.'

Olmy nodded; those were honest sentiments.

'But your abilities . . . you've tended in recent years to feel less regard for your superiors. You say to yourself this is because their abilities have declined . . . But I think it may be suppressed and diverted expression of your own desires to shape history.'

That's my son, Olmy thought. *Quick and to the point. And doubtless right on the mark.* 'Leaving partials with you is like leaving lambs to guard the lion.'

'Thank you, Ser.'

'You're probably correct on all counts. But if you enter that hierarchy, you'll have to supress and divert your own cocky compulsions, too. The most difficult road to leadership is through the defense forces.'

'Yes, Father. That would instill discipline and self-control.'

Unless it shapes you in a mold you're reluctant to break, Olmy thought.

'Do you approve of re-opening?'

No escape, not even in crèche.

'I observe and I serve.'

40

Tapi smiled. 'I've missed you, Father. Not even correct partials shine like the original.'

'I have . . . apologies to make,' Olmy said. 'For past and future actions. I'm going to be very involved in work from here on, more so than in the past.'

'You're working for the defense forces again?'

'No. This is personal. But I may not be able to meet with you any more often than I have in the past few years . . . maybe less often. I want you to know that I am proud of you, and appreciate your growth and maturity. Your mother and I are both exceptionally pleased.'

'Proud of mirror images,' Tapi said with a hint of self-deprecation.

'Not at all,' Olmy said. 'You're more complex and organised than either of us. You're the best of both of us. My absence is not disapproval, and it is not . . . what I would choose.'

Tapi listened, smiling.

'My consent for incarnation is on record,' Olmy said. 'I've assumed responsibility in the Hexamon for your actions. Your mother has done the same.'

Tapi was suddenly solemn. 'Thank you. For your confidence.'

'You are no longer our creation,' Olmy said, following the long-established ritual. 'Now you make yourself. I'll recommend a commission in the defense forces. And I'll try to visit you . . .' *Honesty*, he thought, *would be the best policy*. 'But that's probably not going to be often.'

'I will do you honor,' Tapi said.

'I have no doubt.' Olmy glanced around the decor. 'Now, I'm interested in these Mersauvin structures. Let's quiet this place down a bit and I'd like you to show me how you reached your conclusions.'

Tapi set about eagerly to do just that.

Olmy departed from Axis Euclid within six hours, one of three passengers in a shuttle to Thistledown.

He didn't feel like conversing. The other passengers were too self-absorbed to pay him much attention.

5

Earth

Lanier sat on the edge of the bed to put on his hiking boots. He allowed himself a small grimace as he bent over to tie the laces. It was nine o'clock in the morning and a brief squall had passed over the mountains, dropping a freshet of rain and casting a sweet draft of wind from the sea. The bedroom was still chill. His breath condensed in front of his face. Standing, stamping his boots on the worn rug to settle them, testing the tightness on his ankles, he frowned again at a different kind of ache, another memory he could not blank.

Donning his jacket by the broad window in the living room, he looked over a few hedges and tall ferns at the green and craggy hills beyond. He knew his route through those hills; he had not walked there for years, but today seemed like a good day to reacquaint himself. He sought no panacea, no rigorous exercise to bring back a youth he had rejected; merely a diversion from his thoughts, which of late had been particularly bitter.

Three months had passed since Heineman's funeral.

Karen had not said goodbye before leaving on an errand to Christchurch. She had taken the new Hexamon five-wheel truck; the roads were still rugged in the wet, and the old truck was not always up to country barely fit for horses. Someday, he thought, he would become ill in this house, and it would be a half hour or more until an emergency vehicle would reach them, and then, like Heineman, he would be dead.

One way to rid himself of the bad memories.

'Toll, toll, pay the toll,' he sang softly, his voice husky with the cold. He coughed; age not disease. He was healthy enough. Years more would likely pass, too many, before the memory blotter came and sucked his cares away.

He had done so little in his decades of service, as far as he could tell. The Earth after forty years was still a gaping wound, despite its official name; on its way to recovery, to be sure, but a place of constant reminders of death and human stupidity.

Why did the past come back to him so vividly now, of all times? To distract him from the frustrations of his widening rift with Karen? She had been positively stony since the funeral.

Twenty-nine years ago. A nameless town deep in the forests of southeastern Canada, a cold and snowy trap of three hundred men, women, and children. The men emerged from their solid, low-slung log cabins, emaciated beyond even Lanier's experience, to confront the sky-travelers. Lanier and his partners, two Hexamon operatives, a man and woman, were well-fed and healthy, of course. They walked resolutely across the snowy field between their craft and the nearest hut, addressing the men in French and English.

'Where are your women?' the female operative asked. 'Your children?'

The men stared at them, eyes elfin with starvation, ethereally beautiful, faces white, hair gray and patchy. One man staggered forward, jaw slack, arms out, and hugged Lanier with all his strength. Like being squeezed by a sick child. Lanier, close to tears, supported the man, whose yellowed eyes shone with something like adoration, or perhaps just relief and joy.

A rifle shot rang out and the female operative spun back across the snow, her chest a well of gore.

'No! No!' cried another of the men, but more shots clipped bark from trees, splashed snow, sang off the hull of the craft. A single middle-aged man with a thick black beard, less emaciated than the others, carrying a rifle that seemed even more nourished and fleshy than he, stood in the town's lone road, cursing loudly, 'Eleven years! Eleven! Where have you gods been these eleven awful years?'

The male operative, whose name he could no longer recall,

knocked the man over with a hot flash of ball lightning spun from their only weapon. Lanier stood over the wounded operative, quickly assessing her condition. She would not survive unless they retrieved the marble of downloaded personality from the back of her neck; Lanier bent down and felt her pulse, letting her eyes flutter shut, allowing her to enter the first stage of death. Ignoring everything around him, he took out a folding scalpel and sliced open the woman's neck just below the skull, feeling with his fingers for the black marble, pulling it from its socket, slipping it into a small plastic bag, as he had been trained.

While he did this, the town's men slowly and methodically stomped the rifleman to death. The male operative tried to pull them away, but however weak they were, he was one and they were dozens. The man who had hugged Laneir kept his silence during the operation, frightened out of his wits at this outrage, and then got down on his ragged knees and pleaded with Lanier not to destroy their town.

The women and children emerged from the log huts, more dead than alive.

The people of this makeshift town had survived eleven winters, even the hard first two winters, but they would not have survived this one.

'For whom the bridge tolls,' he muttered. *My wife is vital and young. I am old. We make our decisions and we pay the tolls.*

He stood still in the hallway for a moment, eyes tight shut, trying to force the fog out of his head. Woolgathering, his grandfather had called it. Appropriate in New Zealand. This wool was thick with brambles, however.

We did not save everybody. Not even all the strong and capable. The Death was too universal even for angels from heaven to spread succor to all.

He had not worried about such things for decades, and it irritated him that these thoughts came to him now like pale substitutes for guilt, a guilt he did not believe he should feel. *I did my job. God knows I devoted thirty years to the Recovery.*

45

And so had Karen, but she did not look like a worn-out rag.

Picking up his stick, he opened the door. Gray clouds still skated overhead. If he could catch pneumonia *the old man's friend* he might deliberately try to do so. But among the benefits conferred upon all Old Natives by the Terrestrial Hexamon was freedom from most disease. Their resources in that regard had been ample; every man, woman and child on Earth carried organisms that policed their bodies against any possible outside invaders.

He caught a glimpse of himself in the front porch door's storm-glass pane, face strong but deeply lined, the lines around his mouth curved down, clefts on each side of his nose, eyes sad, upper eyelids drooping, making him appear worldly-wise. It was with a mix of satisfaction and perverse disgust that he realised he felt older than he looked.

Lanier regretted his vow to scale the first leg of the high switchback before resting. At the second bend of the mountain trail, doubled over, hands gripping his trembling knees, he sucked in jagged volumes of air and puffed them out, sweat dripping from his brow. He hadn't done much hiking or even exercise for years, and unless he truly wanted to end his life, to overexert on his first long hike was a foolish luxury. The miracles of Hexamon medicine could only do what he had allowed them to do; that is, keep him reasonably vigorous for his age and disease-free and unaffected by excess radiation, of which he had an abiding horror.

His breath coming back to him, the pain in control now, he looked down from the precipice trail at the valley floor three hundred meters below. Flocks of sheep – maybe they belonged to Fremont, the young owner of Irishman Creek Station – flowed across the mottled green and sun-yellow grasslands, echoed by great rain-heavy gray and white clouds crossing their own intense, dust-blue pastures. Overhead, an eagle soared, the first he had seen this season. The wind this high was cold and bracing even in the November springtime; a thousand and more meters up the mountain there were still patches of snow, dotted with the inevitable filamentary scarlet fungi the shepherds and farmers called Christsblood.

He finally allowed himself to sit on a rock. His shins ached. His calf muscles threatened to knot. For the first time in months, maybe years, he actually felt pretty good, justified somehow for existing.

The wind called his name. Startled, he turned around, looking for a hiker or shepherd on the trail below or above, but saw no one. Satisfied the sound had been an illusion, he pulled a goat-cheese sandwich from his backpack, unwrapped it and began to eat.

The wind called him again, this time more clearly, closer. He stood and glanced up the trail, frowning. The call had come from that direction, he was sure of it. Stuffing the sandwich back in its wrapper, he marched around the second bend and a hundred yards up the trail, boots grinding into the pebbly surface and sliding on succulent grass still damp with dew. He was alone on the trail.

Singing to keep his rhythm, he paused to catch his breath and let the clean air pass into his blood, clear his mind of cobwebs gathered from months of sitting indoors.

He needed to riddle his situation.

While pitying his fellow humans, he had also come to hate them. It seemed that in their agony, more often than not they flailed about in a way that made things worse. Sometimes, those who had been treated cruelly – losing homes, family, cities, nations – had reacted by treating other survivors even more cruelly.

Lanier's favorite reading of late had been the twentieth-century philosopher and novelist Arthur Koestler, who had thought humankind fatally flawed in design. Lanier had few doubts.

He had seen men, women, and even children subjected to deep psychological probing and treatment, plucking out their demons, leaving them better adjusted and better able to effectively confront the reality around them. Lanier had simply stayed quiet in the dispute over such 'healing.' The treatments had cut decades off the Recovery, yet he still could not decide whether he approved. Were human beings such weak, ill-designed machines that so few could heal themselves, self-diagnose, self-critique? Obviously. He had become a pessimist, perhaps even a cynic, but there was a part of himself that hated cynics; therfore, Q.E.D., he was not fond of himself.

A wide mantle of cloud drifted over the land, a circular hole precisely in its middle. He resumed his seat on the boulder by the trail and squinted at the brilliance of the broad beacon of sunlight crossing the valley. So full of warmth, so hypnotic, that kilometer-wide patch; if he simply let his mind rest, sunlight on grass might answer all his questions. He felt vague, sleepy, ready to set all his burdens down, lie back, let the sun dissolve him like warm butter.

A few hundred meters up the trail, a man dressed in black and gray and carrying a hiking stick descended toward him. Lanier wondered if this was the voice in the wind; he wasn't sure whether he appreciated company or not. If the man was a shepherd, fine, he could get along with rustics; but if he was a daytripper from Christchurch . . .

Perhaps the other hiker would ignore him.

'Hello,' the man greeted him, boots crunching in the gravel behind Lanier. Lanier turned. The hiker stood before the brilliant leading edge of the cloud bank. His hair was dark, cut short; he was just under six feet tall, young-looking, broad-shouldered, upper arms heavy with muscle. He reminded Lanier of a young bull.

'Hi,' Lanier said.

'I've been waiting for you to come up here and lead me down,' the man said, as if they were friends of long standing. Lanier identified his mild accent: Russian.

Lanier frowned at him. 'Do I know you?' he asked.

'Perhaps.' The man smiled. 'Our acquaintance was brief, many years ago.' Lanier's mind refused to dredge up where he had seen the man before. Puzzles irritated him.

'Memory fails me, I'm afraid.' He turned away.

'We were enemies once,' the man said, seeming to enjoy the exchange. He did not come any closer, however, holding his stick in front of him. Lanier glanced back at him again. He wasn't warmly dressed and carried no backpack. He couldn't have been on the mountain for long.

'You're one of the Russians that invaded Thistledown?' Lanier asked. His question, asked of a man so obviously young, was not stupid, though it might have been once. The hiker didn't appear to be over forty; still, he might have undergone youth therapy on one of the orbiting bodies or in the Hexamon Earth stations.

'Yes.'

'What brings you all the way out here?'

'There's some work to do, important work. I need your help.'

Lanier held out his hand. 'I'm retired.' The stranger helped him to his feet. 'Those days were very long ago. What's your name?'

'I'm disappointed you don't remember me,' the man said petulantly. 'Mirsky. Pavel Mirsky.'

Lanier laughed. 'Good try,' he said. 'Mirsky's the other side of heaven by now. He rode the Geshel precincts and the Way sealed up behind him. But I appreciate your joke.'

'No joke, friend.'

Lanier searched the man's features carefully. By God, he *did* resemble Mirsky.

'Did Patricia Vasquez ever find her way home?' the man asked.

'Who knows? I'm not in the mood for guessing games. And what the hell do you care?' Lanier surprised himself with his vehemence.

'I would like to find her again.'

'Fat bloody chance.'

'With your help.'

'Your joke is in lousy taste.'

'Garry, it is no joke. I am back.' He stepped closer. The resemblance to Mirsky was uncanny. 'I've been waiting up here for you to come, someone who recognises me, and can take me to the right people. You have been important in the Recovery, no?'

'I was,' Lanier said. 'You could be his brother.' *His exact twin, actually.*

'You should take me up to Thistledown. I must speak with Korzenowski and Olmy. They are still alive, are they not?'

Konrad Korzenowski had designed the Way, once attached to the seventh internal chamber of the asteroid starship Thistledown. Thistledown and two sections of the Axis City were still in a ten-thousand-kilometer orbit around the Earth, one polar 'cap' removed, exposing the seventh chamber. The Thistledown had been blown from the end of the Way to allow the escape of the Naderite portions of the Axis City, forty years ago. The Way had briefly opened into empty space: it had almost immediately sealed itself, closing its infinity off from this universe forever. Those who had elected to stay within the Way – Pavel Mirsky among them – were more distant than the souls of the dead, if the dead had souls.

Lanier stammered something unintelligible, then coughed at a catch in his throat. His neck hair bristled. 'Jesus,' he said into his hand. 'What's going on here?'

'I've traveled a good distance in space and time,' the man said. 'I have a very strange story to tell.'

'Are you a ghost?' That was an old, useless thing to ask; he did not mean 'ghost' in the Hexamon sense. His face flushed.

'No. You shook my hand. I'm solid flesh, mortal . . . in a fashion.'

'How did you come back?'

'Not by the shortest route.' He grinned hesitantly and set his stick down in the grass beside Lanier's boulder, then sat. Mirsky – if indeed it was Mirsky, something Lanier was not willing to concede – looked across the valley with its movements of sheep and cloud shadows, and said again,

'I must speak to Korzenowski and Olmy. Can you take me to them?'

'Why not just go directly?' Lanier asked. 'You've made it this far. Why come back here?'

'Because I think in some respects, you are even more important to me than they are. We must all meet and talk. How long since you last spoke with them?'

'Years,' Lanier admitted.

'There is a crisis coming in the government.' Mirsky glanced up at Lanier, face calm, serious. 'The Way is going to be opened again.'

Lanier didn't react. He had heard rumors, but nothing more. Still, he had isolated himself from Hexamon politics.

'That's ridiculous,' he said.

'No, it is not, actually,' Mirsky replied matter-of-factly. 'Either physically or politically. It is like a drug, that kind of technology, that kind of power. Even the pure of heart cannot hold their convictions forever. Will you arrange a meeting?'

Lanier's shoulders slumped. He felt defeated, too weak to muster up the proper words and defend his sanity. 'I have a radio, a communicator, in my house,' he said, 'down in the valley.' He straightened his back. 'You'll have to prove you are who you say you are.'

'I understand,' Mirsky said.

6

Thistledown

Olmy sat before a personal quarters library terminal in Alexandria, the second chamber city, in a district not yet repopulated. He had installed the terminal just a few days before, in the apartment where he had spent his later childhood – and where Korzenowski's unassembled partials had been hidden, all that had been left of the Engineer after his assassination centuries before. Olmy had located those partials as a boy, and had later been responsible for reassembling and reincarnating Korzenowski, with the help of Patricia Vasquez.

In this obscure location, on a supposedly untraceable private terminal, Olmy received a message from an old acquaintance. The picts, loosely translated, read:

'Have something for you. Crucial to your work.'

The message was completed by coordinates for an abandoned station in the fifth chamber and a time for meeting – 'Alone,' the picts strongly implied. It was signed with the chop of Feor Mar Kellen.

Mar Kellen was an old soldier and gate police comrade, about Olmy's age. He had been born during the later Jart Wars, the biggest push against the Way's invaders before the Sundering, when the Jarts had been repelled beyond two ex nine – two billion kilometers down the Way. Those wars had lasted forty years and had scoured hundreds of thousands of kilometers of the Way. The territory gained had been fortified and gates had been opened to uninhabited worlds ripe for mining. These worlds had supplied the raw materials for the early Axis City, and then had supplied the atmosphere and soil which covered much of the Way's surface.

Those years had been horrible and glorious, years of death and annealing; the Hexamon had emerged from them stronger, ready to command the paths between gates, attracting patrons and partners from inhabited worlds accessed through those same gates. In some instances, the Hexamon had assumed trade abandoned by the Jarts; in this way it had established strong mercantile bonds with the engimatic Talsit. It was the Talsit who had told them the name of their enemies, as closely as it could be translated into human speech.

The Jarts had not been defeated, of course; merely pushed far down the Way, and kept there by a series of powerful fortresses.

Mar Kellen had survived the last twenty years of wars, and had then served in the fortresses beyond 1.9 ex nine. Even those frontier outposts had not challenged him enough. He had joined the gate police, and there had met Olmy.

They hadn't seen each other for centuries. Olmy was surprised to learn Mar Kellen was on Thistledown; he would have thought him the type to join the Geshels in their push down the Way.

Clandestine arrangements irritated him; he had long since ceased to enjoy intrigue, especially when it was unavoidable. . . . But Mar Kellen had suggested he had something Olmy could not ignore; and whatever his old friend's peculiarities, he had never been deceitful.

The fifth was Thistledown's gloomiest chamber, a kind of vast cellar. Many train lines passed through on their way to the sixth and (at one time) seventh chambers, but only one still stopped there, and that infrequently, by special request. There were few restrictions on travel to the only unoccupied chamber in the Thistledown, and each month a few hardy mountain climbers and river rafters visited the grim, cloud-shrouded landscape of raw asteroid mineral, sculpted by centuries of mining into fantastic gray and black and orange peaks and abysses. The excess waters of Thistledown ran red there, thick with rust and other dissolved minerals, not recommended for drinking without having chelation implants to handle the metal content.

The fifth chamber on average was only forty kilometers wide. At the beginning of Thistledown's journey, it had been thirty-eight kilometers wide; the removed material had been used for construction and to replenish volatiles lost through the inevitable leaks in the asteroid's recycling systems. Nobody lived there on a permanent basis; it was patrolled only by remotes.

Olmy took the empty train from the fourth chamber, sitting with arms folded as the black kilometers of asteroid wall between the chambers flowed smoothly by.

Mar Kellen's message had been so unexpected that he did not even try to guess where this would all lead.

Assuming nothing, Olmy wasted little thought on what lay ahead and instead re-explored what little Talsit cultural information had been acquired and stored in the libraries of the Axis City and Thisteldown. He had been over this material frequently, and was now methodically churning it over again, hoping to answer a few intractable questions.

The short journey gave him little time, however, and he watched the tunnel walls give way to a wild, improbable relief of thick black clouds broken by shafts of silver tubelight, racing between sawteeth of somber red and green and gray-blue. The train had emerged from the exit of the curved tunnel at a cant, with windows on the right side pointing up at almost thirty degrees.

He had always found a grim emotional solace in these barren regions.

The train slowed and moved along its three cradling rails to a small cupola-covered station nestled between two rugged walls of dull, oily-looking nickel and red iron. Rain splattered the stone platform beyond the cupola. Not far away came the roar of a tumult of water seeking one of the broad brown lakes that dotted the chamber.

Mar Kellen waited for him inside the small deserted terminal, sitting on a stone bench that seemed more suited to resting machinery than humans. Thunder growled outside, a sound Olmy had seldom heard in Thisteldown; but then, he had seldom had time to visit the fifth chamber, where thunder was common. Mar Kellen lifted two antiquated umbrellas in greeting. He projected a series of biographical picts at Olmy, with sub-signs to indicate degrees of truthfulness and where it might, and might not, be polite to inquire more. Inquiries seemed to be generally discouraged. Olmy did likewise, though with even more equivocation and brevity. The rest of the conversation used both speech and picting.

'I've followed your career, Ser Olmy, as much as was made public. You're an illustrious fellow and a credit to the Naderites.'

'Thank you. I'm sorry to say I've lost track of you, Ser Mar Kellen.'

'Glad to hear it, myself. I made it my duty to be as obscure as possible without downloading into city memory and going rogue.' He picted an image of himself as a free-spirited rogue, crudely sketched, suggesting he might not be terribly successful. They both laughed, although Olmy's humor was more forced.

'I hoped you didn't learn too much about me.' Olmy countered.

'No. Your career was obscure, as well. But parts have become history. And I've learned, perhaps impolitely, of your current interest.'

'Oh?'

'You seem to believe we'll be confronting non-humans again soon. Perhaps even Jarts.'

Olmy said nothing, his lips pressed into a wry smile. His private researchers had been surprisingly public, it seemed; at least for those who thought it worthwhile to know. Mar Kellen's obscurity became more understandable; this man had not downloaded, but he was a rare phenomenon – a corporeal rogue. Olmy picted a yellow half-circle indicating interest and full attention.

'I've come across something you might find useful. A holdover from centuries past. Rather like the Engineer's record.'

'Here?' Olmy asked.

The old soldier nodded solemnly. 'Do we have an arrangement, should you be interested? I assure you, you will be.'

'I'm not a wealthy man. Not even a particularly powerful man.'

'I understand, Ser Olmy, but you still have the support of the Hexamon. You could provide me with all I require in the way of access and privileges, since I'm hardly a fool for Earth's gold.'

Olmy examined the man and closely analyzed his picting style. Mar Kellen was sincere, not bluffing, as far as Olmy could tell.

'I'm retired,' Olmy said. 'My influence isn't nearly as great as it used to be. Within the limits of my present status . . .'

'Sufficient status to procure my needs.'

'If you truly have something I can use, agreed.'

Mar Kellen's abrupt broad smile was wicked. 'Agreed. Come with me.' He handed Olmy an umbrella and showed him how to spread it wide. 'This belonged to my Beni. You'll need it. Shields our tired old bones.'

Olmy held the umbrella over his head and followed Mar Kellen on a narrow trail away from the station. The trail had been cut into a slope of rock and wound through a gorge above a steady red rush of water. Here, tubelight barely filtered through clouds and rain. The landscape was lost in a shadow almost as deep as Earth night. Mar Kellen brought out a light and showed Olmy the way up an incline. The beam caught a hole in the rock. 'It's warm and bright beyond that doorway. Come. Just a few more minutes.' They had been hiking for half an hour.

'I found this while investigating resources for the Thistledown repopulation project,' Mar Kellen said. 'Routine work for a gentleman of leisure. It had been erased from all resource maps but one, and that one must have been an oversight. . . . It didn't seem important to the project, so I didn't tell anybody. But I mentioned it to my Beni, and she – she was my mate,' he confided suddenly, pausing on the incline to look over his shoulder at Olmy. 'Only thirty. Born since the Sundering. Imagine, an old war horse finding a young lady . . . truly a lady. Old Naderite family. But she had adventure in her blood. She far outstripped me for enthusiasm. She wanted to explore. So we explored. We came here, and found – '

He took a spry leap up into the cavity. Olmy followed, more gracefully but with less drama. A smooth black wall at the rear of the cavity reflected a meager dot from the light. Mar Kellen slammed his hand against a smooth black wall with painful force, face locked in a momentary grimace. 'When we found it, it looked just like this. I knew the look. A security wall. Then *I* becme enthusiastic. Nothing like a code to crack! Not easy, though. I had to crack thirty different coded blocks, using analysis invented only in the last century. Math has become my hag, Olmy.' He stroked the blackness, looking between it and Olmy. 'But it's a hag I've mastered. Once upon a time, this place was *very* secure . . .'

He picted a quick flash of symbols and the black wall brightened to gray then simply vanished. Beyond was a well-lit tunnel.

'Once inside, I suspected there were many lethal security measures. We looked for them, and found them – more than I would have thought necessary to guard anything. Most had reached their mandated limits of five centuries and had automatically deactivated. Obviously, nobody knew about it – not even presidents. Or so I assume. I may be wrong there.' Again, the wicked smile.

They approached the wide, half-circle archway entrance. A mechanical voice of ancient style – at least as old as similar voices in Alexandria – requested their identity.

Mar Kellan announced a series of numbers and displayed his palm to an ancient ID panel near the opaqued doors. 'I've recoded with my own patterns,' he told Olmy. The doors cleared and opened slowly. Within, a bare, stripped-down reception area waited in semi-darkness. Mar Kellen beckoned Olmy through, and took him down a hallway to a small room, also lacking furniture or decor pictors.

Mar Kellen stood in the middle of the room's blank white walls, shadowless, hands folded in front of him. Olmy stayed in the doorway. 'This room is the gateway to a very great secret,' Mar Kelen said. 'Of no *practical* use to anybody . . : not now. But once, it must have been very useful indeed. Maybe it was used, and none of us heard about it. Maybe it was considered too dangerous. Come in, come in.'

With Olmy standing beside him, Mar Kellen lifted one hand, extended one finger, and pointed it at the floor. 'Down, please.' The floor vanished. The room was a lift shaft. They dropped quickly, without sensation, into darkness. Every few seconds, a thin illuminated red line marking some unknown depth passed. This went on for several minutes.

Olmy had never heard of inhabited tunnels extending more than two kilometers into the asteroid. They must have descended at least twice that far.

'More and more interesting, hm?' Mar Kellen said. 'Buried very deeply, very securely. What could it be?'

'How far down?' Olmy asked.

'Six kilometers into the asteroid wall,' Mar Kellen answered. 'The lower levels have their own power grid. It doesn't show up on any chamber accounts.'

'It's an illegal data dump,' Olmy guessed. He had heard of such things, super-secure dumps used by police and politicians who in centuries past had feared falling out of favor with the Hexamon. But he had never actually seen one.

'Almost correct, Ser Olmy, but not illegal – *extra*-legal. The lawmakers had this built. Can the lawmakers do anything illegal, strictly speaking?'

Olmy didn't answer. It was a truism, even in the highly ethical world of Hexamon politics, that no governing system could survive a totally rigorous enforcement of its own laws.

A white square rose beneath them to become the floor again. A door opened, and Mar Kellen led him down a short hall into a dim cubical cell, barely three meters on a side.

'This is the memory access terminal,' Mar Kellen said, sitting on a curved metal stool before a broad featureless steel panel mounted at stomach level in one wall. 'I played with it . . . and I found something horrible.'

He touched the panel and faint round lights appeared in two places. 'Access, general key-code. I am Davina Taur Ingel.'

That name would have belonged to an ancestor, probably female, of the former Infinite Hexamon presiding minister, Ilyin Taur Ingel. Mar Kellen handled the board as if he had had some pratice.

'This was the tough part. The security systems have deactivated, but there were access mazes in place beyond them, built into the memory structure. They were very careful, our mysterious extra-legal people. If there had been no mazes, I might have given this to you, for free, jut one old friend passing something useful to another. But I wasn't alone when I made this discovery. I had Beni with me . . .'

Olmy detected a sharp rise in Mar Kellen's emotions. The old soldier was experiencing grief, anger, and finally a grim kind of triumph. Mar Kellen was sincere, but was he *sane*?

He motioned for Olmy to step forward and place his hand on the panel, below a green light.

'Don't worry, just keep your personal barriers ready. You can handle it. I barely managed, but it caught us by surprise.'

Mar Kellen said, 'Access occupant, guest of Ingel.'

Olmy's head jerked back and all his muscles locked. He was getting impulses from something within the panel, something not used to a human body. He saw snatches of visuals, more than just distorted; almost incomprehensible. And he heard a voice far more alien than that of a Frant . . . or even a Talsit messenger.

>> *Time concern. Duty concern. Inactive unknown time.* <<

Olmy jerked back his hand with considerable effort.

Mar Kellen's features had contorted into a rictus of enthusiasm. The old soldier was sincere, but he was also irresponsible. He had been shocked by his experience here, perhaps even emotionally damaged, and yet had managed to almost completely conceal his condition from Olmy until now. Mar Kellen laughed and sucked in his breath to regain composure. 'It killed Beni. After we riddled the maze. It distorted all her neural paths, even reached into her implant memories and scrambled them. There wasn't anything left to download into city memory, but her body was perfectly intact, alive. I killed what was left of her and disposed of it myself. That's why I have to charge you.' His face was blank and pale. 'For her loss. For her pain. What do you think they stored in here?'

'I don't know,' Olmy confessed.

'I have a good theory. If I'm right – ' He stuck his chin out and grinned his wicked grin. ' – They must have captured it a long time ago. They must have downloaded its personality or whatever the equivalent is, in secret, in this clandestine memory store . . . And they they abandoned it. It waited all these centuries, dormant, for Beni and me to stumble across it. You believe we'll face Jarts again, am I right? What would the mentality of a captured Jart be worth to the Hex-amon if that happens, heh?'

Olmy shook his head, too stunned to answer.

'Come look at this. I didn't find it until after she was gone, after we'd . . . Yes. Come.' He stepped toward the wall opposite the doorway. The wall separated in five L-shaped segments and withdrew silently, smoothly. They entered a large dark chamber, cool air eddying around them.

'Show yourself, you *bastard*.' Lights came on in a circle high overhead. A block of transparent crystal lay in the center of the octagonal chamber, occupied by a creature unlike anything Olmy had ever seen. It had a large, blue-gray vertical hammer-like head cut through with three horizontal clefts. Out of the uppermost cleft protruded shimmering white tubes tipped with black – eyes, perhaps – and out of the two lower, long black tufts of hair. Behind the oversized head – roughly the size and shape of a man's trunk – stretched a long, smooth green horizontal thorax. Bifurcated pale pink tentacles each as thick as Olmy's wrist and as long as his arm rose in a crest along the back. To the rear, behind the tentacles, was a bristle of short red barbs or feelers. A thick uplifted tail ended with a purple bugle flare. Perhaps strangest of all, seven pairs of lower 'legs' or supports lined both sides of the body, not legs or limbs in the traditional sense but *poles* or long sharp-tipped spikes, each the color of obsidian, and just as shiny. Below the head, or perhaps emerging from the lower head itself, were two sets of many-jointed arms, one set tipped with appendages remarkably like hands, another with pink translucent palps.

Despite his years of experience dealing with non-humans, Olmy shuddered. As he stepped closer, against his strongest instincts, he frowned, appreciating a deeper truth about the creature; that this body was not alive, merely preserved so that it would not decay. There was something undignified, disordered about its awkwardness that told him it must be dead.

'Beautiful, no?' Mar Kellen circled the transparent block. The creature, fully extended, would have been about four meters long from vertical head to uplifted tail. 'Our ancestral defenders, perhaps people we knew . . . people who trained us . . . they caught a Jart, and he or she or it is stored right here. But why not spread the news? This sort of thing would have been sensational, invaluable . . .'

Olmy knew what he meant. With the weapons possessed by both sides, battles were infrequent and cataclysmic. The Jarts had never responded to diplomatic overtures; in truth, after a few decades of the war, humans had stopped making them. Neither side could ever be certain what its enemies looked like. Decoys and deceptions had been used by both sides; information of any sort was suspect. To capture a Jart – even a dying or dead Jart – and understand something of its thinking . . .

That would have been special, indeed. Why keep it so secret, even down the ages? What had they discovered about their prize that required such caution?

Mar Kellen shrugged, his pictor casting a stray, context-free blue symbol on the ceiling. 'Unless it's not real. Maybe it's a failed simulation. . . .' He tapped the console. 'But I suspect it's real. Our simulations weren't worth much. Though we never encountered Jarts face to face. Nobody ever has, we were told, and returned to tell the tale. But this . . . was kept secret from us all. Whatever, it must be worth *something*, Ser Olmy.'

The old soldier pointed out a white plate to one side of the block. 'There are other ways of examining it. I tried them after Beni – my mate – after she died. I wouldn't touch the direct feed for months. But this is less dangerous. Puts the damned thing on display, an analog of its mental activity. I suppose experts could read the signs back then. I can't.'

Olmy watched the plate. A luminous cylinder formed above the plate. Like a geometric flower, it blossomed and extruded a haze of spinning lines. The lines danced hypnotically. The lower portion of the cylinder splayed out and assumed a tessellated variety of colors; black against gray, blood red against green, white against green, red against black, and so on, fixed and unmoving.

'Tame so far, hm?' the old soldier asked.

Olmy glanced at him, then back at the display. He could not begin to riddle what was being shown. 'This is a diagram of the being's mind?'

'It's a *Jart*,' Mar Kellen said, agitated. 'It must be. This shows the Jart's mind and its *memories*. I've spent hours here, watching it. Sometimes, I've said to myself, "This is what killed Beni . . ." Then I've had to leave or risk going mad.'

Olmy contemplated the pattern, fascinated. He had touched the very edge of the being's personality; not enough to determine whether it was whole or a partial, damaged or intact, or even to guess whether it had been in active memory of inactive. But here was an unparalleled opportunity – and an impenetrable mystery.

Olmy felt his body stabilise a hormonal surge.

'Gives one a chill, doesn't it?' Mar Kellen asked. 'Too many mysteries.'

'Indeed.' He approached the preserved body, letting his own mind and implant processors mull over the problem. 'You've shown this to nobody else?'

Mar Kellen shook his head. 'I've been out of touch. Beni was . . .' His eyes met Olmy's, half-lidded, face wrinkling in pain. 'Healing me. Bringing me back.'

Olmy turned away from the old soldier's anguish.

He had gone in harm's way more often than he could remember. He had tried his courage with perverse regularity. Not even pure Talsit – something he hadn't enjoyed in four years – could relax the hard little knot of desire for challenges. Yet he did not so much relish danger as experience. There had been very little extraordinary experience in the last few decades. He, too, had finally wearied of Earth, with its quagmire of needs and excess of misery.

But never in all of his lives had he felt the kind of fear he did now. Whatever lay within the memory storage – almost certainly a Jart personality, if Mar Kellen's suppositions were correct – had been strong enough to kill Mar Kellen's mate and damage Mar Kellen.

'Don't thank me,' Mar Kellen said, smile gone. 'Now that I've brought you here, I'm . . .' He picted a fury of red and yellow symbols, personal symbols, meaningless to Olmy but structured in an old Naderite prayer-form. 'I don't want anything, really. I don't even care about advantages. There isn't much I do care about, now. I killed her, bringing her down here. . . .'

Olmy broke from his reverie. 'You've found something very important,' he said. 'I'm not quite sure what it is, yet. . . .'

'I'm not curious any more. If it's important, I leave it to you. I've really lived too long,' Mar Kellen said softly, his face glowing by the light of the Jart patterns. He blinked slowly, then licked his lips and glanced at Olmy. 'Haven't you?'

7

Gaia, Near Alexandreia, Year of Alexandros 2345

Rhita stood on the aft deck of the steam ferry *Ioannes*, plying the waters between Rhodos and Alexandreia. To keep away the winter sea chill, she wore an Akademeia brown cape and a butter-colored Rhodian wool gown. Her eyes soft-focused on the ocean and the ferry's broad, churning wake. She was accompanied by a lone gull perched a few arms away on the dark oak railing, beak open, curiously turning its head back and forth. The somber gray sky brooded over a calm ocean the sullen color of iron. Behind her, large motor wagons from Rhodos, Kōs and Knidos hunkered in the shadow of the covered main deck.

At twenty-one years, she felt even more mature than she had at eighteen, and that made her very mature indeed. At least her keen sense of fun had not yet deserted her; she had a healthy awareness of her own capacity for foolishness, and regretted finding little time to indulge it now.

Her hair had kept its luminous reddish-brown shade of childhood, but now she cut it shorter. Little changed were her large, quizzical green eyes, pale skin, and her stature. She had not grown beyond middle height, though her shoulders had broadened somewhat. She had inherited her father's quiet physical strength, as well as long-fingered hands and long legs.

Rhita had visited Alexandreia only twice, both times before she was ten years old. Her mother, Berenikē, had thought it best to keep her only child close to the Hypateion and away from the cosmopolitan seductions of the Oikoumenē's central city.

Berenikē had been an avid disciple of Patrikia, and had married Rhamōn, the sophē's youngest son, more out of duty than love. She had loved her daughter fiercely, seeing in her a young image of Patrikia herself. In looks, however, Rhita resembled her mother more than her grandmother.

Now, with her mother dead a year, and Patrikia dead almost nine years, and her father still locked in a struggle for control of the Akademeia – in competition with theocratic elements her grandmother had openly despised – it had seemed best for her to take her talents and learning to the place where they might do the most good. If the Akademeia declined, at least she would be elsewhere, perhaps to establish a new Hypateion.

These worries were not foremost in her mind, however. They made her feel almost comfortable and secure when compared with her major concern.

For sixty years, Patrikia had searched for an elusive opening into a place she had called the Way. This gate had proven elusive, appearing at various times in various parts of the world only long enough to entice, never to be precisely located. Patrikia had died without finding it.

Rhita now knew precisely where the gateway was. It had stayed in one fixed position for at least three years. Such knowledge did not comfort her. She had become accustomed to her role, though hardly less resentful.

Knowing about the gateway had robbed her of her own life. Her grandmother, she thought, had imposed an almost impossible burden on a young girl by setting the instrument to recognise her touch, and hers alone.

Perhaps Patrikia had been a little crazy that year before she died. Crazy or not, she had given her granddaughter a terrible responsibility.

Everything else – her petition to study at the Mouseion, her personal life, everything – was subordinate to her knowledge.

She had not even told her father.

Rhita had hoped for a quiet life, but with a sigh, watching the seabird preen a wing, she knew that was not possible, not in this world. Even without the Objects, life at the Akademeia was going to be rough. All that she loved and was familiar with lay over the blue-black sea behind her.

She carried the clavicle and life support-machine in a large locked trunk; in a smaller suitcase, she also carried her grandmother's 'slate,' an electronic tablet for reading and writing upon. These were guarded by Lugotorix, her Keltic bodyguard, in her cabin. Lugotorix was unarmed, bowing to the sophē's abhorrence of weapons and warfare, but hardly less lethal for all that. Rhamōn, for all the Hypateion's pacifist philosophy, was a practical man, on occasion surprisingly resourceful and worldly. Lugotorix's service was being paid for in goods more valuable than money; his two brothers now studied at the Akademeia. With such an education, they might overcome the prejudices that had handicapped those of Keltic descent since the uprising of century twenty-one.

Rhita felt a steady, unobtrusive connection with the clavicle; if anything happened to it, she would know, and she would probably be able to find it, wherever it was taken. With Lugotorix standing guard, few would try to take it; but not even the Kelt knew what he was protecting.

In good time, Rhita would petition Queen Kleopatra for an audience. She would present her evidence.

What happened after that, she did not care to dwell upon.

Having had enough sea air for the time – it was thick with cinders as the smoke shifted on the changing wind – Rhita returned to her small, stuffy cabin, sending the hulking, quiet black-haired Kelt to his own cabin for a rest. She removed her clothes and put on a simple Hindi cotton nightshirt. Crawling between the short bunk's thin blankets, she switched on a feeble electric lamp and removed from her suitcase the smaller wooden teukhos, the book-box containing her grandmother's slate and the cubes of music and literature, including her own diaries.

Nothing like the slate existed on this Earth, though in a few years the Oikoumenē mathematicians and mekhanikoi promised to create great electronic calculating machines. Patrikia had provided some of them with the theory of such machines, in meetings conducted just before her death.

Rhita realised her responsibility in caring for these Objects. In a real sense, she carried the fate of the Rhodian Akademeia with her; the Objects were proof of Patrikia's truth-telling. Without them – if, for example, the ferry were to sink in the sea and the Objects were lost – there would be no proof, and in time Patrikia's story would be considered myth, or worse, a lie. But whatever the danger, wherever she went, Rhamōn had ordered that Rhita was to have these objects with her always.

Rhita had read her grandmother's notes many times, comparing the history of her Earth with the history of Gaia. She took comfort in the notes on the slate, as she might have taken comfort from reading familiar fairy stories.

The modern Earth her grandmother described was such a fabulous, if horrifying place – a world that had burned itself alive with its own genius and madness.

One cube held several complete histories of Earth. Rhita had read these carefully, coming to know the other world's story almost as well as the story of Gaia. She knew that on Earth, Megas Alexandros had tried to conquer Hindustan and had only partly succeeded, as he had on Gaia. But on Earth, Alexandros had not fallen from an overturned ferry into the swollen river Hydaspēs, had not contracted pneumonia and been forced to lie sick for a month, to fully recover and live to a ripe old age. On Earth, the Great World-Master had been forced to turn back by his troops, had fallen sick in another location and died young in Babylōn . . .

And there, Patrikia had told her, was the juncture where their two worlds had separated.

Rhita often thought of writing fantastic novels of that other Earth, what her grandmother would have called *romances*. Perhaps in time she would; she favored literature when she wasn't deep in her studies of physics and math.

But who could imagine a world in which the Oikoumenē had fragmented among the loyal Successors? Wars between the Successors, the transformation of Alexandros's empire into competing kingdoms; Egypt dominated by Ptolemaios's dynasty, Syria by the Seleukids, and eventually, with the rise of Latinē, all of the Middle Pontos coming under the control of Rhoma . . .

Rhoma, in Rhita's world, was a small, troubled city in strife-torn Italia – hardly the successor of Hellas! Yet on Earth, Rhoma had risen to destroy Karkhēdōn – Carthago in the Latin language – ending that trading empire's history a century and a half before the birth of the little-known Ioudaian *Messiah* Jeshua, or Jesus. Karkhēdōn would never have gone on to colonise the New World, and Nea Karkhēdōn would never have rebelled from its mother country and asserted itself on the Atlantian Ocean, to become, along with the Libyans and Nordic Rhus, one of the enemies of the Oikoumenē . . .

On Gaia, Ptolemaios Six Sōtēr the Third had defeated the tribes of Latinē, including the Rhomans, in Y.A. 84, thereby guaranteeing that the Ptolemies would be rewarded with perpetual stewardship of Aigyptos and Asia.

On Gaia, there were nuclear power plants, huge experimental things built in the Kyrēnaikē west of the Nilos. There were jet gullcraft and even rockets putting satellites but not men into orbit; but there were no atomic bombs, no continent-shattering missile barrages, no death-ray battle-stations in orbit around the world. Many of these wonders were part of the secret

69

lore of the Akademeia; Patrikia had learned hard lessons in her encounters with Kleopatra's grandfather.

Gaia, despite its troubles, seemed a more secure and livable place to Rhita. Why, then, go hunting Earth? Why ask for that kind of trouble?

She wasn't sure. In time, perhaps, she would understand her own comlpulsions, her own loyalties. Until then, she simply did what destiny had bid her do from childhood; what her grandmother had, without words, asked of her.

Rhita 'scrolled' through the slate texts recorded by her grandmother, and came to the description of the Way, reading it through for perhaps the hundredth time. Here was a world even more fabulous and strange than Earth. Who in the Oikoumenē, or in all this world, could understand or believe such things? Had Patrikia dreamed at least these wonders, made them up out of her nightmares? Humans without human form, a man who had survived death several times, a cosmos shaped like a water-pipe and immensely long . . .

In time, she napped. Soon, the dinner bell rang, and she dressed again, leaving her cabin once more in Lugotorix's charge. He ate alone from a pail provided by the ship's galley.

Rhita ate with her fellow passengers, mostly Tyrians and Ioudaians, in the cramped dining hall above the main deck, ignoring the licentious stare of a richly-dressed Tyrian trader.

She would miss the Hypateion and its easy equality of the sexes, as well.

The skies over Alexandreia were clear, as they almost always were.

The ferry smoked past the four-hundred-arm-high Pharos Lighthouse at dawn the next morning. Rhita stood bundled against the cold at the stern. This Pharos was the fourth of its kind, the tallest of all, an iron, stone and concrete monster built a hundred and sixty years before. The crowded buildings on the low hills

70

of Alexandreia glowed pink in the morning light, dusky green in the shadows. The marble and granite palace buildings on the Lokhias promontory were an orange blaze above the placid gray-blue Royal Harbor. The great caissons, sunk into the harbor floor northeast of the promontory to hold the harbor water back from subsided palace buildings, studded the shore like ivory game pieces, linked by lines of piled stone and masonry.

To Rhita, it hardly seemed real, this most famous of the world's cities, the center of human culture and learning – Oikoumenē culture, at least.

The ferry docked in the Great Harbor and disgorged its motor wagons across a broad steel tongue. Greasy smoke and escaping steam wafted from the wagon deck to the passenger ramp where Rhita and the Kelt lugged their bags.

Crossing the ramp amid Aithiopian businessmen in their formal skins and feathers and Aigyptian hawkers, raucous and insistent in their black robes, the pair managed to cross the quay unmolested. Rhita kept her eye out for somebody to meet them, not knowing quite what to expect if indeed her grandmother's influence still reached to Kleopatra. Off to one side of the pier, in a narrow corridor reserved for motor taxis and horse-drawn cargo trucks, a long, shabby black passenger wagon puffed steam while its driver smoked a foot-long black cigar redolent of cloves. A slate chalked with the message 'VASKAYZA-MOUSEION' leaned against one open door.

'That's ours, I think,' Rhita said. It wasn't the most elegant of receptions. There were no security guards present – none she could see, anyway.

As they approached the passenger wagon, she felt bucolic in her innocence. The city, a palpable, odoriferous presence now – thick acrid fuel oil, sweet spattering clouds of steam, gassy horse dung, unwashed masses of travelers and merchants – could swallow her whole, chew her up, and not be held to any kind of account. For the first time, Rhita acutely felt her lack of power.

Her grandmother had always seemed so self assured; how could she possibly be emulated, in the face of such a huge, overpowering place?

Rhita and Lugotorix presented themselves to the driver, who stubbed out his smoke against an often-smudged door guard, stuffed the butt into a grimy pants pocket, and climbed into the elevated front seat. They boarded the wagon. With a hiss and a jerk, the wagon labored them down a broad boulevard lined with ancient marble colonnades. Turning left into a high marble archway, it took them onto the grounds of the Mouseion, the great Library and University of Alexandreia.

'She's a very handsome young woman,' said the bibliophylax of the Mouseion, adjusting his floor-hugging stool before the queen. 'She has more of her mother's looks than her grandmother's, but her former pedagogue assures me she is the equal of the sophē Patrikia. She's arrived in the harbor with some great Northern brute, a servant, my scouts say, and will be in her temporary quarters within the hour.'

Kleopatra the Twenty-first shifted her short, stout body on the informal throne. The scar that sucked a line across her face from left temple to right cheek, marring the bridge of her nose and half-closing one eye, was a pale shell pink against her fair, otherwise smooth skin. She had little of the beauty of her youth; the Libyan hasisins had seen to that twenty years before, during her state visit to Ophiristan. Having no further interest in lovers – she had lost her three favorite consorts on that one hateful day – she did not mind her appearance any more. Kleopatra was simply thankful she still had her health and a sound, agile mind.

The famous dry Alexandreian sunshine crossed the foot-worn white marble of the royal dwelling's inner porch in a golden stripe and touched the queen's left slipper, hightlighting an unpainted but finely manicured toe. 'You know I indulged that sophē beyond reason,' she said. Her grandfather had decreed that Patrikia Luisa Vaskayza set up an akademeia on Rhodos. The Rhodian Akademeia, named the Hypateion after a woman mathematician none in Alexandreia had ever heard of, had for the last fifty years competed with Kallimakhos's Mouseion for research funding, more often than not receiving substantial royal awards. Useful and even startling work had come out of the Rhodian Akademeia, but everyone in the palace – and in much of the popular press – knew that the sophē's highest priority had been finding a way to return to her home. Most had thought her more than a little mad.

'You are stating a royal opinion, my Queen.'

'Be straight with me now, Kallimakhos.'

The bibliophylax's syrupy expression acidified. 'Yes, my Queen. You overindulged her at the expense of far more worthwhile scholars, with more formal backgrounds and useful proposals.'

She smiled. Hearing this from the bibliophylax made it seem less true. 'No one in the Mouseion has done so much for mathematics and calculation. For *cybernetics*,' she added, pronouncing the word as the sophē would have. She dabbled her toe in the sunshine as if it were a stream of water. For a moment, the simple color of the sunlight – warm and full of God – and the dry, cool breeze from the sea took her away from reality. She closed her eyes. 'Even a queen needs a hobby,' she murmured.

Kallimakhos kept a respectful silence, though he had much more to say. The Oikoumenē Mechanikoi League had made its weapons procurement proposals to the palace two weeks ago. The rebel government of Nea Karkhēdōn, across the Atlantian sea, had twenty times in the past year raided the Oikoumenē's southern hemisphere supply routes. The rebels had, a decade before, repudiated all contracts made by Karkhēdōn and were forming an alliance with the island fortresses of Hiberneia-Pridden and Angleia. The bibliophylax hoped that all the necessary defense work could mean fine rich contracts for his Mouseion. Instead, he sat discussing the sophē Patrikia's granddaugher. The sophē and her family had dogged his footsteps for all the thirty years he had been in office, and the footsteps of his predecessor more decades before that.

Kleopatra smiled at Kallimakhos, a sympathetic, motherly smile despite the scar, and shook her head. 'You must take her into the Mouseion. She must be accorded the rank of her father–'

'No match for his mother, that man,' Kallimakhos said.

'And she must be allowed to continue her search.'

'Pardon my insolence, dear Queen, but why does she not stay at the Hypateion in Rhodos? Surely she could better carry on her grandmother's tradition there.'

'Her petition states she wishes the assistance of your mekhanikos Zeus Ammōn Demetrios. Demetrios has agreed, in a private conference with me. I hope this does not tread on your toes, beloved Kallimakhos.'

She knew it did, and she gambled he would ignore the slight. He benefited too much from his relationship with her highness to let small, if constant irritations like the Vaskayza family irritate him unduly. 'Your will be done,' the bibliophylax said, bowing and touching the collar of his black scholar's robes to the floor.

Overhead came a shrill hawklike scream, followed by a shudder in the palace foundations and a distant, innocuous crump. Kallimakhos got to his feet as the queen rose and followed her deferentially, hands folded, onto the outer porch. She leaned on the railing and saw a pillar of smoke in the Brukheion, right in the middle of the Jewish quarter. 'Libyans again,' she said. He could see deeper red in her scar, but her voice was smooth and calm. 'Have we any news from Karkhēdōn?'

'I do not know, my Queen. I am not privileged in such communications.' The Jewish militia would be even more irritated by this, and already it was common

74

knowledge they did not favor Kleopatra; he wondered how he could use this new outrage to his benefit.

Kleopatra turned around slowly and returned to the inner porch, where she picked up the mouthpiece of an ornate golden telephone. With a nod, she dismissed the bibliophylax.

Within the hour, after a conference with her generals and the head of the Oikoumenē Security Staff, she dispatched a squadron of jet fighter gullcraft from Kanōpos to bomb the Libyan rebel city of Tunis.

She then returned to her simply decorated private quarters and sat cross-legged on a Berber wool rug. Eyes closed, she tried to still her deep rage.

She had very little time indeed for her hobbies, but her word was still law in the Mouseion, if not always in the contentious Boulē. Rhita Berenikē Vaskayza . . .

Kleopatra no longer believed a doorway to another world would ever be found. But even in a time of horrible civil strife, and the worst threat to the Oikoumenē in her lifetime, she believed in allowing herself at just foolish obsession.

8

Earth

Half of the Laniers' house was century-old stone and rough wood, perched on a stone and concrete cellar and foundation dug deep into a tree-shaded hillside. The other half, added forty years before when they had first moved in, was more modern in appearance, white and austere, though well laid out and comfortable, with a new kitchen and accommodations for the equipment he had needed for his work. That equipment still waited against one wall of the study, a small console of communicators and processors that had allowed him to keep track of the state of virtually any spot on Earth; his link with the Terrestrial Hexamon, through Christchurch and the orbiting precincts. He had not entered the study for six months.

Lanier's neck hair constantly reminded him of his guest's presence on the road beside him. They climbed the steps up the hill, Lanier's leg muscles already aching, and stood on the broad covered porch as Lanier opened the unlocked door. He did not know whether Karen had returned home or not; frequently, when busy on her own missions, she stayed overnight or longer in Christchurch or some of the nearby villages. It actually concerned him little that she might have one or more lovers (though he would have resented it if she had taken Fremont into her bed); he had no evidence of such, and besides, Lanier had never been susceptible to that kind of jealousy, sex being among the weaker of his passions.

She was not at home. That relieved him; he didn't know how he would describe or explain their visitor. Still, surveying the empty house, he felt a brief, sharp stab of grief. They had lost so much in the past few years, almost all that had consoled them over the hard cruel decades of the Recovery.

'Come in, please,' he invited. Across the years, he had adopted Karen's precise, almost Oxfordian style of English. Mirsky, or whoever this man actually was – Lanier had an explanation nearly as ludicrous as the visitor's own –, wiped his boots on the porch mat and entered, smiling with pleasure at the house's antiques.

'A fine home,' he said. 'You've lived here since . . .?'

'Between missions, since two-thousand-seven.'

'Alone?'

'My wife and I. We had a daughter. She's lost. Dead.'

'I have not been in a normal house for . . .' Mirsky lifted his eyebrows and shook his head. 'You can talk to Olmy and Korzenowski from here?'

Lanier half-shrugged, half-nodded. 'In my study, at the back of the house.'

Lanier hesitated at the closed study door, glancing back at the man. His theory, which seemed more convincing every minute, was that this fellow did indeed resemble Mirsky, but was not – could not be him. Somebody had created a duplicate of Mirsky, though he could not imagine why. How would he explain to Olmy or Korzenowski – or anybody? They'd simply have to see for themselves.

'Come in,' he invited, opening the door and liberating a faint smell of dust and old, cool air.

From this room, Lanier had worked after his official retirement to advise and guide those following in his footsteps. Karen had wanted them both to continue on full active duty, but he had refused; he had had enough. Perhaps that had been the beginning of their rift. More unpleasant memories returned as he stared at the projectors and control console mounted in the south wall of the room. So much misery and confusion communicated; so many missions assigned here, leading to the diagnosis or treatment of so many indescribable horrors.

Mirsky entered the room. 'Your own Earth station. Very important for you even now?'

Lanier half-shrugged again, as if to be rid of it all. He sat at the console and activated it. A rolling red status pict formed and then resolved into a live picture of Earth as seen from the Stone, wrapped in a coil of DNA. A smooth simulated voice asked. 'What services, please?'

'I need to speak to Olmy. Prior reference individual. Or to Konrad Korzenowski. Either or both.'

'Is this official communication or personal?'

'Personal,' Lanier replied.

The rolling status pict returned, a beautiful spherical skein of intertwined red strands.

'Do you want to meet with them personally?' Lanier asked Mirsky. The man nodded. Lanier lifted his eyebrows and faced the pict again. More suspicious. Yet who could or would want to mount an assassination attempt? Such things were not unheard-of-Terrestrial Hexamon politics – not recently, at least – but they were rare. And Old Natives did not have the technology to create physical duplicates. The more complicated his surmise became, the easier it was to assume the man actually *was* Mirsky.

'Ser Olmy refuses communication at this period,' the console informed him. 'I have located Konrad Korzenowski.'

An image of Korzenowski appeared in the study, projected two meters to one side of Lanier. The legendary Engineer, who had retired from the Recovery to do basic research, glanced with intense eyes at Lanier, smiled abruptly, and faced Mirsky. The image resonated slightly with some unavoidable energy lag or off-world intereference, then steadied, seeming as solid as anything else in the room. 'Garry. It's been years. Is Karen well? And yourself?'

'We're fine. Ser Korzenowski, this man tells me he must speak with you.' Lanier cleared his throat. 'He claims to be–'

'He bears an amazing resemblance to General Pavel Mirsky, does he not?' Korzenowski asked.

'I didn't know you had ever met,' Lanier said.

'We did not meet in person. I've studied the records many times since. You are Ser Mirsky?'

'I am, sir. I am honored to meet such a distinguished individual, and pleased that you are well.'

'Is this man Pavel Mirsky, Garry?' Korzenowski asked.

'I don't see how he could be, Ser Konrad.'

'Where did he come from?'

'I don't know. He met me on a mountainside near my home . . .'

Mirsky listened to this without comment, face bland.

Korzenowski considered briefly. *He still carries part of Patricia Luisa Vasquez*, Lanier thought. *It's obvious in his eyes.* 'Can you bring him to Thistledown, first chamber, within two days?' the Engineer asked Lanier.

Lanier felt a mix of deep anxiety, resentment, and an old, contradictory excitement. He had been away from important affairs for so long . . .

'I think I can arrange that,' he said.

'Is your health good?' Korzenowski asked, some concern in his voice. None but Old Natives and the most fanatically orthodox Naderites refused all methods of prolonging life and health. Lanier was ridiculously decrepit by almost any accepted standard today.

'I'm doing well enough,' he answered shortly, feeling the ache in his legs and now his back.

'Then I will meet you on Thistledown shortly after you both arrive, however long that may take. Ser Mirsky, I must say I am not completely surprised to see you.' The image faded.

Mirsky met Lanier's astonished glance. 'A knowing man,' he said. 'Can we leave soon?'

Lanier turned to the console and made the necessary arrangements. He still had influence, and he had never been displeased to exercise influence.

The situation was evolving; Lanier was no less baffled, no less resentful, but more intrigued.

9

Thistledown

Accompanying the old soldier to the first chamber, Olmy had helped Mar Kellen book shuttle passage to Earth. Mar Kellen seemed to have gained a kind of mystic serenity after revealing his secret. They walked toward the bore hole elevators, Mar Kellen smiling faintly, shaking his head as he ran his eyes along the ground, scuffing his heels on the stone paving.

'All I need is a few weeks to think things over. Might as well do it on the birth world. Beni was not quite orthodox, but she would appreciate my going down there. She told me it was beautiful . . .'

'Star, Fate and Pneuma be kind,' Olmy said.

'Formula, hm? Between two cynical old soldiers?'

Olmy nodded. 'Comforting sometimes.'

'Fairy tales after what we've seen and done.' Mar Kellen looked up at the tubelight, squinting unnecessarily. 'Maybe you'll need comforting now. I'm almost sorry for you. I thought you were the only one who could handle it. But maybe I did the wrong thing.'

'You didn't,' Olmy said, not sure himself.

'I'll climb a mountain for you,' Mar Kellen said. 'A real one, not something in the fifth chamber, all carved away by machines. Tall, with wide glaciers and deep places. Taller than anything on Thistledown.' He winked. 'Good-by.'

Olmy watched Mar Kellen enter the elevator. He received a mental impession – perhaps intuition, perhaps a quick subliminal pict from Mar Kellen's mind – that the old soldier would hike into wilderness, deep into a mountainous region, where he could be sure of never being found.

Olmy returned to the old apartment, relaxing, contemplating. He used the library terminal to communicate with various legitimate (and discreet) research programs in Thistledown's extensive memory stores.

When he had made certain his channels were secure – taking extra precautions to keep Farren Siliom's tracers ignorant of his present location – he called in an old ally, a tracer he had built himself from the memories of a short-haired terrier. The tracer had proven itself to be remarkably thorough, and it seemed to enjoy its work – if enjoyment could be ascribed to something that was, after all, not a complete mentality.

Olmy set the tracer one task: to find any and all references to the downloaded Jart in the records of Thistledown or the orbiting precincts. Many record centers within the asteroid were no longer active; some were carefully hidden. But the tracer could maneuver into the most inaccessible memory, so long as some potential information link existed.

Olmy backed away from the teardrop terminal and folded his hands, face set in an expression of patient watchfulness, eyes glancing this way and that at the picts thrown up almost at random by the tracer's beginning progress reports. This would take time.

He had ascertained that Mar Kellen's implant memory was antiquated and minimal. Beni, as a 'not quite orthodox' Naderite, had had only the legally required memory backups. The Jart records had somehow killed the woman, scrambled her backups, and driven Mar Kellen to the edge of insanity, in less than a second of contact.

It seemed unlikely, but it was possible that beyond the security maze the records had been left open and on download status – ready to be transferred. But the console only supported transfer to human minds or implants – there were no connections for transfer to external storage. He could, of course, rig such an interface . . . But there had to be a reason one did not exist in the first place.

A rapid download of channeled information into an

82

unprepared and unaided brain could, in theory, fatally disrupt someone's mentality. But what kind of machinery or safety circuit would allow *any* damage to an unsuspecting investigator? Obviously, unsuspecting investigators were not expected . . . Only experts.

Prepared experts.

If extreme secrecy was desired, the machinery might be designed to scramble intruder's minds, but Olmy had never heard of Hexamon agencies taking lethal protective measures against citizens in the entire history of Thistledown and the Way.

Beni's first encounter, without implants to buffer the flow, might in fact have kicked in some kind of safety circuit . . . Thus, when Mar Kellen tried the second interface a moment later – not realising Beni was injured – the safety circuit and the buffer of his more extensive implants might have blunted the flow enough to disrupt but not kill him.

So many mysteries and questions . . .

In all of his exploits, Olmy had exercised a maximum of caution, commensurate with the time he was allowed to plan and act. Even so, he had been killed twice . . .

He took risks gladly enough, but he did not seek them. If there was a safe and easy way to accomplish his task, that was the method he used.

Now he was about to break his own rule. He knew he would not go to the Hexamon authorities with Mar Kellen's discovery. That would have been safe, and theoretically his duty would have been fulfilled. Instead, he told no one and pondered different alternatives, all of them deliriously mad.

Olmy had lived through enough history to realise that at most times, major human events were shaped not by rational acts, but by guesswork and something akin to instinct.

To take proper advantage of this mystery, in the time allotted to him, he would have to act alone. Turning it over to the Hexamon authorities would mean delays, investigations by committee, the usual bureaucratic dance around a controversial asset that could very easily be a debit. He strongly suspected – as Tapi's work had probably confirmed – that within less than a year the information this discovery contained would be needed desperately.

Total caution was impossible, even inappropriate. Especially when all that he put at risk – for the time being – was himself.

He journeyed again to the fifth chamber, this time through the bore hole, traveling alone on a small private shuttle. He climbed the trail, followed Mar Kellen's instructions to open the security door, and descended into the asteroid's thick, ancient walls.

In the Jart's crypt, he contemplated the creature's static mind patterns.

The image had changed little since Mar Kellen had first brought up the display for him. He walked around the image, again studying the Jart's preserved body. It was as ugly as he had suspected a Jart would be – and as strange. Perhaps stranger than anything they had met in the Way, and that had included some very odd beings indeed – some difficult to define as 'alive' but for their mental activity. What creature had ever walked on solid sharp-ended poles? How did it eat? It was obviously not designed for speed or flexibility. What function did the tentacles and cluster of spikes serve? How could that narrow body service such a large head?

Olmy sat in the tiny chamber, subduing an old, pale fear of very small places. There was no chair, so he sat on the smooth ancient floor, back against the wall.

Why is it here? A question equally as unanswerable as *Who brought it here?* or *How was it captured?*

Why would a Jart allow itself to be captured and have its personality downloaded?

He stood and stretched his muscles and joints. His body still felt young, fully capable. His mind was equipped with sufficient implant memory and processing modules to house several human personalities beside himself; he hadn't used the excess since he had carried Korzenowski, prior to the Engineer's reincarnation four decades ago. But it was still available. There were few people on Thistledown or anywhere else who matched Olmy's potential either physically or mentally.

Given a few weeks, he could probably riddle the buried chambers and discover how to use the equipment properly. But why would he do that?

For the same reasons he had spent the last few years studying all that was known about the psychology of non-human intelligences. The Terrestrial Hexamon, after decades of concentrating on very different problems, was not prepared strategically or tactically to return to the Way.

Yet they would almost certainly do so. He could feel the pressure of history; a familiar pressure.

If Olmy could give them expert advice, the Hexamon might survive its own foolishness. And of all the beings most likely to confront them in the re-opened Way–

The Jarts were the most formidable. Even captured, imprisoned, quiescent for centuries, somehow they could still kill.

It was essential that Olmy extract what information he could from this source, at any personal cost.

With a grin, he realised much of his rationalising was to hide a basic truth. He did not trust the present leadership. They condescended to the past rather than understanding it. His ingrained sense of soldier's superiority had finally triumphed over his faith in the rightness of the command structure.

'I'm going rogue, myself,' he confessed to the Jart's ancient corpse. 'Damn it all to hell.'

10
Gaia

Alexandreia was a lot filthier than she remembered from her visits years past; it seemed to wear a cloak of smoke and soot as protection against its many troubles. The fabulous marble causeways were pitted with decay. Many of the statues had been shrouded in great sheets of oilcloth.

The representatives of the bibliophylax, the director and archivist of the Mouseion, hurried her and her luggage off the street before the Mouseion's famous Eastern Stoa, then put her in a rickety cart, insisting that she ride rather than walk.

The women's residence hall was a brick and stone two-story block dropped inauspiciously in a dusty, treeless corner of the Mouseion grounds. Rhita's heart fell when she saw it; Lugotorix, riding beside the driver on the cart, gave a low whistle of contempt.

They pulled into the broken brick and pounded-dirt courtyard. An elderly woman in a black shawl swept dust and sand half-heartedly in the shade of the inset double doorway, giving them barely a glance. The door opened and a blond, matronly young woman about the same age as Rhita stepped out with hands clenched over her head in greeting.

'Welcome! welcome!' she shrilled, clicking her tongue and dropping her hands to lift her long brown robe out of the dust. 'You are from Rhodos? From the Hypateion?'

Rhita smiled and nodded at her. The cart jerked to a sudden stop and the driver gave the Kelt some small assistance in dropping her luggage to the curbside. 'You can't stay here, you know,' the woman told the Kelt sharply. 'No men here.'

'He's my bodyguard,' Rhita said.

'My dear, bad as things are for us in the Mouseion, none of us need bodyguards! He'll have to stay elsewhere. You are Reee-ta Berenikē Baskayza?'

'Yes.'

The woman hugged her briskly. 'I am Jorea Yallos, from Galatia. Your houseguide. You study mathematics?'

'Yes.'

'Fascinating. I study animal husbandry in the school of agriculture. I have been told to show you your quarters and answer your questions.'

Rhita's hopes fell when Yallos urged her to the upper floor and bustled before her along a dark hallway. 'We appreciate your coming here. I'm sorry we can't do better for you. In the summer, these rooms cool off more quickly at night. In the winter, that's not what you want. They're comfortably warm during the day, however.' She withdrew a large iron key and inserted it into the padlock, pocketed both lock and key, and pushed and kicked the thin wooden door open. It scraped sadly over the broken tile floor.

'Are you a daughter of Isis?' Yallos asked.

Rhita entered the room. It was like a cell in a monastery, with a pair of small windows mounted high in the outer wall and a leather bed pushed into one corner. Behind the door, a wobbly stand supported a chamber pot and bowl. Against the right hand wall, a scabrous wooden desk had been propped under a faded mural of the Kanōpic Isis with her small, wide-eyed, feathered infant son and protective snake.

'No,' Rhita managed to answer.

'Pity. Dorca, the woman here before you, a lovely helper, she was quite fond of Isis. You can't redecorate without the women's council's permission.'

'I wouldn't dream of it,' Rhita said. She gestured for Lugotorix to bring in her luggage. He squeezed through the door with traveling case and wooden boxes under both arms, gently lowered them to the floor, and stood to one side, away from the suspicious Yallos.

'He's a Kelt, isn't he?'

'From the Parisioi ' Rhita affirmed.

'There are plenty of Kelts in Galatia,' Yallos said. 'I'm of Nabataean and Hellenic ancestry, myself.'

Rhita nodded politely.

'We have a group council at the first hour of sunset. If you'd like to join us, you're welcome. Let me know if you need anything. We women have to stick together here. They don't much care for us, Kallimakhos and his people. We're not good for his defense contracts.' Yallos stood in the doorway. 'The Kelt has to come with me now. I'll get him a room in the old baths, where the groundskeepers bed down.'

Lugotorix flicked his slitted eyes from Yallos, whom he clearly loathed, to Rhita. 'Go,' she told him. 'I'll be okay here.' She was none too sure of that, however. She already felt homesick and out of place. The Kelt shrugged and followed the houseguide. Rhita suddenly thought of something and called to her in the hall. 'Can I have the lock and key?'

'No locks,' Yallos said.

'I need a lock,' Rhita persisted, irritated now and worried for the safety of the Objects.

'Come to the council meeting. We'll discuss it. Oh . . . if you're not a sister of Isis, what are you?'

Rhita made up her answer with surprising speed. 'I belong to the sanctuary of Athēnē Lindia.'

Yallos blinked. 'Pagan?' she asked.

'Rhodian,' Rhita replied. 'It's my birthright.'

'Oh.'

Rhita shut the door and faced her squalid cell. So much for her reception in the Mouseion. Her grandmother's shadow obviously did not stretch this far. Was this the queen's doing, or was Kleopatra even aware of Rhita's arrival?

She sat for a while, shivering in the gloom. A single electric light over the bed cast a yellow glow over that corner and little else. It was already midday and the room was just beginning to warm. How much risk should she take with the Objects, not to mention her own safety? How much risk would she take before – if – she reached her goal?

Prying at a shutter jammed over one small, deep-set window, she broke an already-short fingernail to the quick. She swore beneath her breath, one green eye bright in her meager success, a thin line of indirect sunlight.

Rhita wiped gritty dust from the desk, used a frayed withy broom to sweep the floor, and opened her trunk to put her clothes away. In the late afternoon, the guides had told her, she would meet with the bibliophylax.

She did not look forward to it.

11
Earth

The Russian – so it was most convenient to think of him, at least for the moment – stood with Lanier on the porch, waiting for the wink of a shuttle's lights. The night sky was a smear of aluminum dust across solid black, depth upon depth of stars. The air had cleared since the Death, Earth's natural healing mechanisms removing most atmospheric traces of the conflagration. There were few pollution sources anywhere now, even with the Recovery well along. Hexamon Technology was non-polluting, self-contained.

The first lights they saw were not in the sky, but along the road leading up the side of the valley to the cabin. Lanier pursed his lips and met the Russian's glance with a shrug. 'My wife,' he said. He had hoped to get the Russian away before her arrival.

The rugged All-Terrain Vehicle, modeled after types used by the first investigators on the Stone, ground its tires along the gravel drive to one side of the cabin and stopped, its electrical motors cutting abruptly. Karen swung down from the cabin in the automatic glare of the outdoor floodlights, saw Lanier on the porch and waved at him. He waved back, feeling older just looking at her.

In their life together, he had seen her age a decade or two, *grow old along with me*, then regress under therapy, the same therapy he had turned down. She looked a youthful forty at most.

'I've been in town,' she called out in Chinese as she dragged her duffel from the rear of the ATV. 'We're setting up an artificial social network, so the – ' She saw the Russian and stopped on the porch steps, biting her lower lip. She looked over her shoulder at the drive;

no other vehicles. Then she queried Lanier with one raised eyebrow.

'This is a visitor. His name is Pavel,' he said.

'We have not met,' the Russian said, stepping forward and extending his hand. 'I am Pavel Mirsky.'

Karen smiled politely, but her instincts had been aroused.

'How are you feeling?' she asked, shifting her eyes to her husband. She glanced between them quickly, brow furrowed.

'I'm fine. His name,' Lanier repeated with some deliberate drama, 'is Pavel Mirsky.'

'I know the name,' she said. 'Wasn't that the Russian commander on the Stone? Went with the precincts down the Way . . . didn't he?' Her eyes fell accusingly on Lanier: *What is this?* She had seen pictures of Mirsky in the history tapes. The game was up. She recognised him. 'You look just like him.'

'I hope I haven't disturbed you,' the Russian said.

'He's a son, a look-alike?' she asked Lanier.

He shook his head.

She stood on the top step, hands clasped before her. 'You're sure everything is all right? You're joking with me.' She climbed up one step, paused again. Then, in Chinese, she asked Lanier, 'Who is this man?'

In Chinese, Lanier responded, 'He's a good imitation, if not the real thing. I'm taking im to meet with Korzenowski.'

Karen walked slowly before them, examining the Russian, biting her lower lip. 'Where did you come from?'

The Russian looked between them. 'I have not explained that yet,' he said. 'Better to wait until it all comes out.'

'You can't be Mirsky,' Karen said. 'If you're trying to hoodwink my husband . . . All we heard would have to be a lie.'

Surprisingly, Lanier hadn't considered that possibility. He had not, of course, actually *seen* Mirsky go down the Way.

'No lies,' the Russian said. 'I am pleased to finally meet you. I have always thought your husband a fine man, a true leader, with sound judgment. I congratulate both of you.'

'Why?' Lanier asked.

'On having found each other,' the Russian explained.

'Thank you,' Karen said sharply. 'Have you offered our guest any refreshment Garry?' She carried her duffel into the cabin. Her suspicion had turned into anger.

'We're expecting the shuttle any minute,' he answered. 'We've eaten a little, and had a beer.'

The Russian smiled at the mention of the beer. His enjoyment had been obvious.

Karen made various small noises in the kitchen, then continued her interrupted conversation through the screened window opening onto the porch. 'We're going to get twenty or thirty village leaders and political science students from Christchurch and fly them to Axis Thoreau. It's going to be a kind of conference, all in city memory, to establish social ties it would take years to make otherwise. They'll all act as if they were family afterwards, if it goes well. Think of all politicians having family ties with each other, and their constituents? It could be wonderful.' Her tone had changed; now she was ignoring the mystery.

Lanier suddenly felt exhausted. All he wanted was to lie back on the old couch before the cabin's fireplace and close his eyes.

'Here comes the shuttle,' the Russian said, pointing. A blip of white soared across the opposite side of the valley, then swooped in low, just above the trees. Karen returned to the porch, face strained, and looked up at her husband.

'What in hell are you doing?' she demanded in an undertone. 'Where are you going?'

Lanier shook his head. 'To the Stone.' Everything

was losing its edge of reality. Nothing seemed very probable. 'I don't know when we'll be back.'

'You shouldn't go alone. I can't go with you,' she said. 'I have to be in Christchurch tomorrow.' She glanced at Lanier. Karen was no fool, but she was having a difficult time shifting gears. Her expression said that she knew just how odd this really was; and how important it might be. 'Maybe you can explain to me after you get to the Stone?'

'I'll try,' Lanier said.

'I am sorry for the disruption,' the Russian said quietly.

'You shut up,' Karen cried, turning to him. 'You're just a goddamned ghost.'

At that, Lanier smiled. He put his hand on Karen's shoulder, both to reassure her and stop her from saying more. *The gestures come easily enough*, he thought. *Why not the feeling?*

They were off, cushioned in the free-form white interior of the shuttle, flying high above the dark Earth. In the sky, staring out across the black, ridged horizon, where bloom of stars met mountains, Lanier felt free. He hadn't flown in years, had almost forgotten the feeling. As soon as the shuttle pointed its blunted nose straight up, and the view through the transparency in the hull tilted, his exhilaration changed to an opposite dread.

Space.

How nice just to fly in the thin film of air, and avoid the larger issues. Flying was like a marvelous kind of sleep, above the hard reality of waking, but below the greater blackness of death . . .

Across the aisle, the Russian stared straight ahead, not bothering to examine the view, as if he had seen it all so often it could not affect him one way or the other. The Russian did not look thoughtful. He did not look concerned. There was no way to know what all this meant to him, or how he felt about the meeting with Korzenowski . . . or about returning to the Stone.

If he was Mirsky, his return to Thistledown should hold a true emotional charge. The last time he entered the Stone, it had been through a fury of projectiles and laser beams, as part of the Russian invasion force, just before, perhaps as prelude to, the Death.

Lanier realised that if this was Mirsky, then from that fateful moment until he came to the valley, he had not seen Earth again.

The flight, smooth and quiet, seemingly effortless, did not reduce Lanier's sense of unreality. *If he is Mirsky, where has he been since – what has he seen?*

12
Gaia

The Mouseion had expanded considerably into the Neapolis and Brukheion – the Hellenic quarter – since ancient times, and had even set a foot – the school of medicine – into the Aigyptian district. The buildings of the school of medicine, the Erasistrateion, abutted the smaller, less reputable Library of Domestic Oikoumenē Studies, the one-time Serapeion. The university, research center and library – actually, seven buildings spread around the original library – occupied a square about four stadia on a side in the middle of the city. Scattered throughout the older marble and granite and limestone buildings were new, boxy iron and glass centers for the study of science and mechanics. On top of the steep hill of the former Paneion, the university had installed, five centuries before, a huge stone observatory. It was more a relic than a functioning center of astronomical research, but its grandeur was impressive.

Rhita's neck ached from twisting back and forth. Her carriage rolled with an irregular rhythm over the cobbled and slated paths, between feathery trees and stately date palms. The sun dipped in the west, throwing an orange light across the city, just as she had seen it the day before on entering the Great Harbor. Smoke drifted in the thin dark ribbons from a tall brick stack appended to one science building. Students in white and yellow academic robes – mostly male – passed them on the path, eyeing Rhita curiously. She returned their stares frankly, calmly, though feeling none too calm inside. She didn't like this place much – not now, perhaps not ever – and that bothered her. This was the center of culture and science in the Western World, after all. There was much for her to learn in Alexandreia

– if the circumstances had been such that she could just study.

The oldest intact building in the entire Mouseion, the original central library, now housed the administrative offices and academic quarters. Once it had been ornate and lovely; now it looked a little bedraggled, though still magnificent, three stories of marble and onyx, decorated with gold-leaf-covered bosses and thousand-year-old grotesques from the time of the Second Occupation, during the Third Parsa Uprising. Sheets of paler marble had been added less than fifty years before to repair time-damaged walls. Thus far, none of the Libyan rockets falling on the delta had struck the Mouseion grounds.

The path led through an archway into the courtyard, polished granite and onyx paving stones arranged in a checker-board cross with exotic plantings from Aithiopia and the Southern Great Sea occupying the corners, and an Arsakid Parsa stone lion fountain adorning the center.

The cart lurched to a stop and she stepped down. A young, small man in a black tunic and Teutonic-style leggings – a popular street fashion in the city now – came forward, a large toothy grin on his narrow brown face. 'I am very pleased to meet the granddaughter of the sophē Patrikia,' he said, dipping forward slightly and passing his hand over his head in salute. 'My name is Seleukos, and I am from Nikaea near Hippo. I am assistant to the bibliophylax. Welcome to the Library.'

'Thank you,' Rhita said. He dipped again and beckoned her to follow. She closed her eyes briefly, checking on the status of the clavicle – it had not been moved or approached – and then walked after the young man.

The ground-floor office of the bibliophylax was not large for his station. Three male secretaries worked busily at a triangle of desks in one corner, beneath the light of an open window. Beside them, a press reaching to the ceiling overflowed with stacks of papers. A large electric graphomekhanos hummed and clunked on a heavy wooden stand beside the press. The bibliophylax himself worked behind a four-part Ioudeian hand-carved cedar screen, beneath the largest window in the room, in the opposite corner. The young man ushered her politely behind the screen.

The bibliophylax raised his shaven head and surveyed her coolly, then smiled the merest hint of a smile. He stood and passed his hand over his head. Rhita did likewise, and took a withy-cane seat at his request.

'I trust everything is in order with your quarters?' he asked. She nodded, reluctant to quibble about small things. 'It is an honor to have you here.' He pulled forward a file – a finger's-width of papers pressed between two paper-board sheets – and pulled out a long document. She recognised it as the transcript of her Akademeia studies and appended progress report. 'You are a distinguished student indeed, especially in the area of mathematics and physics, I see. And you have chosen a similar curriculum here. Our professors have much to offer you. We are, after all, a much larger institution than the Akademeia, and we draw our teachers from around the Oikoumenē, and even outside.'

'I look forward to beginning my studies.'

'One thing interests me. You made an unusual request, even before you arrived,' the bibliophylax observed. 'Besides your appointment to the office of the mekhanikos Zeus Ammōn Demetrios, unusual in itself, you wish a private audience with the Imperial Hypsēlotēs. Can you tell me the purpose of your visit to her?'

Before Rhita could speak, the bibliophylax raised a hand and said, 'It is our business, because we look after the welfare of all students in the Mouseion.'

She closed her mouth, waited for a moment, and then said, 'I bring a private message from my grandmother.'

'She's deceased,' the bibliophylax observed, deadpan.

'Through my father. A message the sophē felt the queen would be intersted in.' She paused, her lips set in a grim line. She could feel opposition radiating from the bibliophylax, even a professional kind of hatred. 'A private message.'

'Of course.' His face soured slightly, and he flipped through more papers. 'I have reviewed your course requests, and they are all in order. You are seeking a fifth in mathematics, and a third in physics, as well as a second in science of city leadership. Can you handle such an academic load without strain?'

'It's similar to my load at the Akademeia.'

'Ah, but Mouseion professors will not be awed by your ancestry. They might treat you less leniently.'

'I was not treated leniently on Rhodos,' Rhita said, keeping her irritation in check. She wanted to laugh at the man, kick her slippers off and show him the bottom of her foot – but she stayed outwardly composed, though her stomach twisted.

'No, I am sure you weren't,' the bibliophylax said. His small black eyes dared her to say something more.

'I do have one problem,' she said, facing his stare.

'Oh?'

'My manservant. He is with me for protection, at the direct request of my father, yet we have been separated – '

'No servants or guards are allowed in the Mouseion. Not even for royalty.'

As it happened, there were no royal youths studying in the Mouseion; the queen was childless, and most of the rest of the royal family had long since retired to Kypros for safety.

'Please feel free to consult this office at any time,' the bibliophylax concluded abruptly, closing her file and slipping it into a small square withy basket on the left hand corner of his desk. He smiled and passed his hand over his head, dismissing her.

When she returned to her quarters, she sat in the cool of the room for an hour, trying to regain her composure. The Objects had not been disturbed, but could she count on complete privacy and security for much longer? She did not trust the bibliophylax; the only hope she had was that the queen had already taken up her case, and was protecting her. Whatever, she hoped her audience would be soon.

She suspected, once she told the queen what she knew – and demonstrated its truth to her – that she would not long remain a student in the Mouseion. She would no longer be allowed the luxury of scholarship and studies.

Discouraged, she left her room to attend the meeting of the women's council. The least she hoped to accomplish there was to get the lock back.

Is everybody here my enemy? she wondered.

13

Thistledown

The Thistledown's axis bore hole opened tiny and black in the middle of the vast depression marking the asteroid's south pole. The opposite pole – 'north' for a sense of direction only, since the asteroid had no natural magnetic field – was now a gaping, rough-edged crater with the seventh chamber opened wide to space. Using ships equipped with traction fields, the Hexamon had long since swept the debris of the Sundering away from the seventh chamber, making it serviceable as a spaceport. Someday, the orbiting precincts would need extensive repair; the seventh chamber dock would be ideal.

For small ships like the shuttle on which the Russian and Lanier rode, the south pole entrance was more practical.

Lanier hardly noticed the darkness swallowing the craft. His mind was still elsewhere. He felt a stronger queasiness, and a flash of anger at his eternal unease. He closed his eyes tight, then opened them suddenly as the shuttle latched onto the rotating interior dock.

'We are here,' the Russian said.

The first chamber had changed little. Even the de-rotation and re-rotation of the Thistledown had left it relatively unmarred. Of course, there had been little but sandy desert on the first chamber's floor in the first place. As they departed the elevator, a steady, cool breeze fell on them from the face of the chamber's southern cap, a great, demeaning gray wall behind them. Around the axis shimmered the hazy white light of the plasma tube, twenty kilometers above them where they now stood on the 'valley' floor.

To each side, the chamber stretched as flat and normal as could be imagined for a dozen kilometers, then with a slow, lazy vault began to creep upward, finally rising in an impossible vertical curve to meet overhead, behind the plasma tube, like some bridge for gods. After a good many years – how long had it been since his last visit, ten, twelve? – the dimensions of the Thistledown's inner chambers struck Lanier all over again. He remembered the feeling of those awful months before the Death, when he had been swamped by administrative duties, by intrigues on Earth and within the Stone, by mystery and foreknowledge. He had called it being Stoned.

The rush of memories did not cheer him. He found it difficult to believe men had ever dwarfed themselves by such a creation. That was how he felt; small, over-powered. Stoned again.

They were greeted by a tall man, skeletally slender and very bald, an assistant to Korzenowski. 'My name is Svard. Ser Korzenowski sends his regrets that he does not meet you personally.' He gave the Russian a quick appraising stare, then he led them toward a tractor. 'The Engineer has a research compound in the middle of the valley, and he invites you to join him there.'

They boarded the tractor. The eight-passenger vehicle rode over the sand on a traction field, not treads or tires; it had been manufactured aboard Thistledown and was sleek and beautiful, with a pearly white exterior and a soft, adaptable gray interior that shaped itself to spoken or picted commands.

Svard wore a pictor hidden within his low collar. Lanier had never quite learned the art of picting. 'I trust you've had an interesting journey, Mr. Lanier, Mr. Mirsky,' Svard said. Lanier nodded abstractedly. The tractor floated smoothly and swiftly over low scrub and brown and white patches of sand and soil.

'What keeps Ser Korzenowski busy now?' Lanier asked. 'We haven't spoken for some time.'

'He has been doing research,' Svard said.

'For the Hexamon?' Lanier asked.

'In part. Mostly to satisfy his own curiosity.'

'Who pays the bills?'

Svard smiled over his shoulder. 'Really, Mr. Lanier. You should know that Ser Korzenowski has – what is the old phrase? – carte blanche to spend any reasonable amount, either in resources or money. He was given that privilege before his death, and the circumstances did not change with his resurrection.'

'I see,' Lanier said.

Directly ahead lay a complex of low, flat buildings, their walls gently curved to merge with the sand. The air above the complex shimmered like a mirage; was it because of rising heat, Lanier wondered, or something else? He squinted through the tractor's transparent nose, trying to define the shimmer.

The tractor stopped a few dozen meters from the southernmost building and eased to the sand with a low sigh. The door flowed open and Mirsky stepped out first, Lanier following, watching the man's reaction closely. The Russian looked around the valley floor, glancing up at the plasma tube. *He knows the Stone*, Lanier thought. *He's been here before. It doesn't hold pleasant memories for him.*

Svard bent low to exit the tractor and rose gracefully to his full height, large eyes blinking. 'This way. Ser Korzenowski is in his private quarters.'

Lanier savored the extra spring in his step. The Stone's spin imparted a pull of six-tenths of Earth's gravity on the floor of each chamber, one of the few qualities of the Thistledown that had always been pleasant to him. He remembered, decades ago – before the Death – exercising in the first chamber, swinging vigorously on parallel bars . . . That reminded him of his once excellent physical conditioning. He had been a gymnast in college.

A hundred meters to the east of the main complex, a smaller anonymous blister of white rose a few meters out of the sand. Svard escorted them along a gravel path and picted a greeting to the dome's receptor as they approached. A green icon of an outspread hand floated before each of them. 'He wants us to come right in,' Svard said. A square door in the wall curled aside, and Konrad Korzenowski emerged, dressed in a simple dark blue caftan.

Lanier had not seen him in person in over thirty years. He had changed little in that time; a simple, spare frame, round face topped by a short crop of pepper-gray hair, a sharp, long nose and penetrating dark eyes. The eyes were more haunted – and haunting – than when they had first met. Having absorbed part of Patricia Vasquez's mystery, that part of the human personality which could not be synthesised, Korzenowski had seemed to carry in ineffable aspect of the mathematician. His look had been enough to spook Lanier. Patricia was still discernible in the Engineer's makeup, if anything, more pronounced. *What does he feel, with part of her making up his core?*

On Earth before the Death, heart-transplants had been commonplace before the perfection of prostheses. *How does one feel about carrying a transplanted part of someone's soul?*

'Good to see you again, Ser Lanier,' Korzenowski said, shaking his hand. He hardly glanced at Mirsky, treating him less as a guest and more perhaps as an unresolved curiosity. He beckoned them enter and take seats. The free-form white interior of Korzenowski's quarters was cluttered with white and gray cylinders of all sizes, draped with lumps of what looked like white bread dough. He pulled a few of these aside – as he lifted them, they elongated in his hands, hissing faintly – and ordered the floor to form chairs, which shaped themselves rapidly. The Russian sat and folded his arms, appearing at ease. The trace of apprehension he had exhibited outdoors was gone.

Svard made his farewells, picted something rapidly to the Engineer, and departed. Korzenowski folded his arms decisively, echoing Mirsky's gesture, and stood before Lanier and the Russian. The Engineer's expression had become stern, irritated.

'We have a genuine puzzle here, Ser Lanier,' he said, regarding the Russian. 'Is this truly Pavel Mirsky, or a clever imitation?' He looked sharply at Lanier. 'Do you know?'

'No,' Lanier said.

'What's your intuition?'

Lanier didn't answer for a moment, a little startled. 'I can't really say. If I have any intuition, it's fogged by all the impossibilities.'

'I know for a fact that Pavel Mirsky went down the Way in one half of the Axis City, and that the Way closed up behind him, and all who accompanied him. I know there has been no gate opened to this Earth since. If this is Pavel Mirsky, he's returned to us by some avenue we can't begin to guess at.'

The Russian shifted a little in his seat, folded his hands in his lap, and nodded agreement, content to be spoken of as if he were not there.

'He seems self-satisfied,' Korzenowski said, rubbing his chin speculatively. 'Cat with a canary feather. I hope he pardons a candid examination. Our instruments tell us that he is solid and human, down to his atomic structure. He is not a ghost in the old or new sense, and he is not a projection of any kind familiar to us.' Korzenowski uttered these observations as if going through a string of obvious truths simply to get them out of the way. 'His genetic structure is that of Pavel Mirsky, as recorded in the medical records of the third chamber city. Are you Lieutenant General Pavel Mirsky?'

The Russian glanced between them. 'The simplest answer is yes. I think it is close to the truth.'

'Do you come here of your own free will?'

'With the same qualifications, yes.'

'How did you come here?'

'That's more complicated,' the Russian said.

'Do we have time to listen, Ser Lanier?'

'I do,' Lanier said.

'I would like Ser Olmy to be here,' Mirsky said.

'Unfortunately, Ser Olmy does not answer his messages. I suspect he is on Thistledown, but I don't know where. I've sent a partial to locate him and tell him the circumstances. He may or may not join us. I'd like to hear your story as soon as possible.' Korzenowski sat and pulled one of the white lumps into his lap, kneading it between his hands.

Mirsky stared at the spotless floor for a moment, then sighed. 'I will begin. Telling it all with words would be painfully slow and clumsy. May I borrow one of your projectors?'

'Certainly.' Korzenowski ordered a traction beam to lower the nearest projector. 'Do you require an interface?'

'I don't think so,' Mirsky said. 'I'm somewhat more than I appear.' He touched the teardrop-shaped device with a single finger. 'Pardon me if I don't completely reveal myself to your apparatus.'

'Quite all right,' Korzenowski said, with absurd cordiality. Lanier's body hair tingled again. 'Do begin.'

The quarters interior vanished, replaced by something difficult for Lanier to comprehend at first – a condensed representation of the Way, the Axis City, Mirsky's first few days in the forested Wald of the Central City, the journey down the Way, accelerating along the flaw . . .

The projected information spun and dazzled. All sense of present time ended. Mirsky told his story in his own way. Korzenowski and Lanier lived it.

*Call it escape or the grandest defection of all time. Running
from the horrid past, my own death, the death of my nation,
the near-death of my planet. If you can refer to as 'running'
the flight of half a city, filled with many tens of millions of
souls and perhaps a dozen million corporeal human beings,
down an infinite tunnel in space-time, fleeing through the*

fury of a star's heart on the rail of an elongated 'knot,' an umbilicus of impossibilities . . .

The tunnel itself an immense tapeworm curling through the guts of the real universe, pores opening onto other universes equally real but not our own, other times real and equally real . . . Those pores cauterised by our passage, the tunnel itself changing or having changed because of our flight, warping and expanding from the moment it was made with the prior knowledge of our escape; how do you explain this to an unaugmented human being?

You cannot.

I had to change to know all this, and change I did, many times across decades and centuries of flight. I became many people, and sometimes one of me would hardly know another until they could mesh with each other, exchange personal gossip. I was no longer the Russian Mirsky – had not been perhaps since my assassination in the Thistledown library – but an inhabitant of the Geshel neighborhoods of Axis Nader and Central City. A citizen of a new world, adapting to it's unlikely environment. We were no longer masters of all we surveyed, as the Axis City had once nearly been . . .

I watched the humans who had come with me from Earth evolve, as I did, or eventually fade away – die in the last way left to immortals, to forget one's self and be forgotten by others. The rest of us lived, and merged.

The journey lasted, from our point of view, centuries. You know that time is a variable thing, far less important than our youth and weakness once made us think; flexible, but ever-present, warped and twisted into some barely recognisable form or another.

I lived many different times: the time of the city traveling down the Way at relativistic velocities, my time on the high-speed level of city memory, the time spent communicating directly with my fellow travelers, as I do now with you. Time bunched and coiled like a spring. If all my time were stretched out in a straight line, I might have lived ten thousand years, by your scale . . .

We had long since passed beyond the point in the Way where the last moments of this universe might have been accessed. Had we opened a gate there, something not possible to us, we might have witnessed the death of all we had ever known, all that was — however remotely — connected with us . . . And still we fled. I had defected from my own universe.

Strangely, that moment was not particularly momentous. We had already closed in upon ourselves in an extraordinary way, like a pupating insect. We had isolated ourselves from our surroundings, even as we continued to study them.

The Way opened into an immense, twisted tunnel. Our passage down this tunnel no longer followed any rational geodesic. There was no longer a flaw, a singularity, in the middle; the city could not draw its power from the flaw generators, so it sucked power from the very thin atmosphere of particles and stray atoms within the Way. And because of this, we slowed . . . rapidly. Within ten years of our own basic time, the city traveled at less than relativistic velocities.

The Way grew broader around us. We studied this increase, and foresaw what awaited us . . . A vast blister of space-time, capping but not ending the Way, finite but unbounded . . .

We had entered the egg of a new universe. We could not survive as material beings within this egg. We would have been dissolved by the nascent plasma of potential mass and energy as salt vanishes in water. But we learned how to cope with such an eventuality.

The entire city, all of its citizens, worked to transform itself. We expected at any moment to simply die, cease to exist, for we were children facing a raging furnace. But there was another possibility, very remote . . .

The possibility that we could adapt to the furnace-egg, live in it, and finally shape it to expand into a mature universe. It would sever its connection with the Way, drift free in superspace, and within the furnace-egg, our transformed selves would expand butterly wings, reborn.

Is it immodest to say we planned to become gods? We had no choice. We had reached the end of the Way, such as it had any end, and we could not go back . . . We had no choice but to make our own universe.

To do so, we had to shed all of our material connections.

107

We had to impose ourselves on the foundation of all space and time, beyond and below energy and matter, beyond the touch of the plasma amnion.

I watched my companions wall themselves up in light, great rose windows of personality spreading and blurring at the edges, painted across the walls of the city, using the city's mass as a temporary restraint against simply dissolving away. The light of each of us touched the light of all. We were drunk with oneness. It was an orgy of incredible proportions. All the remnants of our humanity distilled into a vast merging sexuality. We almost lost sight of our goal. We might have become stunned by our own self-immersion in recognition, love and pleasure, and plunged like a lovesick moth into the furnace . . . But we regained control, and managed to take the next step.

All that we were, now united, was a frail and very delicate tissue of thought wrapped in and around the remains of the city. We spread those tissues out to the particle winds within the Way, much hotter now with the furnace-egg so near. We toughened, condensed, and finally pushed ourselves through to a level beneath even that of light and energy.

We flowered into the furnace, imposed our will, gave it the impetus to expand by converting the remaining mass of the city into energy, tipping the balance. The unbounded egg began to swell and cool, its plasma amnion condensing and taking shape . . .

We became shapers of worlds. For a moment, we considered simply reproducing our own birth universe, making galaxies and stars and starting things anew. But we learned quickly that we could not do this. This universe was far more constrained than ours had been. Its roots were humbler, coming not out of the ground of superspace itself, but from the tortured extending of the Way. It would be smaller, less complex, far less ambitious. Still, we could shape it into a fascinating place, a universe that would absorb all our creative abilities . . . if we were careful.

It is far more difficult to be a god than we could possibly have imagined. We had assumed, from the beginning I suppose, that one conscious will, or a combined conscious will, could shape and control a universe. We focused our pinpoint of will and shaped and made, guided and tuned, in ways that of course I cannot begin to describe, because in this body I cannot remember them, or fit them into my thoughts even if I could remember.

For a time, it seemed all would go well. We rejoiced in our mastery. We were like a child in a vast playground. The universe became beautiful. We began to shape the equivalents of living and thinking beings, to be our companions, perhaps to hold our own personalities in time. We still yearned for material form. We were still influenced by our origins.

And then it began to fail. The universe ruptured, decayed, rotted. Its boundaries shriveled inward, eating and transforming what order we had established into sour, hot chaos. We had miscalculated. A single will could not create a stable universe. There had to be contrast and conflict.

We desperately tried to separate ourselves into opposing forces to repair the damage. But it was much too late.

The god we had become, failed.

We would have all ceased to exist, dissolved in the falling shreds of our failure. But we heard another voice. It was a less exalted, less ecstatic voice than ours, and it seemed far away. But it was much more practical and experienced, much more diverse. We thought for a time we had heard the voice of another god, or gods, but that was simply our ignorance. However advanced we had become, we were incredibly ignorant and naive.

What we heard was the voice of our descendants, reaching us from the end of our own universe. All the intelligent beings who had grown up and grown old with the cosmos we had been born into, had detected our failure, and felt us trapped within. They were no more material, no more distinguishable as individuals than we were, but theirs was a hardier, more practical intelligence. They had become the Final Mind, at once united and coherent, and yet made up of many individual communities of minds.

They rescued us. Pulled us back along the still-open cord of the Way, never quite severed from our furnace-egg.

Their rescue was not magnanimous. They had a use for us.

Is it appropriate to describe the emotions of a failed god? We were chagrined, deeply embarrassed. We measured ourselves against this other matrix of thought, and saw we were less than infantile: we were puerile. We were young wine aspiring to vintage. We had begotten vinegar.

But we were forgiven, and treated, brought back to the equivalent of health. We were welcomed into the community of thinkers, one and separate at once, who occupied the end of the old universe. They revealed many things to us.

I was reconstituted from the whole of my matrix, isolated – an experience worse than death, I can assure you, worse than loss of family or city or nation or planet. I mourned and went crazy, and they reconstituted me again, with refinements. Finally, after many attempts, they made me stable, and sent me back here.

I carry a message, and a request – if it can be called a request. They have their limitations, these descendants of all intelligent beings now alive. And they have their duties. They must bring the universe to an honorable and complete end, an aesthetic conclusion. But they do not have infinite resources.

I am more than I seem, but I am far less than those who sent me here, and I must persuade you of one thing.

I have described the Way as a great tapeworm, winding through the guts of the universe. It extends beyond our universe, as you know. The universe cannot die with such an artificial, such a young construct winding through its body; rather, it cannot die well. It can only die badly, and our descendants cannot accomplish all they hope to.

Lanier swam out of the projection and re-focused his eyes on Mirsky. One particular image lingered in his mind. It terrified him. He tried to remember it clearly, but all he could retrieve was a vague impression of certain galaxies being chosen, throughout time, for sacrifice . . .

Galaxies dying to provide the energy for whatever the Final Mind was trying to do.

His head throbbed and he felt mildly nauseated, as if he had eaten too much. Moaning, he leaned forward between his knees.

Korzenowski put a hand on his shoulder.

'I share your distress,' the Engineer said quietly. Lanier glanced up at Mirsky, who had released the projector.

'What in hell are you?' he asked weakly.

Mirsky didn't answer that question. 'You must re-open the Way, and you must destroy it from this end. If you do not, then we have betrayed our children at the end of time. The Way, to them, is a kind of magnificent hairball, an obstruction. We are responsible for it.'

14
Gaia

On the evening of her fourth day in Alexandreia, after seven frustrating hours trying to find her way around the maze of buildings, walking from classroom to distant classroom, as Rhita sat alone in her room, digesting another unfamiliar and faintly nauseating meal eaten in the tiny dining hall reserved for women, she allowed herself a moment of supreme homesickness and misery. There was nothing she could do but cry. After a few minutes of that, and no more, she sat up on the hard cot and grimly considered her situation.

There had been no word yet from Kleopatra.

She had not yet met with the mekhanikos Demetrios, her appointed didaskalos. On a rare occasion of providing useful information, Yallos told Rhita that she should meet with the didaskalos within a week or so, otherwise her standing in the academic competition might slip. She felt lost; she had had an appointment with the man since the week before sailing from Rhodos. Inquiring at his office, in a dark, ancient and ill-tended building in the western quarter of the Mouseion grounds, she had been told by a waspish male assistant, 'He had been called to Krētē for a conference. He will be back inside a month.'

What was worse then the indignity was her sense of loss and alienation. Nobody here knew her; it seemed scarcely anybody cared about her. The women – with the unfortunate exception of Yallos, whom Rhita had taken a strong disliking to – ignored her or slighted her. Yallos, with an air of coming to the aid of a simpleton, had appointed herself Rhita's informal advisor.

To the women in the dilapidated two story building,

she was 'an island girl,' unsophisticated and boorish. Worse, she was also from a well-known family, and yet had not been graced by the Mouseion with any apparent privileges. Her social status was a puzzle, then; she was fair game for their disdain. Within earshot, they gossiped about her, speculating wildly. She had heard whispered rumors that the Kelt was her 'island lover.'

That, she thought, was probably envy.

She was not free to leave the Mouseion and wander the streets of Alexandreia; she knew very well what might happen to an innocent 'island girl' there. And walking with the burly, taciturn Kelt at her side was not the sort of stroll she fancied just now, though in time she might resort to his company, just to get away from the Mouseion.

She hadn't seen the ocean since leaving the quays in the Great Harbor.

Rhita longed for Rhodos, for the prancing sea-laughter of the waves when a storm sat offshore, the dusty green smell of olive groves and the play of dazzling clouds against lapis blue sky. What she missed most of all was the company of Rhodians, simple and sun-wise, as the island saying went; especially the beach children.

Perhaps she was just an 'island girl.'

At almost any hour of the day, sometimes even at dusk or after the twilight had faded, on the rocky and sandy beaches of Rhodos could be found a few scampering adolescents, brown and naked but shifts or lioncloths. Usually they were Avar Altais from the south of the island or the old refugee slums in Lindos, swarthy, oriental-eyed, round-headed, mouths full of curses, sun-gold limbs flashing as they spear-fished in the tidepools or carried makeshift metal detectors in search of lost coins or buried wrecks. She had stolen away as an adolescent from her studies to run with them, laughing and learning their language, their curses and sunny expressions of enthusiasm, musical and harsh at once, so alien or her Hellenised tongue. Her mother had called

113

them 'barbarians,' an old word seldom used now. Most of the citizens of the Oikoumenē were barbarians by her mother's definition.

When Rhita's breasts had developed, and the shoulders on the beach boys had grown broader, something new had come into their play – a tender roughness. She had almost appreciated the curses thrown at her, half in jest, half as if growled by carnivores wanting her flesh. Had she been less protected, a bit more worldly and less enshrouded by the Hypateion gymnasion's code of behavior, one of those boys might have been her first lover. The Great Mother knows she had had enough caresses and kisses stolen from her.

She still remembered their jokes, born out of centuries of struggle and desperation, not at all tempered by the tolerance and clime of Rhodos. There were cruel, wild jokes about ill-timed death spoiling great plans, raucous fables about separated families and lost relatives, about herd animals never seen on Rhodos.

Once, she had sat talking with a boy perhaps a year younger than she. He had told her his family's story, unnumbered centuries tangled up with the lives of other families, other tribes, perhaps even other nations; and she had tried to fit that in to what she knew about the old Rhus-Oikoumenē-Parsa alliances and the extinguishing of the Steppes tribes. In return, he had listened to her formal history with unusual politeness and attention, and then had told her, 'That's what you winners say.' Leaping up, he had brayed at her like an ass, and run across the beach, his bare feet unerringly picking a path on flat sun-heated stones.

With a sigh, Rhita opened her eyes, losing that hot pale noon sky and distant running boy. She picked up the electronic teukhos that had belonged to her grandmother, switched it on, selected a memory block and began to search through the volumes listed. Then, realising she might be taking a risk, she turned the machine's lighted screen off. Examining the frail door, she decided the least she could do was block it with the

114

room's single cane chair. She hadn't dared listen to any of the music cubes since her arrival; discovery would be at best embarrassing, and at worse, disastrous. The Mouseion might confiscate the Objects. They might accuse her of all sorts of ridiculous crimes; how could she know?

Rhita hated this strange, difficult, clannish Mouseion, with its ancient, mazy gounds . . .

She felt out of place among the city-wise students, drawn from all around Gaia. To her surprise, she had seen young men dressed in the peculiar fringed leather clothes sported by Nea Karkhēdonians, in imitation of the indigenous peoples they had subjugated a century ago. These were the children of the sworn enemies of the Oikoumenē. What perversion of diplomacy allowed them into Alexandreia? She had even seen students dressed in the shifts and leather skirts of Latin tribes. Not that she disliked any of them personally; Rhodos seemed so remote from all that, though having studied her history, she knew nobody was truly isolated from such conflicts.

Rhita drew the gap in the curtains tighter, old nutshell curtain rings rattling against the cane rod, and returned to her bed, feeling without reason a little more secure. Switching the screen back on, she surveyed the list. She had read or looked through virtually all of the two hundred and seven books listed.

This time, however, her eyes alighted on a title she had not read. She could have sworn it was newly added. It said simply, 'READ ME NOW.' She called it up on the screen.

The index card preceding the display of the first page told her the volume was three hundred pages in length – about a hundred thousand words – and it was in Hellenic, not English, as all the other books in the cubes were. She halted the display of the index as she saw a flashing cursor next to a description she had not seen before. 'Contents and catalog display suppressed until 4/25/49.'

That had been two days before.

Rhita pressed the keypad to read the first page.

Dear Granddaughter,

You have the name of my mother. Is it all my fancy someday you will meet her? When you were younger you must have thought I was a crazy old woman though I think you loved me. Now you have this, and I can talk to you though I have never gone home, not really. Some say even here that dying is going home.

Imagine that world I have told you about, and you have read these books, if you are my granddaughter, and I know you are. You have read these books and they must tell you I made nothing up. All is true. There was a place called Earth. I did not come out of a whirlwind.

I clung to this slate and the few blocks brought with me – all by accident, by chance! – for years when it seemed even to me I must be crazy. Now you are burdened by my quest. But all things are connected, even such faraway things as my world Earth and yours Gaia. My fancy could be important to you and all on Gaia. If there is a gate. And there will be again. They have come and gone on the clavicle like dust-devils. Who would taunt an old woman so?

On certain days, I will leave you something here to read, like the unrolling of a scroll, to be revealed only that day and after.

She could not get the machine to display any more of the large file's contents. The machine had apparently been set to portion it out to her a bit at a time. Rhita turned off the slate and screwed her knuckles into her eyes. She could not get away from Patrikia. She had no life of her own.

But if there was such a thing as a gate –

And there was! Who could deny machines that spoke to her mind, or hundreds of books her grandmother could not possibly have imagined, much less written?

If the gate was real, then there was more of a burden on her shoulders now than just responsibility to her grandmother. All the people on Gaia weighed her down.

Rhita was beginning to imagine what such a thing as a gate would mean to this world. Not all that she imagined was pleasant. It would bring change, perhaps immense change . . .

15

Thistledown City

The tracer transferred itself to Olmy's library terminal
and signaled with the black and white pict of a grinning
terrier that it had completed its search. Olmy switched
on blowers to collect the remnants of a meager cloud of
pseudo-Talsit, pushed himself off the couch and stood
before the teardrop terminal, concentrating on the tracer's picted condensation of its findings.

*No relevant file sources in Axis Euclid or Thoreau or
copies of library records of Nader and Central City. All file
sources classified in Thistledown libraries; classification limit
has expired, but no records of access to files since the Sundering. Last access –52 years remote from Axis City, no identifi-
cation, but likely from noncorporeal in city memory. Thirty-
two files containing references to Fifth Chamber Repository.*

By law, all security classifications in libraries and city
memory storage were voided after one hundred years
without application and approval for renewal. Olmy
inquired of the tracer how many applications for extension had been made on the files. The tracer replied *Four.*

The files were all older than four hundred years.

'Records of file authors,' he requested.

All author records deleted.

That was highly unusual. Only a president or presiding minister could approve of deletion of authors or
originators from file records in libraries or city memory
storage; and even then, only for the most pressing
reasons. Anonymity was not an approved concept in
Hexamon history; too many of the Death's perpetrators
had hidden themselves away from responsibility before
and after the holocaust.

'Description of files.'

All are brief reports, in words only.

The time had come. Olmy was surprised to realise his reluctance. The truth might be worse than what he had imagined.

'Show me the files in chronological order,' he said.

It *was* worse.

When he had finished and stored all the files in implant memory to mull over at leisure, he gave the tracer its reward – the free run of a simulated grassy field on Earth – and released the meager cloud of pseudo-Talsit into the room again.

His decision was made infinitely more difficult by what the tracer had retrieved.

Reading between the lines – the whole story was by no means contained in the files, which were adjunct files only, bare scraps left over after some hasty and none-too-thorough purge – Olmy put together his half-educated surmise.

A living Jart had been captured some five centuries before, under what circumstances there was no knowing. It had died before being returned to Thistledown and its body had been preserved after its mentality was crudely downloaded. Not knowing Jart psychology or physiology, the downloading had been only partly successful. How integrated the Jart mentality was, how true to its original, not even its captors had known. They had even suspected the body; several researchers felt that Jarts, like humans, could adapt their biological forms and even their genetic makeup to fit the circumstances. Hence, the Jart's physiology had been studied, but the studies were inconclusive; they had not been passed on to military commanders or other researchers.

At first, the investigations into the downloaded mentality had been conducted in secure but relatively open situations, with perhaps ten or fifteen individual researchers. Nine had died in the process, two irretrievably – their implants hopelessly scrambled. Direct or indirect mental links with the downloaded personality had been forbidden at that point. Research, so encumbered, came almost to a halt.

Even then, Olmy knew, indirect examination of mentalities had been a highly developed art. He found it difficult to believe that a Jart, fragmented or whole, could injure investigators in such circumstances. And yet, Beni had been killed and Mar Kellen damaged . . .

Olmy controlled another hormonal surge. Were he not so altered and augmented, the surge would indicate a condition called *fear*.

For centuries, there had been a law in cybernetic research: 'For any program, there is a system such that the program cannot not know its system.' That is, a program, however complicated, even a human mentality, could not always be aware of the system it was running on, if no clues were provided by that system; it could only know the extent to which the system allowed it to run.

But less than a century ago, Hexamon investigators headed by a brilliant team-leader, homorph Doria Fer Taylor, had found mathematical algorithms which allowed programs to completely determine the nature of their systems. Thus, a downloaded mentality could tell whether or not it had been downloaded; Olmy could, in theory, know under any circumstances whether his focus of personality was running in implants or in his organic mind.

In theory, such algorithms, fully developed, could allow a mentality or program to change the nature of its system, to the extent that a system could be changed. Because of the existence of rogues in city memory, such information could have had disastrous consequences. The rogues – even one rogue – could have destroyed city memory and all that was in it. Human mentalities were not disciplined enough to be given such power. The researches had been classified. Olmy had learned of them through his police work, when he had been ordered by the presiding minister to investigate whether any mentalities in remote gate memories – human or otherwise – had independently discovered such power. None had.

Olmy searched his deepest levels of implant memory for the Taylor algorithms. He had often tucked away such items, trusting himself to keep them secure, unable to resist the chance to incorporate them into his personal data file. They were still available. He would have to purge them before – if – he ever downloaded into the current city memory.

Not likely, he thought.

Judging from what had happened to Beni and Mar Kellen, as well as the early researchers, the Jart mentality was aware of and fully capable of using the Taylor algorithms. But at the time of its capture, humans had not even known of their existence.

The Jart mentality, still an unknown quantity, had been removed to complete isolation in the fifth chamber, to be studied now and then across some number of decades, apparently less than a century, and then to be forgotten, but for an occasional inquiry as to status. Too valuable to be destroyed, too dangerous to be investigated . . .

The investigators had apparently all passed into city memory in their allotted times. Most had been Geshels. Equally apparent, all of them had chosen to go down the Way during the Sundering. That could explain why there had been no further inquiries in the last forty years; it did not explain twelve years of silence before that.

He called up the complete list of data and looked at the file access dates. *Why check on static files if not to see whether somebody else has accessed them?*

The access dates were all between five and thirty years apart over the last century and a half. The name of the accessor had been erased after the fact in each case; a clever trick, but perhaps not clever enough. Olmy requested the string length of the erased void in each access record. In every case, the name had filled fifteen spaces. It seemed probable that only one person had accessed the files for at least one hundred and fifty years, checking to see if the footprints were still hidden, if the danderous skeleton in the closet was still secure.

Someone, of course, could have accidentally stumbled on the security door in the fifth chamber, or found out about it as Mar Kellen had. But Mar Kellen had used code cracking techniques developed comparatively recently to open the door.

In all likelihood, nobody in the Terrestrial Hexamon but Mar Kellen and now Olmy knew anything about the captured Jart.

Mar Kellen was finding his way to an honorable obscurity.

That left Olmy.

16
Gaia

The Boulē conference on the Libyan attack on the Brukheion had been discouraging. Jewish militia stationed all around the Nilos delta had already shown their displeasure in demonstrations that bordered on mutiny; the Boulē was now reacting. Kleopatra, attended by her usual midge-cloud of counselors and advisors, had emerged from the session into the glare of lights wielded by an official Boulē recording crew. She had enough vanity to hate bright lights and cameras, and enough sense of duty to smile.

Her position as queen was shaky indeed. She had long since come to regret the power she had regained for the Ptolemaic Dynasty in the past thirty years; power enough to take blame, yet not enough to assume control. She did not have the power to defy the Boulē completely and take charge of the military; yet she was held responsible by many groups if the Boulē military policy was a failure. Rumours of plots were thick in the air; she almost wished they would come true.

The day did not improve when her Mouseion spy reported on how Rhita Berenikē Vaskayza was being treated.

Her Imperial Hypsēlotēs had long since learned to take every possible advantage of a situation. She had suspected for over a decade that the Mouseion's interests were drawing apart from her own, but not so far apart that they would be openly defiant. The Akademeia Hypateia on Rhodos was a thorn in the bibliophylax's side; Kleopatra had thought she could provoke an interesting response, then, by allowing Patrikia's grand-daughter to come to the Mouseion.

And if this young woman brought better news than Patrikia had . . . So be it.

Either way, she was useful.

But what the spy told his queen was infuriating.

She listened to the spy's testimony while seated on a campstool in her private study. Her scar whitened as her jaw muscles tightened. She had not believed that the bibliophylax Kallimakhos would be so willing to flout her authority.

Kallimakhos had sent Rhita's chosen didaskalos, a young physics and engineering professor named Demetrios, away on extended sabbatical, against his own expressed wishes. (Demetrios, the spy said, was a fine mathematician as well as a promising inventor, and had looked forward to working with the daughter of the sophē Patrikia.) Kallimakhos had then rudely treated Rhita, ignoring her privileged visitor's status, forcing her to live separately from the Kelt bodyguard who might very well be necessary for her safety . . .

Rhita Vaskayza, the spy said with some professional admiration, was bearing up well under these disgraces. 'Is she a royal favorite?' the spy asked.

'Do you need to know?' Kleopatra asked coldly.

'No, my Queen. If she is a favorite, however, you have chosen an interesting woman to favor.'

Kleopatra ignored the familiarity. 'It's time to play the chosen piece,' she said. With a deftly pointed finger, she ordered the spy from the room. A secretary appeared in the doorway. 'Bring Rhita Berenikē Vaskayza to me, tomorrow morning. Treat her exceptionally well.' She hummed and stared at the ceiling, thinking what else she could do. Something for her simple satisfaction, without derailing any larger plans. 'Send the tax auditors to the Mouseion. I want every administrator and didaskalos on the premises – understand that, only those who are immediately present – audited for tithe performance and royal taxes. With the sole exception of Kallimakhos. Tell him I wish to meet with him within the week. And see to it that any royalties and benefits transferred from palace funds to the Mouseion are delayed for three weeks.'

'Yes, my Queen.' The secretary touched clasped hands to chin and angled back through the door.

Kleopatra closed her eyes and stilled her dull anger with a slow breathy moan. She found herself wishing more and more for something apocalyptic, to cut cleanly through the political morass that was her life now. Neither supremely powerful, nor weak enough to be ignored, she had to ply her power like a sailor with a ragged boat on Lake Mareotis.

'Bring me something distracting and wonderful, Rhita Vaskayza,' she murmured. 'Something worthy of your grandmother.

The residence hall echoed with women's voices speaking Hellenic, Aramaic, Aithiopian, and Hebrew. Today was the beginning of classes, yet Rhita had no didaskalos, no assignments, and hence, no classes beyond the basics accorded to all Mouseion students: orientation, language – of which she had no need – and Mouseion history. By the second hour of morning – beginning after sunrise – the hall was nearly empty, and she sat in a dark mood in her cramped room, wondering about the wisdom of coming to Alexandreia at all.

She heard two pairs of heavy footsteps outside her door and felt a moment of anxiety. There was a rap on the doorframe, and a male voice inquired, 'Rhita Berenikē Vaskayza?'

'Yes,' she said, standing to face whoever might come in.

'I'm here with your bodyguard,' the man said in polished common Hellenic. 'Her Imperial Hypsēlotēs requests your presence by the sixth hour of this day.'

Rhita opened the door and saw Lugotorix standing behind a tall, bulky Aigyptian in royal livery. The Kelt nodded at Rhita and she blinked. 'Now?'

'Now.' The Aigyptian confirmed.

Lugotorix helped her gather the cases containing

Patrikia's Objects. She felt faintly ridiculous, having tried the Mouseion at all; but that had been her father's strategy, at her mother's suggestion, years back. *Best not to approach her Imperial Hypsēlotēs directly*, her mother had advised. *Especially after the fiasco of the disappearing gates.*

A much larger motorised wagon waited for her on the cobble road curving past the main archway of the residence hall. Three other Aigyptians, also in royal livery, carefully loaded her cases into the back. The Kelt took a seat beside the driver, and the guards stood on running boards. With a wind-horn roaring, she was driven from the grounds of the Mouseion, west to the palace.

Leaving the main gate, she looked back and realised, with an intuitive shudder, that her brief sojourn in the Mouseion was at an end.

17
Thistledown

Once, before the age of thirty, life had been bordered by walls of reasonable proportions; Garry Lanier had not had to face a constant barrage of explosive re-evaluations of reality and where he fit in. Since the arrival of the Stone, he had had to come to grips with mind-stretching truths so often, he had once thought nothing would amaze him any more.

He lay in the bunk prepared for him by Svard, Korzenowski's assistant. In the dark, on his back, half-covered by a sheet, he sighed and knew that he was not so jaded after all. The Russian's story had flabbergasted him.

Mirsky had returned, after traveling beyond the end of time and becoming at least a minor deity.

He was an avatar, a reincarnated symbol of forces outside even Korzenowski's comprehension.

'Jesus,' Lanier said almost automatically. The name had lost considerable power in the past few decades. After all, the miracles at the foundation of Christianity were almost all duplicated weekly in the Terrestrial Hexamon. Technology had superseded religion.

But what was Mirsky, that his reappearance should supersede even the abilities of the Hexamon? Had wonders gone full circle, back to the realm of religion again?

What Mirsky had shown them . . . The combination of simplified visuals and words and incomprehensible *sounds* projected into their minds . . . His innards still curled at the memory of the experience.

What would Karen have thought, from her less Western perspective? Born in China of parents defected from England, her capacity for wonders might be increased by a different attitude toward reality. At least, she had never seemed quite as culture-shocked, future-shocked, as Lanier had felt. She had accepted the inevitable and undeniable with calmness and pragmatism.

Lanier knuckled his closed eyes and turned over, trying to find elusive sleep. Now that he could not possibly see her, he realised he missed Karen. Even with the hidden bitterness of their last few years together, they shared something with her when they were together: a common link with the past.

Was it that he was simply *too old* to accept these new realities? Would pseudo-Talsit help, or a cleansing of his mental channels through a new youthfulness?

He swore under his breath and started to get out of the bunk, but there was no place he could safely go in the compound, no place where he was unobserved. And he needed isolation now, needed darkness and freedom from stimulus. He felt like a transported animal clinging to the security of an enclosed cage. Opening the door, he might be assaulted by another barrage of impossibilities.

While Lanier tried to sleep, Korzenowski was arranging a meeting with the president and several key corpreps. There was a good possibility that Judith Hoffman, Lanier's boss and mentor four decades ago, would be present.

Lanier had not kept up with her activities for years. He was not surprised to learn she had undergone pseudo-Talsit and transplant rejuvenation, but it came as something of a shock when Korzenowski informed him she was leading the Thistledown faction that supported re-opening the Way.

The trains between Thistledown's chambers were as efficient as ever, sleek silver millipedes gliding at several hundred kilometers an hour through their narrow tunnels. Lanier sat beside Mirsky, and Korzenowski sat opposite, all lost in silence.

Theirs was a cosmic shyness with little room for small talk – not after what Mirsky had showed them.

Mirsky took the silent treatment stoically, peering through the windows at the surrounding tunnel darkness and the sudden explosion of cityscape as the train emerged into tubelight.

The third chamber metropolis, Thistledown City, had been designed and built after the asteroid's launch, taking advantage of lessons learned in the construction of Alexandria in the second chamber. Its enormous towers rose from slender bases to wide tops five kilometers above the valley floor. Soaring suspended structures reached across the curve of the chamber like skyscrapers strung along a curtain. The glittering megaplexes, each as capacious as a good-sized town on prewar Earth, seemed poised for imminent disaster. Much of Thistledown City was an architectural nightmare to unaccustomed eyes, always teetering, threatening to collapse in a stray wind.

Yet these buildings had survived the stopping and re-rotation of the asteroid during the Sundering, with comparatively little damage.

'It's truly beautiful,' Mirsky said, breaking the silence. He leaned forward and shook his head enthusiastically, grinning like a boy.

'Quite a compliment from a man who's seen the end of time,' Korzenowski observed.

He doesn't act like an avatar, Lanier thought.

After the Sundering, Thistledown City had been reoccupied by citizens from the precincts. An abortive attempt to bring Old Natives to the asteroid and settle them had been called off after the new immigrants expressed great unhappiness; most had been returned to Earth, where they would not be overawed by unnatural splendor. Lanier sympathised.

Now, the city was about one-fifth full, citizens clustering together in certain areas, others in less populated regions often living one or two families to a building. If ever large numbers of Earth's inhabitants could be persuaded to make Thistledown their home, space aplenty waited for them.

All of the city's parks had been restored, unlike in Alexandreia, where restoration was still in progress. Some had been replanted with flora brought up from Earth. Conservators were encouraging endangered animals from Earth to breed in various spectacular zoos completed with the past two decades. The second and third chamber libraries contained the genetic records of every Earth species known at the time of Thistledown's launch, but a large number of species had vanished in the years after the Death; now was their chance to prevent those extinctions.

The Terrestrial Hexamon Nexus met in the middle of a thousand-acre rain forest. A wide, low translucent dome the color of a clear twilight sky vaulted over much of the forest and the Nexus meeting chambers; under the dome, the tubelight was transformed into glorious sunlight and clouds.

The Nexus was not in session this day. The meeting chambers, a circular arena and central stage, were almost empty.

Judith Hoffman sat in an aisle seat near the central stage. Lanier, Mirsky and Korzenowski walked down the aisle abreast, and she turned in her seat, cocking an eyebrow. With a quick glance, she summed up Mirsky and Korzenowski, and then she smiled at Lanier. He stepped aside and met her welcoming hug while Mirsky and Korzenowski waited.

'It's wonderful to see you again, Garry,' she said.

'It's been too long.' He smiled broadly, feeling more energetic and reassured just in her presence. She had allowed herself to age a little, Lanier noted, though she still appeared twenty years younger than he; her hair was steely gray and her face carried a look of tired, careworn dignity.

She had deliberately ignored the more advanced fashions of Thistledown City, where apparel might consist of illusion as much as cloth. Instead, she had chosen a stolid gray pants suit with just a hint of feminine cut to her lapels. She wore a pictor necklace and carried a small slate at least four decades old, the equivalent here of a quill pen.

'How's Karen? Have you been keeping up with Lenore and Larry?'

'Karen's fine. She might be here now. She's working with Suli Ram Kikura on a social project.' He swallowed. 'Lenore is in Oregon now, I believe. Larry died a few months ago.'

Hoffman's mouth made a surprised O. 'I hadn't heard . . . Damn. That's a Christian for you.' She clasped his hand and sighed. 'I'll miss him. I've been out of touch up here – too much so. I've missed you all, but there's been a lot of work.' The other three representatives approached from another aisle: David Par Jordan, Assistant and Advocate to the President, a small, delicate Thistledown-born man with white-blond hair; Sixth Chamber Supervisor Deorda Ti Negranes, a tall, lithe female homorph dressed in black; and Eula Mason, a squat, powerful woman with hawk-like features, corprep for Axis Thoreau, an orthodox but not extreme Naderite with substantial power as a swing vote in the lower Nexus.

Mirsky watched them all with his mild, distanced expression, like an actor waiting to be called on stage. Hoffman shook hands and exchanged pleasantries with Korzenowski, then turned to Mirsky. She folded her hands in front of her chest. 'Garry,' she said, 'is this man who he says he is?'

Lanier knew his judgment would be relied upon implicitly. 'I wasn't sure to start with, but now, I think he is, yes.'

'Ser Mirsky, my pleasure to meet you again,' Hoffman said. 'Under circumstances more peaceful, and certainly more mysterious.' She unfolded her hands and extended one with some hesitation. Mirsky grasped it by the fingertips and bowed.

Chivalry from the end of time, Lanier thought. *What next?*

'Indeed, Ser Hoffman,' he said. 'Much as changed.'

As they adjourned to a meeting room in the complex beneath the arena, introductions were made all around, with a social awkwardness that Lanier found amusing, considering the circumstances. Human convention could trivialise even the most momentous occasions, and perhaps that was its purpose – to bring enormous events down to a human scale.

Korzenowski pointedly did not go into detail about Mirsky.

'We have some complicated and important evidence to bring before the Nexus and the president,' Korzenowski said as they took seats around a small round table.

'I have one question, and I can't wait to ask it,' Eula Mason said, features stern. 'I know very little about Ser Mirsky. He's on Old Native – pardon me, a Terrestrial – and he has Russian ancestry, but your introduction doesn't explain his importance, Ser Korzenowski. Where does he come from?'

'From a great distance in space and in time,' the Engineer said. 'He's presented us with some disturbing news, and he's ready to testify before this select group. I warn you – you've never experienced anything like such testimony, even in city memory.'

'I make it a habit to avoid city memory,' Mason said. 'I respect you, Ser Korzenowski, but I dislike mystery and I certainly dislike having my time wasted.'

For ostensible allies united against the re-opening, Lanier thought Mason was being remarkably uncongenial to Korzenowski.

Korzenowski was unfazed. 'I've asked the four of you here because this is so unusual a circumstance, and I'd like a kind of rehearsal before we go on to the full Nexus.'

'Will we need aspirin?' Hoffman asked Lanier, leaning in his direction.

'Probably,' Lanier said.

Negranes's design as a homorph was a little too extreme for Lanier's tastes; her facial features were too small on her head, and her body was proportioned in ways that exceeded the natural – emphasis on length of legs and thickness of thighs. extremely long fingers, an almost masculine chest. Yet her bearing was regal and it was obvious she knew her place in this room, and on Thistledown. 'Is this evidence designed to discourage re-opening, Ser Engineer?'

'I think it may allow us to reach a compromise,' Korzenowski said.

That's a bit optimistic, Lanier thought.

Mason squinted with unconcealed suspicion. Obviously, Korzenowski was not completely trusted in his own camp. That was hardly surprising; he had designed the Way in the first place.

'Then let's have it,' Par Jordan said.

'This time, I will not use a projector,' Mirsky said. 'I will spare Sers Korzenowski and Lanier . . . They have suffered my story once already.'

When the presentation was over, Hoffman laid her head on the table and sighed. Lanier rubbed her neck and shoulder gently with one hand. 'God,' she exclaimed, her voice muffled. Par Jordan and Negranes seemed stunned.

Mason stood, hands trembling. 'This is a farce,' she said, turning on Korzenowski. 'I'm amazed you believed this willful deception. You are certainly not the man my father put his confidence in – '

'Eula,' Korzenowski said, facing her coldly, 'sit down. This is not deception. You know that as well as I.'

'What is it, then?' she asked, voice shrill. 'I don't understand any of it!'

'Yes, you do. It's quite clear, however amazing.'

'What does he want us to do?' she continued. Korzenowski raised his hand and nodded his head, asking for patience. Mason found just enough patience to fold her arms and sit rigidly back in her chair.

'Do you have any questions?' he asked Negranes and Par Jordan.

Par Jordan seemed the least disturbed of them all. 'You think the president should see this? I mean, experience it?' he asked.

'It must be the entire Nexus, please, for a decision,' Mirsky said. 'As soon as possible.' They looked at him as if he were an unexpected ghost – or perhaps a very large insect. They were noticeably reluctant to speak to him directly.

'Ser Korzenowski, that's going to be difficult. I sympathise with Ser Mason's reaction . . .'

She slapped her open hand on the table, vindicated.

Negranes lifted her head. 'I've never felt anything like it,' she said. 'It makes me feel immeasurably small. Is everything so futile, that we simply vanish and are forgotten in time?'

'Not forgotten,' Mirsky said. 'Please. You are not *forgotten*. I am here.'

'Why you?' Negranes asked. 'Why not some better-known figure from the Hexamon?'

'I volunteered, in a way. I offered myself,' Mirsky said.

Hoffman fixed Korzenowski with her clear brown eyes. 'We've been opposed on this question for a long time. I'm sure Garry is surprised to hear I've been supporting re-opening. How do you feel, experiencing this? Have you changed your mind?'

Korzenowski didn't answer for a moment. Then, using a tone of voice that made Lanier jump – a familiar tone, that of Patricia Vasquez – he said, 'I've always known it was inevitable. I've never enjoyed inevitability. I don't enjoy this, now. I designed the Way, and was punished for doing so by assassination. I was brought back, and I saw what progress we had made, and how much we had gained as human beings – not lost. We were trapped by our own glories.

'I was certain that returning to Earth would balance out our problems, but the Way is like a drug. We have been using this drug for so long, we cannot break free of it, so long as the possibility for re-opening remains.'

'You sound ambivalent,' Mason said.

'I think the Way must be re-opened. And then it must be destroyed. I see no alternative to the method presented by Ser Mirsky.'

'Re-opening,' Mason said, shaking her head. 'Finally giving in.'

'Our responsibility is a heavy burden,' the Engineer continued. 'The Way must be dismantled. It blocks the designs of those whose goals are far larger than anything we can easily imagine.'

'Count on this,' Mason said. 'If we favor any kind of re-opening, *they* will not let us dismantle.' She nodded at Negranes and Hoffman.

Hoffman looked at Lanier, her face only now regaining some of its color. 'By all means. The Nexus must see this. I believe this man is Mirsky, and that's remarkable enough to convince me.'

Par Jordan stood. 'I'll make my recommendation to the president.'

'What is your recommendation?' Mirsky asked.

'I doubt we can block testimony before the Nexus. I don't know whether we'd want to. I just . . . don't know.' He took a deep breath. 'The disruption is going to be unbelievable.'

Lanier suddenly longed for a chance to relive that moment on the mountain, when he had first seen the hiker descending the path.

Given another chance, he might run away as fast as cramped legs allowed.

18

Gaia, Alexandreia, Lokhias Promontory

Kleopatra the Twenty-first greeted the young woman warmly in the sitting room of her private quarters. The queen's hair was shot with gray and her eyes lackluster. The scar across her cheek, a badge of honor well-known throughout the Oikoumenē, appeared red and puffy. She looked exhausted.

The Kelt was not allowed into the private quarters. Rhita felt vaguely sorry for the man, always cooling his heels someplace away from his primary duty – protecting her.

'You were not treated well at the Mouseion,' Kleopatra said, sitting across a transparent rose-veined quartz table from the young woman. 'I ask your forgiveness and understanding.'

Rhita nodded, not knowing what to say, thinking it best to let the queen speak. Kleopatra seemed agitated, ill at ease.

'Your request for an audience was expected, and welcome,' she continued. 'I'm afraid your grandmother thought I lost faith in her.' The queen smiled faintly. 'Perhaps I did. It is easy to lose faith in a world of disappointments. But I never doubted her word. I *needed* to believe in what she said. Is that easy to understand?'

Rhita realised her silence might be interpreted as shock at being in the presence of royalty. Strangely, she was not nervous. 'Yes. I understand.'

'From what I've been told, you were not close to your grandmother, not all your life.'

'No, my Queen.'

Kleopatra waved away the formality, fixing her tired eyes on Rhita. 'She chose you for something?'

'Yes.'

'What?' The queen's hand gestured for her to be more forthcoming, as if urging her closer.

'She put me in charge of the Objects,' Rhita said.

'The clavicle?'

'Yes, my Queen.'

'Is it busy disappointing us again?'

'It shows a new gate, your Imperial Hypsēlotēs. This one has stayed in place for three years.'

'Where?'

'In the steppes of Nordic Rhus, west of the Kaspian Sea.'

The queen thought that over for a moment, brows drawn together. Her scar lightened in color. 'Not easy to get to. Does anybody else know it's there?'

'Not that I know of, my Queen.'

'Do you know where it leads?'

Rhita shook her head.

'There's nothing . . . more convincing about this particular gate?'

'In what way, my Queen?'

Try as she might, Rhita could not change her method of address. It seemed almost sacrilegious to speak to the woman baldly, without some kind of obeisance.

'I suppose I'm asking for security. If I outfit an expedition, brave the diplomatic difficulties of sending it to Nordic Rhus – should we be caught, I mean, since there's no question of asking permission – and it's all for nothing, a hole to nowhere . . .'

'I can't guarantee anything, my Queen.'

Kleopatra shook her head sadly, then smiled again. 'Neither could your grandmother.' She took a deep breath. 'She was, and you are, both very lucky to have me as queen. Someone more intelligent, more pragmatic, would not listen to either of you.'

Rhita nodded solemnly, braced for rejection.

'Do you have any idea what lies on the other side of this gate? Any notion at all?'

'It may take us back to the Way.'

'Patrikia's big water-pipe world.'

'Yes, my Queen.'

Kleopatra stood, holding her finger to her temple on the upper end of her scar, clenching and relaxing her jaw. 'What would your expedition need? More than what Patrikia once requested?'

'I don't believe so, Hypsēlotēs.'

'Not a great expenditure. The Objects are all working properly? The Rhodian mekhanikoi have kept them in good shape?'

'They have required no maintenance, my Queen. Other than changing batteries . . . They are working properly.'

'You could guide this expedition?'

'I think that is what my grandmother wished.'

'You're very young.'

Rhita did not deny it.

'Could you?'

'I believe so.'

'You lack your grandmother's passion. She would not have hesitated to say yes, even if she doubted herself.'

Rhita did not deny this, either.

Kleopatra shook her head slowly, walking around the table. She stopped with her hands resting on the back of Rhita's chair. 'It's political folly. Risking a confrontation with the Rhus, and a storm in the Boulē should secrecy be broken . . . My position is not enviable now, young woman. There's a part of me irritated – no, not just irritated, angry! – at your simply being here, making your tacit request. And another part . . . the part your grandmother took advantage of . . .'

Rhita swallowed, locking her neck muscles to keep from constantly bobbing her head in agreement.

'I've already spread some minor punishments for your ill-treatment in the Mouseion. In a way, I've already supported your cause. But it is not easy for me to simply give in to my desires. And I do desire that you find something . . . wonderful, maybe even dangerous, wonderfully newly dangerous. Something far above this incredible tangle of low-level threats and high-level hatred and intrigue.' She bent beside Rhita, bringing her face close to the young woman's, eyes shifting over her features. 'What collateral do you offer?'

'Collateral, my Queen?'

'Personal guarantees.'

'None,' Rhita replied, her heart faltering.

'None at all?'

Very softly, hating herself, fearing herself and her own uncertainties, Rhita said, 'Only my life, Hypsēlotēs.'

Kleopatra laughed. Straightening, she took Rhita's hands in her own and raised her from the chair, as if they might dance. 'There's some of the old girl in you after all,' she said. 'Can you show me?'

Rhita unlocked her neck muscles long enough to nod once.

'Then bring your clavicle here and show me, as your grandmother did. I enjoyed that experience.'

19

Thistledown, Fifth Chamber

After thirty-one days of investigation, Olmy had reached a decision. The Jart mentality, in its present location, could not be studied safely. He knew too little about the system it was stored in, whereas the Jart apparently knew everything.

He stood in the second room, jaw muscles working. The mentality's displayed image had not changed noticeably in all the time he had studied it. Placid, undisturbed, timeless; soon to be reborn, and perhaps to attempt its higher purpose yet again . . .

Olmy had never put himself into a situation where his inner being could be violated. He had even shied away from mixing personalities with lovers and friends, not uncommon back in the heady days of the Jart Wars. Whenever he had joined entertainments in city memory, he had always carefully wrapped a tight shell around his self.

He regarded this foible with as much amusement as anyone; but he had violated the rule only once, when he had down-loaded Korzenowski's reassembled partials into his implant memories. Korzenowski's scattered mentality had been close enough to share only his outer layer of thoughts, and nothing deeper, however.

In a way, he detested deep intimacy. He valued his singularness. He had never subscribed to the old poet's maxim that to be alone was to be in bad company. Olmy clearly understood why he rejected deep intimacy; he did not want to know himself completely, or to have anybody else know him. He did not relish the thought of exploring his own mentality, as others did.

But to know the Jart, the best way would be to download it into an isolated implant within himself. He could not trust any device to resist the Jart's explorations; inside, he could constantly monitor the downloaded mentality, and even shift it from an implant using one system to another with a different system. He had three large memory implants, one of them only five decades old, the extra two installed in anticipation of carrying the Engineer's partials, all of Talsit construction. Each could be modified at will, isolated, examined from outside with little or no chance of unwanted output from whatever was kept in memory . . .

The plan had been inevitable all along.

Olmy had simply avoided the obvious.

How much was he willing to sacrifice for the Terrestrial Hexamon? His mentality, his *soul*? If the Jart somehow managed to *corrode* its way through all internal barriers, to outwit and outmaneuver him, then more than that would be lost.

The Jart had allowed itself to be captured.

It was a Trojan Horse.

Of this much he was sure.

And he was about to take the horse within the walls of his own precious citadel, his mind.

If his safeguards failed, the Jart might do what it had probably planned to do all along. It could become a spy, a saboteur in human form, within the Hexamon. It could control all of his memories, even, in the worse case imaginable, convince his enslaved personality that he was acting of his own violition.

Hormonal implants kept his body chemistry in relative balance, but the sharp bite of fear was still apparent. Olmy had never been so unsure of the outcome of his plans.

He returned to the first room, where Beni had died, and opened a small box of equipment. Onto the panel's output device he locked a data valve. Drawing several leads from the valve's smooth round surface, he fastened them to the curved band that would slide tightly around the base of his skull.

The downloading could take hours; the equipment

141

here was ancient. The valve would not allow any unregulated surge of information.

You're about to become a bomb, he told himself. *A very dangerous rogue indeed.*

The room was silent but for the faint hum of the valve. He thought of the fifth chamber landscape, six kilometers above, and of the mass of the Thistledown all around them; even more ancient than this equipment. A weight of history and responsibility that he had carried for most of his life.

If he were to die right now, killed by this rash process or by some unexpected irregularity in his body – rare, but not unknown – he knew he would have performed his duty to the Hexamon many times over. He would not regret simply ceasing to be. And perhaps Korzenowski or someone else would pull the Hexamon through these dangerous times.

He reexamined the wires. All fittings were correct. First, however, he had to take a few precautions. He rigged a strong traction field near the door, laying two small nodes on each side. The nodes would draw from the room's hidden power supply. If he simply tapped a remote button, or sent a sharp whistle, or blinked his eyes in a rapid code, the field would activate . . . And there was no way to turn it off or harm the nodes, since they would lie within their own field.

He would not be able to escape. Nothing inside him would be able to escape. This would be a tomb for both of them.

If necessary, Olmy would stay in the room for several weeks, waiting to see if the process was successful. He had rigged other traps for himself in Alexandreia, in the fifth chamber near the train station, in the third chamber. All he had to do, should something go wrong away from this small sanctuary, would be to make his way to one of those traps, activate traction fields, and wait to die – or wait to be discovered.

Nobody knew of these traps. Nobody knew of his plans.

And then, there were the traps within his own mind . . . Mental trip-wires controlled by the same internally-down-loaded partial that would oversee the Jart's mentality.

If he felt himself losing all control, and could not make it to a trap, a blunder across these trip-wires would release a small explosive charge in his chest.

Satisfied that everything was in order, he reconnected the leads and sat on the floor, legs in a lotus, before the panel. He removed a small vial of nutrient fluid from his equipment case, lifted it to the silent air in toast, and said, 'Beni. Mar Kellen. Nameless researchers. Star, Fate and Pneuma be kind to you all.' He drank it down and laid the vial aside.

Then he reached up and touched the valve.

The transfer began.

20

Gaia, Alexandreia, Lokhias Promontory

The evening after their meeting, Rhita dined with the queen on sturgeon, lentils and fruit in the hall of Ptolemaios the Guardian. They took their seats at a marble table, a servant standing behind each, and looked out over the parapet at the sun setting on the ancient capital.

Kleopatra explained the unusual menu as each dish was served. 'This is a royal fish, flown in fresh from Parsa, a fish beyond price, garnished with its own roe. The lentils are a common dish, coarse and healthy, served with unleavened bread made of bleached maize from the Southern Continent. The fruit is Gaia's gift to rich and poor, common to us all. Would that all commoners could eat as well as their rulers.' As they ate, they did not discuss the gate or anything else of immediate consequence. 'We've made enough interesting decisions today,' Kleopatra averred.

After the dinner, Rhita was shown by a wizened white-haired chamberlain to a windowless room deep in the ancient, cool lower floors of the royal quarters, in the palace's north wing.

'Do you trust him?' the chamberlain asked her just outside her door, jabbing his finger at Lugotorix.

'Yes,' Rhita said.

The chamberlain looked him over with a squint. 'If you say so.' He raised his hand and a servant at the end of the hall advanced. A few mumbled words of Aigyptian – which Rhita did not understand – made the servant run to the end of the hallway. A moment later, while all three stood waiting in awkward silence, a dour, stocky old man in a leather apron and arm-chaps brought forward a Ioudaian machine gun and a bullet-proof vest.

'This is the palace armorer,' the chamberlain explained. He took the weapon from the armorer and handed it to the Kelt, who accepted it with obvious admiration. Then the chamberlain ordered the armorer to instruct the Kelt in its usage, which he did, using Hellenic and a touch of Parisiani.

'You wear an armored vest, and she doesn't,' the armorer explained, 'because you should always be between her and a hasisin. Understood?' The Kelt nodded grimly.

At another gesture from the chamberlain, two massive Aithiopians stalked toward them from the end of the hall. The Kelt raised his new weapon instinctively, but the chamberlain tapped the gun's black barrel with a disdainful finger and shook his head. 'Ceremony,' the chamberlain explained. 'You're to join the Palace Guard.'

The Kelt was initiated on the spot in a brief blood-sharing ceremony with the Aithiopians. Judging by his astonished expression, he was quite impressed. Rhita was less enthusiastic; she was tired, and vaguely wondered why she had to witness all this.

A cot was brought into the corridor and placed near the door of her sleeping chamber. Then the chamberlain gestured to the armorer and the Aithiopians and they left.

'You're going to be comfortable here?' Rhita asked him, standing in the doorway. He patted the cot with the splayed fingers of one huge hand and shrugged.

'It's too soft, mistress, but it won't hurt me.'

'What do you think of all this?' she asked, her voice lower.

The Kelt pondered for a moment, thick dark-blond eyebrows knitted. 'Will I go with you, or stay here?'

'You'll come with me. I hope.'

'That's okay, then.' He was obviously unwilling to comment further. Rhita closed her door and walked around the room, trying not to feel closed in. The fanciful murals painted above a wainscot did little to add to the room's size. They depicted crocodile and hippopotamus hunters on Lake Mareotis, and were doubtless very old – perhaps two thousand years. Their sense of perspective was primitive. Rhita suspected she could do better herself, and she had never been a quick study at drawing.

After examining the exquisite furniture – ebony and ivory and highly polished silver and brass – she lay on the feather mattress and stared at the purple silk canopy hanging from the ceiling.

What in hell am I doing?

Teeth clacking together with exhaustion and anxiety, Rhita remembered she had not yet looked at the slate to see if there was a message for her today. She removed the slate from her case and turned on the display.

My dear granddaughter,

If you have met the queen, you know she is a very smart woman, tough and quite capable of holding her own in a troubled Oikoumenē. But she is also a woman who will die shortly – politically, perhaps, before her body dies. The Oikoumenē will soon be run by aristocratic administrators, men for whom politics is a precise and clear-cut science. They already resent her for her intuitions and unpredictable decisions. That is why the gates must be found and examined before she dies or is deposed. She is our last chance. No reasonable politician would allow an expedition such as this. For one thing, no reasonable man would believe in the existence of something like a gate. Kleopatra believes because it gives her a much-needed thrill, a sense of bigger things in a life focused on day-to-day crises. I have disappointed her once, but I think the need is still in her. All the same, do not be arrogant with our queen. Exercise your inborn caution. And beware the lure of the palace. It is a dangerous place. Kleopatra lives there as a scorpion among snakes.

Rhita thought about the chamberlain, the armorer, the Aithiopian guards, and the ceremony she had been made to witness. Somehow, it all made a little more sense. She turned off the slate, grateful to the sophē for her foresight – and insight. But her teeth still chattered, and sleep was not easy to find.

Planning for the expedition to the site in Nordic Rhus began the next morning, in secret. The pace of the next two days was dizzying; the queen and her advisors seemed to be racing against time to get their preparations made, and Rhita was soon made privy to the reason for speed and discretion.

Kleopatra had once, decades before, controlled most matters involving exploration and research in the Oikoumenē. She had assumed this royal prerogative in her youth, even before the influence of the Boulē had waned and Kleopatra had gathered more and more power to the Ptolemaic Dynasty and away from the Alexandreian and Kanōpic aristocracies.

'Your grandmother cost me dearly when her gates wandered and vanished,' Kleopatra said, lips twisted in a wry smile. She shuddered and dismissed the past with her hand. 'But the aristoi have been getting into a fair amount of trouble lately. Farmer and klēroukhos revolts, conscription failure in the Kypros crisis . . . They've been in hiding for the past few months, letting me take the fall, and that gives me some room to breathe. If I breathe secretly. Secrets don't last long in Alexandreia. I have to have this expedition outfitted, and on its way, within five or six days, or chances are it'll be stopped by the Boulē Counselor.'

Kleopatra introduced her to a trusted advisor, Oresias, an explorer and expert on the Nordic Rhus who had a fierce loyalty to Kleopatra. Oresias was tall and lean, of late middle age, strong and aquiline and white-haired; centuries past, he might have been one of Alexandros's generals. With his help, Rhita hastily prepared a list of supplies and people necessary to the expedition. On something more than whim, she included the name of Demetrios, though they still had not met; she thought she might enjoy the company of a fellow mathematician.

Oresias consulted with another trusted advisor, Jamal Atta, a short, black-haired man, retired general of the Oikoumenē Overland Security Forces. Jamal Atta was of Berber ancestry, but affected the style of an old Persian soldier. Together, they plotted the difficulties and dangers of entering unfriendly territory.

Rhita thought about the long journey to Nordic Rhus with no small amount of trepidation. As Oresias spread the plans before her on a cards-and-jackals table in the royal game room, his strong, badly-scarred index finger tracing the likeliest routes, she wondered what the queen's motivations really were. Had Patrikia read Kleopatra's intentions truly?

The expedition would be politically risky; they would have to avoid detection by the Nordic Rhus high-frequency towers placed along their southern borders, from Baktra to Magyar Pontos. The independent Rhus-allied republics of the Hunnoi and Uighurs also lay in the path, and both were renowned for fierce and heartless warriors. Intrusions might be regarded as justifying counter-intrusions, or even lead to small border wars. Jamal Atta mentioned these possibilities in passing, as simple comments on Oresias's plans.

The expedition's vehicles would be Ioudaian beecraft, large hovering vehicles powered by Syrian jet turbines. Atta fanned out a handful of pictures of these beecraft with their top-mounted long broad spinning blades and forward canopies like bug's eyes.

'I cannot say how reliable they are,' Atta said in his deep, froggy voice, with his face even longer and darker than usual. 'We can get two of them from the palace secret police. They have a range of five hundred parasangs. A parasang is about three hundred Oikoumenē schoene – rope-lengths.' Rhita said she knew military and Persian measures. Jamal Atta lifted an eyebrow, pursed his lips and continued. 'Weapons we can get plenty of – black markets flourish in the delta, if we can't transfer them from the palace armory or the weapon factories at Memphis. The question I need answered is, why are we going? What do we plan to do if we find what we're looking for?' Both Atta and Oresias had been told some details, but not all, about the unlikely thing for which they would search.

Rhita stared at the plans spread on the game table. 'We'll try to enter the gate,' she said.

'Where will this door take us?'

'Into a place called the Way.' She described it for him, but Atta's eyes glazed after a few minutes and he raised his hand.

'If we can live there, then others can live there, too. Will they resist us?'

'I don't know,' Rhita said. 'They might welcome us.'

'Who will they be?'

'The people who made the Way. Perhaps.'

Atta shook his head dubiously. 'Whatever someone has, they protect from intruders. This all sounds dangerous and badly thought out. I would feel safer with an army in front of me.'

Oresias, sitting to one side, said, 'Obviously, an army is out of the question. If this young woman is prepared to go, can an old strātegos be less willing?'

Atta held up his spread hands, 'You're damned right I can. But her Imperial Hypsēlotēs commands.' He fixed his weary eyes on Rhita again. 'What kind of weapons might they have?'

'Nothing we could defend ourselves against,' Rhita said.

'What does that mean?'

'From what my grandmother told me, they have weapons we might dream of making in a hundred or a thousand years.'

'What are they, gods?' Atta asked with a gloomy edge in his voice.

'An old klēroukhos on his plot might think they were gods, yes,' Rhita said. She blushed slightly, realizing she had used a queenly tactic against the stratēgos.

'What about an old soldier hoping to live on his pension?' Atta asked. 'An old man who's seen all the

149

things this world has to offer, from the forests of Nea Karkhēdōn to Africa's bottom?'

'You've seen nothing like the Way,' Rhita said, staring at him without blinking. Atta refused to engage in this kind of contest. He casually turned to Oresias.

'Wonderful,' he said. 'Her Imperial Hypsēlotēs wishes us to end our days of service eaten by monsters or burned to ashes by gods.'

'Or being met by friends.' Rhita said, angry now at the stratēgos's cynicism. 'Friends who could bring the Oikoumenē back to its days of glory.'

'Treasure beyond the monster's jaws,' Oresias said.

'Try to be more specific about their strengths and weaknesses . . . if they have any weaknesses,'' Atta urged her gently. 'We only have a few more hours before we start putting everything together. Help an old ass carry a heavier load.'

'I've never seen these things. I've only been told about them,' Rhita said, suddenly afraid again.

'Try to remember,' Atta said with a sigh. 'Any scrap can only help.'

21

Thistledown, Fifth Chamber

The Jart bided quietly within Olmy, apparently unaware of any change in status. Olmy lay in the second room, eyes closed, probing delicately at his new companion, like a surgeon seeking the best point of entry to a sleeping but dangerous beast.

He could feel the depths of the asteroid all around him, unchanged across billions of years, implacable as time, primordial rock and carbonaceous materials and water that had fed and housed his people for centuries.

He looked at the empty plate which had once revealed the Jart's placid patterns. Now the memory stores were empty; all that there was of the Jart had been successfully uploaded into Olmy's implants.

His first discovery, in the first few seconds of investigating the Jart, was that a kind of translating shell, or interface, had been developed, either by the Jart itself in reaction to the probes of early researchers or, less likely, by the researchers themselves. Without the shell, Olmy would not have picked up sensible communications when Mar Kellen first hooked him to the system. The shell was incomplete but useful for a beginning.

Having confirmed that translated communications was possible, Olmy now double-checked his precautions. He had set both the Jart mentality – which occupied one implant – and a downloaded partial of himself apart from his primary self, and erected a number of barricades, not the least of which was a timer that regulated access to all of his implants. The partial conducted the early investigation and reported to him periodically.

In the super-fast world of implant functions, all of

this took place within ten minutes of the uploading. Olmy's partial determined that the Jart mentality was almost intact – that is, its major routines and subroutines appeared to follow the accepted rules for intelligence ordering. They were not fragmented. The Jart's lesser routines did not appear to function properly, but he would reserve judgment on that until later.

One never assumed that any part of a ticking bomb was inert until one completely understood the bomb.

Within the first hour, Olmy's partial had located some pieces of Jart experience-memory. The first attempts to transfer these disturbed the Jart. Parts of its mentality seemed to wake briefly from its timeless slumber, and once again Olmy received a cacophony of anxiety messages:

>*Duty unclear. Presence of Duty arbiter(?)*<
>*Unable to locate (self?)*<
>*(Abominations)*<

And then a lapse back into the quiet pool of seeming repose.

The memories he retrieved were far from clear or easy to translate. Jart sensoria were very different from human equivalents; 'eyes' were sensitive to both light and sound, combining such signals in a way unique in the Hexamon's experience. This did not cause Olmy's major difficulty with the memories, however; algorithms had been known for centuries which could interpret nearly all sensory messages. What puzzled him (or rather, at this stage, his partial) most of all was the de-emphasis on individual perception to the advantage of larger cultural conditioning. A Jart individual's personal perspective seemed almost irrelevant; and there was substantial evidence that this Jart at least acted more as a remote sensor than a self-willed individual.

Yet other indications contradicted this. The Jart had a strong, independent motivation routine – what in human terms might be analogous to an ego. There were enormously difficult associated complexes of social and hierarchical responses which meshed with this motivation routine, however. The Jart was strong-willed, yet in certain situations – when enmeshed in it social environment – it would be completely docile and obedient, lacking almost any will at all. And it would find no contradiction between these states.

For a Jart, obedience was undistinguishable from self-will, yet Olmy was certain Jarts did not comprise a group mind – at least, not this Jart. Perhaps the Jart carried a model or artificially imposed simulation of the Jart hierarchy, a kind of monitor or conscience.

For a time, as Olmy received data through the one-way link with his partial, he wondered if in fact two or more mentalities had been downloaded. It was difficult to accept such primary contradictions in the routines of an individual.

The partial was finally able to assemble a series of sensory memories that could be translated into human terms.

Not surprisingly, since the Jart had been highly stressed, the most prominent images were of its capture. Olmy saw what had to be the Way – quite flat and colorless – and brilliant objects in the foreground, picked out with amazing detail. The details changed frequently, making him wonder whether his partial was translating properly. The partial, anticipating the reactions to its primary, assured Olmy its interpretations were correct.

The Jart was perceiving objects from multiple and almost independent viewpoints, not in a Picasso-like Cubist fashion, but by processing the visual input through many different routines.

It then came to Olmy – and his partial independently concurred – that the Jart was using sensory interpreters adapted from other species. The Jart contained many visual 'brains', almost certainly patterned after those of non-Jart species.

During its capture, the Jart had apparently shuffled

through these alternatives, trying to duplicate a human viewpoint by using routines from beings thought to be similar to humans.

Did this explain some of the confusion as to ego and motivation routines? Did Jarts literally engulf the mentalities of other species, carrying them around like tools in a kit?

How many intelligent species, how many cultures and societies had the Jarts conquered? What had happened to them?

Olmy worked for an additional hour, trying to make sense of the visual memories. Finally he was able to piece together a reasonably clear picture of the capture.

First level sense interpretation (perhaps the Jart's natural routine):

The surround is pitchy black and cold, absent of sound. The foreground is occupied by hot and noisy objects moving very rapidly. The objects are machines, but the Jarts do not build machines like these (an image of seeding and virus-like development).

Second level sense interpretation (foreign?):

The background is filled with detail, sharp to the point of distraction; the foreground objects seem irrelevant, ignored. This routine simply cannot interpret machines or perhaps close objects at all.

(Is this an adapted sense routine, Olmy wondered, designed to augment or supplement the others? It seemed to have a minor place in the totality.) Olmy had no difficulty recognising the Way. Tractor fields stretch across the vast expanse, brilliantly colored – purple and red.

Some fields recede in sparkling tatters from penetration beams. The beams pierce through and intersect – but again, this routine cannot interpret machines.

(An odd lack, Olmy thought; seeing was akin to thinking, however, and it was possible the species this routine had been 'borrowed' from had no knowledge of technology.)

Third level (adapted Jart? Similar to the first):

The actions of the foreground objects are clearly understood, in the abstract. Each machine is sharply delineated.

Olmy recognised human armored physical penetrators (unmanned except by partials) and automated seek-and-destroy units, great and small – all nasty and black and seething with field energies. He shuddered. He had always disliked such weapons. They were simple and direct and unstoppable. They destroyed whatever they captured within their fields, reducing it to component atoms, pulses of heat and gamma rays.

The Jart had witnessed such weapons – yet had survived to be captured. And this Jart had been in the *front lines* of whatever skirmish in the Way these images represented. Humans sent only partials into such action.

Was this Jart a natural organism in any way, or an artificial creation entirely? The original human captors had not trusted the physical form to be typical of Jarts. Why trust the mentality?

Olmy concentrated on the sequence of events in the Jart's capture. As more sense-memories arrived, he pieced together a humanly linear story.

The Jart occupies a small vehicle, weaving through tractor field boundaries like a dragonfly through walls of reeds. Above, throughout this section of the Way –

Very likely in the million kilometers or so of disputed territory at 1.9 ex 9 –

Jart and human weapons engage in fierce combat. There is stalemate; this situation has continued for a considerable time.

(The Jart measures of time are not clear to Olmy)

The Jart's vehicle encounters and destroys numerous small human machines scouring the Way's barren surface. It encounters seek-and-destroy units and somehow evades them. It is now in territory behind the region of impasse, in human territory, where it will attempt to inflict a devastating blow to some command center – a large flawship or armored fortress. But its next encounter is with a cloud of penetrators.

– and vehicles Olmy himself does not recognise

and before it can maneuver it is caught in thick layers of traction, the shell of its vehicle stressed and mangled. A research and reconnaissance machine quickly seals off the crash site in a traction bubble. The Jart lies within its environment cradle, pulses of light crawling over the surface of this transparent shield as its generator begins to fail. Remotes shaped like giant black beetles push through the bubble and neutralize the weakening environment cradle, pulling the Jart from its controls. The Jart body is already severely damaged. Another vehicle almost as large as a flawship, moves over the surface of the way.

– and the sense images blurred and came to an end.

Olmy opened his eyes. The Jart's mission had been hopeless; he had never heard of organic forms occupying the Jart equivalent of penetrators. The entire action was more than suspicious – it was uncharacteristic, ludicrous.

Yet the humans had taken the bait, hoping – perhaps believing – that they had at last captured a Jart.

Perhaps they had. Perhaps the Jarts had been willing to give up the advantage of an enemy's ignorance in order to slip their Trojan Horse past the walls. But then, why kill researchers immediately? Why open the belly of the horse before night has fallen and the Trojans are asleep?

Olmy closed his eyes and recalled the last few scattered visuals sent by his partial. They were too fragmentary to reassemble –

But connected to the last was a *scouring*, biting node of corrosion. Olmy withdrew from this acid sting and

156

shoved the entire sequence into his third implant, isolating it immediately.

He then purged the third implant of all data contents.

The Jart was not slumbering.

Olmy waited for the downloaded partial in the second implant to deliver a self-analysis. When the data came through, the initiation string was badly flawed. The partial had been compromised.

The Jart was active. His precautions had almost failed.

Olmy raised more barricades around the isolated implants and prepared another partial. Sending partials into that alien hell was like sending himself – the partials were duplicated pieces of himself. His hormonal levels surged again and he fought back a sick, claustrophobic terror that almost overwhelmed his peripheral controls.

Less than two hours had passed since the uploading.

Studying the Jart was obviously going to involve a battle of wits. After wiping the second implant and putting another partial in to replace the one that had been compromised, Olmy waited for results from a new series of probes. The Jart mentality did not attempt to tag the data with corrosives, nor did it corrupt the partial.

They were taking each other's measure.

Despite its attack on the first partial – a circumstance Olmy had been prepared for – the Jart had not yet succeeded in altering the basic system of the implants in which it was stored. Olmy believed the Jart did not understand the system it now occupied, but it probably knew that its status had changed.

His safeguards were effective. Having accomplished this much, he decided to leave the buried memory storage rooms and continue his interior researches in the fourth chamber.

The cramped quarters and the sensation of being surrounded by kilometers of rock had become oppressive. However, he was not yet ready to return to human society. There were a great many more probes to make and tests to run before he took that risk.

If the Jart was reawakening, the time had come to expose it to some of the greater reality of human existence.

22

Gaia, Alexandreia

Within the cavernous palace garage, Rhita stood at the center of the circle of members of the queen's expedition. Clavicle in both hands, she closed her eyes and focused on the spinning globe. Continents raced beneath her disembodied eyes, their features etched in bright relief. There were many things about the display she did not understand. Certain features flashed as if they might be of interest; others were crosshatched or dotted. Some land masses or ocean areas were outlined in red or yellow. Yet the clavicle did not reveal the meaning of these functions; it simply rotated the globe to the Kanōpic mouth of the Nilos, then twisted and rolled the globe again to the position of the gate, marked by a cross. Her point of view 'fell' to the surface of the globe, and she crossed bright, feverishly colored landscapes to a grassland that burned with green fire. There was the gate, marked only by an unlikely cross with wide-splayed armpits.

She opened her eyes.

'It's still there,' she said. Oresias stood beside her. She hesitantly took his hand and placed it on hers where it gripped the clavicle bar. 'Close your eyes,' she said. He did, and she felt the projection move through her, into him. He stiffened as he had the first time they had shared the images, then forced himself to relax. After a few seconds, he opened his eyes.

'I confirm that,' he said. 'We know our goal.'

Kleopatra sat in a portable throne on a stone platform above the circle. All turned toward the queen. She stood and held her hand out over them. 'The blood of the keepers of Alexandros the Uniter, the Conqueror, flows in my veins.' Her lips twisted in that peculiar smile

Rhita had seen several times. 'However diluted by Persians and Nordic folk. To some, this seems like a royal whim, the shadowy wish of a weak queen. But can you feel this day's importance? What you find, what you learn and bring back with you, could mean rebirth for the Oikoumenē, and a century of order and prosperity, rather than decline and strife. We might look for a talisman, for the penis of Aser or the lost magic of Neit; we might be fools. What we seek instead is real, and I only regret I cannot share your danger.' Her tone was convincing; none, Rhita saw, doubted the words of their Imperial Hypsēlotēs.

'Go with the gods and the spirits of your loved dead. Apollo shines upon you all. I love you as my children. I envy you.'

Sour, long-faced Jamal Atta's eyes filled with tears. Oresias saluted the queen with a hand held high, fingers splayed – Alexandros's sign of friendship and cooperation. 'We will return, my Queen,' he called out.

'We will return,' the members called out in unison.

Kleopatra nodded and kneeled before them.

Rhita felt Oresias's hand on her arm. He led her to the cab of a covered steam freight wagon. Seven such wagons waited to carry them and their equipment from the staging area in the garage to the aerodromos in the western desert, beyond the old nekropolis. 'This had better be worthwhile,' he murmured in her ear, not in accusation, but in camaraderie.

Jamal Atta accompanied a tall, black-haired man with ruddy skin. Both climbed into Rhita's wagon and found their assigned seats. When they were settled, and the wagons began to roll from the garage, the military advisor introduced the stranger. 'This is your long-missing didaskalos, if I recall correctly,' Atta said. 'He has just returned from Kallimakhos's exile. Demetrios, this is your patient and disruptive student, Rhita Berenikē Vaskayza. She asked that you accompany us.'

Demetrios turned his genial features on Rhita and

smiled with a mix of confidence and shyness that Rhita found disconcerting. 'I am honored,' he said.

'As am I. I hope you weren't . . . troubled by your journey. I seem to have been the reason for it.'

'Irritation, no more,' Demetrios said. 'I'm still not sure what I'm doing here . . . We seem to be going on a long journey, and the queen personally told me I was needed. I can't imagine why.'

'Because you're the mekhanikos with the most advanced ideas,' Oresias said. 'Her Imperial Hypsēlotēs expects we'll be seeing some real marvels, and hopes you can explain them to us, if our mistress Vaskayza cannot.'

'She did discuss wonders. I confess I couldn't understand all she said . . . Are we looking for the door that opened for the sophē to enter this world?'

'Maybe,' Rhita said.

'That would be a marvel, indeed.' He shook his head in wonder, and then looked at the box holding the clavicle. 'Is that one of the Objects?'

Rhita nodded. Demetrios had the features of an aborigine from Nea Karkhēdōn, but with lighter, more olive-toned skin. There was perhaps some Latinē blood in him, or Aigyptian.

'You will pardon my reverent curiosity,' he said. 'Mechanikoi in my studio have been taught about the sophē's Objects from childhood. To actually see one . . .' He seemed about to ask if he could touch it, but Oresias shook his head discreetly.

'I am pleased to meet you,' Demetrios concluded, smiling again. Rhita glanced at the other men in the wagon. She was the only female in this wagonload. There were only two other women in the entire expedition. She had hoped there might be more, but even under Kleopatra's influence, the attitudes of Alexandreia were very different form those of Rhodos.

The steam wagons wound through the Brukheion and Neapolis in the early dawn, passing a few market owners and fishermen walking or riding donkeys to their stalls. The air was crisp, cleaner than it had been the past few days, which seemed auspicious. Alexandreia had once been renowned for the purity of its air; the factories of the delta had changed that.

Once through the Neapolis and Aigyptian district – where the roadway rose above the hovels on disdainful concrete pillars – the nekropolis spread out before them on the city's western border, a jumble of limestone, red and gray granite and marble tombs. They were not stopped at the city's gates; the queen's influence among the police was still strong.

The sun was well up as they passed through the city of the dead. The poor had invaded the nekropolis centuries before, moving into the tombs of forgotten families and setting up a unique, violent social structure that had become a way of life unto itself. The most the police could do was keep the nekropolis from moving into the Neapolis; the Aigyptian quarter acted as a buffer. Still, the caravan was not bothered on the rutted, potholed highway through the tombs.

The queen had her contacts and supporters here, as well.

Beyond the last dismal scatter of old graves, a military highway rose out of the scrub grass and sand like an inky mirage. The caravan followed this route to the aerodromos, an additional ten schoene to the west. Upon their arrival, the morning was well under way. Rhita could smell kerosene and oil on the wind, and heard a continuous low roar as jets and other gullcraft took off to patrol the Libyan borders. She could see little through the plastic windows in the canvas covering the wagon; they faced away from the aerodromos.

'We're here,' Oresias said, standing and flexing his knees. Demetrios stood beside him, still unsure of his place.

The caravan had stopped on an apron of asphalt near a broad concrete quadrangle. As he stepped down, glancing left, Rhita saw long rows of gleaming silver gullcraft, sleek fighters that were all wing and larger needle-shaped bombers with markings of the provinces of Ioudaia and Syrian Antiokheia. Beyond them lay the western desert, a narrow ribbon of cream above the white concrete and black asphalt. A fighter screamed down the closest runway, passing within barely a hundred arms of the line of wagons. Rhita shifted the box with the clavicle to one arm and covered her left ear, wincing at the din.

As they walked around their wagon, she saw the two beecraft squatting on the apron, sullen and nondescript brown with patches of yellow and white. They seemed ugly and ungainly compared to the fighters, like flying houses. Their wide horizontal blades drooped, man-sized nacelles on the tips coming within three arms of the ground on each side. A few men in red and white flight outfits stood beside the beecraft, engaged in conversation, watching the wagons' passengers disembark.

Climbing down from the back of the next wagon in line was the Kelt and a small contingent of the palace guard; all to protect her, she realised.

She stifled a sudden urge to drop the clavicle and run into the desert.

A whistling breeze riffled little lines of sand on the asphalt, scattering grains about her feet. She looked up at the sun, shading her eyes against the brilliance.

It was a perfect day for flying. She had hoped it might be otherwise. She thought of the sanctuary of Athēnē Lindia, with its stone steps hot in the sun and the lapis-blue water beyond.

'Time to board,' Oresias said. 'Didaskolos, assist your student, if you please.'

Demetrios offered his hand but Rhita declined, moving ahead of them with quick, small steps to show her determination.

'Ours is the machine on the right,' Jamal Atta instructed.

Oresias shaded his eyes and looked across the field to the low buildings nestled among sand hills to the south. 'Are we expecting a reception?' he asked. Rhita followed his pointing finger and saw a line of distant vehicles about half a parasang from the asphalt apron.

'No,' Atta said, tensing. 'We have this part of the field to ourselves.'

'Then we'd better hurry.'

Demetrios moved up behind Rhita as if to protect her. The palace guards and the Kelt joined their group at the beecraft hatchway, falling in line at Atta's command. The military advisor cursed repeatedly under his breath, eyes flicking between the people and piles of supplies yet to be loaded and the approaching wagons.

Oresias rapped on the plastic canopy and the kybernētēs opened a small window. 'Get this thing off the ground first if you have to. Get her out of here if they reach us before we're ready.'

'I've got a query on the radio,' the kybernētēs said.

'There weren't supposed to be any *queries*,' Oresias told him sharply.

'Then I don't suppose they expect an answer,' the kybernētēs replied casually. 'Everybody has to be loaded two minutes before we can leave the ground. I need time to get my blades up to speed.' He snicked the window shut.

Rhita found her seat within the narrow fuselage, a thinly padded canvas square stretched across two parallel iron bars. Demetrios handed her the case containing the slate and helped her secure the clavicle in its box behind a net in an overhead rack. The whine of the jet motors directly overhead was hideously loud, disorienting. A crewman handed them ear-covers and motioned for all to be seated and strap themselves in.

Outside, the last of the supplies was being hastily piled into the second beecraft. The wagon drivers retreated to their vehicles and spun them away from the apron toward the military road. Rhita wondered what would happen if they were caught; why had things gone wrong? *Had* they gone wrong?

She clapped her hands over the ear-covers and closed her eyes. She had never flown before.

Oresias tapped her shoulder and she opened her eyes.

We're going, he mouthed to her. She glanced out the square window between the explorer's seat and her own and saw the ponderous jet nacelles blurring as the blades picked up speed. The roar seemed to turn her entire body to liquid. She hadn't urinated in hours. The need was intense. She clenched her teeth.

The two beecraft left solid ground and drifted off the apron, accelerating north. She couldn't see what the soldiers in the vehicles behind them were doing. She hoped they weren't shooting.

Demetrios, sitting beside the Kelt across the aisle, grinned despite his gray face and strained expression. Rhita closed her eyes again.

She knew she would never again see Rhodos or Rhamōn or the sanctuary of Athēnē Lindia. The feeling came to her as an absolute certainty, beyond question.

For the first time, she actually understood the parallels between her grandmother's journey and her own. Her grandmother had been young, too; only a couple of years older than Rhita was now. She had not just flown from her home, but had been lifted by rockets into space, away from Gaia – from Earth.

So who was responsible? What could she have done to avoid this misery? Rhita prayed, remembering the comfort and peace of sitting quietly in the shadow of Athēnē's sanctuary, and for the merest instant she was back there, with Athēnē towering above her in the dark wooden shed.

Then the beecraft lurched sharply and she saw dazzling iron-pewter sandpaper through the window – ocean directly below them, hundreds, perhaps thousands of arms away.

'We're turning east,' Oresias shouted in her ear. 'I think we've gotten off without any damage. At least we're not being followed.'

'What will we come back to?' Atta shouted. Even at high volume, his voice expressed dismal unhappiness.

He flung his hands out and rubbed his temples with his fingertips. 'What went wrong?'

The question remained unanswered. As planned, they kept radio silence, staying five or six parasangs off the coast.

The pressure in her bladder was becoming too much. She leaned forward, gestured for Oresias to lift an earcover, and said something in a low voice. He still could not hear her.

'I have to urinate,' she shouted. The explorer raised an eyebrow and pointed to the back, where a crewman was pissing into a metal canister. 'There's a curtain.'

Rhita nodded. Not too embarrassing for a former gynandros – what Patrikia called a *tomboy*. When she was done, as a small sign on the canister instructed, she poured the contents into a funnel in the floor. Presumably, it fell from the beecraft and dribbled across the sea, her own personal rain.

She finally became used to the noise, and ate from a packet of dried fruits and nuts, drinking wine thoroughly diluted with water. One of the three crewmen handed out plastic packets of olive oil, telling everyone, 'For your health. Suck it down.'

Rhita glanced at the overhead rack and saw the clavicle secure behind its netting. She tried to persuade herself that the expedition was under way and there was no sense feeling regret, but regret dominated her thoughts anyway.

In an hour, her attitude began to change. She was almost used to the bobbing and the rising and falling in her stomach. Looking out the window and seeing the clear, cloudless air of the coast – and then, far to the southwest, the smoggy haze above the delta – gave her a new perspective that was actually exciting. She listened to Oresias and Jamal Atta plotting their course with the kybernētēs, who had left the beecraft in charge of his assistant. Behind and to their right flew the second craft, matching course precisely.

The Kelt and the palace guards took the situation

quietly and stoically. Rhita thought there was a kind of contest between them – the first to show any sign of unease, lost.

Demetrios no longer looked so gray, but he was obviously unhappy. Rhita leaned across the aisle and then unbuckled her harness to get closer to him. She tapped his ear-covers and he lifted one side away.

'Let's have a contest,' she said, giddy.

'What kind of contest?' he shouted.

'The first one to look scared or sick or upset, loses.' She nodded at the guards and the Kelt and grinned. 'Game?'

'Game,' Demetrios said, returning her grin. 'I've lost already, though,' he said ruefully.

'Starting now. Let's sober up.'

Atta looked at them with patent disapproval.

'Where are we?' Rhita asked him, lurching near the group of three and grabbing hold of an overhead rack. Her bravery seemed unlimited now.

'West of Gaza,' Oresias said. 'Making good time. We're following Alexandros's route! Sort of. We have a stop in Damaskē for refueling, then Bagdadē, then on to Raki below the Kaspian Sea, where we're followed by an aeriel tanker. We refuel in mid-air over the Hunnos Republic, and within two hours we're at your site in the prairie steppes. I hope our allied provinces are good on their pledges to the queen.'

The sound of the beecraft's engines equated with security for Rhita now. She napped for an hour, dreaming of sandy wastes, and found they had crossed Ioudaia and were nearing Damaskē. Like an enormous pastry fresh from the oven, the sand and rock and crusted mountains passed below. She thought of caravans and days of travel, of dying of thirst and digging for water in ancient wells . . . That was romance.

Crossing it all like god's bird was simply unreal.

Out of the baked pastry desert came a distant patch of green, spread across the sands like a spill of paint. Rhita smelled Damaskē before she actually saw it; a smell of life and water and greenery that made her lift her head and twitch her nose, hoping for more. Demetrios and Oresias were deep in expedition plans; the mekhanikos was catching up on what he had missed. She wondered how she would feel if she had been conscripted, as Demetrios had. *But I was conscripted*, she reminded herself. *My grandmother chose me.* She crawled from her harness and looked through a window.

Damaskē claimed to be the oldest city in the world. Excavations at Jericho in the last century had challenged that claim, but Jericho was a much smaller community, hardly more than a village; Damaskē had truly been a city for millennia. It was the major trading center of Syria, surrounded by orchards and fields, squat glass and steel and stone ziggurats rising from the Jewish quarter and the Horian quarter, the massive stone Persian fortress dominating the south of the city, and south of that, the international civilian aerodromos of El Zarra.

Atta returned from the kybernētēs cabin and told her they would be landing on the outskirts of El Zarra for refueling. 'I hope to get some news there, if anybody's talking.' He shook his long head gloomily.

The beecraft dropped low and approached the aerodromos just above tree-top level. Rhita smelled dates and cookstove camel-dung smoke and smiled despite the tension. She had never been to any of these places; if she lived, she would be a very well-traveled young woman.

The beecraft set down on a flat concrete pad near a few ragged old fuel wagons. Tired, dusty men approached the two craft, dragging long, flat sand-colored hoses behind them. They waited for the props to stop spinning, then tugged the hoses to within a few steps of the side doors. Oresias swung their door open and jumped down, followed by Atta, the bodyguards and Demetrios. The Kelt took a deep breath and shook his head as if to clear it.

Atta conferred with the closest field attendant, who seemed reluctant to say anything, concentrating on hooking up the hose and starting the fuel pumping. Atta then walked over to speak to a wagon driver, and seemed to have better luck. When he returned, he appeared, if such a thing was possible, even more desolate.

Rhita stood beside the mekhanikos as Atta told them what he had heard. 'There's no communication out of Alexandreia. We're getting our fuel, but we were supposed to get aerial charts of the steppes from the Syrian Map Center, and they haven't shown up.'

'What do they mean, no communication?' Oresias asked.

'Just that. No radio, no telephone, nothing, as far as the driver knows. He's an officer, too; he talks with pilots coming in to the aerodromos. All flights are being held in Alexandreia. Ours are the only craft to land today.'

Oresias circled his fingers around his wrist and twisted them. 'Something's gone wrong.'

Demetrios squinted quizzically. 'What – '

'We're being slighted,' Atta said. 'We get our fuel, but the powers in Damaskē are being spare with other amenities. That tells me the queen's influence may now be less important to them . . .'

Oresias chafed his wrist until the skin seemed about to rupture. 'A blow against the palace?'

Atta shook his head, unwilling to speculate. 'We still have our mission. But something's wrong. It must have begun just before we left. We can't radio back . . . it would take an hour or more to go into the city, or to the acrodromos administration and place a cable . . .' He shrugged. 'We have no choice but to go on.'

Rhita stared at the distant towers and squat ziggurats of Damaskē, realising she was not scared, but should be. The flight's mixed exhilaration and boredom still had a grip on her, like a drug.

'Check with your clavicle, please,' Oresias told her

softly as they re-boarded the beecraft. 'I want to know whether our goal is still there.'

She pulled the box from its rack and opened it, touching the handlebars with one finger. The brilliantly colored world spun before her again, and the cross reappeared in the same position, unchanged.

'Still there,' she affirmed. Oresias strapped himself into his seat, leaned his head back and closed his eyes.

In a few minutes, the beecraft were refueled and ready for the flight again. Atta came aboard at the last and angrily slammed the sliding hatch shut. 'What about our aerial tanker?' he muttered. 'What about the return leg?'

23

Thistledown

Olmy arrived in the fourth chamber an hour after hiking to the abandoned station in the fifth chamber. The train crossed over a broad expanse of shimmering, silvery water and dropped him off at a rest station on Northspin Island, in the first quarter, near the northern cap. Avoiding the few other hikers, he rented a tractor, drove ten kilometers to a distant trail head, and walked into the dense coniferous forests.

Within his implant memories, isolated from his primary personality, the freshly created partial conducted its more cautious investigation of the Jart mentality.

Three hours later, he stood beneath a thousand-year-old redwood, a light mist drifting from spinward, his feet sinking into ancient loam.

Whatever isolation and abstraction he had felt before, after his months of research on nonhuman psychology, was nothing compared to his sense of self-exile now. He kept thinking of Tapi, perhaps even now working through his incarnation exams. He did not think he would see his son for some time, if ever; or Suli Ram Kikura. It seemed unlikely their paths would cross.

He felt the redwood's thick, tough bark and wondered if he should feel a kinship with this old tree. In truth, he felt a kinship with nothing, not even his fellows, and that disturbed him. It was barely possible his implant regulators were not working properly, and that he was experiencing an unhealthy mental state. Just to be sure, he ran a test string through his primary mind and through the regulatory implants.

No inappropriate states, the results told him.

Merely extreme stress and danger.

All of these trees had survived the re-rotation after

the Sundering. They had lasted through temporary weightlessness, floods, chaotic weather, and years of neglect, and now they seemed to thrive. Why couldn't he feel simple encouragement from their example'

Why can't I feel anything at all?

A scheduled status report emerged from behind the barriers. His partial sent a string of information indicating successful penetration of the Jart's cultural and personal memory stores. In addition, the partial had exchanged cautious 'greetings.'

Olmy sat back against a tree and took a deep breath. A kind of dialogue was happening a lot sooner than he had expected. The Jart, for the moment, was finding some advantage or other in cooperation. He might soon be able to tell how much of the Jart's ostensible memories were real and how much manufactured; it seemed unlikely the Jart would willingly give up actual information about its kind. But then, everything about this situation was unlikely . . . and Olmy still had no idea what a Jart's psychology was like, what it was capable or not capable of doing.

When the partial transferred its findings to Olmy, for a time, as he sat with eyes open, he saw both the forest and

Great prism-shaped Jart flawships, moving with majestic slowness over a colonized segment of the Way.

(again in several visual layers, but these more ordered, less frantic)

and dancing clouds of midge-like attendant machines and vehicles moving from the flawship to broad curving ramps on the floor of the Way.

With a start, replaying the memory, Olmy realised that beneath the nearest ramp was an inverted image of the exterior of a planet. He tried to reinterpret but could not; it seemed that at least in this case, Jart gates were

172

not circular holes, but slashes in the Way several kilometers wide. There was always the possibility that all the information he had received this far was deception, that the Jart itself was a ruse; one way to find out would be to ask Korzenowski about the possibility of elongated gates in the Way. Even if they were possible, other details might be distorted . . .

Another memory:

mingling with other beings

(Jarts? Clients of the Jarts?)

in a thick green liquid, much smaller silver worms passing between them, occasionally wrapping around one individual or another and cinching tight enough to crease flesh. Some of the beings resembled the Jart body in the fifth chamber memory store's second room; others were flat white speckled black carpets with undulating fringes, flying through the liquid, or trilaterally symmetric 'starfish' with flexible mandibles or fingers on the end of each arm, or thick shapeless extrusions from colorless tubes . . .

All seemed to have some remote and nightmarish sea floor as a common origin, and none of them did anything Olmy could even begin to understand.

There were other images, too many to experience for the moment. Storing these findings without examination, he moved on to the exchanged 'greeting.'

Partial: (*Replay of capture memories and a string signifying awareness of the Jart's existence and status.*)
Jart: >*I am beyond reach of duty? Where is duty expediter label?*<
Partial: *You are* >*beyond reach of*< *all your kind.*
Jart: >*What is brother/father status? Is this communication from command oversight?*<
Partial: >*Brother/father status*< *not known. Not command oversight. You are captured and under examination.*
Jart: >*Acknowledge personal status as captured.*<

The partial then sent a long list of questions. Those

were being processed now. At least, for the time being, he had an illusion of progress.

The partial passed along another string:

Jart: >*Cooperation and transfer of status information? Replacement of command oversight and command?*<

This seemed to be a kind of surrender. Olmy marked the phrases 'duty expediter,' 'command oversight' and the isolated 'command', wondering if they were levels in Jart society. The partial had agreed to the condition offered by the Jart, subject to further explanation. The limits and methods were being worked out now, with the barriers still up and not likely to be lowered except for the transfer of more findings and status checks.

Olmy dug his hand into the loam and stared up at the tree branches overhead. All of his defenses were on alert. It was possible the Jart was simply preparing for another assault.

Somehow, he didn't think it was that simple. Having failed to immediately kill or subdue Olmy, the Jart was apparently taking a different tack. Where it would lead, Olmy had no idea.

But a detailed exchange was beginning.

24

Gaia

Elamite Bagdadē was a ruin slowly being rebuilt by the Mesopotamian Nekhemites, who had moved west in armored, mechanised hordes and sacked the city twenty years before, while the Oikoumenē concerned itself with one of the endless Libyan incursions on its own borders. The Nekhemites had proved themselves barely able to control the effete but efficient people they had so piously slaughtered in the name of their faceless, demanding god; they had then turned to Kleopatra, one of the few queens left on Gaia, and requested that she be a 'bride to Nekhem.' The request was so ludicrous and so opportune that it could not be denied; henceforward, her Imperial Hypsēlotēs was worshiped in effigy in Bagdadē, and Oikoumenē money and technical assistance flowed into the ancient city. In return, the Nekhemites guarded the frontiers of the Hunnos Republic and Nordic Rhus.

Jamal Atta thought it very unlikely they would face any trouble in Bagdadē, and indeed, after three hours of flight from Damaskē, the turbaned and red-robed attendants at the new aerodromos gave them all the fuel they needed, and maps of the Kazakh, Kirghiz and Uzbeki territories of Nordic Rhus. As they departed sad Bagdadē, the Kelt bent over to investigate the floor and held up something, grinning foolishly. Tiny plastic statues of Kleopatra mating with Nekhem had been tossed through the beecraft doors along with their supplies.

The Kelt gave her his find. Rhita fingered it thoughtfully, fascinated by its crude vigor. Inelegant, ignorant, vicious and cruel beyond her experience, yet honest and full of life, the Nekhemites might someday own all the middle lands of the old world. She hoped they had deposed Nekhem by that time. He was an ugly god.

From Bagdadē, they crossed the land of the Nekhem and picked up a tailwind, which brought them in two hours to Raki, Raghae of old, once again on Oikoumenē territory. Raki was an isolated city on an island of peace heavily fortified on all its borders. There, Oresias learned from a military field inspector that no news had been heard from Alexandreia, and that their air transport escorts – an aerial tanker and an old cargo plane that would be abandoned – were ready to accompany them from that point.

They now began their incursion into truly dangerous territory. Fifteen hundred years before, the Persians and the Oikoumenē in Europe had been swept to the west and then driven to the seas – the Priddeneian Sea and the Middle Sea – by the Alanoi and Hunnoi, working their nomadic peoples and subject Teutonic tribes into a vast mobile nation of warriors. An empire had been set up from the shores of Galleia and Kimbria to the great walls of Chin, the greatest the world had ever known – and the most fragile. In fifty years, that empire had vanished like a dream of blood and smoke, and the Skythians and Nordic Rhus had moved into the void. The Alanoi and Avars had finally held their ground east of the Kaspian, and the Hunnoi north and east of them. For a thousand years, these territories had been in flux, but had kept their basic shapes, until the arrival of the Aigaian Turkmenoi, pirates and ravagers of Hellas.

The Turkmenoi had carved their own niche, transferring their piratic tendencies to the Kaspian, and it was over that slender mountainous territory between the Altaic republics that the beecraft now flew. The Turkmenoi recognised no one as their betters or their masters. They isolated themselves and tried to hold back the incursions of the outside world. There would be no mercy for gullcraft should they be forced down; but it was unlikely the Turkmenoi could muster such weapons.

Rhita looked at the hundreds of miles of broad naked mountains passing below, and felt lonelier than ever before. She realised the variability of human thought and human history, the contradictions of cultures, as unmappable as these rocky passes and pinnacles, and it seemed that humans would never share a single truth. That meant either there was no single truth, or humans would kill themselves trying to find it. . . . Either way, thinking about it depressed her.

Her exhilaration of a few hours before had faded into dark unease. She was tired; sleep on the beecraft was not refreshing, accompanied as it was by the unending roar of the jets. Her stomach was touchy again; she did not feel it was safe to eat any more, yet she was hungry. She complained about nothing, but the flight was dragging on and on . . .

They refueled in the air near the northeastern border of Turkmenia. That process was interesting, what little she could see of it. The tanker veered away from their group and flew back to Raghae, leaving them with the cargo plane as escort. So far, despite her unease, she had to admit the expedition was going well.

Against her will, her thoughts wandered to home. She had never had opinions one way or the other about the Oikoumenē; it had always been there; it seemed to be immortal. Within her lifetime, there had never been disaster broad enough to affect her world. Still, Rhodos had been peaceful for only eighty years. As a youngster, she had swum in huge rain-filled pockmarks in the hills, shell-holes from bombardments older than almost anyone alive. But if the queen herself was in peril . . .

The entire Oikoumenē could change its character. There might not be a home she could safely return to. Rhita squirmed on her seat, thinking of war, rebellion, death.

The mountains below gave way to ochre flatlands, with raw, rounded naked-looking hills and rocky promontories. The ochre became patchy green, and long ribbons of green bordered shallow streambeds.

'We've passed over the southern extremes of the Hunnos and Alanos republics,' Oresias said, returning from the front cabin.

They swooped close to ground level for twenty minutes. Atta seemed especially forlorn, shaking his head and pounding his hands despairingly on his knees, waiting for the Nordic Rhus Uzbek and Kazakh watchtowers to sense them. But defenses never appeared; they apparently had passed through, either unseen or a blip too small to be credible.

'One hour,' Oresias said. The jets droned and wind rushed by, whistling through cracks in the beecraft hull. She tried to sleep again, but could only close her eyes, not bring on oblivion. She ached all over from tension and trying to hide how uncomfortable she was. The men sat still as statues, stoic, faces dull, rocking back and forth in unison as the beecraft maneuvered or hit a pocket of air.

How could she be so uneasy, and yet so bored? She might die, and not be excited when death caught her. . . . Would death – she imagined a large black serpent with skulls for teeth – recoil from such a cool, calm victim? Was it against death's principles to eat the uncaring?

Looking out the window. Squinting in the sunlight. Using the can in the back again and voiding it, watering the steppes. Sitting, strapping herself in.

'How close?' Oresias asked, bending over her. She had managed to fall asleep somehow, dreaming of turtles flying. She rubbed her eyes and gripped the clavicle. The globe seemed much larger now, and the sweep across the surface much shorter, with more and more strange symbols and abstract shapes flashing by, unexplained. Then she was in the swale, and the cross was still there, vibrant red.

'Let me sit up front,' she said. They made way for her to the kybernētēs' cabin, and the assistant gave her his seat. She clutched the clavicle, feeling its responses, and looked out over the endless grasslands. 'Down, please,' she said.

'How far?' the kybernētēs asked.

'Slow down, and descend to . . . a hundred arms? Less?'

She looked back at Oresias. Demetrios had crowded in the hatch behind him, eyes wide, face still pale.

'Fifty arms,' Oresias said. 'Will we see it?' he asked her.

'I don't know. It might not be large . . . but I'll know when we're there.'

The two beecraft slowed and descended, while the cargo plane and the tanker began to make wide turns over the landscape, flying above them every few minutes as they searched. Rhita concentrated on the prairie, trying to match the terrain with what she felt in the clavicle . . . an exercise not really necessary, as it turned out.

'Here,' she said. 'Stop here.' The clavicle had simply told her, in no way she could specify, that they were over the site. The beecraft overshot and she guided them back, until both craft were within a hundred and fifty arms of each other, and the site lay beneath them, recognisable now: a grassy fertile swale around a small muddy streambed. She could not see the gate with her eyes, but the clavicle told her its precise position.

'Let's land,' Oresias instructed the kybernētēs. The kybernētēs spoke with his counterparts on the other beecraft, and they descended the last fifty arms, touching down with a gentle bump on the grass, their blades causing rippling waves to spread and clash between them.

'Stop your engines,' Atta instructed from behind Oresias. 'We want silence. We've come here like a horde of drunken demons. No sense overdoing it.'

'Is there a place for the gullcraft?' Oresias asked Rhita. She was confused for a moment – how could *she* know? – when she remembered that the clavicle could tell her. In the clavicle's display, she flew over the simplified landscape and searched for a flat, undimpled area several stadia in length for the plane to land. 'Northeast a few hundred arms,' she said. 'It looks smooth though there's probably a few holes . . . might be rough.'

'From which direction?' Oresias asked.

'They should fly in from the south. They'll see it – it's quite broad.'

'Wish them luck,' Oresias instructed the kybernētēs as he relayed her message. 'Is it safe to go out?'

'I don't see why not,' Rhita said, though she trembled. Not seeing the gate with her eyes disturbed her. She could not tell anything about it except its position.

Perhaps it's nothing at all.

The doors were pushed open and a sweet, clean cool breeze blew into the stuffy interior. Grass-smell like a horse barn. Tang of something else, wet soil perhaps.

From horizon to horizon, the prairie steppe rolled with dominant confidence, ignoring them, ignoring all humans, concerned only with its dreaming fecundity. Its surface provided some of the richest land on Gaia, where water was available. To the west, a clean orange-yellow sun was within half an hour of falling below the horizon. The sky was cloudless and pure, the blue of Athēnē's hemline spread over her domain, with a few bright stars or perhaps planets twinkling in the expanse, drops of glitter from Aphrodite's makeup box.

The cargo plane made its descent to ground a couple of stadia distant, followed by the tanker, their motors obscenely loud in this calm, this aloofness.

They stood, all the expedition, beneath the still blades of the beecraft, looking down the gentle slope into the swale. They had arrived at their destination without real difficulty. Nobody, judging from their expressions, expected the absence of trouble to continue. Atta kept glancing at the horizon all around, one heavy eyebrow lifted doubtfully.

The Kelt stood beside Rhita with his weapon ready. The other palace guards followed a few moments after,

180

expressionless, alert. Birds returned to the grass, tiny feather bullets shy and curious.

Rhita lifted her clavicle. 'It's there,' she said. She swallowed. 'I'll go down and look at it. Nobody comes with me . . . except him.' She indicated the Kelt. It would deeply insult her bodyguard to keep him away when she walked into danger.

Demetrios stepped forward, still pale from his ordeal on the beecraft. 'I'd like to go with you,' he said. 'I'm here to make an opinion about what we're seeing . . . I'm useless if I just stand here.'

Rhita was too tired and nervous to object. 'Just Lugotorix and you, then,' she said, hoping there wouldn't be any more brave men volunteering. There weren't. Oresias and Atta stood at the edge of the swale, arms folded, surrounded by the beecraft crew and kybernētēs and the other expedition members, while Rhita, the Kelt and Demetrios walked down the gentle slope to the muddy streambed.

Not of her own volition, Rhita lifted the clavicle into a better position and carried it before her. She saw the gate in the display as a red circle now, barely five arms ahead of them. 'Is it close?' Demetrios asked.

Rhita pointed. 'Right there.' She could make finally it out with her eye, an almost invisible lens floating about eight arms above the ground, slightly darker than the sky around it. It seemed quiescent, but still it terrified her.

The clavicle told her things she barely understood, and she had to ask it silently for a repeat. Not using words, it informed her again that this was an incomplete gate, requiring very little energy to maintain; a test gate, through which probes might be dropped and samples taken. It was not large enough for anything wider than a hand to pass through, and it was not at this moment open for passage anyway.

She relayed this to Demetrios. They walked around it, heads inclined, while the Kelt stood a few arms away, weapon ready. *Can I open the gate myself?* she asked.

The clavicle responded that there was a possibility the gate could be expanded from this side, but that such an action would undoubtedly alert anybody or anything monitoring the gate, whatever they might be.

Do you know who opened this gate?

No, the clavicle said. *Gates at this stage of their creation are pretty much all alike.*

She turned to Oresias and Atta and said, 'It's too small to pass through. If I try to open it wider, people on the other side will know we're here.'

Oresias considered this for a moment, then he and Atta conferred in low voices. 'We'll think about this overnight,' Oresias said. 'Come back to the beecraft. We'll set up camp.'

The sun was already below the horizon and the sky over the grassland darkled quickly. Rhita squinted at the lens again, seeing a watery star distorted through it, and nodded at Demetrios. 'Let's go,' she said.

Camouflage nets were thrown over the beecraft, making them look like grassy hillocks – not a very good disguise, she thought, considering how flat everything was around them, but better than nothing. Oresias and Atta met with the kybernētēs of the cargo plane while four large tents were erected. Rhita listened to their plans for the next day from her cot on a pad of grass flattened by a canvas sheet. Flies and moths buzzed around her light in the corner of the tent. She was exhausted; hardly able to keep her eyes open, and yet she could not seem to drift off. Demetrios brought a can of soup from the makeshift galley and she sipped it, asking herself silently, again and again, *Why here? Why open a gate here?* Who could have followed Patrikia to this Gaia, and who would want to?

There had been no messages on the teukhos for the past two days. This evening, however, she flipped the switch and saw her grandmother's words again. She had been no witch, after all; she was still advising Rhita about politics in Alexandreia, a world to all intents and purposes lost to her granddaughter now. Rhita read the long message and closed her eyes, somewhat relieved; for a time, she had thought perhaps Patrikia was staring over her shoulder, holding her accountable. Now it was apparent that the sophē had been mortal, after all.

Exhausted, Rhita turned off the slate, packed it into its goatleather case, and turned down the kerosene lantern. In other parts of the tent, all was quiet. Outside, the day's gentle wind had settled, and the prairie was wrapped in expansive silence, with thousands of stadia of emptiness all around.

25

Thistledown City

Lanier, feeling a need for simple amusement, rearranged
the decor of his guest quarters below the Nexus dome.
He walked from room to room in the palatial suite,
giving voice instructions. 'Polynesian,' he said in the
dining hall, currently austere, sharp-edged and classical.
The decor projectors searched their period memories
and produced a fire — and torch-lit ceremonial chamber,
matted with brown and white tapas, set with wooden
bowls. The walls were constructed of palm logs and
faced with more matting woven of grass and palm
leaves.

'Very good,' he approved. By making fun of such
marvels, he felt he could soothe his wizened little ego,
or at least put himself in a better mood.

Once, powerful governors – senators, presiding ministers and even presidents – had lodged in these quarters.
The rooms had been empty for centuries after the
exodus down the Way, and were now used only for
ceremonial occasions.

Korzenowski had gone off to make arrangements
for the full Nexus conference; Mirsky was in his own
quarters, similar to these; Lanier had nothing to occupy
him but his thoughts. He felt like a fifth wheel. He was
old, if that mattered; his understanding had never been
adequate to a problem like this. Yet he had not
expressed his reservations to anyone yet, and that worried him still more. It meant the administrative dog
within him was starting at last to grip the bone being
forced between its teeth. He did not want that; he
wanted repose, not mind-bending excitement and challenge. He wanted –

Not to put too fine a point on it, Garry Lanier realised he wanted to be *dead*.

His eyes opened a little wider and he sat on the step of the staircase leading into the dining hall (carved from volcanic rock, the projectors perceived). He felt as if his heart had skipped a beat. Always willing to hide his feelings from himself, he had never directly confronted this particular personal truth.

An end to life and experience. Acquiescence to rest of the final sort. Reassurance that whatever the advances in medicine and technology, for him at least all life could end in darkness and quiet.

Lanier had lived through more unusual things than he could clearly recall; much of his memory was clouded by simple incomprehension. He might spend a century researching what he had seen, and be only a little wiser; so he would chuck it all and lie back.

Still, the admission shocked him. He rubbed his hollowing cheeks with his long, thin, still-strong fingers and repeated this interior revelation several times, savoring its bitterness. Whatever he had been, he had never been a quitter, and yet this was nothing if not wanting to quit.

Heineman had not wanted to quit. He had accepted mortality, but had enjoyed life to the end, and he had survived as much trauma as Lanier; perhaps more. Lenore Carrolson's spirit was intact; she still had vitality and purpose. And Karen relished life so much she refused to think of dying, postponing that day with Hexamon technology.

No wonder he and Karen had parted ways. Like Lenore, she had not been blunted by all she had seen, and she had seen as much as he. She had grieved for their daughter as deeply as he – grief made all the more difficult because it was mixed with an impossible hope . . . that they might someday recover Andia's implant. Where was his failure, then?

The room's voice announced a visitor at the main entrance. Lanier groaned, hoping for time to chew this over before having to confront his fellows, but that was not to be. He could not deny visitors now. 'All right,' he said. He walked to the suite's main entrance, a five-meter-long, two-meter-wide steel bridge suspended in a hollow sphere of meteoric crystal. A slice of the crystal moved aside from the opposite end of the bridge. Pavel Mirsky stood there, smiling his usual chagrined smile.

'Am I interrupting?'

'No,' Lanier said, spooked more by the man's normality and solidity than by anything else. *Why couldn't he come dressed as a god, at least? A thunderbolt or two flickering in his hair . . .*

'I do not sleep normally, and I am bored just searching for information . . . I need company. I hope that is fine with you?'

Lanier nodded weak assent. *Of course he would be bored. Even the Stone's incredible libraries would seem childish to him . . . wouldn't they?*

'I haven't apologised for imposing on you, have I?'

'I believe you have,' Lanier said. *Surely, his memory can't be faulty?*

'Perhaps I have.' He smiled again and crossed the bridge, passing Lanier. 'These are spacious living areas, yet not, I think, much more luxurious than where common folks lived? Technology finally made equals of leaders and led.'

'It's too rich for my tastes.'

'I agree,' Mirsky said as they crossed the reception rotunda, passing beneath a dome depicting the heavens as viewed from the Thistledown's northern pole. At the moment, the Moon was visible and full, and its light cast shadows under their feet. 'This is a nice effect, though, no?'

He seemed more like a child now. More spontaneous, playful, yet in control.

Lanier followed Mirsky into the suite's small informal sitting room. The Russian tried out a stylish and neutral chair – neutral in that it did not possess traction cushions or any other field effect. He bounced on the centuries-old cushions, still pliant, and shook his head with mock sadness. 'I was such a mess when I left this place, this starship,' he said. 'I had lost much of my personality, or so I thought . . . very confused. I remember one thing clearly, however.'

Lanier cleared his throat. Mirsky's long stare was unnerving.

'My admiration for you. I found you an incredible force. You faced all from the beginning, and did not . . . crack?'

Lanier shook his head slowly, not quite denying that he had kept his sanity. 'Those were hard times.'

'The worst. I can hardly believe what I am now came out of those times, those circumstances. But this evening, I feel this urge to talk, and I want to talk more with you. You and I are not much alike, most would say, but I see similarities.'

'Even now?'

Mirsky's face became bland. 'You are not enthusiastic. I fear you have come to the end of your rope.'

Lanier barked a laugh. 'Yes,' he said. 'How true.' Softly.

'You know, a man reaches the end of his rope, he falls off.'

'Hangs himself, actually,' Lanier said. 'That's the cliché'.

'But a dog, he reaches the end, bites the rope . . . he's free.'

'Old Russian wisdom?'

'Hardly,' Mirsky said, still bland. He did not quite look at Lanier, not quite away from him. He seemed a kind of pudding into which one could comfortably fall, to live a life of vanilla and sleep. The itch to confess flared.

Lanier sat opposite him, trying to revivify that fluid body motion of his youth, just to compete with this avatar. Competition not being practical, but –

'All right,' he said. 'I'm tired. I've lived too long.

You've lived out a universe and you're not bored or tired.'

'Yes, but I have been bored and tired in ways I cannot see clearly now. Exhausted by failure. We who went down the Way failed miserably, and it cost us in ways . . . well, it cost dearly. We were scarred. We suffered what I can only call an ego-loss, and that alone was almost enough to bring us to self-extinction. When you exist in a nullity, ego-loss is like loss of blood. We nearly sapped ourselves away.' Mirsky rested his hands on his thighs and splayed his fingers, examining them as if looking for dirt or hangnails. Almost shyly, he asked, 'Are you curious about me, what I am now?'

'We're all curious,' Lanier said, again softly, gently, as if not to disturb Mirsky's enchanting blandness.

'I am back to my old self, mostly. Sometimes I do not control my capabilities, and that is when what I must do exceeds the comprehension of my old self.'

Lanier raised his brows, not understanding. Mirsky continued without elaboration.

'But I come to talk about you, and why I came back to you. I owed you a debt. I could not discharge that debt across all of time. In some of my forms, this debt did not bother me, since all my past was tucked away like an old book, unread. But when I knew I would return as my old self, the debt surfaced.'

'I don't know of any debt.' Lanier felt the impulse grow, not just confession but a bursting, an exploding. He wanted to hold his head and keep himself together.

'A simple debt. I need to thank you.'

Tears came to Lanier's eyes, unbidden, unwanted.

'You were decent. You did your work and did not ask for thanks. You are the reason I survived to make our long journey, and come back now. In every situation, there can be a seed crystal of goodness and decency, of sensibility. You were that crystal on the Stone.'

Lanier leaned his head back on the chair, tears streaming down his cheeks. Had it been in his character, he would have sobbed. He held those spasms in, but felt a release none the less.

'A simple thanks,' Mirsky reiterated.

How incredible that in all the time he had worked on the restoration, he remembered no one thanking him. Not even Karen, too close to see the need. He had sacrificed life and time for the people he had administered, yet because of his manner – a confident self-sufficiency – he had never been thanked, or because of some personal flaw could not remember the thanks. Perhaps he had never put himself in a position to be thanked. The release now was like the unwinding of an ancient spring that had pinched his vitals.

He lifted his head and stared at the Russian's blurred face, embarrassed and grateful at once. 'I was your enemy,' he managed to croak. He touched his face and was surprised to find old skin, soft and yielding.

Mirsky clucked his tongue, a startling mannerism in an avatar. 'To have a decent enemy is a blessing beyond measure,' he said, rising. 'I have disturbed your rest. I will go.'

'No,' Lanier said, lifting his arm. 'No. Please. I do need to talk with you.' The fear and envy this man aroused had turned in a moment into a kind of love, a homecoming of feelings he would never have acknowledged four decades ago. With these feelings came a sudden wary, almost painful concern for Karen. What was she doing now? He needed to speak to her, too. His skin . . . so *old!*

'Shall we reminisce? There appears to be time enough now, and may not be later.'

Mirsky nodded and sat again, leaning forward, elbows on knees, hands clasped. The blandness had gone from him.

'Maybe we both need memories refreshed,' Lanier said. 'I wanted to tell you how tired I was, but I don't feel very tired now.'

Mirsky waved his hand nonchalantly. 'Old warriors always chew the bull long after.'

'Chew the fat,' Lanier said, smiling. It seemed very unlikely Mirsky made an unconscious error. 'I'd like that.'

'Tell me what happened after I defected.'

'First, I'd like to ask a question . . . A thousand questions.'

'I cannot answer a thousand questions,' Mirsky said.

'Then one or two.'

Mirsky nodded skeptically.

'Your presentation . . . there was so much *power* there. You tell us they'll take – they are taking – whole galaxies and converting them, destroying them . . . Lifeless galaxies?'

Mirsky grinned. 'Wise question. Yes. Stillborn, you might say . . . Huge, full of too much energy, burning themselves out anyway, or quickly falling into frozen stars at their center . . . You call them black holes. No life, no order in those galaxies will survive. The Final Mind accelerates and controls their death.'

Lanier nodded stupidly, caught himself, and licked his dry lips. 'With so much power, why not just force us? Send a kind of army of people like yourself, or . . . something stronger.'

'Not subtle. Not the right way.'

'What if you fail?'

Mirsky shrugged. 'Even so.'

'What will happen . . . between now and the end of time?' There it was, bald; he had had his interest in the future renewed, and with that came curiosity.

'I remember only what I need to remember. If I remembered more, I would not be allowed to tell you . . . not everything.'

'How long will it be – until the end?'

'Time means less and less in that region of history,' Mirsky said. 'But an estimate – a ballpark figure – is not too misleading. About seventy-five billion years.'

Lanier blinked, trying to absorb such a span.

Mirsky shook his head sadly. 'Sorry. I am not trying to be evasive, but there can only be so much revelation now. Perhaps later . . . much later, when humans join the communities . . .'

Lanier shivered and nodded. 'All right,' he said. 'But I'm still curious. Others are probably more curious than I am . . . The very people you have to convince.'

Mirsky agreed with a wry expression. 'Now, Garry, I have my own questions. Can we talk about what happened after the Geshel precincts left?'

'Starting from when?'

'From the return to Earth.'

Lanier thought, found a starting point, and began his confession, after the need for it had finally passed.

26
Gaia

Birds sang and something else was in the air – something electric. Rhita pulled down her covers and listened to the men moving around in the rest of the tent, grumbling. She rubbed sleep from her eyes; she had been exhausted, strained to the breaking point, she realised now. For a moment she simply hung on to the comfort of her bed, refusing to listen to her instincts. Then something exploded not far from the tent and she was on her knees, and on her feet, dressed only in loose-fitting underwear. The air crackled and wind beat the outside of the tent. A few men screamed questions and orders at each other. Demetrios lifted the edge of the tent flap, stared at her, embarrassed, and said almost sternly, 'Thunderstorm. It's going to pour rivers on us any minute.'

'Just what we needed!' She stepped into her pants, not at all embarrassed to be seen by him. In fact, she found the moment slightly arousing – the appraising look in his eye before his politeness made him look down . . .

'It adds to the excitement,' he admitted, back turned. She looped her shirt closed and zipped up her jacket, then bent down to put on her shoes, buckling quickly. In seconds, she was fully dressed. She brushed past Demetrios and skipped by a kybernētēs and a soldier, down the covered gap between two sections of the tent, into the outside.

Oresias and Jamal Atta stood at the edge of the ravine, Oresias with hands on hips, Atta speaking into the mouthpiece of a mobile radio mounted on the back of a soldier. *What happened to radio silence?* she asked herself. Demetrois came through the tent door behind her, just as big drops of rain splashed on her face and hands and darkened the fabric of her jacket. Atta lifted his hands and shook his head; the last straw, more than any human could bear.

The two beecraft seemed hunched under the onslaught, blades drooping almost to the level of the grass. Soldiers stood in the hatchways, smoke rising from several long pipes as they casually watched the downpour grow more intense. Oresias handed the soldier the mouthpiece and drew his jacket up over his head, running toward them. Lightning flashed to the south, lighting up the canopy of clouds and the steppe around them with cold, pale brilliance.

'There's disaster in Alexandreia,' Oresias shouted over another crack of thunder. He pushed Rhita and Demetrios back through the door into the tent and threw aside his jacket, running his hand like a comb through his wet hair, rubbing water out of his eyes with his knuckles. Atta remained standing in the middle of the storm, raising his arms now and then, shouting or whispering, they couldn't tell over the noise.

'He wants lightning to hit him. Might be better for all of us,' Oresias said. 'There's been a revolt. Elements in the Mouseion, I gather . . . and the Jews. The Lokhias is under siege and the palace has been locked up. Soldiers loyal to the queen have dropped bombs on the Mouseion – '

'No!' Rhita felt the word leap out of her, a futile, outraged countermanding order.

Oresias grimaced in shared pain. 'We should have known from the attitude in Bagdadē and Damaskē. We have no protection on the way back. For all we know, the Hunnos and Rhus border stations are being alerted now. I don't think they have a radio fix on us yet, but they will if we have to send any more messages.'

Lugotorix stood tall and protecting over Rhita, his eyes dark under a heavy frown.

'What do we do here?' Demetrios asked, apprehensive but not fearful.

'Our mission,' Oresias said. 'We have two hours before I order a pull-out and we try to get back. We'll unload what we need from the cargo plane.' He ordered several soldiers to organise the transfer of supplies. Outside, the tanker's engines roared over the storm. The fuel had been transferred, and now it was taking off. 'A long, leisurely expedition is no longer possible, but we can investigate this gate, learn as much as we can, and save our skins before the Kirghiz or Kazakh Tatars or their Rhus masters are upon us.'

Atta had given up imprecations against the thunder and joined them under the tent. 'Lightning hit the gate,' he said breathlessly. 'It glowed like a lantern.' Simultaneously, he and Oresias looked at Rhita.

'My turn, isn't it?' she said.

'I will bring the Objects,' Lugotorix said. She looked at the Kelt's retreating back with some surprise. *Everybody pushes me to this. I don't like the feeling I have; my instincts say no. . . .*

Or was she simply afraid?

'Will lightning strike the clavicle, too?' Oresias asked.

'I don't know,' she said softly.

'What?'

'*I don't know!*' she shouted. Demetrios nodded phlegmatically and she turned away from him with a flash of disgust contradicting her earlier attraction. *He can't help. Nobody can help. I'm trapped.*

Lugotorix returned with the large case. She unlocked it with her keys and removed the clavicle, holding it low before her, feeling its power in her hands and thoughts. *It tries to reassure me.* The Kelt adjusted his machine pistol and shifted from one foot to the other behind her. Oresias smiled and pulled aside the tent door.

Without hesitation, refusing to show any weakness to anybody, disgusted with herself and everything else – especially with her weak-minded notions of *adventure* the day before – she stalked out into the driving rain.

She stopped and turned, eyes blinking against the

pounding drops. 'That way,' Demetrios said, pointing her in the direction of the swale.

'It'll flood soon,' she called over her shoulder. The men followed her, all but the Kelt hunched over. Lugotorix strode through the storm like a walking tree, hair plastered across his face, eyes mere slits, teeth bared in a grimace.

The bottom of the swale was already ankle-deep in rushing water. She slipped and stepped gingerly down the bank, somehow staying upright with both hands gripping the clavicle, until she splashed across the bottom and stood beside the shivering lens of the gate, seeing it with her eyes and also in her mind, undisturbed by the storm or the lightning strike.

The clavicle showed her how wide the storm was, and odd symbols flashed through the display, bunching up at one point in the clouds and blinking green –

Just as lightning brightened the grassland yet again.

The clavicle kept her informed about all conditions around the gate. *A pity Grandmother didn't tell me about all this*, she thought. *She might not have known.*

'It's still here, and it hasn't changed,' she called to the men. Only Lugotorix followed her into the swale. Demetrios stopped halfway down the bank, not, she surmised, out of fear, but in deference to her position, her control of the situation.

'Do you need help?' he asked, holding out his hands.

'I don't know,' she said. 'I've never done this before'.

What do I do to widen the gate? she asked the device. She assumed that was what they were all after, with no time to be extra cautious. She could hardly conceive of who or what might be waiting for them on the other side: ogres or gods.

She was still a child of Rhodos, however sophisticated she might pretend to be. She did not have her grandmother's upbringing.

The clavicle instructed her below a level she could follow with her conscious mind. Her hands tingled; the effect was almost painful. Her muscles jerked minutely, growing used to new directives, new channels of command being blazed through her nervous system in just a few seconds. For a moment, Rhita was both tired and nauseated, but that passed and she straightened.

Surprised, she blinked away a few drops of water. The rain had stopped and she hadn't noticed. Had she fainted or blacked out? She turned and saw Lugotorix behind her, eyes focused over her head. Demetrios halfway down the bank, and Atta and Oresias and the soldiers along the edge, all stared at the gateway.

Rhita looked up.

The lens had risen and expanded, flattening. It gleamed oddly in the fresh rays of a morning sun shining at a low angle between parting clouds. She consulted the clavicle.

The gateway's changed. What's happening?

We have made it expand, the clavicle told her. *You ordered it so.*

Can I go through it?

Not advisable, the clavicle said.

Why?

We cannot know what is on the other side.

Rhita thought that made a great deal of sense, but their time was limited. *There's no way we can find out?*

None.

But it is open?

Yes.

Can someone come through from the other side?

Yes.

The enormity of what she had done began to sink in. She stood below and to one side of the gate, admiring its uncanny beauty, like a suspended raindrop, or the lens from the eye of some huge fish.

Water had risen above her ankles in the swale. It tumbled in glassy sheets over the bent grass, muddy foam catching against the bank. Rhita glanced down at it, annoyed, and decided it would be wise to climb up the bank, away from any possible flood. She stood beside Demetrios, holding the clavicle level with her knees, breathing heavily. 'It's open,' she told him quietly. He glanced at Atta and Oresias, then back at her.

'Don't you want to tell them?'

'Of course,' she said. 'It's open,' she called back over her shoulder. 'I opened it. The clavicle opened it.'

Atta nodded, lips drawn down, eyes squinted in speculation. Oresias gave her a short smile. 'We can pass through?'

'It says we can, but that we shouldn't. It doesn't know what's on the other side.'

Oresias walked down the bank. 'We came here to investigate,' he reminded them. 'Whatever's happened in Alexandreia, that's our mission. You're too valuable to send through,' he told Rhita, 'and we need Atta to command the pilots and soldiers in an emergency. Which this situation is, probably. Demetrios – '

'I'd love to go,' the mekhanikos said, eyes sparkling.

'No.' Oresias lifted his hands and shook his head. 'You didn't sign on to take risks. I did.'

Lugotorix watched them all closely, his eyes following the circle of conversation.

'Bring down the second Object,' Oresias ordered one of the soldiers. The man ran off to comply.

'I don't know how to use it,' Rhita said. 'Grandmother didn't tell me.'

'Careless of her,' Oresias said, face glowing with the challenge. 'We'll see if it still works, and whether or not we can work it. If it works, I go through. If not – '

'I'm responsible for all of the Objects,' Rhita said.

'And I'm responsible for you,' Oresias said. 'If it doesn't work, we can at least poke one of our caged animals through first, and then I'll follow – if the animal comes back alive.' He touched Rhita's arm lightly. 'I'm not a complete fool, and I don't want to die. We'll be cautious.'

The case containing the second object was brought down into the swale by the soldier. Rhita opened the lid while he held it, and brought out the control box and recirculation box, both attached to a thick black belt. 'It's very old,' she said.

Oresias held up his arms and she wrapped the belt around his waist. 'How would you make it work?'

Rhita thought for a moment, then touched the control box with her hand. The device did not communicate with her mind; apparently it was less sophisticated than the clavicle. *What would Grandmother do?* she asked herself.

She'd talk to it.

'Please turn on,' she said in Hellenic. 'Please protect this man.' Nothing happened. She thought about that for a while, and then decided to use her grandmother's English, a difficult language she was not at all fluent in. 'Please turn on,' she said. 'Protect this man.'

Again, no response.

Rhita felt a flush of anger at her own ignorance. *Why didn't Grandmother teach me how to use all the Objects?* Perhaps, toward the end of her life, Patrikia's brilliance had faded. 'I can't think of anything else to try . . .' she said. 'Unless . . . it might work if I'm wearing it.'

Oresias shook his head firmly. 'If her Imperial Hypsēlotēs still sits on her throne, she'd have my head if I put you in any danger. We'll try the animal first.' He ordered that a cony be brought forward.

'I'll go,' Lugotorix told Rhita in confidence, speaking softly in her ear. She shook her head; everything was confused. They were amateurs; none of the others – probably not even her – had any idea of how momentous this occasion was, how *dangerous* and not just for them.

The cony arrived, a small bundle of fur in a wicker cage, twitching a pink nose, its cage suspended by a metal hook on a long wooden pole. The water had not risen appreciably, so he took the far end of the pole and stepped into the stream, walking awkwardly with the cage dangling before him. 'Where should I put it?' he asked.

Despite herself, Rhita grinned. 'In the center.'

Lugotorix seemed to find this amusing, too; the Kelt seldom found anything worth smiling about.

Oresias lifted the long pole and maneuvered the cage up to the center of the glimmering lens. 'Like this?' he asked. The cage and cony disappeared, as if by some magician's sleight of hand.

'Yes,' Rhita said softly, awed. She tried to visualise Patrikia falling through such a lens, landing in an irrigation channel . . .

'I'll leave it there for a few seconds,' Oresias said, the pole trembling in his grip.

Rhita heard a deep pounding sound to the north. Jamal Atta looked up from the swale and flinched. 'Tatars – Kirghiz!' he shouted. 'Hundreds of them!'

Oresias's face blanched, but he continued to hold the pole in position. 'Where?'

Lugotorix leaped to the rim of the swale. Rhita was torn between staying near the gate and Oresias and following the Kelt to find out what was happening. Soldiers shouted around the beecraft. The pounding grew louder.

'Horsemen and infantry!' Lugotorix called down to her. 'They're close – a couple of stadia.'

'What banner?' Oresias asked, his entire upper body trembling with the weight of the cage and pole. The lens hung steady and undisturbed, absorbing the cage just as an invisible doorway swallows the top of a magician's rope.

'No banners,' Jamal Atta said. 'They're Kirghiz! We must leave!'

Oresias pulled the cage from the gate convulsively. Rhita saw a limp blur of red and gray in the cage as Oresias swung the pole out over the stream to the bank. They both peered down at the cony. It was dead; it hardly resembled an animal at all.

'What happened to it?' Rhita asked.

'Looks like it exploded, or something tore it apart,' Oresias said. He fingered the wooden bars; they were intact, their contents dripping a thin fluid of blood onto the grass and dirt. He unhooked the cage and stuffed it hastily into a rubberized sack. Lugotorix came down the decline to grab her arm. 'We go now,' he said firmly, machine pistol in hand. She did not resist.

They stood on the edge of the swale for a moment to get their bearings. Soldiers ran through the grass to the beecraft with boxes of supplies. One stumbled and fell, screaming; Rhita thought he had been shot, but he regained his footing and picked up his load. She looked to the north, beyond the beecraft, and saw a line of dark riders moving rapidly toward them, horses up to their withers in grass. Clods of mud flew up behind them, and their voices joined in a heavy, ululating song above the pounding of hooves. Some waved swords and long rifles in the air. Hidden by a low hill until just this moment, a flimsy multiple-winged gullcraft suddenly vaulted into view behind the riders, buzzing like a summer dragonfly. The gullcraft flew over the line, gained more altitude, and passed above them at about fifty arms, wings dipped almost vertical as the kybernētēs and one observer in a rear seat tried to see the invaders. She clearly made out a long black telescope in the observer's hands, and then Lugotorix lifted her by her arms, pinned to her sides by his huge hands, and ran with her to the nearest beecraft. Oresias tried to keep up with them. She turned and saw Jamal Atta scrambling with arms outflung, cape billowing, in the direction of a clump of soldiers bearing yet more boxes of supplies from the cargo gullcraft.

'Drop them! Get to your craft!' he ordered. But it was too late. The horsemen were already riding through the camp, some plunging into the swale, barely missing striking the gate, and up the other side, horses chuffing and flinging ribbons of foam, their nostrils flaring.

The riders wore black leggings and dark gray pants, with loose magenta tunics belted and tied around the wrists with rope. Their hats were made of skins, ear coverings flapping loose as they bounded around the tent, pointing their rifles and laughing and screaming.

Soldiers cowered in the grass, on their knees, or stood their ground with wide eyes, cringing this way and that, not daring to bring up their own weapons.

They were clearly outnumbered. To add to the confusion, it began to rain again.

Lugotorix lifted her into the beecraft and leaped up after her, pushing her behind a bulkhead with one boot while he took a position with pistol behind his back near the open hatch. Other soldiers hid in the craft, and some crawled beneath it, seeking refuge from the pounding hooves. There were at least three hundred riders.

The second beecraft started its jets. Rhita crawled to a low window on the opposite side and saw the props rotate ponderously, jet pods low, almost in the grass. Horsemen rode around it rifles pointing at the forward compartment, shouting and swinging their free hands down. Oresias crawled up beside her. Demetrios coughed behind him. 'They won't let any of us leave,' he said. Jamal Atta strode with some dignity between four riders on plunging and rearing horses, glancing this way and that with a fierce grin. *He's showing them he has no fear*, Rhita thought. Atta turned and approached the area of the rotating blades. The pods were picking up speed now, the props rising slowly and the grass bending outward. The horsemen rode clear, rifles still at ready. Atta shouted at the beecraft, but from inside their own vehicle, they could not hear what he said.

'He wants them to stop the engines,' Oresias guessed.

Demetrios found his own position near a second window. 'What happened to the cony?' he asked.

'It's dead,' Oresias answered bitterly. 'Our luck has been steady throughout this expedition.'

'Dead how?' Demetrios persisted.

'Like something ate it and spit it out!' Oresias replied, eyes wild. 'We may all be dead in a few minutes anyway.'

Encircled by riders, Jamal Atta spoke with a brawny

fellow in a thick black wool coat, shiny with rain, that made him seem twice his already formidable size. The Kirghiz swung a long curved sword idly near Atta's ribs. Atta seemed to pay little attention to this, maintaining an admirable calm despite being soaked to the skin, his hair hanging in long strings. Other riders herded scattered soldiers before them. The second beecraft's engines moaned sadly, turbines dropping in pitch, and the props swung to halt, pods undulating.

'He's surrendering,' Oresias said. 'Not much choice.'

Rhita still held the clavicle. She had ignored the device for several minutes, yet she clutched it firmly in both hands. Lowering her head from the window, shaking her aching hands out one by one, she returned her full attention to what the device was telling her. Her thoughts filled with the display again. She saw the gate – still represented by a red cross – and she saw what must have been a haze of rain drops around the swale. The riders did not seem significant to the clavicle – she could detect no symbols indicating their presence. But something was happening to the red cross. It was surrounded by one red circle, and then by another, and a third. The circles broke into three equal segments and spun about the cross.

What's happening?

The gateway is still expanding, the clavicle told her.

How?

Controlled from the opposite side.

Rhita's heart fell. She had not been truly frightened – exhilarated, shocked, surprised, but not afraid – until now. 'What have we done?' she murmured. Once again she prayed to Athēnē Lindia and closed her eyes, wishing Patrikia were here to advise her.

A trio of riders seemed to rise up out of the ground before the beecraft hatchway, screaming and waving their rifles and swords. Oresias stood and faced them, hands outstretched to show he was unarmed. The lead rider, bareheaded, bald and with a long, thin mustache, leaned forward in his minimal saddle and motioned for Oresias to approach.

'You speak Hellenic?' the rider asked.

'Yes,' Oresias said.

'Our stratēgos, he wishes a word with you – you are Oresias?'

'Yes.'

'You command with this *arabios* Jamal Atta?'

'Yes.'

'Why are you here?' The bald-headed rider leaned forward with an expression of intense, solicitous interest. Then he leaned back, shaking his sword vigorously. 'No. You tell the stratēgos, with the *arabios*, all together!'

Oresias climbed down from the hatch and followed the trio across the grass, around the beecraft, to where Atta conversed with the man in the wool coat.

Rhita still had half her attention on the clavicle display. The circles spinning around the cross had become a blur; that, the clavicle told her, was an indication of the strength of the gate. A great deal of energy was being expended. She could not see the swale or the gate directly.

'Something's happening,' she told Demetrios. He knelt beside her, hair dripping rain. They all resembled drowned cats. He held out his hand, and she released the clavicle to clasp it, then pull it down to touch a handle. His eyes grew large.

'God!' he said. 'It's a nightmare.'

'I guess the Tatars don't see anything unusual,' Rhita surmised. 'But it's getting wider, stronger.'

'Why?'

'Something's going to come through,' she said.

'Maybe more people like your grandmother,' Lugotorix said. He laid the machine pistol behind the winch housing, out of sight but quick to hand; not, however, immediately in hand, in case they were searched.

Rhita shook her head, feeling hot, almost feverish.

They are not human, the clavicle told her. *They do not use human methods on the gate.*

Demetrios stared at her, having heard the message as well, but not knowing what to make of it.

How soon? she asked.

The gate is open. When they will pass through cannot be known.

27
Thistledown, Fourth Chamber

There was no time to worry about the Jart's almost total cooperation with his partial; Olmy could hardly keep up with the flow of information they were exchanging. Some risk was involved; a particularly subtle corrosive or worm could be embedded in the Jart's flood of information, and might even make it past Olmy's filters and other defenses, but that was a risk Olmy was willing to take.

The exchange was not one-way. Olmy's partial was providing the Jart with selected information about humans.

Physically, Olmy sat on a rock by a narrow streamlet, tubelight filtering through a haze of pollen that dusted the quiet pool near his feet. Mentally, he explored the labyrinth of Jart social strata, convinced by now that the Jart's information was accurate and not made-up. It was too convincing, too true to what little humans had learned about their long-time adversaries in the Way.

This Jart was a modified *expediter*. Expediters carried out orders passed through *duty expediters,* slightly different in mentality and form. An expediter might be thought of as a laborer, although their tasks were often non-physical; expediters might just as often be assigned thought processing as physical work. Duty expediters designed practical ways of carrying out policy. They decided who should be called up from a pool of expediters, who were stored, Olmy learned, in a kind of city memory, but kept inactive. If physical forms were required for their labor, they were assigned to bodies which might be either mechanical, biological, or a mix of the two.

Another description of another kind of body existed which Olmy was not sure he understood: the translation came across as *mathematical* form, but was not complete by any means.

The Jart was not above holding back key information. Neither was Olmy.

Above duty expediters was *command*. Command made policy and foresaw the results through intense simulation and modeling. Command was always made up of Jarts in their original natural bodies, without augmentation of any kind. They were mortal and allowed to die of old age. They were never downloaded. Olmy puzzled at this bottleneck in an otherwise extremely advanced and amorphous group of beings; why not give what was obviously an important level in the strata more flexibility, and more capabilities than they naturally had? He made a note to have his partial ask the Jart about this.

Above command and all other ranks of Jarts was *command oversight*. At first, Olmy could not understand what role command oversight played. Individuals in this rank were immobile, lacked any bodies, and resided permanently in a kind of memory storage different from that where inactive expediters were kept. Command oversight Jarts—if they could be called Jarts at all—were stripped of all but pure reasoning faculties and rigorously modified for their tasks. Apparently they gathered information from all levels of the strata, examined it, made judgments of goals achieved and efficacy of actions and presented 'recommendations' to command.

In all of Jart cybernetic technology, as far as Olmy was being informed, there were no artificial programs; all processing was accomplished by Jart mentalities which had, at one time or another, occupied natural and original Jart bodies. However far from their natural origins, however duplicated, modified and customised, these mentalities always had a connection with their original memories. It was possible, then, that there were Jarts still active who remembered a time before their occupation of the Way, who perhaps remembered the Jart home world.

If there had been a single home world . . .

The Jarts might not be a single species, but a combination of many species—a kind of *volvox* of beings and cultures.

The only level within the strata allowed to breed naturally was command. No impression of what command looked like came through in the information; Olmy was beginning to realise that understanding Jart physiology was much less important than humans had once thought.

Jarts, far more even than humans, had superseded their physical origins; most had been consumed by their cybernetic structures.

But in all honesty, Olmy could see that had the Infinite Hexamon continued its development, humans might have ended up in a society not qualitatively different from that of the Jarts. They might yet; neo-Geshels were pushing the Terrestrial Hexamon to return to the old ways.

Did freedom or individuality mean anything at all in such a culture? Another note, another question.

In all the information, Olmy found nothing that could be considered directly strategic: nothing about the Jart activities in the Way, about their trading partners (if any) or their ultimate goals (again, if any). He decided it would be best not to press for this information until he saw fit to provide the Jart with similar insight.

It was a kind of dance, this exchange of information. The moves had started out awkwardly, rapidly become fast and furious, and might soon slow to a measured back-and-forth rhythm.

For the time being, there was almost total cooperation. Olmy doubted that would last; the Jart had its mission, after all, and probably suspected that a great deal of time had passed.

Vigilance was the order of the hour.

28
Earth

There was no physical sensation when the shuttle lifted off from the landing field at Christchurch. Karen Farley Lanier closed her eyes briefly and listened to the exclamations of the delegates, many of whom had never flown until the last few weeks, much less traveled in space. They would spend seven hours in transit before docking with the Stone – Thistledown, she corrected herself. Only the Old Natives referred to the orbiting asteroid as the Stone.

Still slender, her blond hair graying into sunlit ash, Karen seemed mature, but nowhere in age near her sixty-eight years. She might have been a well-preserved forty. Pride in her appearance and fitness had been part of her bulwark against the Death; if she could maintain her strength and youth, she felt more subconsciously than otherwise, then the Earth could regain her vitality. Sometimes she accused herself of self-serving vanity, but what did she have to be vain about, or for that matter, who could she be vain *for*? Her husband hadn't complimented her on her looks in at least five years; they hadn't made love for three years; she had neither time nor inclination for affairs.

Life had made her almost completely self-contained, a kind of emotional analog to the homorph Olmy.

The atmosphere in the shuttle was electric with excitement. The delegates sat glued to the ports, eyes wide. After an hour and a half, the novelty passed sufficiently for some of the delegates to turn away from the view of stars and Earth. Karen looked around the broad, dimly-lighted white interior of the cabin. As with almost all Hexamon shuttles, the furnishings resembled ingeniously molded soft white bread dough:

couches arranged almost casually for maximum efficiency, all capable of customising themselves to fit their occupants' bodies; opacity where no windows were needed, transparent ports where passengers wished to see out; pools of light where a delegate read a small stack of papers (archaic in this setting!), and shadow where another slept.

This Hexamon shuttle was much larger than most, easily capable of carrying several hundred passengers. There were forty-five aboard now, forty-one men and women from around the Earth, as well as herself. It was going to be a grand experiment – a by-your-bootstraps knitting of these individuals into a single family, teaching them to see that their problems were not separate but intimately linked, and to see their companions not as competition, but as helpers.

The introduction at Christchurch had gone smoothly enough; Karen had blended in, despite her rank as Chief Earth Coordinator, and had been accepted by most of the group as a peer.

A number of delegates had attached themselves to her in an attempt to form a proto-ruling-class. One such was a middle-aged Mainland Chinese woman whose community, near Karen's home province of Hunan, had not known the touch of the Terrestrial Hexamon until just five years ago. Another was a badly scarred, very proud Ukrainian, representing a group of Independents who had held off the would-be-salvagers of their villages and towns for nearly twenty years after the Death. Yet a third was a North American from Mexico City. Mexico City had survived the bombs only to succumb to lethal radiation, and had been repopulated by Latinos from Central America and refugees from the border cities . . .

Karen appreciated their confidence in her but she subtly discouraged the hierarchy they were unconsciously forming. She did not desire eminence or power, only success. Theirs was a unique opportunity. The circumstances had to be handled carefully.

Their faces bore the mark of Earth's agony, even though some had been born after the Death. Few of these people had received pseudo-Talsit mental therapy, having kept their sanity and abilities even in the worst of times; they were incredibly tough and resilient. They had been hand-selected by Hexamon sociologists who had spent months searching the Recovery census – completed only in the past four years – for just their kind. 'We call them high primes,' Suli Ram Kikura, the project coordinator, had told Karen. 'Strong naturals with little or no previous tampering.'

Most of them were natural leaders, having come to power without Hexamon help. They seemed at ease together, though few had dealt with each other as leaders before. Their communities were far enough apart that the borders did not touch, and there had been little commerce between them; but with the completion of the Hexamon social structure over the next ten years, their peoples would certainly interact, and the experience they received aboard the Stone would make them all – it was hoped – a kind of seed, broadcast over the Recovered Earth.

Ser Ram Kikura's prejudice against the Hexamon's extensive psychological meddling still showed; it made her the perfect coordinator for this project, an attempt to let Earth stand on its own feet.

Some citizens of the Terrestrial Hexamon seemed to feel the Hexamon would not remain stable for the indefinite future. The shortage of materials necessary for the maintenance of society aboard the Stone, the shifts in deeply held attitudes, the repercussions of dealing with their own origins on the post-Death Earth – all were taking their toll on Hexamon stability.

If Earth had to survive a crisis among its saviors, it would have to be weaned . . .

Karen spoke Chinese, English, French, Russian and Spanish, having brushed up on her Russian with Hexamon devices, and having learned Spanish the same way. That was enough to communicate directly with most of the delegates. Those few whose language she didn't speak – including three whose dialects had arisen since the Death – could usually communicate with others in the group through a shared second language. No outside human or machine translators diluted this early stage of their interaction; they were being taught to rely on each other. Before the week was out, they would all speak each other's languages – having acquired them within the third chamber's city memory – and many more, besides.

For the first time in years, Karen felt on the edge of fulfillment. She had suffered as much as Garry during the last four decades, traveling around the ravaged Earth, seeing more death, destruction and seemingly unending agony than she thought she could stand. Losing their daughter. Her breath still took a hitch at that memory. But she had dealt with her grief in a very different manner, not internalising it as world-guilt, but finally rejecting it, setting her personality aside as a separate thing, and dealing with her work as a nurse might. She did not succeed entirely – she had her own hidden scars – but she had not declined into a permanent funk.

She forced the thoughts back again, a little surprised they had gotten loose. Karen had long ago learned when and how to block off the area of her mind having to do with her husband; she usually managed not to think much about Garry when they were separated, concentrating on the delicate tasks at hand. But their last meeting . . . Garry, nervous, perhaps even frightened, though doing his best not to show it, escorting a man who could not possibly be on Earth . . .

She glanced out the shuttle window at stars, temporarily ignoring the steady, polite conversation of three delegates sitting beside her. Was Garry aboard the Stone, with the impossible Russian? She had, in her own stubborn way, come close to resolving the mystery by deciding that someone had played a trick on her husband; that Mirsky had never gone down the

Way. But the more she thought about it – and she could not help thinking about it now, with little else to do – the more she realised how unlikely this was.

She felt a flush of anger. Something was going to happen. Something momentous. She *resented* the mystery of Mirsky's return, feared it might drive Garry deeper into his funk by making him face cosmic imponderables even farther outside his control than Earth's pain.

She frowned and turned away from the stars. Unlike Lanier, Karen felt little dismay at the changes in her life. She accepted change easily enough; spaceflight, the Stone, the opportunities offered by the Hexamon. But Mirsky's return slipped from her understanding like a fish through her fingers.

'Ser Lanier,' the Chinese delegate called, smiling broadly and inclining her head as she sat beside Karen on the free-form couch. Her face was wreathed in fine sun-wrinkles; she was small and round, matronly, probably ten years younger than Karen. 'You seem pensive. Are you worried about this conference?'

'No,' Karen said, smiling reassurance. 'Personal difficulties.'

'Your mind should be at rest,' the delegate said. 'All will go well. We are friends already, even those whom I worried out.'

'I know,' Karen said. 'Its nothing, really. Don't trouble yourself.' *He's doing it to me again*, she thought. *I cannot get away from him*. She closed her eyes and forced herself to sleep.

29

Thistledown

Korzenowski's partial located Olmy in the fourth chamber forests of Northspin Island two days after Lanier's arrival. Downloaded into a cross-shaped tracking probe, the partial searched the fourth chamber with infrared sensors and located seven hundred and fifty humans. Most were in groups of three or more; only seventy were solitary, and only two, across half a day of activity, showed signs of deliberately avoiding company. The partial analysed the heat signatures of both of these possibilities and settled on the one most likely to be a self-contained homorph.

Under any other circumstance, this kind of search would have been unthinkable, a gross invasion of privacy. But Korzenowski knew the importance of having Olmy speak with Mirsky. And he needed Olmy for the upcoming Nexus debate on the reopening of the Way. The Engineer could no longer completely oppose that project; Mirsky's arguments were too persuasive, however bizarre. How could one deny the requests of gods, even if they existed only at the end of time?

It was not the partial personality's duty to analyse these problems. It flew above the valley floor to hover near Olmy's campsite, and then projected an image of Korzenowski with the appropriate picts revealing its status as an assigned ghost.

From Olmy's point of view, Korzenowski seemed to walk out of the forest, his face wreathed in a smile, his eyes cat-like, piercing. 'Good day, Ser Olmy,' the ghost said.

Olmy pulled himself away from the flow of Jart information and hid his all-too-human irritation at being found. 'You've gone to considerable trouble,' he picted.

'Something extraordinary has happened,' the ghost informed him. 'Your presence in the third chamber is required.'

Olmy stood by the tent, unsure of his emotional state for the moment, neither moving nor picting nor speaking.

'A decision is to be made regarding the Way. Your presence is requested by my original.'

'Is this a Nexus summons?'

'Not formally. Do you remember Pavel Mirsky?'

'We never met,' Olmy said. 'I know who he was.'

'He has returned,' the ghost said, rapidly picting the few salient details.

Olmy's face seemed to contort with pain. He shuddered, then his shoulders sagged and the tension left him. He pushed aside the Jart information, refocusing on his humanity and on his relationship with Korzenowski, once his mentor, the man who had shaped much of his life – or rather, lives. The fact of Mirsky's reappearance then assumed its proper color – deeply bizarre, more than puzzling: entrancing. He did not doubt the ghost's message. Even had someone besides Korzenowski summoned him, this news alone would suffice to bring him out of the forest and away from his meditations.

Events were moving more rapidly than he had imagined.

'Is there time for me to hike out?' Olmy asked, smiling. The mild social humor was as sweet as sugar in his mind, and he realised how starved he had become for human company. The ghost returned the smile. 'Quicker transportation will arrive soon.' it said.

'The prodigal son,' Korzenowski said, hugging Olmy firmly in the Nexus antechamber. 'I apologise for sending a partial to hunt you down. I assume you didn't want to be found.'

Olmy felt a kind of shame, standing before his

214

mentor, unwilling to speak of what he had been doing. He still had to keep his balance within his own head, watching the implants he had given over to the Jart. 'Where is Mirsky?' he asked, hoping to sidestep questions.

'With Garry Lanier. The Nexus is meeting in two hours. Mirsky is testifying before the full chamber. He wants to speak with you first.'

'Is he real?'

'As real as I am,' Korzenowski said.

'That worries me.' Olmy forced a grin.

He has an amazing story to tell.' Korzenowski, unwilling to find humor in anything now, looked away from Olmy at a wall of natural asteroid iron, his reflection milky and distant in the polished metal surface. 'We've caused a lot of trouble.'

'Where?'

'At the end of time,' Korzenowski said. 'I remember thinking about this possibility centuries ago, when I was designing the Way . . . It seemed a vain fantasy then, that anything I could be involved in would have such repercussions . . . But the idea has haunted me. I half expected someone to return from the precincts, like a ghost.'

'And here he is.'

Korzenowski nodded. 'He hasn't pointed any accusing fingers. He seems happy to be back. Almost childlike. Still, he frightens me. We have such responsibilities, now.' Korzenowski turned his square, discerning eyes on Olmy. 'Would you resent a request for help?'

Olmy shook his head automatically. He owed more to the Engineer than he could ever repay – more than even bringing him back to life could tally against. Korzenowski had shaped Olmy's life, opened vistas to him he would have missed otherwise. Still, he was not sure how his plan – already fixed and irrevocable – might match Korzenowski's . 'I am always at your service, Ser.'

'Sometime in the next few months, perhaps even today if the time is right – if Mirsky puts his story across as clearly to the Nexus as he did to us – I am going to recommend that the Way be opened,' Korzenowski said.

Olmy's smile was faint, ironic.

'Yes, I know,' Korzenowski said gently. 'We've been opposing forces on this.'

It seemed no one understood his position, not even his mentor. Olmy did not think it worth the time to correct him. Still, he could not help but gently chide the Engineer, if only to make sure he was keeping everything in perspective.

'I hope I don't presume when I say that you are not completely unhappy with this turn?'

'There is excitement and challenge,' Korzenowski said, 'and then there is wisdom. I've been clinging desperately to wisdom. Which of us is more eager to have this monster back?'

'Which of us really wants to face the consequences?' Olmy asked.

Lanier and Mirsky left the elevator and approached them. Mirsky walked ahead of Lanier, smiling expectantly, and extended his hand to Olmy. 'We have not met,' he said. Olmy shook the hand firmly. Warm and human.

'You are the expediter of our duty,' Mirsky said. Olmy could not completely contain his reaction to that choice of words. Mirsky paused, examining his face. *Who is he looking at?* Olmy wondered. 'You understand the problems, no?'

Olmy hesitated, then said. 'Perhaps some of them.'

'You've been preparing?'

There was no question now of not understanding. 'Yes.'

Mirsky nodded. 'I would expect nothing less from you. I'm anxious to testify,' he said. 'Anxious to get things moving.' He walked away with an abruptness that puzzled all of them.

Olmy turned to Lanier while the Russian paced near the door to the Nexus chamber. 'How have you been?' he asked. 'And your wife?'

'She's fine, I suppose, working on a project . . .'

'She's just arrived on Thistledown,' Korzenowski said. 'She's working with Ser Ram Kikura.'

'Will the Nexus listen to me?' Mirsky asked, walking back toward them. 'I am nervous! Can you believe that?'

'No,' Korzenowski said in an undertone.

Mirsky suddenly turned and faced Olmy. 'You believe the Jarts will oppose us,' he said. 'And you suspect they won't be the only ones. You know the Talsit were Jart allies before – you think they probably are again. You have been working on this, haven't you? It's what I expected from you!' he said again, staring earnestly at Olmy. Olmy nodded.

'Is he the same Mirsky?' Olmy asked Lanier when Mirsky returned to the opposite side of the room.

'Yes and no,' Lanier said. 'He's not human.'

Korzenowski glared at Lanier. 'Knowledge, or supposition?'

Lanier pursed his lips. 'He can't be human. Not after what he's gone through. And he's not telling us everything yet. I don't know why.'

'Does he know whether he will succeed?' Olmy asked.

'No. I don't think he does.' A dreaming expression came to Lanier's face. 'I've never met anybody like him. I envy him.'

'Perhaps we should all be cautious in our evaluations,' Korzenowski suggested dryly. 'Having an *angel* in our midst.'

Mirsky paced back yet again. 'Nervous! I haven't felt nervous in . . . a *very* long time! It is exhilarating.'

Korzenowski's irritation grew. 'Are you beyond caring?' he asked.

'I beg your pardon?' Mirsky stopped pacing, facing the Engineer with an intensely puzzled expression.

'We are – *I* am being forced to make a decision I have tried to avoid for forty years! If we do have to fight the Jarts, the results might be disastrous – we might lose everything.' He grimaced. 'Including the Earth.'

'I am more concerned than you know,' Mirsky said. 'There is more at stake than just the Earth.'

Korzenowski was not mollified. 'If you are indeed an *angel*, Ser Mirsky, you might not be as concerned as we are about our own skins.'

'Angel? Are you angry with me?' Mirsky asked, his face bland again.

'I am angry with this situation!' Korzenowski said, drawing his head closer to his shoulders. 'Pardon my outburst.' He looked to Olmy, who had stood with arms folded throughout the exchange. 'We are both torn by our emotions. Ser Olmy would love to get back to his paper work, keeping our Hexamon intact in the Way, and I am fascinated by the prospect of re-opening. The part of me that remembers Patricia Vasquez . . .'

Lanier almost flinched as Korzenowski glanced in his direction.

'That part is eager. But what our less responsible selves want, and what is safe for our Hexamon, could be very different things, Ser Mirsky. Your reasons are compelling . . . I am just irritated by your carefree attitude.' Korzenowski looked down at the floor and took a deep breath.

Mirsky said nothing.

'In truth,' Olmy interceded, 'the pressures on the Hexamon to re-open would be strong even without you.'

'Thank you for your guidance,' Mirsky said quietly. 'I lack perspective. I must approach the Nexus carefully.' He spread his arms and looked down at his body, still clad in hiking clothes. 'To have *limitations*, to think in channels. It's exhilarating to be back in flesh again! A wild, half-drunken blindness . . . a fleshy peace.'

The Earth circled by a strand of DNA, the symbol of the Terrestrial Hexamon Nexus in session, appeared by the doors to the chamber. A partial of Presiding Minister Dris Sandys materialised beside the symbol.

'Full chamber,' the partial said. 'Please enter now and be sworn in.'

Mirsky squared his shoulders and smiled, walking through the doors first. Lanier held back, entering the chamber behind Korzenowski and Olmy. Guided to his assigned seat in the lower circle, he was reminded of the time when he had testified before the Infinite Hexamon Nexus on the Axis City. Now, that time didn't seem so long ago. Earth's wounds had been raw and fresh then, nearly fatal.

Mirsky stood patiently in the armillary sphere of testimony before the presiding minister's dais. President Farren Siliom occupied the dais beside the P.M. Lanier faced the pictor near his seat, aware that the experience would drain him again, but eager to see what Mirsky would say this time, whether he would elaborate.

An orthodox Naderite corprep seated beside him smiled politely, picting polite curiosity about Lanier's age.

'I'm from Earth,' he answered.

'I see,' the corprep said. 'Do you know anything about this testimony?'

'No fair telling ahead of time,' Lanier said conspiratorially. 'Get set for the ride of your life.

30

Gaia

The Kirghiz in the black wool coat held court in the expedition's tent, sitting cross-legged in the middle of a circle consisting of five of his troops, Oresias, Jamal Atta, Demetrios and Lugotorix. Rhita stood with the others outside the circle, hands bound with strong thin rope. Women were anomalies on a military expedition, apparently; they did not believe she was among the leaders, and no one made them any the wiser.

A translator entered the circle, short and wiry, wearing a drab uniform cut in a modern Rhus manner, with scalloped collar and tight-wrapped linen leggings above short, supple boot-slippers. The bull-like, black-coated Kirghiz leader spoke, and the translator converted his words into common Hellenic.

'I am Batur Chinghiz. I control this square of the grass for my esteemed masters, the Rhus of Azovian Miskna. You are trespassers. I need to know your reasons, to report by radio to my masters. Can you enlighten me?'

'We are here on a scientific expedition,' Oresias said.

The translator smiled before converting those words into Kirghiz. Batur smiled also, showing even yellow teeth.

'I am not stupid. Surely you would ask our scholars to do this thing for you, not risk your own lives.'

'It is an urgent matter,' Oresias said.

'What about the dark one, the *arabios*. What does he say?'

Jamal Atta nodded in Batur's direction. 'I concur.'

'With whom, me or the light-skinned leader?'

'We are on a scientific expedition.'

'Ah, so it is. I will report you are lying, and they

will tell me to kill you, or perhaps cage you and send you to Miskna. Are you part of the revolt in Askander-gul? He means,' the translator added, 'Alexandreia, of course.'

'I don't understand,' Oresias said.

'Are you fleeing from the palace, perhaps, cowards in search of sanctuary in our wide territories?'

'We know little about a revolt.'

'We have only received news in the past few hours ourselves.' The Kirghiz lifted his broad shoulders and raised his chin, staring at them across his flat brown cheeks. 'We are not speakers of nonsense here. He means Barbarians,' the translator added again. 'We have radios, and we are in touch with our fortresses. We even bathe when the rivers are full or we are garrisoned.'

'We have all due respect for the illustrious Kirghiz soldiers of the Rhus of Azovian Miskna,' Atta said, glancing at Oresias. 'We are intruders, and we humbly beg your mercy, which under the sky of God and the grass of the Riding Devils, we feel sure the great horsemen Batur Chinghiz will grant us.' Oresias nar-rowed his eyes, but did not object to Atta's attempt at formulaic diplomacy.

'I am pleased by your kind and understanding words. But mercy is not mine to give. I am, as you say, soldier and not master. Enough of this. Can you enlighten me further before I request orders for your disposition?'

Rhita shivered. The clavicle had been taken from her when they had been dragged out of the beecraft; she had no idea what was happening with the gate, but darkness was coming. More than anything, she wanted to be away from this place, relieved of responsibility to her grandmother, to the Akademeia and her Imperial Hypsēlotēs – whatever had happened to *her* now . . .

She was terrified. The past few hours had given her time to absorb a few facts she had until now managed to ignore. She was mortal; these people would gladly kill her and all her companions. Lugotorix could not protect her, although when the time came – if it came – he would attempt to die first trying.

This situation was her doing. She could not easily pass the blame on to her father or Patrikia. She had agreed to come; the outcome of bringing the news to Kleopatra could not have been foreseen, but . . .

She shivered.

The Kirghiz troops prodded and shoved them out of the tent and into a hastily made enclosure of tent poles and canvas gleaned from the emergency supplies in the cargo gullcraft. The enclosure had no roof; it lay open to the cool wind and the deepening twilight. 'I think we're dead,' Atta murmured as the final section of canvas was erected and tied by a Kirghiz infantryman, who regarded them with narrow, curious eyes.

Their prison was flimsy at best, but they didn't dare even touch the canvas; they had been given, by gestures of rifles and hands striking the fabric, the distinct impression that bullets were ready for anyone who made a ripple in the barricade.

Rhita squatted on the dirt, arms across her knees, and rubbed her face wearily. Her entire body ached; hours of fear had done this to her. She needed desperately to urinate, but no one had yet made provisions within the barricade for a latrine, and she was too angry and confused to take the lead. Soon, however, she might be forced to.

She turned slitted eyes up at the stars, as miserable as she had ever been in her life, and felt their coldness sink into her face. *They don't know, they don't care.*

All absolutes meant nothing; how far could a goddess such as Athēnē extend? She seemed wholly inadequate beyond Gaia. The comfort of prayer meant little if she was going to die soon, and die in discomfort and ignominy, far from Rhodos.

'Damn it, I have to piss,' she said aloud. Jamal Atta stared down at her, his dark brows knitting.

'So do I,' he said. 'We'll – '

Rhita ignored him, fascinated by something above

his head – a luminous green straight line, singular, unembellished, silent.

'– make an area over here – ' Atta continued.

The line passed smoothly over their enclosure; she could not tell whether it was near or very far. Another green line crossed it and both lines moved their juncture rapidly to the edge of the enclosure. That made them seem close.

The gate. Something was happening at the gate.

The lines passed out of view. There was no unusual sound outside the enclosure – men conversed in soft gutturals; boots scuffed dirt, grass rustled in the cool evening wind. Darkness was almost complete. She smelled raw dirt and scared men and the green of the steppes.

Like an automaton, she followed Atta to the designated latrine, marked by boot-scuffed lines of sod. She pulled down her pants and relieved herself. A few men glanced in her direction, never too frightened to catch a glimpse of a woman's naked flesh. Pulling back her pants, she stepped out of the scuffed lines and looked closely at her companions within the enclosure. They stood in dejected postures, heads hanging, faces coldly outlined by a faint crescent moon and the starlight.

This is what it had come down to. In truth, she now hoped something *would* come through the gate. It might be their only chance at reprieve.

Had the green light been real, or were her eyes playing tricks?

She stood still for several minutes with arms crammed beneath her jacket, the cold sapping her strength and numbing her face. The fabric of the barricades tensed and bellied in a freshet of wind; expecting a bullet, she flinched as a teardrop of rain splatted on her eyelid. A black wall of cloud slid smoothly over the moon. She could barely see around herself.

More raindrops fell. She listened for sounds outside the barricade, suddenly alert, her arm-hairs pricking. No voices. Not even the hoof-clomps or neighing of horses complaining of the wet. Darkness, scattered rain and wind whipping the canvas.

The moon gleamed through a rift. Lugotorix stood beside her, huge and bedraggled. Saying nothing, but touching her arm, he pointed above the barricade to their left. Something tall and sword-shaped, as wide as a man's spread arms, towered over their flimsy prison. Its edges rippled like water. Smoothly, quickly, it curved to one side and dropped out of sight. *Death*, she thought. *It looks like death.*

'Kirghiz?' the Kelt asked quietly. Nobody else seemed to have noticed.

'No,' she said.

'I didn't think so,' Lugotorix muttered. Rhita tried to locate Oresias or Jamal Atta in the temporary illumination; they were hidden among the men. Before she could find them, the moon vanished again.

A hideous ripping noise on all sides startled her. She gave a small scream and reached for Lugotorix, but he was not there. The canvas barricade was being torn to shreds. Wind rushed by, the wake of the passage of something huge. Nails drove into her back, knocking the breath out of her; *one* pause *two* pause three and four and five. She could not fall over. Lugotorix whimpered nearby like a struck dog, a sound she had never heard from him before. Head slung back, jaw open, scalp and neck resting on something icy cold, she saw once again the straight green lines cross above them.

Something lifted her. She had an impression that the grass had grown huge and metallic; the camp was covered with swaying, supple steel blades, edges rippling like water, topped with smooth green shields or hoods. Her spine stiffened until she wished she could scream, but all her muscles had frozen. She could still see, but gradually she realised she was losing the ability to think.

For what seemed a very long time, she saw everything, and nothing; she might as well have been dead.

31
Gaia

The clavicle came into her hands and comforted her. It knew her; for the moment, that was enough. The clavicle was withdrawn and she missed it deeply.

No time at all later, but later nonetheless, she realised the clavicle had told her the gate was fully established, a 'commercial width.' There were other gates. This did not comfort her.

Lugotorix, standing naked between two huge snakeswords, touched on arm and thigh by dots of luminous green.

You are connected with this man?
Yes.
Do you need him?
Yes.
And the others?

She thought of Demetrios and Oresias.
They saved them.
She wondered what would happen to the others.
It did not comfort her that she was a center of attention. For a time, there were many of her, and some of her selves were subjected to unpleasant experiences. That was all she remembered. Her body was not injured.
She had no privacy.
They asked her if Athēnē had opened gates to Gaia; or Isis, or Astarte. Rhita said no. She did not believe these beings, gods, actually existed. That interested them. *Are the gods imaginary companions to console you for the possibility of dying?*

She didn't know how to answer that.

You did not make the clavicle.

No answer required. That much must have been obvious.

How did you find it?

She told them.

They believed her.

They became very interested in the sophē.

She's dead, Rhita informed them.

You are from her.

Again, no answer was required.

Some time of intense discomfort, worse than pain.

It was almost worth the experience to feel time passing.

Without memory, she stood in a place of blue sky and crumbling marble overlooking the sea.

That went away, and came back, and she was years younger, standing in the sanctuary of Athēnē Lindia. She remembered everything, including her life after this moment. A young man stood near her, vaguely handsome; his face was not clearly defined. He wore a white byssos shirt and dark pants with legs split and tied; like a fisherman, but not. She wondered if this was a lover but he was not; nor was he a friend.

'Is this pleasant for you?' he asked, walking around her. 'Please be truthful.'

'It doesn't hurt.'

'I hope you'll pardon our intrusion. We've had few opportunities to work directly with your kind. You've been treated rudely.'

She forgave nothing. Her confusion was too great for such niceties.

'Would you prefer I have a name?'

'I won't know you, anyway.'

'Would you prefer we stay here?'

It seemed wise to say yes. She nodded, appreciating the sun on her face and the cool reassurance of the abandoned temple in the rock. She did not believe she was actually there.

I am Rhita, she told herself. *I am alive. Maybe I've been taken through the gate.*

Maybe Grandmother came from Hades.

32

Thistledown City

For reasons clear only to himself and his advocate, the president had decided not to lodge in the formal Nexus quarters beneath the dome. Instead, he chose temporary quarters in a small, plainly decorated apartment in a Journey Century Five building adjacent to the arboretum, a kilometer from the dome. Four hours after Mirsky's testimony, Farren Siliom held audience there with Korzenowski, Mirsky, Olmy and Lanier. His manner was sharply formal. He seemed to be controlling anger.

'Pardon my forthrightness,' he picted to Korzenowski. 'I have never, in my existence in the Way and now near Earth – never seen such a treacherous about-face by a celebrated Hexamon citizen.'

Korzenowski bowed slightly, face stiffening. 'I make these requests reluctantly, and under pressure,' he said. 'That should be obvious.'

'I'm sure the entire Nexus needs a Talsit session,' Farren Siliom said, pressing on the bridge of his nose. The president glanced at Lanier, seemed to dismiss him with a leisurely blink, then focused his attention on Mirsky. 'The Hexamon considers itself an advanced society, whatever our self-ordained limitations . . . but I find it very hard to believe our work could have such far-ranging consequences.'

'You are at a crux,' Mirsky said.

'So you claim. We are not complete innocents, however. I well remember Olmy's deceit before the Geshels some years back, when he brought the Engineer back to us. He did all true Naderites a service. But is this another kind of deceit, another manipulation?'

'The truth of my story should be obvious,' Mirsky said.

'Not so obvious to someone who has spent the last ten years fighting a tide of sympathy for re-opening. Fought with the Engineer by my side, although that seems difficult to believe now.'

Lanier swallowed. 'May I sit?' he asked.

'By all means,' Farren Siliom said. 'My irritation obscures my manners.' The president ordered a chair to be formed for Lanier, and as an afterthought, ordered chairs for them all. 'We're going to talk for some time,' he told Korzenowski.

'I'm a reasonably practical man,' Farren Siliom continued, 'as practical as a politician can be in charge of a nation of dreamers and idealists. That's what the Hexamon believes it is; has been for centuries. But we've also been hard-headed, strong and willful. We met the challenge of the Way once. But we nearly lost to the Jarts, and they have had decades since to refine their tactics. We all believe they've occupied the entire Way – don't we?'

Lanier was the only one to abstain from agreeing. He felt like a dwarf among giants here; again old, a fifth wheel.

'Do you understand my confusion?' Farren Siliom asked Korzenowski.

'Yes, I do, Ser President.'

'Then clear it up for me. You've been convinced, but do you swear to me by the Good Man, by the Stars and Fate and Pneuma, that you are not involved in a plot to re-open your creation, and you have not somehow fabricated this entire episode?'

Korzenowski regarded the president for several seconds in offended silence. 'I so swear.'

'I regret calling your integrity into question, Ser Korzenowski. But I must be absolutely certain. You had no prior knowledge of Ser Mirsky's return?'

'I half-expected something of this sort; I cannot say

I believed it would happen. No, I did not have prior knowledge.'

'You are convinced the Way has done this damage?'

'Not damage, Ser Minister,' Mirsky said. 'Obstruction.'

'Whatever. You are convinced?' He stared sharply at Korzenowski.

'Yes.'

'You understand that most of the corpreps and senators have the highest regard for you, but that your motives in this case must be suspect. You spent much of your life creating the sixth chamber machinery and the Way. You must have felt some justifiable pride at changing the course of Thistledown's history. It would be understandable if you felt your status had decreased since your reincarnation and since the Sundering. Personally, I'm well aware you've had nothing to do with encouraging our neo-Geshels.' Calmer now, the president rubbed his hands together and sat among them. 'If we open the Way, will we be at war with the Jarts, Ser Olmy?'

'I believe we will.'

That's it, Lanier thought.

'If we do not open the Way, Ser Mirsky, and make preparations to close it from our end, will we block the distant, noble efforts of our descendants?'

'Of the descendants of all intelligent creatures in our universe, Ser President. Yes.'

Farren Siliom leaned back in his chair and closed his eyes. 'I can replay parts of your testimony. I'm sure most of the corpreps and senators are doing so now.' He grimaced. 'The procedure for voting on this is going to be difficult. We've never called for a complete Hexamon plebiscite. Do you understand the problems?'

Mirsky shook his head.

'Let me enumerate them. Voting procedures on Thistledown and in the orbiting precincts are very different from those on Earth. Most citizens on Earth must vote physically. It would take months to make arrangements for such a vote; we simply haven't prepared.

'Each citizen in space must download a special partial into a *mens publica* in city memory. The partials are assembled into a unified whole, using methods strictly outlined in the Hexamon constitution, and can vote within two to three seconds on any subject, though by law they are given much more time to make a decision. Citizens can update their partials once a day if they wish, to reflect changing personal attitudes; the partials cannot evolve opinions on their own.

'Those are the technical considerations. Considered as a problem of public policy, if we re-open the Way only to destroy it, we aggravate those who wish the Way to remain closed, and to avoid conflict with the Jarts. We certainly do not satisfy those who wish to reoccupy the Way. And the Jarts will no doubt resist our efforts fiercely. They may have more at stake in the Way now than we ever did; they seemed much more singular in their pursuits. Am I correct, Ser Olmy?'

'Yes.'

Farren Siliom folded his hands. 'I do not know how our Terrestrial citizens will view this problem. Or even whether they're capable of judging now. For most Old Natives, the Way is a very foggy concept, at best. Earthbound citizens do not have direct access to extensive city memories or libraries yet. I suspect, however, that the neo-Geshels will invoke the Recovery laws and cut Earth out of the voting entirely . . . That would be exceptionally distasteful.'

'Earth's senators would fight it every step of the way,' Lanier said.

'The Recovery laws haven't been used for a while, but they're still in place.' Farren Siliom raised his hands, face drawn. 'The way I read the Hexamon's temper now, those who want to re-open are about evenly divided with those who don't. Social condensations and coalescences are not at all unlikely in such a split; rapid formation of power groups . . . perhaps even a neo-

Geshel domination in the Nexus. The neo-Geshels could force me to act as they decree, or resign and let them form a new government. These problems are not specifically your problems, my companions. But you bring them to me, and I can't say I'm grateful to you. Nor can I say how the vote will go. We face a number of problems, a number of decisions, and now that the genie has finally crawled – or exploded – out of its bottle again . . .'

Farren Siliom stood and picted a query at the quarters' monitor. 'If you could stay here for another few minutes, gentlemen, I've arranged for another Old Native to join us. Ser Mirsky should remember him. You were companions, fellow soldiers, during the invasion of Thistledown by forces of the Soviet Union, before the Sundering . . . before the Death. He returned to Earth after the Sundering, and has lived in what we now call Anatolia.'

Mirsky nodded, face composed. Lanier tried to remember the surviving Russians who had worked with and around Mirsky, and found only a few faces weakly linked with names in his memory. The sharp, acerbic *zampolit* Belozersky . . . assured, calm, doomed Vielgorsky, senior engineer Pritikin.

The monitor flashed and Farren Siliom ordered the door to open. 'Gentlemen, this is Ser Viktor Garabedian,' he said with a look of triumphant expectation. *He believes he'll expose Mirsky*, Lanier thought.

Garabedian entered the room, white-haired, thin, slightly stooped. His hands were hideously scarred. His eyes were half-lidded, rheumy. Lanier could read his condition almost immediately. *Talsit-cleansed radiation damage . . . he must have tried to return to the Soviet Union, decades ago.*

Garabedian looked around the room, obviously not prepared for this meeting. His eyes lit on Mirsky and an ironic smile crossed his face. Mirsky seemed stunned.

'Comrade General,' Garabedian said.

Mirsky rose and approached the old man. They stood

232

apart for a moment, and then Mirsky spread his arms and hugged him. 'What happened to you, Viktor?' he asked in Russian, holding the old man at arm's length.

'A long story. I expected another old man. They didn't tell me you'd look the same. Ser Lanier, I recognise him, but he looks dignified, not like a youngster.'

Farren Siliom folded his arms. 'It took us several hours to locate Ser Garabedian.'

'I live as near Armenia as I can,' Garabedian told Mirsky. 'The homeland will be cleansed in a few years, and I can return. I've worked as a policeman with the Soviet Recovery Forces . . . I fought in the Armenian Liberation against the Hexamon . . . Not much of a war, like children fighting their doctors and teachers with sticks. When that was put down, I became a farmer. Where have you been, Comrade General?'

Mirsky glanced around the room, tears in his eyes. 'Friends, Viktor and I must talk.'

'They want me to ask you some questions,' Garabedian said.

'Yes, but alone. All but for you, Garry. Will you come with us? We need a room.' He glanced at the president.

'You can use one of my work rooms,' Farren Siliom said. 'We will record your meeting, of course . . .'

Lanier observed the change in Mirsky's expression. He seemed sharper, more hawk-like, less serene; much more like the Pavel Mirsky he had first met in the Stone, four decades ago.

'I'd like to speak with Ser Lanier for a moment, then he'll join you,' Korzenowski said.

The two men left the room, guided by the president to another section of his temporary quarters.

'Ser Lanier?' Korzenowski asked.

'He's Mirsky,' Lanier said.

'Did you doubt?'

'No,' he said.

'But this is additional proof?'

'For the president,' Lanier said. 'It has to be the clincher.'

'The president's reservoirs of doubt are vast,' Olmy said quietly. 'Matched only by political expediency.'

The president passed Lanier in the wide cylindrical hallway, nodding at him. Uncomfortable, Lanier followed Mirsky and Garabedian into the work room and stood beside them. A small round table rose out of the floor, surrounded by several free-form chairs. The room smelled vaguely of clean snow and pines; a residue, Lanier suspected, of some previous environment.

Garabedian, cap clutched in gnarled pink and white hands, examined his old comrade with the childlike eyes of the old and weary, eyes empty of any emotion but a kind of stunned wonder.

'Garry, Viktor was with me when the Space Shock Troops invaded the Potato – Thistledown,' Mirsky said. 'He was with me when we surrendered, and he advised me during the bad times after . . . I last saw him before I volunteered to go with the Geshel precincts. You've lived through hard times, Viktor.'

Garabedian continued to stare, his mouth slack. Then he turned to Lanier. 'Sir,' he said in halting English, 'You have not stayed youthful. Some have. But Comrade General Mirsky . . .'

'No longer a general,' Mirsky said quietly.

'He has not changed at all, except . . .' Garabedian squinted at Mirsky again, and said in Russian, 'When you were shot, sir, you changed. You became more resolved.'

'I've been on a very long journey since.'

'The people who brought me here . . . we seldom see them in Armenia. They come to break up our little wars, to stop our plagues, to repair our equipment. We were like children. We hated them so much. We wished to be let alone.'

'I understand,' Mirsky said.

'This time, they did not ask me . . . *Pavel*.' Using

234

Mirsky's first name seemed to strain the old man. 'They came and said I was needed. They said I was a witness. They were like police in the old times.' His voice rose. 'How can they treat us so like children? We have suffered! So many died.'

'How have you suffered, Viktor? Tell me.'

Lanier saw Mirsky's face become bland and accepting again, and a chill made him clench his jaw muscles. Mirsky put his arms on Garabedian's shoulders. 'Tell me.'

'Nothing is like it was,' Garabedian said. 'Nothing will ever be. There is good and bad in that. It seems all my life I have been confused, having seen this, and then gone back to the villages where my forefathers lived. Having fought against the Hexamon, having lost . . .'

'Yes?'

Garabedian held up his hands. 'We went into poisoned lands. The soil had become a serpent. It bit us. We were taken out by Hexamon angels. They apologised for not giving us new bodies. I could not go home. There was nothing there. I moved into Armenia . . . they call it North Anatolia now. No nations, they say. No factions. Only citizens. I farmed and raised a family. They were killed in an earthquake.'

Lanier felt the familiar sinking sensation in the pit of his stomach. *Couldn't save them all.*

'I raised horses. I joined an Armenian cooperative for protection against the Turks. Then the Turks made peace, and together we fought against immigrant Iranian farmers raising opium. The Hexamon came in there, too, and pulled us out . . . Then they gave people something that made the opium useless.'

Mirsky looked at Lanier.

'Some sort of immune response, blockers . . .' Lanier said. He knew very little about this aspect of the Recovery. Mirsky nodded.

'Go on.'

'It has been a long life, Pavel. I have suffered and

seen many die, but until now I have forgotten much of the pain. I see you, so young. It is indeed you?'

'No,' Mirsky said. 'Not the same one you know. I've lived a much longer time than you, Viktor. I've seen much myself, triumph and failure.'

Garabedian smiled weakly, shaking his head. 'I remember Sosnitsky. He was a good man. I think often that we could have used him in Armenia . . . Me! An Armenian, thinking that about a White Russian! Everything has been turned upside down, Pavel, and it is still upside down. I hated the Turks, now I am married to a Turkish woman. She is small and brown and has long gray hair. She is not a city girl, not like my first wife, but she's given me a beautiful daughter. I'm a farmer now, growing special plants for the Hexamon.'

Lanier thought of the Frant farmers on Timbl, the Frant homeworld, walking through their fields, growing biologically altered crops for export to the Way.

'Is it what you wanted?' Mirsky asked.

Garabedian shrugged, then smiled ironically. 'It's a living,' he said. He grasped Mirsky's left hand in his and prodded him with a scarred finger. 'You! You must tell me.'

Mirsky looked at Lanier with a sheepish expression. 'This time I'll tell it in words,' he said. 'Garry, you must go back to the others now. Viktor, tell Ser Lanier. Am I Pavel Mirsky?'

'You say you are not exactly him,' Garabedian said. 'But I think you are. Yes, Ser Lanier. This is Pavel.'

'Tell the president.'

'I will,' Garry said.

Mirsky smiled broadly. 'Now sit, Viktor, because I doubt that you will believe what has happened to this Ukrainian city boy . . .'

33

Thistledown City

Little of the Nexus debate took place in real time. Korzenowski and Mirsky answered questions and discussed the problem in detail within an isolated Nexus branch of Thistledown city memory; Lanier 'listened in' to the debate. Hours of argument and information exchange whisked by in seconds.

The debate was not nearly as exhausting as it would have been in open session. Geshels, neo-Geshels and all but the most orthodox Naderites participated; off and on, it lasted three days. It seemed to last several months. Not an aspect of the re-opening was neglected, not a nuance left unexplored.

There were proposals of such scale that Lanier's mind reeled; some firebrands – if you could call any Nexus member a firebrand – wanted the Way opened, scoured of Jarts, and then human hegemony pushed even farther, opening new wells every few dozen kilometers, establishing broad lengths of territory before Jarts or other forces could push them out again. Others scoffed at the grandiose schemes; still others, presenting dispositions from colleagues of Korzenowski who had been in precinct city memory for decades and even centuries, theorised that the Way could be destroyed from the outside, without re-opening.

This suggested two possibilities: that those who wished to unravel the Way could do so without the risk of confronting the Jarts; and if the Way were re-opened and the Jarts defeated, they might exact revenge by destroying it from outside. Mirsky, unveiling yet more of his character and capabilities, demonstrated through complex mathematics – equations that made even Korzenowski furrow his brow – that this was unlikely.

The Russian seemed in his element during the debate. The level of discussion was usually far beyond Lanier's comprehension, even when his mind was augmented by loaned talents – a service he had never used before.

But Lanier could sense one thing perhaps not so obvious to the corpreps and senators. Reverence for the Way was deeply branded into even those who were terrified of re-opening. The Way had been their world; most of them had grown up in it, and until the Sundering, most of them had known no other existence. The debate, however fiery, was one-sided; the question rapidly became not whether to re-open, but what to do after the Way was linked again to Thistledown.

They gathered now in physical session to hear what the Nexus would recommend to the Hexamon. In addition, a vote would be taken on whether to pass the matter on with Nexus recommendations to the Hexamon as a whole, or to restrict voting to the Thistledown *mens publica*, or to launch an educational campaign on Earth and postpone the voting until that effort was complete, which could take years.

Lanier entered the Nexus Chamber alone; Mirsky, Korzenowski and Olmy had preceded him for some pre-session discussion with the president. The chamber was empty but for two corpreps across the circle picting at each other. He stood in an aisle, oddly at peace. He was still out of his depth, but since his confession to Mirsky, he no longer felt the inner turmoil, the dark, confused exhaustion.

He had toured the third chamber city for a few hours earlier in the day, riding in a spinward train to the main library where he had once spent hours learning Russian, and where Mirsky had been shot and resurrected. The library had been reactivated thirty-five years ago; it was now a busy facility, its wide floor of pictors and seats often serving hundreds of corporeal scholars at once. The library had been built about the same time as the Nexus dome. What had once seemed monumental, alien and frightening – containing as it did the news of Earth's death before it had happened – was still monumental, but familiar now, acceptable to him.

His attitude towards the starship had certainly changed. He thought he wouldn't mind living on Thistledown for a few years. The lighter pull of the asteroid's spin agreed with him; he was tempted to try some gymnastics. Parallel bars had helped keep him sane when he had administered the exploration of the Stone. Glancing at his clawlike hands, he winced, thinking of what he had allowed to slip away. . . .

He still resisted the idea of rejuvenation. He wanted to discuss things with Karen, to see if their bonds hadn't been cut completely.

But he would not interrupt her conference. That was important to her. Besides, while the debate was still relatively closed, he did not think it was politic to talk with those not directly involved.

The members entered the chamber and took their seats with little talk or picting. The air in the chamber was charged with something ineffable; history, Lanier thought. Decisions had been made here that had altered the fate of worlds. Now, the fate of more than worlds was at hand.

Mirsky and Korzenowski entered behind him and walked down the aisle. Mirsky smiled at Lanier and took a seat beside him. Korzenowski nodded at them both and walked farther down to sit beside the panel of six men and women currently in charge of the sixth chamber machinery.

The president and presiding minister Dris Sandys came in last and took their seats behind the armillary sphere of testimony.

The presiding minister announced, 'The Nexus *mens* has cast its vote on the proposal of Sers Mirsky, Korzenowski, Olmy and Lanier.'

Lanier was surprised to find himself designated as one of the proposers. A flush of excitement and nervous pride went through him.

239

'Now it is time to confirm this vote by a physical plebiscite.'

Lanier glanced around at the corpreps and senators, hands clenched in his lap. He did not know how the vote would be taken; would they all pict their decisions, the whole chamber lighting up like a Christmas tree?

'The final recommendation of this Nexus having been determined first in the Nexus *mens*, must now be confirmed by a voice vote. Each voice will be recognised and tallied by the chamber secretary; the votes will be cast at once. Members, is it your decision to proceed with the basic proposal of re-opening the Way? Signify by aye or nay.'

The chamber was a chaos of ayes and nays. Lanier thought he detected a preponderance of nays, but that apparently was nerves on his part. The presiding minister glanced at the secretary, seated beside the sphere of testimony, and the secretary raised his right hand.

'Aye it is to the proposal. Is it to be the recommendation of this Nexus to open the Way with the intent of ultimately destroying it, as Ser Mirsky has requested?'

The Nexus members voted again, their voices a warm murmur in the dome.

'Nay it is to this decision. The Way is to be kept open. Is it the decision of this Nexus to create an armed force with the express purpose of securing the Way for the benefit of the Infinite Hexamon and its pledged allies?'

The voices seemed to rise in volume. Lanier could not tell whether ayes or nays led now; the vote was very close, and some corpreps and senators had dropped out, bowing their heads or leaning back, faces strained.

'The decision is aye. Is it the decision of this Nexus to put the issue with our recommendations before a full vote of the Terrestrial Hexamon, including the *mens publica* and the corporeal voters of Earth?'

Again the voices spoke out in unison.

'Nay it is to this plan. Is it the decision of this Nexus to take a vote solely from the *mens publica* of the seven chambers of Thistledown and the two orbiting precincts?'

And again.

Lanier closed his eyes. It was happening. He might actually stare down the throat of the Corridor, the Way, again . . . There might even be a chance, someday, of learning what had happened to Patricia Luisa Vasquez.

'Aye it is. The vote shall be taken solely before the *mens publica* of the three orbiting bodies. Ser Secretary, do these votes tally with the Nexus *mens*?'

'They do, Ser Presiding Minister.'

'Then the recommendations are set and the voting process will begin. A Nexus advisory will be issued to all citizens of the three orbiting bodies tomorrow at this time. There will be a week-long period of individual research and contemplation, with all information and testimony presented to the Nexus available to the voters. Within twenty-four hours of the end of that week, all citizens will inform their partials within the *mens publica*, and another period of twenty-four hours will pass before a vote is taken there. The decision of the citizens of the Hexamon will be ratified by the Nexus within one week, and the implementation of the new policy will be made binding upon the Nexus and the president and presiding minister. It is the law that the president may delay this entire process by as long as one month of twenty-eight days. The president has informed me that he does not wish to delay the process. This meeting is hereby adjourned. Thank you all.'

Uncharacteristic pandemonium broke out in the chamber. Lanier watched the corpreps and senators flashing bright picts at each other, some meeting to embrace, others standing in stunned silence. A contingent of conservatively dressed Orthodox Naderites came forward to meet with the president and presiding minister beneath the podium.

Mirsky pinched the bridge of his nose. 'This is not good,' he said quietly. 'I have opened the bag and the winds are escaping.'

'What will you do?' Lanier asked.

'Much thinking. How could I not have convinced them?'

'During your journey, you might have forgotten one thing about humans,' Lanier suggested.

'Obviously. What thing?'

'We're a perverse group of sons of bitches. You've come to us like an avatar. Maybe they resent being dictated to by a demigod, just as much as people on Earth resent being saved. Maybe they simply don't believe you.'

Mirsky frowned deeply. 'My physical powers are not great,' he said. 'I come as catalyst, not as an explosive. If I fail, however, there will be grave times ahead.'

Lanier felt his old instincts coming to the surface. 'Then use judo on them,' he said. 'Think of the power to the directed when the Way is opened.'

'Power?' Mirsky turned his placid gaze full on Lanier.

'The social disruption.' He might not be a fifth wheel after all; he saw a crazy plan coming together in his head.

'Yes?'

'I think perhaps we should go with Olmy to Suli Ram Kikura.'

'You are thinking about something interesting, then,' Mirsky said.

'Perhaps. I need to talk with my wife, too. Earth has been cut out of the decision. There's a lot of resentment already; this could be explosive, even if you aren't.' He had taken the bone in his teeth and was clamping down hard. His neck ached with tension. He rubbed it slowly with one hand.

'Lead on, my friend,' Mirsky said. 'This avatar bows to your judgment.'

34

Thistledown City Memory

The valley of Shangri-La lay below the walls of the palace in shadowy emerald splendor, mountain crests touched with gold in the last light of the sun. Karen gripped the cold stone rail of the balustrade with fingers clenched white.

The conference had begun to unravel on the first day.

The fighting among the delegates had begun in the third chamber city when they had been taken to their apartments, located on the lower floors of a huge gray and white Journey Century Nine building shaped like a golf tee. A woman from North Dakota had protested that their quarters were entirely too luxurious. 'My friends back home are living in wooden and sod shacks. I can't live like a queen.'

Suli Ram Kikura had suggested, somewhat innocently, that the quarters could be made to seem as spare as they wished. The North Dakatan had scoffed. 'Fake hovels in a palace won't disguise the palace,' she had answered contemptuously.

A shack had been built for her in a nearby park. The expense of wiring an extension pictor and building the shack had cost more than her simply living in temporary luxury; but there had been no criticism of her choice. This was to be an exercise in understanding and unanimity, after all.

Then had come the disputes over which fantasy environments the delegates would interact in. 'We can't expect lasting results if we lose all touch with reality,' a male delegate from India had declared. He had then demanded a setting similar to an early-nineteenth-century mogul's palace. When none of the other delegates had agreed with this, he had threatened to leave the conference.

He was back on Earth now.

What had seemed straightforward and promising to begin with had rapidly turned sour.

The remaining delegates had finally settled on a suitable environment for interaction – a duplicate of James Hilton's Shangri-La, created for downloaded Thistledown vacationers centuries ago. Within a few hours, more disputes had broken out. Two delegates had become enamored of each other and complained when the environment would not allow them to have sexual relations.

'That's not what we're *here* for,' Karen had tried to explain. They had not been mollified. Suli Ram Kikura had put her foot down, explaining that the environment had been modified to forbid sexual interactions. In this project, the delicately balanced psychological atmosphere would be damaged by allowing them. The two delegates had grudgingly given in, but even now complained about other petty issues.

Karen realised now that she and Ram Kikura had approached this project with entirely too much idealism. This shamed her; she knew humans too well to have been so naive. But Ram Kikura's attitude had affected her deeply; she had approved of the advocate's upbeat approach, and had unconsciously hoped against her better judgment that it would all turn out well, that people would after all be reasonable . . .

But even those with the very best attitudes and records were only human. Taken from the surroundings in which they had proven themselves, they had become little better than children.

City memory's ideal environments were too seductive for Old Natives, and for that reason unsuited for what Karen and Ram Kikura hoped to accomplish.

Besides, there was a tension in the air . . . even in Shangri-La – something she could not define, but which seemed to put large obstacles in the way of their project's success.

Suli Ram Kikura appeared on the balcony behind her and put a hand on her shoulder. 'I think it's time you took a rest.'

Karen laughed. 'This place was made to be restful.'

'Yes, but for you, it's not right.'

'So what are we? Wild flowers that wilt in the greenhouse?'

Ram Kikura's brow wrinkled. Physically, she had changed little since Karen first met her, four decades before; she was still striking, with strong, pleasingly irregular features and golden-brown hair. 'I've never thought of Thistledown as a greenhouse.'

'It's Shangri-La to these people, even without going into city memory. I should have known.'

'You're tired.'

'I'm mad, goddammit.'

'I was wrong. It is not your fault.'

'No, but I was *hoping* so much you'd be right, and we could bring them all together here . . . forge a bond. It was such a wonderful plan, Suli. How could it have gone so wrong, so quickly? We explained it to them . . . They're acting like children!'

Ram Kikura smiled grimly. 'They know what they need better than we, perhaps. I wanted to force things. Like a parent watching a child play with toys . . . trying to teach them how to grow up more quickly.'

'That's not fair . . .' Karen cut herself off, surprised that hearing the delegates compared to children made her angry. She felt close bonds with these Old Natives . . . was one herself, of course. 'They've lived through hell, most of them.'

'Maybe they thought of this as a vacation,' Ram Kikura suggested. 'And we were tour guides. We disappointed them by being so bossy.'

Despite herself, Karen laughed. *She's a master, really, however naive she is . . . we've been.* 'So what do we do now?'

'I have just enough stamina to give it one more try. But you, dear Karen, are at the end of your rope.'

'I must be. I want to kick them.'

'So you must take a break. We've been in this environment for an objective ten-hour period. Return to your apartment – '

'Back to my body. Out of the dream.'

'Precisely. Out of the nightmare. And get some genuine rest, in your own head, natural rest without city memory's overtones.'

'How could this be anything but restful?' Karen asked wistfully. The stars were coming out above them, as sharp and real as any she had seen on Earth. The night winds smelled of jasmine and honeysuckle.

'Do you agree?' Ram Kikura asked.

Karen nodded.

'Then go now. I'll report to you if anything improves. Otherwise, I'll close this whole charade down and send them all back to their bodies. We'll escort them back to Earth and start planning all over again.' She lifted her eyebrows and inclined her head, staring levelly at Karen. 'All right?'

'Yes. I . . . how do I get back?'

'Ruby slippers, my dear. Remember the code.'

Karen looked down at her feet. Instead of soft doe-skin boots, she now wore ruby slippers. She tapped them together. 'There's no place like home,' she said. Ram Kikura vanished.

An objective hour later, in her temporary apartment, Karen put on a silk kimono, given to her by a group of survivors in Japan thirty years before, and lay back on a couch with a cool glass of Thistledown Chardonnay, a Haydn quartet playing softly in the background *sans* pictor accompaniment. The apartment environment had been adapted to resemble an open-air porch looking across a tropical island beach. Across the broad, dazzling blue ocean, a nub of volcano smoked casually, its plume mingling with stacked white anvil-head clouds. Warm, salty breezes played over her wicker chair.

She might have never left city memory, the illusion was so complete, but there was a certain sensation, a *knowing*, that her body was being deluded and stimulated, and not just her mind. It was a moot distinction. So many distinctions were moot on Thistledown.

We are all such children! she thought, sipping her glass and considering the distant volcano. *Maybe Garry's right to chuck it all and let old age claim him. Maybe we are all burned out after forty years, and he's only being honest.*

The room control chimed melodiously. She leaned back in the chair and said languorously, 'Yes?'

'Two men wish to speak with you, Ser Lanier. One is your husband and the other is Pavel Mirsky.'

Involuntarily, she shivered. *Speak of two devils.* 'Drop the islands and give me the standard setting.' The porch, beach, volcano and ocean vanished and were replaced by a small room decorated in classical Hexamon spareness. 'All right.'

Garry appeared in the middle of the room. 'Hello, Karen.'

'How are you?' She fingered the cool bowl of her wineglass, both glad to see him – she had not blanked out her worry – and curiously irritated. But their quiet discord had gone on for so long, she did not want to let him know her emotions. That was *her* armor.

'I'm fine. I've been thinking about you.'

'I wondered if you were up here,' she said defensively, struggling to keep her voice mellow.

'I wanted to talk to you before now, but I didn't want to interrupt your conference.'

'Please do,' she said. An image came to her mind of whom she wanted to be like now: the American actress of the early twentieth century, Bette Davis, cool and contentious, armored but desirable. The apartment pictors could not do that for her, however.

'We need to speak with Suli Ram Kikura.'

'She's still in city memory, keeping the chickens from pecking at each other.'

'Problems?'

'It's not going well, Garry.' She looked away from the image, noticed her finger actually *in* the wine, removed it, and set the glass down. 'I'm resting. What about Mirsky? What's happening?' There; the curiosity had escaped.

'Have you been following the Nexus proceedings?'

She shook her head.

'There's very big trouble coming.' He explained the situation.

The time had come to shift gears; this was not strictly a personal call. Still, the shift did not come easily. 'That doesn't sound like the Nexus at all. Without consulting Earth?'

'Mirsky's told us some amazing things,' Lanier said, 'and frankly, I don't like the Nexus denying his request. I think re-opening the Way, and leaving it open, is a very bad idea.'

'Suli hasn't heard his story?'

'No.'

She thought quickly, her conflicts temporarily suspended. They were almost a team again, working together on a problem. Something had changed about her husband. What had Mirsky done to him – to all of them? 'All right. I'll contact her in city memory and tell her it's urgent. Then I'll set up a meeting. Where are you?'

'Nexus dome quarters.'

'Mirsky . . . he *is* Mirsky?'

'Yes.'

That answer, unequivocal, brooked no argument; she knew Lanier better than to think he had come to such a judgment lightly. Somewhat to her surprise, she found she still trusted her husband's judgment on these matters . . . perhaps on many other matters as well. Why was that surprising? She did not dislike Garry; she disliked the thought of losing him forever. Their discord and separation were certainly not based on distrust or aversion.

'This is very big, then.' A note of wonder and speculation crept into her voice.

'It is indeed,' Lanier said. 'And Karen . . . I don't want our problems to get lost in it.'

Her face flushed. 'What do you mean?'

'I need to talk about other things, too.'

'Oh?'

'When there's time.'

'Fine,' she said lightly.

'I love you,' Lanier said, and his image faded.

Completely against her will, and to her surprise, her breath caught in her chest and she had to struggle to hold back tears. It had been years since he told her that.

'Damn him,' she said.

35
Rhita

Before the memory of her capture was lost to her completely, bleached away by the false Rhodian sun, she asked the youth, 'Where are my friends?'

'Preserved,' the youth replied. She tried to ask more about them but could not. Her thoughts were restricted into certain channels. With a wrenching awareness of the falseness of this place, she forced herself to think, *I am not free*. She felt a shiver of horror. She could not be among her grandmother's people. The sophē would have told her about such horrors . . .

Who had her, then?

She did not understand how such things could be; how could she be someplace and yet not be there? This was not a dream, however devious; it did not feel like a dream. Whatever it was, they took it from her, but it was not hers; she did not control it.

She walked through the stone house where Patrikia had lived, bare feet stroking cool tile with each step, peering into this room, then the next, aware somehow that they wished to know more about the sophē but unwilling to tell them. Or show them. She was blocking her grandmother from her mind. How long could she do this? They seemed very strong.

She decided she would ignore the youth. He did not answer her questions fully. There was no way of knowing whether the little he did tell her was the truth.

A flash of anger and scattered confused thinking made her vision darken and Patrikia's library room fade. When her vision cleared, the Objects lay on the floor around her, clavicle revealed in its wooden case.

'This is a device for passing from the Way to other

worlds. You attracted our attention by using it on the gate.'

Rhita glanced over her shoulder to see the youth behind her. His face was still indistinct.

'Where did you get it?' he asked.

'You know that already.'

'Where did your grandmother get it?'

She closed her eyes and still saw the clavicle before her and felt the unanswered question.

'We are not going to torture you,' the youth said. 'We need your information to take you where you want to go.'

'I want to go home,' she said softly. 'My real home.'

'You did not make this device. Your grandmother did not make it. Your world has no use for such things. We are curious how it came to be here. Did you once commune with the Way, far back in history, perhaps?'

'My grandmother. I told you.' *What* had *she told them? And how often?*

'Yes. We believe you.'

'Then don't ask me again and again!' She turned on the youth, anger again dimming her vision. Each time she got angry, it seemed they knew more; yet she was not actually trying to hide anything from them. She surmised she could not hide facts if they were capable of making her think she was on Rhodos when she wasn't. *I should be nearly dead with fear.*

'There's no reason for you to be afraid. You are not dead, you are not injured.'

The youth's face suddenly became distinct, as if a shadow not of darkness but of ignorance had passed. He had regular features, black eyes, black hair and a slight growth of beard. He might have been a Rhodian beach boy. 'I take this shape because you are not familiar with us.'

'You're not human?'

'No. We come in many different forms, unlike your people. We are all unified, but . . .' He grinned. 'Different. So please accept me in this more pleasant shape for the time being.'

They seemed to have changed tactics, or perhaps learned how to make their deception even more convincing. Rhita turned away from him and from the vision of the Objects. 'Please leave me alone. Let me go home.'

'I will not conceal the truth from you. Your home is undergoing changes now, to make it more efficient.'

Rhita looked at her hands. She wanted to shiver, but she couldn't; she could, however, feel more anger. She restrained herself. 'I don't know what you mean.'

'We've laid claim to your Earth. I suppose it's time we drop this pretense and acquaint ourselves more fully. Are you prepared for that?'

'I – '

'Let me explain. This is a kind of waking dream, made up by our investigators to introduce you gently to your new life. I am a superior officer among the investigators. I have just arrived to speak with you. Until now, you've been speaking with an inferior officer. I am more acquainted with your people than he was. Is that clear?'

'I think so,' Rhita said.

'You've been in this state for several years of your time. Since there's nothing you can do to hurt us, and since we have enough information from you for the time being, there's no need for pretense, so I've decided we will let you awaken. When you are ready, you will be able to use your real body, and the environment you see around you will be real. Understood?'

'I don't want any of this,' she said. *Years?* That took a moment to sink in; the despair she felt spreading through her thoughts was a dark, freezing thing. She realised she might as well have been dead from the moment she boarded the beecraft; perhaps from the moment she had left Rhodos. She – and Patrikia – had opened a true Pandora's box; she still had no idea what had emerged. *Years.*

I am too young. How could I have known? Patrikia did not know. Is the world dead, too?

The cold sensation passed and she felt a series of small aches. The illusion of Rhodos and Patrikia's home faded. She opened her eyes and found herself lying on a hard, warm surface beneath a square of light the color of embers. The light slowly dimmed. Her skin felt sore, as if it had been sanded; indeed, looking at her arms, they seemed flushed, sunburned.

A man-shaped shadow stood just beyond the reach of the light. An olive-colored darkness surrounded them, the hue of a dream before it begins, or after it ends. She did not feel well.

'I'm sick,' she murmured.

'That will pass,' the shadow assured her.

'Are you a Jart?' she asked, trying to sit up. She had not voiced that question until now because she had hoped never to have to know the answer. Now, hopeless, she faced the shadow.

'I've tried to decide what that word means. It's possible we are; but you've never encountered Jarts, nor did your grandmother, who told you about them. The word does not connect with us; the humans your grandmother seems to have known could not have spoken our true name . . . They might have known a name used by others, not human. The answer, at any rate, may be yes.'

'She told me you fought humans.'

The figure in shadow did not directly respond to this. 'We are many and varied, and we can change our shape if we wish, change our functions.'

Rhita felt better, physically if not mentally. The despair faded with an odd sensation of hot chill that diminished with the overhead glow, now cinnamon. Other lights came on, vague and soothing, in the olive gloom.

'Am I on Earth?'

'You are within what you call the Way.'

Her breath shuddered and she suppressed a moan.

That meant nothing and everything to her. Could she believe them? 'Are my friends alive?'

'They are here with you.'

That, she decided, was evasive.

'Are they *alive?*' she asked again.

The shadow stepped forward, its face falling within a nimbus of light. She shrank back, sensing very strongly this was not a dream or an illusion, but a physical being. The face was masculine but without much character, smooth-skinned, narrow-eyed. Not a face she would look at twice in a crowd. It was neither godlike, nor some monstrous horror. It wore a jacket and pair of pants similar to that worn by the soldiers she had traveled with . . . years ago, if that wasn't a lie.

'Would you like to speak to them?'

'Yes,' she said, breathing more rapidly. She held her hand up to her face; it felt the same. She had not been changed; why should she expect such a thing? Because her captor looked human?

'All of them?' the Jart asked.

She looked down for a moment, lips moving. 'Demetrios and Oresias,' she said.

'Allow us some time, please. We discard nothing.'

36

Thistledown

'I hadn't expected to see you again,' Suli Ram Kikura
picted at Olmy, her symbols cool blues and greens.
Olmy smiled enigmatically and followed Korzenowski
and Mirsky into the corporeal meeting area reserved
for Ram Kikura's fellowship project. Befitting the Terrestrials' home surroundings, the room had been decorated in mid-twentieth-century industrial boardroom –
spare metal and wood chairs, a long wooden table, bare
bone-white walls, with a display board on one end.
'Excuse the primitive conditions,' Ram Kikura apologised in speech.

'Brings back memories,' Lanier said, catching the
chill between the advocate and Olmy. Olmy seemed to
take it in stride; but then, Lanier had never seen him
nonplussed. 'I spent many a long hour in rooms that
looked like this.'

'Our Earth guests are still in city memory. We're
trying to repair a complete fiasco,' Ram Kikura said.
'Karen will join us in a few minutes. From what she
tells me, some unholy alliances have been forged the
past couple of days. The Nexus has decided to re-open
the Way?' She pointedly avoided Olmy's eyes.

Korzenowski stood by one of the chairs, fingering it
with a puzzled expression. 'Yes,' he said, coming out of
his brief reverie with a quick blink. 'A Nexus advisory
subject to Hexamon voting. Precints and Thistledown
only.'

'I presume they're invoking the Recovery laws. We
should have wiped those from the statute books years
ago.' Ram Kikura seemed more radical and bitter to
Lanier than when they had first met. Age and the
Recovery had worn on her, as well, yet she did not

appear any older than when he had first met her. She had kept her style and looks largely unchanged the past four decades.

Olmy complete a slow walk around the table, his gait smooth and leonine. 'You've absorbed Ser Mirsky's story?'

Ram Kikura nodded. 'As much as I care to. It's hideous.'

Mirsky's eyes widened in surprise. 'Hideous?' he asked.

'The ultimate pollution. The ultimate sacrilege. I was born and raised in the Way, and yet now . . .' She looked as if she might spit. 'To open the Way again, and keep it open, is more than folly. It's evil.'

'Let's not get extreme,' Korzenowski said mildly.

'I beg the Engineer's pardon,' Ram Kikura said.

'You're being shrill,' Olmy picted privately to her. She turned on him with a stone-heavy glare. 'These men are here to ask your help. So am I. There's no sense being self-righteous before you know what we need. Or what we believe.'

This message passed in an eye's blink. Lanier only knew that Olmy had picted with her; he was not in the line of picting, of course, and did not consider himself adept at translating picts anyway. Ram Kikura's shoulders slumped and she stared at the carpet, eyes closed, taking a deep breath.

'My apologies. Ser Olmy reminds me of my manners. I happen to be passionate about these things. Seeing the aftermath of the Death gave me a strong impression of what our hubris can do.'

'Please remember, until now I have opposed the reopening of the Way,' Korzenowski said. 'But the pressures on the Hexamon are enormous. And Ser Mirsky's return – '

'Excuse me, Ser Korzenowski,' Mirsky interrupted. 'I am curious why she calls my story hideous.'

'You tell us the Way clogs up our universe like a snake,' Ram Kikura said.

'Not precisely. It makes a project carried out by our very distant descendants more difficult, perhaps impossible. But the Way itself is not thought of by these being as "hideous." They regard it with wonder. That such a tiny community, traveling between worlds, still locked into the realm of matter, should accomplish so much in so short a time . . . this is unprecedented. Constructs similar to the Way exist in other universes, but none of them were created by beings so early in their development. To our descendants, the Way stands out as the Egyptian pyramids did in our history, or Stonehenge. If they had their preference, it would be preserved as a monument to early brilliance. But that is not possible. It must be dismantled in a particular fashion . . . and that can only begin here.'

Ram Kikura's anger faded. She regarded him with deep interest. 'You aren't concerned with our petty politics, are you?' she asked.

Mirsky rapped his fingers on the table, an impatient gesture Lanier found intriguing. 'Politics . . . never petty to those caught up in it. I am concerned only insofar as politics might prevent dismantling the Way.'

Karen entered the conference area and stepped forward to kiss her husband. The kiss was short but apparently sincere; there was no need, she seemed to tell him, for personal problems to come to the fore now. Nevertheless, he took her hand and squeezed it.

'The timetable is short,' he said, forcibly interlacing his fingers through hers. Her jaw tightened and she glanced around at the others, wondering what they were making of this, quickly seeing that social nuances and speculations were the last things on anybody's mind.

Lanier did not loosen his grip. 'Ser Korzenowski?'

'The Way could be opened in less than six months. I'm afraid Ser Mirsky's story drove a wedge into the Nexus, and the neo-Geshels used that wedge to open a wide split. The Nexus will advise a permanent re-opening. Nobody doubts what will happen then – if the

257

Jarts aren't waiting for us, I mean. There'll be a rush of entrepreneur legislation – permits to open "test" gates, some of which of course will lead us to Talsit concessions . . . And if we establish commerce with the Talsit again, we'll never shut the gate down. The Talsit are damnably seductive salesmen, and besides, many Hexamon citizens *need* their goods too much right now. There's an air of desperation . . . Ser Olmy?'

'Even Naderites enjoy their longevity,' Olmy said. 'Within the decade, millions will have to give up their bodies and download into city memory . . . or die. Naderites dislike the idea of living permanently in city memory. They accept artificial life enhancements, but city memory is a kind of Gehenna, a limbo to the orthodox.

'That sounds a lot like hypocrisy to me,' Lanier said dryly.

'It is, of course,' Korzenowski said. 'Committees of partials are being formed in city memory to study the possibility – that's all the neo-Geshels will call it – of Jarts reoccupying the Way. If they agree with Ser Olmy, they might delay the re-opening until an adequate defense is in place – perhaps even a workable offense.'

'My God,' Karen said. 'They'd fight the Jart Wars all over again?'

'They are being very optimistic,' Korzenowski observed darkly.

'What if the Jarts are right there, waiting for us?' Lanier asked.

Korzenowski grimaced. 'Such a nightmare has occurred to me often the past few days. I have partials in city memory listening to all planning sessions. And I must participate in the defense of the Hexamon, if I am so ordered . . .'

'How can we defend ourselves?' Karen asked.

'It used to be a secret, very closely held,' Korzenowski said. 'But even the deepest secrets can be declassified when the ruling powers think it expedient. We have immensely powerful offensive weapons stored in Thistledown. They were too ungainly for pure defense; useless in the Way fortresses. No military planner gives up weapons that might someday have a use . . . So they were kept in the asteroid walls. Ancient, but still effective and deadly.'

Ram Kikura covered her nose and mouth with prayerful hands and shook her head. 'Star, Fate and Pneuma,' she murmured. 'I didn't know. The people were told – '

'All politicians will lie,' Mirsky observed, 'when it is politically expedient. The people demand it of them.'

Lanier's face had gone pale. 'Weapons?'

'Surplus from the last Jart War, stockpiled in Thistledown's secret chambers,' Olmy elucidated.

'They've been there all along? When we first boarded?' Lanier asked.

Olmy and Korzenowski nodded. Ram Kikura watched his reaction with grim irony.

'What if we had found them . . . ?' He did not finish his speculation.

'The Death happened anyway,' Korzenowski said, waving a hand, irritated at being sidetracked. 'Even if the Jarts are in the Way, we can at the very least establish a "beachhead," I believe the strategic term is.'

'Unless they've progressed beyond our old technologies,' Ram Kikura said dourly.

'Indeed. At any rate, I have been given a Nexus command to render technical assistance. That I cannot refuse. I've had my special research privileges for too long to play the upstart now. Our problem is, how to change the Hexamon's collective mind . . .'

'Go around the Nexus,' Ram Kikura said. 'Go directly to all citizens, including terrestrials.'

'Without the Earth, a bare majority would agree with the re-opening,' Lanier said. 'We've done opinion modeling. Or rather, Ser Olmy did.'

'They cut the Earth out because it's too ignorant?' Karen asked.

'Too provincial and too self-absorbed,' Korzenowski said. 'Which, of course, it is . . . but the procedure is very irregular. The threat of encountering Jarts could be made more evident . . . Even the existence of the weapons might be used to convince the *mens publica* to vote against the advisory. Ser Ram Kikura's suspicion that the Jarts have advanced beyond us – that could make a useful counter-argument. And before the advisory is made, I think we can attack it through the judiciary on the grounds that no segment of the Hexamon should be disenfranchised.'

Mirsky had taken a seat in one of the conference room chairs. He clasped both hands in front of him, then lifted his arms over his head. 'Delicate job,' he said. 'No doubt Garry understands how delicate?'

Karen looked at her husband.

Lanier decided to emulate the Russian's familiarity. 'Pavel says the Way must be dismantled.'

'And if it isn't?' Ram Kikura asked.

'It will be,' Mirsky said. 'One way or another. I did not count on such difficulties. Even with a better mind than I now have. If I fail, the consequences will be spectacular . . .'

'Is that a threat?' Ram Kikura asked.

'No. It is a certainty.'

'How spectacular?'

'I do not know. I did not make the contingency plans. I probably would not understand them in my present form, anyway.'

'Too many questions,' Korzenowski said unhappily. 'Ser Mirsky, when your story is made public . . . how many of our citizens will believe you, and how many will think your appearance here is an Orthodox Naderite trick to keep us locked to Mother Earth?'

'I can be no more convincing than I am now,' the Russian said, releasing his hands and stretching. 'Do *you* not believe me?' He looked around the group, thick eyebrows raised in query.

Karen, who had yet to see his presentation, ventured

no opinion. Korzenowski, Olmy and Lanier did not hesitate to express their belief. Ram Kikura reluctantly said she concurred.

'We have to set our strategy,' Lanier said. 'Between us, we can devise something worth presenting to the opposing corpreps and senators. They can make their case – Ram Kikura can carry the case to the judiciary. A two-pronged assault.'

'I think I'd better start on Earth,' Ram Kikura said. 'There's a meeting of the Earth Hexamon Council in a few days. We were going to report our conference results there anyway – nobody in the Nexus will be any the wiser if Karen and I leave and attend that meeting. How much of this is officially confidential?'

'All of it,' Korzenowski said. 'Until the advisory is made, none of us is supposed to talk.'

'That's not strictly legal either,' Ram Kikura mused. 'The Nexus neo-Geshels have become an eager group, haven't they? I'm surprised Farren Siliom would go along with them . . .'

'He'd rather keep his government together than turn everything over to his opponents,' Lanier said.

Ram Kikura picted a complex symbol he could not read. 'I'll steer clear of mentioning the weapons. That could involve me in defense law – and I'm no expert there.'

'Somehow, when I was not in this body, and my mind was immense, I thought all rational people would agree,' Mirsky said, shaking his head. 'What a surprise to be human again!'

Lanier smiled thinly. 'Back to being thick as a brick, hm?'

'Not thickness,' the Russian said. 'Perversity, twisting.'

'Amen,' Karen said, glancing at Ram Kikura. 'People are the same all over.'

37

The Way

The ghost of Demetrios hung translucent and unhappy before Rhita. Her face was white with horror; she had expected nothing like this. Now she understood she was beyond the reach of any god or gods; or in the hands of the wrong gods.

The escort told her, 'His mind patterns have been stored. His body is also in storage. He is not using his body at this moment; nor are his thoughts moving through his brain. They move through a different medium, where you also were once stored.' He stood beside Rhita, examining her face, gauging her reactions. 'Are you in distress?'

'Yes,' she said.

'Do you want the display ended?'

'Yes! Yes!' She backed away, hiding behind her clenched fists, and began to cry hysterically. Demetrios reached out with ghostly arms, beseeching, but could not speak before he vanished.

In the indefinite chamber that was her prison, she squatted on the soft floor and buried her face in her hands. All of her remaining scant supply of courage had fled her. She realised, beneath her horror and hysteria, that at this moment she was completely vulnerable to her captors. They could put her back in a fantasy, in a dream, and she would live there happily without protest, answering their questions, just to be in some place like home, away from this nightmare.

'There is no reason for your fear,' the escort said, stooping beside her. 'You would be speaking to your friend, not to an image we have made. He is still thinking. He occupies a pleasant illusion, as you did before you insisted on returning to your body.'

The escort waited patiently, saying nothing more as the paroxysm faded and she regained control of herself. She had no idea how long this took. Time was not her strong point now. 'Oresias and the others . . . are they dead, too?' she asked between her last few sobs and gulps.

'Death has a different meaning for us,' the escort said. 'Some are active in illusions; others are inactive, as if in deep sleep. None are dead.'

'Can I speak to any of them, if I want to?' she asked.

'Yes. All are available. Some might take more time to be brought here than others.'

She decided it would be best to try again, although she was not at all sure she could control herself. 'Can you make Demetrios seem more real? He frightens me . . . He looks like he's dead. He looks like a ghost.'

The escort seemed to savor the word 'ghost,' repeating it several times and smiling. 'He can be made to seem as solid as you and I, but that will still be an illusion. Do you want such an illusion?'

'Yes. Yes.'

Demetrios reappeared, more substantial but no less miserable. Rhita got to her feet and approached him, leaning forward, arms stiff by her side, hands clenched into fists. 'Who are you?' she asked between gritted teeth. Still, her body shivered.

'Demetrios, mekhanikos and didaskalos of the Mouseion of Alexandreia,' the figure replied. 'You are Rhita Vaskayza? Are we dead?' He spoke as a shade might speak, voice slow and quavering. Rhita could not stop her teeth from chattering.

'I d–don't think so,' she said. 'We've been captured by demons. No.' She shut her eyes tightly, trying to think how Patrikia would have approached this situation. 'I think we've – we've been captured by people who are not human, but with very advanced . . . machines.'

Demetrios tried to take a step forward, but seemed to be walking on ice. 'I can't reach you,' he said. 'I should be frightened, but I'm not . . . Am I the one who's dead?'

Rhita shook her head. 'I don't know. He says you're still alive. You're dreaming.'

'*He* says? What is he?' Pointing to the escort.

'One of our captors.'

'He looks human.'

'He's not.'

The escort didn't seem to think it was necessary to pay attention to the image. He focused on Rhita. This frightened her even more.

'Are the others dead?'

'He says they're alive.'

'What can we do?'

The escort, eyes still on Rhita, said casually, 'Nothing. Escape is not possible. You're all being treated with respect, and no harm will come to you.'

'Did you hear him?' Rhita asked, jerking her thumb vehemently at the escort. She really wanted to strike him, but knew that would accomplish nothing.

'Yes,' Demetrios said in a thin voice. 'We opened the wrong doorway, didn't we?'

'He says years have passed on Gaia.'

Demetrios looked this way and that, squinting as if through smoke. 'It seems only a few hours ago . . . Can he take us back to the real Gaia?'

'Can you?' Rhita asked.

'It's possible,' the escort answered diffidently. 'Why would you wish to return? It's not the same world you once knew.'

Demetrios did not react. Rhita felt sick to her stomach; she had enough of her grandmother's knowledge and instincts to half-visualise what that meant. These were Jarts; Jarts were rapacious. So Patrikia had been told by the people in the Way.

I may be responsible for the destruction of my home. Her hands rose automatically, like symmetrical claws, to just under her chin. 'Demetrios, I am so *frightened.*

These . . . people don't seem to care. They just want information.'

'On the contrary,' the escort said. 'We're really quite passionate. We're very interested in your welfare. Very few people have died since we claimed your planet. A great many of them are in storage now. We waste nothing. We cherish all thoughts. We have scholars, and we save as much as we can.'

'What are you talking about?' Demetrios demanded. His voice was so calm, calm and deep and thin; Rhita remembered what that felt like, to be in the illusion and not feel true fear.

'Do you wish me to address your companion?' the escort asked Rhita.

Dumbfounded, aware there was some protocol here of which she was ignorant, she gave her permission with a nod.

'It is our duty and destiny to study and preserve the universes, to spread our own kind, the best and most efficient of all intelligences, to serve the ends of knowledge. We are not cruel. Cruelty is a word and concept I learn only from your language. It is wasteful to cause pain and to destroy. It is also wasteful to let other intelligences advance to a point where they will slow our growth by resistance. Wherever we go, we gather and store, we preserve, we study; but we do not allow resistance.'

Demetrios absorbed this soberly, with a puzzled expression. He knew next to nothing of Patrikia's stories; only what she had told him on the grasslands, before the arrival of the Kirghiz horsemen.

'I would like to see my home,' Rhita said resolutely. 'I would like Demetrios and Oresias . . . and Jamal Atta, as well, to accompany me.'

'Only part of your request can be granted. Jamal Atta killed himself before we could capture him. Not enough of his personality has been preserved, I fear, to present a complete image, or to control a rebuilt body.'

'I *must* go,' Rhita said, sticking to this one demand,

unwilling to be distracted by her own mounting horror. If she wept, if she let her hands reach her face, she might lose all control, and she would not shame herself before these monsters. Or before pale Demetrios.

'We will take you there. Do you wish to observe the process, or would you like your journey to be instantaneous?'

Demetrios looked at her pointedly; she wasn't sure what he wanted her to say, but it was obvious to both of them that she was the important one to their captors. 'I want to see everything,' she said.

'It might be confusing. Do you wish for me to accompany you, and explain, or would you like a supplement added to your own psyche, to your memory, to guide you?'

She bowed her head, face almost touching her hands. She did not understand the first alternative, or perhaps she refused to understand it. *Can they make me more than what I am?* Perhaps she had already been changed. That thought was almost unbearable. 'Please,' she said, her voice little more than a harsh whisper. 'Come with us. Just take us.'

She had one hope left; that the Jarts were liars.

If they were not, then she might as well be dead, and she would work very hard to die. Somehow, she did not think the Jarts would let her. To their way of thinking, it might be a waste.

38

Thistledown City

Ram Kikura wondered what it would be like, some day, to fall into city memory, never to return; trapped away from life, in a world indistinguishable from life but for all its mutability, its extraordinary privileges. That would make city memory either heaven or hell, albeit a comfortable enough hell . . .

She had been born in city memory, incarnated much as her son would be, and feeling uncertain about city memory now was both premature and foolish. She had at least one more incarnation to go, her life was not hazardous; she might live for millennia before the problem became practical . . .

But she mulled it over as a natural youth on Earth might mull over death. The youth on Earth, however, would not be allowed to sample the afterlife; she could do so whenever she wished, for as long as she wished, and visiting her 'unborn' son was the usual reason.

Her visits seldom lasted more than five minutes, external time; those five minutes in city memory could extend for months. The last time she had visited, she had accompanied Tapi on a tour of an imaginary and highly embellished Amazon, something he had created as a personal project. The simulation was selected for a permanent place in city memory recreations, something of an honor.

Their time would be more limited on this visit. She was entering Axis Euclid's city memory remotely, from Thistledown. That reduced both the time and complexity of her experience.

When she accessed Tapi's personal space, he was involved in 'limiting' himself, cutting away unnecessary mental adjuncts to prepare his mentality for birth. By law, no newborn could enter its body requiring implant memory; every incarnate had to design and choose a core mentality that could fit within the limits of a normal human brain.

'It's painful,' he said ruefully. 'So much freedom here. Makes the real world seem harsh and confined!'

'Sometimes it is.'

'Makes me wonder if incarnation is such a privilege . . .'

She moved through his personal space, looking over what he had already cut away. 'Wise choices,' she said. Extraneous subroutines, modified personalities adapted to abstract environments he was unlikely to encounter when he became incarnate, sexual image experimentations probably prompted by fellow unborns . . . all stored away, to be accessed at some future date should he wish, or permanently discarded.

'There's a lot of *me* disappearing,' he complained. Around Olmy, Tapi did not complain; he enthusiastically demonstrated and explicated, but never revealed his doubts. That was reserved for his mother, and she took some pride in seeing this other side.

'Doesn't look like anything essential,' she commented dryly.

'Fewer voices in the chorus,' he said. 'But I'm seeing what I'll be more clearly. I think Olmy will approve, don't you?'

'Has he been to see you?'

Tapi nodded. 'Some time back. He gave his approval.'

She withheld some half-sarcastic comment. 'He knows quality when he sees it,' she said instead.

'Father's facing some very large problems.'

'Aren't we all.'

'Perhaps larger than you think.'

She examined her son's present image – very close to the appearance of his chosen body-form – and asked, 'Has he told you anything . . . surprising?'

'No,' Tapi said. But he was holding something back.

He knew the present status of his parents' relationship; he would not carry tales.

'I'm concerned about him.'

'So am I.'

'Should I be more concerned?'

'I don't know,' Tapi said, honestly. 'He tells me very little.'

Ram Kikura set her mind on the task at hand, finished examining the deleted adjuncts, and embraced her son. 'All right,' she said. 'I think you're ready.'

'Your approval?' he asked, an eagerness in his voice that belied his previous complaining.

'Registered already,' she said. She did not go through the age-old formula, as Olmy had; she resisted that kind of traditionalism.

'Have you decided where you're going to be born?'

'Yes,' he said. 'On Thistledown.'

Olmy had been born within the asteroid; she had been born on Axis City. Still, she knew Tapi was not slighting her.

Tapi arranged his personal space to hide the discarded adjuncts. 'Do you approve of my plans once I'm born?'

'It's not my place to approve or disapprove. You'll be independent.'

'Yes, but I appreciate your opinion.'

'My opinion is,' she said, 'like father, like son. Olmy's part in you is very strong. Mine seems subdued at the moment. But I have no doubt you'll make us both proud.'

Tapi literally beamed, filling the space with light. He embraced her again. 'You're as much a soldier as Father,' he said. 'You just fight different battles.'

Olmy felt more in control among his fellows, and less strained by the circumstances than he had thought. Still, it was good to be alone, if only for a few hours. He missed the isolation of the fourth chamber forest.

He did not return to the Thistledown City apartment; instead, he had accepted temporary quarters beneath the

Nexus dome. Whoever so desired could spy on him all they wished; he was certain they could not discover what he carried in his implants.

There was a strong temptation to simply lie still and study what his partial was sending to him; he resisted that temptation and went through the intricate steps of the Frants' *relsoso* dance, taught to him over a century ago on Timbl, the Frant homeworld. He stretched out his arms and lifted his legs, twisting smoothly from corner to corner of the small quarters. Frant anatomy was inherently more subtle and flexible than human; Olmy had to refashion some of the basic movements. Still, the *relsoso* did its job. He felt more relaxed and stronger afterward.

'*Now* I'll sit and vegetate,' he announced out loud, squatting in the middle of the blank, unfashioned parlor and its white furniture-forms.

The exchange with the Jart mentality was proceeding smoothly, according to his partial; in a few more hours, more information would be passed through the barriers.

What he already had to digest was considerable. There was little room left in his implants to process the material more rapidly; between the Jart, his partial, the various barriers and safeguards, and the cleared and uploaded information, the implants were filled almost to capacity. His study consequently was slow, limited to a natural human rhythm. There were some advantages to this; implant processing of information was rapid but sometimes lacked the cross connections of more natural thinking.

Olmy closed his eyes and was bathed in Jart philosophy. Translating the concepts into human language or even thought was difficult at times; other times, the ideas seemed directly analogous. He mused on the possibility that the Jart was releasing this part of itself in order to persuade its captor; propaganda certainly was not out of the question.

He instructed his partial to match the cultural and

270

philosophical exchange with an equal emphasis on persuasion.

Jarts were voracious conquerors, much more so than humans. While humans desired commerce, Jarts seemed to relish domination and complete subjugation. They were unwilling to share hegemony with non-Jart species, making exceptions only when they had no choice. The Talsit, for example, had traded with Jarts before humans had retaken the first few billion kilometers of the Way. The Jarts must have known that conquering the elusive Talsit was virtually impossible. Talsit were after all representatives of a much older race, even more mysterious – and certainly far more advanced – than Jarts.

The question was, why such voracity? What lay behind the push to control everything?

Command has duty established by > ancient command < *Gather and preserve that* > descendant command < *may complete the last duty. Then there is repose for expediters and all others, and in repose we will become ourselves again, relieved of duty, relaxing the* > image of strained materials < *that is our thought and being. Why is this not what humans do?*

Olmy tried to riddle this apparently key passage. It had such a formal air that he surmised it might contain quotes from some ethical or semi-religious work of literature or indoctrination.

The notion of *descendant command* was particularly intriguing, with its overtones of Jart evolution, transformation and transcendence. Oddly, in this idea there was also the only hint that Jarts and other beings could equitably cooperate and share responsibility. There was an implication of vast enterprise behind descendant command, of work that surpassed the capabilities of any individual group of beings.

Gather and preserve. That string/image was particularly striking. Olmy searched the background behind it, opening up layer after layer of complex instruction.

The Jarts were collectors, and more than that; they transformed what they collected, hoping to prevent self-destruction of the collected objects, beings, cultures, and planets. Nature was, for them, a process of decay and loss; best to take control of all things, stop the decay and loss, and ultimately present this neatly beribboned package to . . . descendant command.

Olmy felt a mixture of attraction and horror. Theirs was not a selfish greed; it was a compulsion of incredible depth and uniformity for such a diverse and advanced culture, and it had little to do with their own welfare and progress. Jarts were simply the means to a transcendent end. They believed they could rest only when the task was done, when the neat package of preserved galaxies (such maniacal ambition!) would be given up to this nebulous entity; their reward would consist of being gathered and preserved themselves. And what would descendant command do with the package?

It wasn't a Jart's duty to speculate. Certainly not an expediter, however modified.

Olmy found a list of supremely forbidden actions and inactions. While it might be necessary to destroy in the struggle to completely preserve – as the Jarts had to destroy human forces to try to keep control of the Way – to destroy unnecessarily was hideous sin. There was not a hint of cruelty in any portion of the Jart philosophies; no enjoyment of victory, no petty satisfaction for the success of a moment's work, no savoring of an opponent's defeat. Ideally, Jart actions were to be motivated only by desire for the transcendent goal. Satisfaction would come when the package was presented.

Olmy doubted that this kind of purity was possible in any living being, but that at least was the ideal; and in its rigor and selflessness it put to shame a good many exalted human philosophies. There was a neatness and finality about it that denied change of mission without denying progress; progress in speeding achievement of the goal was highly desirable, and any level of Jart from expediter to command could make improvements subject to command approval.

Human history had seldom managed that neat trick; fixed goals almost inevitably fixed change, causing a strain in human history that usually led to denial or reshaping of the goals.

Even in the Hexamon there was the dichotomy of accepted philosophy – Star, Fate and Pneuma and the rule of the Good Man Nader – and the contradiction of actions necessary to preserve institutions and advantages for individuals, groups and the Hexamon as a whole.

Jarts could fit war and destruction neatly into their philosophy, encompassing contradiction of goals in a tight wrap of necessity while controlling excess and bloodlust. Humans had never been so neat about their paradoxes, nor so capable of reining in excess.

Olmy realised there was an element of propaganda here, very effective propaganda. He was not seeing Jart history; there seemed very little of that. He was simply being fed the ideals with no information as to how closely they were followed.

He withdrew from the philosophy and sped through an overview of the Way's role in the Jart scheme.

When the Jarts had first entered the Way through a fortuitous test gate, they had quickly understood the principles behind this marvel. They had thought themselves either the creators of this infinite tube-shaped universe, through a rationale Olmy found difficult to follow, or they had postulated that descendant command had sent it to them to help them reach their goals. And the Way could not have been more neatly designed for them; by understanding its principles, as they quickly did, Jarts could open gates to any point in the universe, and even find means to enter other universes. They could travel to the end of time. In this Jart's memory, they had not done so, apparently, never having mounted an expedition like that of the Geshel precincts after the Sundering . . . Perhaps they felt it was best to leave such things to descendant command, or at least to wait until their task was finished.

As a tool, the Way fit into their plans perfectly. Through the Way, Jarts could wrap up and even present the package in record time.

Olmy barely touched the image connected with this idea: a static, perfectly controlled universe, all energies harnessed, all mysteries removed, unchanging, ready for consumption by descendant command.

It was a logical conclusion.

Still, it made him feel justified for all the resistance he had offered to the Jarts. Theirs was the purity of a kind of death. Jarts did not savor or enjoy or suffer or exult; they merely performed their roles, like viruses or machines . . .

He knew the simplification was unfair, but a feeling of deep abhorrence was upon him. Here was an enemy he could understand and hate at the same moment.

His partial signaled that more information was ready for transfer and consideration.

Olmy opened his eyes. It was hard to reorient after such strange journeys. Having barely skimmed the data already available, he packed it away and cleared the path for more.

39
The Way

Her captor's scrupulous attention to leading her step by step to Gaia began to wear on Rhita early in the journey. Nothing, not even the scale of what she was seeing, was familiar or comprehensible.

First, she was taken from her chamber – actually quite a small room, nowhere near the cavern she had imagined – and placed inside a protective oval bubble, where they stood on a flat, railed platform four or five arms wide and as black as lamp soot. The escort accompanied her in the bubble, which seemed to be made of exquisitely thin glass.

Or perhaps soap. She was not willing to place any limits on what her captors could do.

'Where are my companions?' she asked. The image of Demetrios had been left behind; they were alone in the bubble.

'They are taking a much quicker route. What I am doing with you is, if I may borrow a word, expensive; it consumes energy. I am given only so much energy for my tasks.'

The bubble hung suspended in blackness. Ahead of them, at the far end of the blackness, a brilliant triangle of white light grew as large as her outstretched hand, and then stopped. For a moment there was no further action; the escort stood in silence, staring at the light ahead.

Rhita shivered. Something animal in her looked for a way out, hoping that some magic had suspended all this reality and provided her with a chance to escape. But she did not try. Left idle with her thoughts, she turned and saw an opaque wall behind them, covered with the sheen of an oil slick on black water, gold and silver and all the colors of the rainbow besides. The wall stretched off above them in shadowy darkness. It was hauntingly, massively beautiful; it gave her no clues whatsoever as to where she was, or what would happen next. The silence terrified her; she had to speak to keep from screaming.

'I don't know your name,' she said quietly. The escort turned to her, smooth face all attention, and she was oddly ashamed for even wanting to know such things about her enemy. The shame came in part from realising that she could not hate this figure standing beside her; she wasn't even sure what it was. To learn more, she would have to ask questions that might make her seem weak.

'Do you want me to have a name?' the escort asked pleasantly.

'You don't have a name of your own?'

'My companions address me in a wide variety of ways. In this form, however, since I am to be viewed and accessed only by you, I have no name.'

His seeming obtuseness renewed her irritation. 'Please choose a name,' she said, turning away from him.

'Then I will be Kimōn. Is this a suitable name?'

She had had a third school paidagōgos named Kimōn. He had been a round, pleasant man, gentle and persistent but not quick. She had felt deep affection for Kimōn as a young girl. Perhaps the escort hoped to play on that. *And perhaps he doesn't need to use any such obvious subterfuge.* 'No,' she said. 'That isn't your name.'

'Then what should my name be?'

'I will call you Tȳphōn,' she said. From Hēsiodos: the horrible being who fought with Zeus, son of Gaia (hence the escort's human appearance) and Tartaros; a deeply buried monster of limitless evil . . . That name might keep her on her guard.

The escort nodded. 'Tȳphōn it is.'

Without warning, the bubble sped away from the rear wall. There was no way she could judge their

276

speed; she felt no motion. All around, the darkness seemed filled with subliminal rainbows. Glancing up, she saw a myriad faint beams of light traveling in parallel from the triangular whiteness ahead, over and behind them, into the wall, where they vanished. The triangle grew larger and brighter; they were obviously approaching something, but what she could not be sure.

Hypnotised, Rhita stared until the whiteness filled her vision, a brilliant, almost dazzling luminosity with a pearly quality that both awed and soothed her. This was the light in which a god might come clothed. *Those gods I don't really believe in,* she thought. *They're still inside me, though. Athēnē and Astarte and Isis and Aser and Aserapis and Zeus . . . and now Tȳphōn.*

Suddenly the light surrounded her, and the blackness became a yawning wall or hole behind. With a sudden reorientation, she realised that she had emerged from a huge triangular prism into a surrounding bath of pearly light. She turned and saw the dark equilateral mouth receding. It was framed by a thin line of sullen red of a richness and elegance hard to describe – a color that seemed to carry within it the qualities of serene dignity, vibrant life and horrendous violence all at once.

'Where am I?' she asked, her voice no more than a whisper.

'Behind us is a vessel. We are in a vacuum, within a tube of glowing gases. We will descend through this tube momentarily.'

She still had no clear idea *where* they were. Her stomach had knotted; so much strangeness, she decided, was not good for her. How had the sophē reacted, seeing so many strange things? There was a time when Gaia herself must have seemed strange and perhaps awful to Rhita's grandmother.

She held her fists to her eyes and rubbed them. They hurt. Her neck hurt from so much tense craning. Her head hurt; she felt miserable again, and yet there was a beauty to the light . . . She was ashamed to be in pain.

I'm not reacting well, am I? Perhaps I should be grateful to still be sane.

The glow intensified and she felt a momentary tingle. They passed through the boundary of the tube of pearly light. Below lay something incomprehensible, intricate like an enormous map, pale green in color, covered with white and brown lines, dotted at rhythmic intervals with processions of cone-shaped towers made up of stacked disks with rounded edges.

Again she felt a reorientation, and *saw* with understanding instead of just coordinated sensation.

They were within a closed, elongated surface round like a cylinder or a pipe, but enormous. The surface of the cylinder spread out like a Krētan textile design, all pale greens and browns and whites, or like . . . she quickly ran out of comparisons.

Rhita knew where she was now. Patrikia had described many of these things – though not these patterns or colors. Above their bubble stretched the wide band of the plasma tube, much fainter now, and the impossible region called the flaw, the singularity. Perhaps the prism rode the flaw, like the Hexamon's flawships.

She was seeing the Way.

40

The Hawaiian Islands

The Terrestrial Senate was in recess, its members scattered around the Pacific Rim. One influential Terrestrial senator had remained in Honolulu, however, and Garry Lanier arranged for a meeting with him.

Suli Ram Kikura and Karen accompanied Lanier to Earth; their object was sabotage.

Lanier knew Robert Kanazawa, senior senator from the Pacific Nations, from fifty years before; they had met as young officers in the Navy. Kanazawa had gone on to become a submariner, Lanier a pilot; their ways had parted until the Recovery, when they had met again in a Nexus plenary session on Thistledown. They had managed to cross paths every few years until Lanier's retirement. He deeply respected Kanazawa; the man had survived the Death in a U.S. Navy submarine, had worked in California to reestablish civilian authority, and had become senior senator twenty years before.

During the Death, around the world, Allied and Warsaw Pact military facilities had been targeted repeatedly. Yet due to some vagary in Soviet planning, or wholesale missile failures, Pearl Harbor had been hit by only two warheads. Other bases on the islands had been struck by one warhead, some by none at all. Honolulu had suffered widespread damage from the Pearl Harbor attack; still, as a city, it had not been obliterated.

After the Sundering, as Hexamon investigators – Lanier among them – chose sites from which to begin the Recovery, the islands had offered themselves as a prime location for mid-Pacific support services. The weapons used there had been relatively clean; the radiation, after five years, was not especially dangerous, and could certainly be countered by Hexamon medicines and treatments.

In ten years, the lush growth of Oahu's jungles and grasslands returned. Cities rose again, feeding both on the Hexamon activity and on trans-Pacific trade between New Zealand, North Australia, and Japan and Indochina.

Because Hexamon communications did not make geographic positions crucial to centers of Recovery Government, the Terrestrial Senate had established its capitol on Oahu, at the site of old Honolulu. There had been a hint of power and privilege in this decision, but the Nexus overseers did not attempt to change it; they knew that few terrestrials would participate in such an unpleasant task as leading the Recovery without substantial perquisites.

Kanazawa lived in a long wood-frame and stone house a mile from the fused glass shore of Waikiki. With a moist, warm southerly breeze rustling palm fronds overhead, Karen, Garry and Ram Kikura walked up the pumice path to be greeted by a Nexus security device, a long polished white tube about a meter long and fifteen centimeters wide, floating beside the porch.

'We're pleased to see you again, Ser Lanier,' the device said in a higher-pitched version of Kanazawa's voice. 'You are all expected. Please enter and excuse the mess. The senator is doing research for a trade bill to be considered next session.'

They walked up the stone steps and entered the porch breezeway. Wicker furniture rested on polished dark wood floors. Papers and folders lay in haphazard piles around the living room; advanced electronic storage media were still something of a luxury on Earth. Ostentation was not Kanazawa's style; he relied on paper.

'I like this,' Ram Kikura said, fondling Polynesian print fabrics on sofa and chair. 'The real thing.'

Kanazawa stepped from his rear office wearing a blue and white Japanese cotton print robe and tabi slippers.

'Garry, Karen! I'm delighted to see you again.' He smiled at Ram Kikura. 'If I'm not mistaken, this is Earth's advocate and a former colleague, Ser Suli Ram Kikura?' He offered his hand; Ram Kikura shook it and bowed slightly. 'To see all of you here at once worries me, pleased as I am by the visit. Something important is happening in the Nexus, I take it?'

He led them to a back porch and ordered drinks from a mechanical servant. Since his second wife had died ten years before, Kanazawa had not remarried; instead, he had plunged more deeply into his work, establishing a reputation as exceptionally polite, exceptionally capable, but also exceptionally stubborn, even obsessive.

'There's an advisory about to be issued by the Nexus on Thistledown,' Lanier said.

'I've heard nothing about it,' Kanazawa said, tilting his head to one side with curiosity. His broad, rugged face carried a vivid white scar across one cheek where he had received a flash burn while standing on the sail of the U.S.S. *Burleigh*, his submarine. A similar scar marked the back of his right hand, ending at the shadow of the long jacket sleeve he had worn. The submarine had been sailing north along the coast of California, three days after the inception of the Death; the flash had come from a Spasm re-nuking of San Francisco.

'Chances are, the Old Natives will not be allowed to vote on this issue,' Lanier said.

Kanazawa's expression did not change, but his voice took on an edge. 'Why not?'

'They'll be excluded by Recovery regulation,' Lanier said. 'Unfit for the making of decisions involving the parent Hexamon.' By a peculiar twist of legal language, in the early years of Recovery legislation, the Thistledown and Precinct ruling bodies had become the parental legislatures.

Kanazawa nodded. 'Not invoked for eleven years, but still in force. Should it concern me?'

'It concerns all of us, I think,' Lanier said. 'It's a rather long story.'

'I know it is worth my time, coming from you. Tell me.'

Lanier told.

41

Thistledown

Korzenowski walked across the sixth chamber terminal to join Mirsky under a transparent skylight. The avatar – Korzenowski found it easiest to think of him that way – stared up across the chamber at the carpet of machinery on the opposite side of the chamber. Clouds moved swiftly over the view, both on their side and the far side; the colors, gray and green and mottled, traversed by the glow of the plasma tube, soothed Korzenowski in a way he found puzzling. He had cut himself loose from all this, yet it continued to fascinate him.

Like Olmy, he now believed that the Hexamon would re-open the Way no matter what obstacles they faced; would he be sorry?

'It's magnificent,' Mirsky said. 'A magnificent achievement.' He smiled at the Engineer. 'When I first saw this, it was beyond anything I could imagine. I was dwarfed. I had not been introduced gradually, had not had the time Lanier spent in the Potato – that's what we called Thistledown. We had not entered peacefully. It felt impossibly alien and disturbing, and fascinating, too. Yet Ser Ram Kikura called it "hideous." '

'Her passions do not lie in machinery; she's spent her life with huge machines. She takes them for granted. It's not unusual for Naderites to be blind to their actual environment, in quest of some perfection. We're a mystical group, all in all; Star, Fate and Pneuma lie deep in us.'

'How long will it take you to complete this diagnostic?' Mirsky asked.

'Three days. There are partials and remotes all over

the chamber now. Everything crucial seems in working order.'

'And the weapons?'

Korzenowski stared intently at the view through the skylight. Rain began to fall in gentle patters, mottling the glass; the same water that had cooled and cleansed the machinery in the sixth chamber for centuries. 'I did not build them. I know very little about them. I suspect they're in working order, also. The Hexamon spent much of its history relying on machinery to stay alive; we respect our creations, and by instinct, we build them to last.'

'How long until the re-opening, then?' Mirsky asked.

'The timetable hasn't changed. Unless Lanier and Ram Kikura succeed in blocking the advisory and the vote, perhaps two weeks; no more than a month.'

'You'll do it, if they order you to? Open the Way again?'

'I'll do it,' Korzenowski answered. 'It seems to be Fate acting, doesn't it?'

Mirsky laughed. For the first time, Korzenowski heard a timbre in the avatar's voice that did not seem entirely human, and it chilled him. 'Fate indeed,' Mirsky said. 'I have been with beings like gods, and fate puzzles them, too.'

42
Hawaii

'I would be honoured to have you stay here,' Kanazawa said. 'My hospitality is not what it was when my wife was alive – only mechanical help donated by my constituents, but the kitchen treats my guests and me well.'

'We'd be delighted,' Lanier said. 'We leave in the morning to visit Oregon, then fly on to Melbourne and back home, New Zealand . . . Christchurch. We haven't much time.'

From the front porch, they saw the sun decline in splendor beyond the palms and beach, setting the slopes of Barber's Point aflame with a gentler fire than that area and its Naval Air Station had known during the Death. A Japanese graveyard lay just west of the senator's property, behind fresh-painted white picket fencing; Suli Ram Kikura stood there now, Karen beside her, examining the carved lava pagoda-shaped headstones and crosses.

'There's something the old Axis City lacked,' Lanier said.

'What's that?'

'Graveyards.'

'Far too many here,' Kanazawa said quickly, 'Many things must be different up there – we have such close ties, and yet, I sometimes think, so little understanding of each other. I wish I were not so afraid of space travel. My only trip was the last time we met. My weeks in the *Burleigh* cured me of cramped quarters, I suppose. I left the ship when we beached her at Waimanalo, and I swore I would never sit in an iron tube again. I flew up there sedated.'

Lanier smiled sympathetically.

'You've worked with them – hell, Garry, you were

one of the first to meet them, Surely you understand what motivates them.'

'I can guess.'

'Why suddenly consider us weak partners, when this could affect all of humanity?'

'We *are* weak partners, Senator.'

'Not as weak or naive as they must think. We can encompass many strange things before breakfast.'

'I think the quote is more like, "believe six impossible things before breakfast." '

'Impossible things! That we have a man returned from the dead, or very nearly . . .'

'We've had lots of those,' Lanier said. 'I've even helped resurrect people. Mirsky is something much stranger than that.'

Kanazawa turned his back on the twilight. The flames past Barber's Point had died to purple dream-tones. Sunsets were not as spectacular now as they had been for years after the Death, but in Hawaii, they were still memorable. 'All right. Perhaps we are naive. Does *she* accept such a thing?'

'Karen, or Ram Kikura?'

'Ram Kikura.'

'I think she accepts it one way, and finds it difficult to accept another way . . . She accepts that we have to act on what Mirsky says. But she deeply regrets his return. She believes he catalysed this whole mess, which of course he did; it would have happened anyway, however.'

'Spreading word across the Earth can only increase resentment, however many believe you,' Kanazawa said. 'We resent our saviors. We resent having our childhood stolen from us.'

'I'm not sure I understand, Senator. Surely the Death did that.'

'No. The builders of Thistledown – *they* survived the Death, grew out of it, developed a new civilisation. They invented their own marvels, struggled to supremacy, launched their asteroid starships. We cannot do that. They've come to us with hands full of marvels, like parents raising children, giving us miracles here and wonders there, sometimes forcing them upon us. They did not let us make our own mistakes–'

'Thank God,' Lanier said dryly. 'We'd screwed up badly enough already.'

'Yes, but do you see what I mean?' Kanazawa asked plaintively. 'My constituents feel lost when confronted by these saviors; they think of them as angels. A visitor from the precincts or the asteroid is still rare; they are respected and feared. We are left on Earth like backwater bumpkins.'

'If the shoe fits,' Lanier said.

'You've grown cynical, Garry.'

'Not without reason, Senator,' Lanier said, smiling wryly. 'But I understand what you're saying. Still, we have to make more of an effort. Earth can't live in resentment and bitterness and envy like some twisted postbellum South. Maybe a larger issue like this is what we need to spark enthusiasm down here.'

'They will not understand, Garry,' Kanazawa said. 'It is beyond their experience. A fairy tale. It's the stuff myths are made of. Myths don't play well in politics. You have to disguise them, make them seem down-to-Earth.'

Ram Kikura and Karen came back from the fence, both looking somber. 'Mortality is not the only thing that separates some of us,' Kanazawa said in an undertone.

Dinner was served by robots. The four of them sat around the table, Lanier and Karen and Kanazawa feeling slightly giddy with big tumblers of rum after the day's solemnity and worry. Lanier hadn't been even mildly drunk in decades; he found more knots loosening, and regarded Karen with eyes of a distant, more youthful self. She was truly a lovely woman; however young she seemed, she had much of the wisdom of age, and that made her even more beautiful. Lanier did not despise youth; he was simply unwilling to let its attractions dominate him.

Working together might be a remedy, he thought; but she was still not as warm to him as he felt toward her, and they behaved as an old married couple might, talking more with others at the table than between themselves.

Ram Kikura was reluctant to try rum. 'I've heard about alcohol,' she said with a voice of temperance caution. 'A narcotic poison.'

'Was Thistledown *dry* during its voyage?' Kanazawa asked, astonishment creeping into his voice.

'No, not at first,' she answered. 'Though alcohol played second fiddle, if that's still a current idiom. Or third or fourth. Early voyagers were more interested in direct mental stimulations, a problem we carried with us from Earth. The stimulations became more sophisticated, and safer, and we found ways to treat personalities devoted to excess, chemical or neurological . . . Alcohol was never a major worry, or a major recreation. Wines, if I remember, were cultivated . . .'

She seemed to enjoy a chance to talk history, especially when it delayed her decision on the rum. 'But when the Way was built, and we had pushed back the Jarts, trade began through the wells. Talsit and other substances became known to us . . . complex intoxicants, enhancers, augmenters, not to mention the nuances of complete downloading. Alcohol and other chemical intoxicants were like *kazoos*.' (she emphasised the word, enjoying its alienness) 'compared to a symphony orchestra.'

'Primitive treats still have their charm, though,' Kanazawa said.

'I'd hate to make a fool of myself,' Ram Kikura said softly, dipping her finger into the small glass, lifting it to her nose. 'Esters and ketones. Very strong.'

'Destroys the brain,' Karen said, on the edge of being tipsy. 'Might need to rent another.'

'Alcohol,' Ram Kikura began, pausing, realising she

was about to be sententious, 'is still a problem on Earth. Am I right?'

'You are absolutely right,' Kanazawa said. 'And a balm for our manifold wounds.'

'I dislike not being in control of myself.'

Karen leaned forward. 'Drink it,' she said. 'It actually tastes good. You don't have to drink it all.'

'I know what it tastes like. I've had biochrones in city memory.'

'Biochrones?' Kanazawa asked.

'Not as popular now as they once were,' Lanier said. 'Simulated full-life experiences. Edited, usually; the more extreme remove your awareness that they're simulated. You live another life.'

'Jesus,' Kanazawa said, making an astonished, strongly disapproving face. 'That's almost like being . . . I know. Unfaithful to yourself.'

As they discussed the ethical dilemma of whether or not sex in a biochrone was tantamount, by older Earth standards, to cheating on one's wedding vows, Ram Kikura brought the rum glass closer. Lanier could see she was attracted to it; she had always felt a connection with the past. When they had first met, she had picted an American flag over her shoulder, proud of her ancient ancestry; here was a bit of the past she knew little about, directly. Biochrone memories, he had heard, were not nearly as vivid as real ones; they couldn't possibly be, without extraordinary implants, larger than practical in homorphs.

'All right,' she said, steeling herself and picking up the glass. 'To being human!' She drank a much larger swallow than Lanier would have recommended. Her eyes widened and she spluttered, choking. Karen pounded her back unhelpfully.

'Ah, Pneuma!' Ram Kikura croaked when she was halfway in control again. 'My body hates it!'

'Go slow,' Kanazawa recommended. 'If that's too strong, I have some wine . . .'

Ram Kikura waved away their attentions, embarrassed by her ineptitude. She wiped away tears and lifted the glass again. 'What were the toasts?' she asked, still slightly hoarse.

'Down the hatch,' Lanier suggested.

Ram Kikura sipped more moderately. 'Makes my throat close up.'

'I don't understand,' Kanazawa said. 'It's very good rum, Oahu's best.'

'At least three hours old,' Lanier said. Kanazawa gave him a twinkling look of senatorial disapproval.

'From my district,' he said.

'This half of the world is your district. Surely you don't drink everything bottled by your constituents!' Karen said.

Ram Kikura sat quiet for a moment, contemplating the effect. 'I don't think I'll become drunk,' she said. 'My implant metabolisers are converting the alcohol to sugars faster than I can drink.'

'What a pity,' Kanazawa said.

'I could fine-tune them . . . if I will fit into the occasion less sober . . .'

Kanazawa glanced meaningfully at Lanier. Karen sighed. 'You are not a natural party girl, my dear,' she said.

The night sky of Hawaii was a cold blaze, reminding Lanier of Van Gogh's *Starry Night*. Kanazawa brought a low-powered red laser pointer onto the back lawn. They sat on the grass, eating Brazilian chocolates and sipping aperitifs.

'This is my private planetarium,' the senator said, crouching carefully, kicking out one foot, almost falling over, then settling back on his butt and crossing his legs. 'Nothing comparable to actually being up in space, I suppose. . . . But I'm happy with it.'

He switched on the laser and lifted it. In the moist sea air, the beam cut a straight glowing path hundreds of feet up to the stars, seeming to touch them individually. 'I know all the constellations,' he said, 'the

Japanese and Chinese and the Western. Even some of the Babylonian.'

'It's beautiful,' Ram Kikura said. She had allowed more than a little of the alcohol to have an effect on her; her eyes were half-lidded and she seemed relaxed, almost sleepy. 'The sky is more . . . human down here. More friendly.'

'Yes, I see that,' Karen said. She and Lanier sat back to back on the grass, heads touching. 'But when I was a girl, it still seemed immense. Frightening.'

'Yes, I see that,' Ram Kikura said, imitating Karen's tone and smiling broadly. 'I really do.'

'My own planetarium,' Kanazawa repeated. 'I can just point the laser and move the beam and watch and nobody knows or cares. Their problems–' He flicked the beam across the entire sky, from cloud-darkened horizon to clear open sea, '–are not my problems.' He sighed over-dramatically. 'It is good to see you again, Garry, Karen. And it is good to meet someone from the precincts on less than formal terms. We have such distance between us, for being parents and children . . .'

'Who are the parents,' Karen asked, 'and who the children?'

'You are the parents,' Ram Kikura said.

'And the children, too.' Karen bumped her head gently against Lanier's, and then harder, as if to attract his attention.

'Ow,' he said. 'What?'

'Just bumping, you old son of a bitch.' She giggled. 'Sorry. Rum talk.'

'Keep bumping, he said.'

Ram Kikura held her hands up. 'I would love to see crowds of Earth children now. Healthy children, happy children. I love to watch Hexamon children through my apartment window, in Axis Euclid. You've never had more children, Karen . . . Why?'

'Much too busy,' Karen said. She bit her lower lip.

'How can anyone be too busy to have children?'

291

'Naturally, or the Hexamon way?' Karen said. The pain had been blunted by time but she still shied from the center.

'The Hexamon way, I think,' Ram Kikura said. 'My son Tapi is an old-fashioned child.' She smiled and shook her head. 'He will pass his incarnation exams. He will follow in his father's footsteps . . . Olmy's,' she added.

'I never knew you had a son,' Lanier said.

'Oh, yes. I'm very proud of him. But I did not give birth to him in the very old sense. To have children is important, though, however you have them . . . whether or not they are raised first in city memory. Allowed to grow like flowers, to make mistakes.'

'And to die,' Lanier mused, his eyes closed. Karen stiffened and leaned forward, breaking their back-to-back contact, and he instantly regretted his words.

'There are graveyards on Thistledown,' he said defensively, avoiding Ram Kikura's steady gaze. 'I've seen them. Columbaria, even pretentious tombs. Your people once knew what death was like.'

'Death is *failure*,' Ram Kikura said, her tone angry.

'Death is completion,' Lanier said.

'Death is a waste and a loss.'

'I'll go along with that,' Karen said, bumping him again pointedly. 'More life.'

'Robert!' Lanier pointed a finger at him. In exchange, Kanazawa pointed the laser beam's arrow on his chest.

'Garry! What?'

'You decide. You're a natural man. No implants, nothing but radiation therapy – you've even kept your scar–'

'White badge of courage,' Kanazawa said. 'Helps me stay in office.'

'Is death completion or waste?'

'We're far from the subject of the evening, aren't we?' Kanazawa asked.

'You have Japanese ancestry. They look upon death

in a different way. Honorable death. Death at the right time.'

'Do you have Amerindian blood?' Kanazawa asked him.

'No.'

'Well, you look as if you might. When people have to die, they look upon death differently. They dress it up and dance with it and put it in black robes and fear it. I have many disagreements with the Hexamon, but I do not regret their giving us the choice. Those graves – most are from the years just after *the* Death. Most of my constituents have chosen to live longer. Some hope to live forever. Perhaps they will. Death is not failure, it may even be completion, but only so long as it is not master.'

'Right,' Karen said.

'Have you chosen to live forever?' Lanier asked.

'No,' Kanazawa said.

'Why?'

'That is personal.'

'Sorry,' Karen said. 'This is not a pleasant subject . . .'

'No. It is important,' Kanazawa said. 'Not too personal to talk about. Rum talk, even. I cannot forget certain things. Unpleasant memories. I cannot use Talsit or pseudo-Talsit, even if we could get them, wonderful as those treatments are; these memories are a fixed part of me, and have made me what I am now. I fight with them always. In the morning I wake to them. Sometimes they hang over my whole day. You know what I'm talking about, don't you, Garry?'

'Amen,' Lanier said.

'When I die, those memories will be gone. I will be gone, and perhaps someone better will come in my place. He may have knowledge of the history I've lived through, but he will be able to lift above them. There will be no waste. What I cannot assimilate, he or she will.'

'Amen,' Lanier repeated in a whisper.

'We will agree to disagree,' Ram Kikura said. 'You are a wonderful man, Senator. Your death would be a loss.'

Kanazawa tilted his head to acknowledge her compliment.

'We cannot cry, you know,' Ram Kikura said. 'We feel many of the same emotions, but we have . . . not risen above them. Transcended them. We assimilate and remain ourselves, but . . .' She shook her head vigorously. 'I can't think straight! Rum thought, rum talk.'

'We are too close to a lot of death to look at individual death objectively,' Kanazawa said. 'Karen, do you approve of your husband's age?'

'No,' she said after a long pause.

'I can't keep up with her,' Lanier said, trying for a pleasantry.

She looked down from the stars at the dark grass. 'It's not that. I don't want to lose you. I don't want to sacrifice myself to stay in step with you, either.'

'Lance that boil, doctor,' Lanier said.

'Shut up.' She pushed away from him again and stood up. 'We're talking stupid talk now.'

'Rum talk,' Kanazawa said, swinging the beam across the sky again. '*In vino, veritas.*'

'This is noble,' Ram Kikura said. 'This is human.'

Karen ran for the house. Lanier stood, brushed grass from his pants, and said, 'I think I'm going to follow her and then we'll go to sleep.'

Kanazawa nodded sagely.

Lanier walked back to the house, found the bedroom, and stood in the doorway, watching Karen undress. 'I remember the first time you made love to me,' he said. 'In the jumpjet. On the tuberider.'

She made a little noise, unhitching her bra.

'It took me many years to really appreciate you. Not until after we were married. After we had worked together.'

'Please shut up,' Karen said, but not angrily.

'You became like one of my arms, one of my legs,' he pursued. 'I took you for granted. I thought everything I'd do, you'd do. I loved you so much I forgot you weren't me.'

'There was work to do.'

'No excuse, even so,' he said. 'I think you lost sight of me, too.'

'You're not the only one with bad memories,' Karen said sharply. 'I went back to Hunan. Remember? I saw my town, the farmlands. I smelled *death*, Garry, *waste*. Skeletons of infants by the roadside, you couldn't tell whether they had been there for months or years, from the Death or after, when their parents dropped them because they couldn't feed them. We couldn't get to everybody in time. *You are not the only one with memories!*'

'I know,' Lanier said, still leaning on the door frame.

'I can handle them. I can love you for a lot longer. I don't want you to go away from me. I hate that thought.'

'I know.'

'Then come back to me,' she said. 'You can still become young. There are centuries left to us. Centuries of work yet to do.'

'That's not my way,' he said. 'I wish you could accept that.'

'I wish you could accept my . . . fears,' she said.

'I'll try. We're working together now, Karen.'

She half-shivered, half-shrugged and sat on the bed. He remained standing by the door, still dressed. 'What about Mirsky?' she asked. There was a look of patent wonder on her face, forehead smooth, eyes wide, lips drawn down as if in a pout. 'Is he going to bring the gods down on us? Is that what he's really saying? He's a *horrible* thing, Garry.'

'I don't think so.'

She shook her head. 'A nightmare.'

'A vision,' Lanier countered. 'Let's wait and see.'

'I am afraid,' she said simply. 'Will you allow me that?'

If he came forward now, he knew, and tried to hug her, she would not accept; she would push him away. But he could see that the time might come, and for now, still mildly buzzing with rum, that was enough. 'Of course,' he said.

'I'm going to sleep.' She lay back on the guest bed and pulled the covers up.

He watched her for a moment, then shut out the light, turned, and stood alone in the dark and quiet hallway. Out on the grass, he heard Kanazawa and Ram Kikura talking.

'I would be honored if you would share my bed with me this evening,' Kanazawa said.

'I'm not even mildly drunk now, Ser Kanazawa,' Ram Kikura said.

'Nor am I.'

Ram Kikura said nothing for a moment. Then, 'I'd like that.'

Lanier contemplated his wife in bed, the quaint comfort of the guest room, and shook his head. Still too many walls between them. He walked to the front porch and lay down on the padded wicker sofa there, plumping an old tattered silk pillow under his head.

In the morning, Lanier walked along the beach before Karen awoke. A kilometer away, he spotted Ram Kikura, walking around a tongue of exhausted surf, tall and slender, surrounded by wheeling gulls. Without gesture, they walked toward each other, and Ram Kikura smiled at him as they closed.

'Am I a *brazen hussy?*' she asked, turning to match his pace and direction.

Lanier returned her smile. 'As brazen as they come,' he said.

'In all my years as Earth's advocate, I've never made love to an Old Native,' she said.

'Was it quaint?' Lanier asked. She scowled at him.

'Some things stay remarkably the same, in basics,' she said. They walked on in silence for a while, watching gulls prance on the wet sand ahead of them, avoiding the slick rising curves of water. 'Ser Kanazawa is furious,' she finally said. 'He's angrier than I've seen any man in a very long time. He didn't show it to all of us . . . He's going to call a meeting of all of Earth's senators and corpreps. Through me, they'll challenge the *mens publica* vote. I can make a strong argument that the Recovery laws cannot apply in this case.'

'Will you win?' Lanier asked.

She bent down to pick up a glass Japanese float. 'I wonder low long this has been here?' she asked. 'Do they make these now?'

'I don't know,' Lanier said. 'I suppose they do. Will you win?'

'Probably not,' she said. 'The Hexamon isn't what it used to be.' She held the float up close, examining its tiny starlike bubbles floating in green glass. She returned the float to the sand.

'The president seems to be swinging with the tide,' Lanier said. 'He claimed he violently opposes re-opening.'

'He does. But there's not much he can do if the Nexus supports it. And I fear that like the captain of a troubled ship, he won't hesitate to cut the Earth loose, if it's necessary to save what's left of the Hexamon.'

'But the Jarts–'

'We beat them back once, and we weren't prepared for them,' Ram Kikura said.

'You sound proud, almost supportive,' Lanier said.

She frowned again, shaking her head. 'An advocate needs to understand how the opposition feels. I'm as furious as Kanazawa, myself.' She swung her arms and bent to pick up a crumbling piece of plastic bottle. 'How old is *this*, do you think?'

Lanier didn't answer. He was thinking of Mirsky, surprised by the refusal of the Nexus to go along with his request. 'What chance is there for a negative vote?' he asked.

'None,' she said. 'Without a persuaded and informed Earth, and that seems to be an impossibility in the near term.'

'Then why are we here? I thought this was a good idea . . . I thought we might have an effect.'

Ram Kikura nodded. 'We will,' she said. 'We'll hang on their damned heels and slow them down. The tide is coming in, don't you think?'

The tide was going out, as far as Lanier could tell, but he understood her meaning.

'What will we say in Oregon?' he asked.

'The same thing we've said here.'

They turned around to walk back toward the house. When they arrived, the others were up and about, and the robots were serving breakfast. Kanazawa and Ram Kikura were friendly, cordial and no more.

Lanier was thoughtful. He had had a burst of youthful enthusiasm shot down. There was chagrin, but there was also the realisation he could still be young and foolish. He could still fight for hopeless causes. Somehow, that made him feel even more alive, even more resolved.

Besides, he suspected Mirsky – or the beings at the end of time – were far more resourceful than even the Hexamon.

They packed their few pieces of luggage. Ram Kikura and Karen spoke with Kanazawa as Lanier carried the small bags to the shuttle. As he entered the shuttle doorway, the automated pilot flashed a red pict before his eyes.

'Speak in English, please,' Lanier said, vaguely irritated.

'Our flight has been held,' the pilot said. 'We are to stay here until precinct police arrive.'

Lanier set the bags down, stunned. 'Precinct police? Not terrestrial police?'

The pilot did not respond. The interior lighting

dimmed. The white interior relaxed and turned an inactive blue.

'Are you still functioning?' Lanier asked. There were no further answers. He looked around the darkened interior, opening and closing his fists. He stepped down from the doorway, face red with anger, and confronted Karen.

'I think we're being intercepted,' he said. Ram Kikura and Kanazawa came from the house.

'Problems?' the senator asked.

'Precinct police are coming,' Lanier said.

Kanazawa's face hardened. 'Not if I have anything to say about it.'

'You probably don't,' Ram Kikura said. Kanazawa stared at her as if she had struck him. 'This is very serious, Garry. How did you—'

Karen looked out to sea. Beyond Barber's Point, three aircraft flew toward them, sharp white against the billowing gray mid-morning clouds. They banked and approached the house, slowing and hovering, their flight fields knocking bits of gravel and dirt from the senator's driveway and yard.

'Ser Lanier,' a voice from the craft boomed above them. 'Please respond.'

'I'm Garry Lanier.' He stood away from the others.

'Ser Lanier, you and your wife are to return to New Zealand immediately. All Old Natives are being returned to their homelands.'

Ram Kikura stepped out beside him. 'Under whose orders, and by what law?' She lowered her voice. 'There are no such laws,' she muttered.

'By Revised Recovery Act. Direct presidential authority. Please board your shuttle. Its flight plans have been changed.'

'Don't go,' Kanazawa said. He lifted his eyes to the three craft and raised a fist. 'I am a senator! I demand a meeting with the president and the presiding minister!'

The hovering craft did not reply.

'You won't board the shuttle,' Ram Kikura said. 'We'll all stay here. They won't dare use physical force.'

'Garry, they said all Old Natives were being returned – even those with permanent residency on the orbiting bodies?' Karen's face resembled a child's, horribly disappointed, disbelieving.

'I don't know,' Lanier said. 'Senator, we can do more in our own territory . . . unless we're under house arrest, in which case it doesn't matter where we are.' He turned to Ram Kikura. 'I assume you'll go back to Thistledown.'

'Assume nothing,' she said tightly. 'All rules are off. I certainly didn't expect this.'

'They do this,' Karen said, her face red, 'and they'll really have a fight on their hands.'

I doubt that, Lanier thought. *The fight is probably over right here and now. They feel the need to play dirty.*

The three craft held their position, implacable. A light sun shower began to fall. Ram Kikura wiped wet hair from her face. 'We shouldn't just stand here like disobedient children,' Lanier said. 'Senator, thank you for listening to us. If we can talk again, I'll–'

'Please board your shuttle now,' the voice boomed.

Lanier took his wife's hand. 'Good-by,' he said to Kanazawa and Ram Kikura. 'Good luck. Let Korzenowski and Olmy know what happened here.'

Ram Kikura nodded.

They boarded the shuttle and the door flowed shut behind them.

43

The Way, Efficient Gaia

A maze of brilliant green lines sketched themselves in parallel around them, breaking pattern to draw a harness or cage about the bubble faster than Rhita could move her eyes to follow. After a brief pause, another array of lines rose from the surface of the Way, far below, originating at a single dazzling vertex near one of the stacked disk towers. The lines connected and the oval bubble descended with alarming rapidity, though again with no sensation.

Rhita felt faint. There was too much stimulation, too much to absorb. 'I'm going to be sick,' she told Tȳphōn. The escort took hold of her left arm – the first time he had touched her. His touch was warm but unconvincing; through her constricting circle of thought and vision, she was faintly repelled. Then she was on her knees and past caring.

She half-expected Tȳphōn to do something to her, to fix her and banish the spell of dizziness. But he simply stood behind her, keeping her from falling on her back. For a moment, she restrained an impulse to heave, and then shut her eyes tightly, deciding darkness would be better for her health.

After a time, the dizziness faded and she felt better. 'If you are thirsty,' Tȳphōn said, 'drink this.' She opened her eyes and saw a glass cup of clear liquid in his hand. She took it and sipped cautiously. Water; nothing more, as far as she could tell. This disappointed her. She had expected some elixir. Of course, where the escort had found a cup of water in the bubble was a puzzle. . . . She imagined him opening a hole in his body and drawing it out, or perhaps spitting into the glass. She shut her eyes again, fighting another rising plume of nausea.

Rhita used the railing to regain her feet, waving off his hand, and hastily returned the half-full cup. Partly to distract herself from the panorama outside, partly to subdue her queasiness, she directed her full attention to what he did with the glass.

He held it. Nothing more. Shivering, she turned back to the view. They had dropped much closer to the surface now, and flew – guided by the green lines – toward a white tower. Trying to judge scale, she decided the tower was at least as tall as the Pharos at Alexandreia, and much more massive. But the scale of the Way dwarfed all structures.

Rhita forced herself to lean her head back and look up. Her neck protested. Her lips parted and she sighed, despite herself. Far behind and above them, the triangular prism hung huge and blunt and graceless in the center of the pearly ribbon of light, like a long black crystal suspended in milky water.

Something much farther down the throat of the Way, a blinking beacon, caught her attention. She shielded her eyes, although the tubelight was not excessively bright, and squinted to focus on a moving speck. It, too, was within the ribbon of light, but many stadia away, moving rapidly in their direction. She jerked her neck back as it reached a point just above them, saw that it was another huge rainbow prism, and realised it would collide with the first prism. Twisting about, she gasped as the prisms struck like trains on a rail. For a moment, they were one long green mass, and then the second prism passed through the first without damage to either, continuing its travel unimpaired in the opposite direction.

Patrikia had never described anything like *that*.

'I feel numb,' she said, glancing resentfully at Typhōn.

'It was your choice to see it all,' the escort said mildly. 'None of me take this route often, themselves.'

She pondered that syntax for a moment, decided the view was less disturbing than what she suspected Tȳphōn meant, and faced forward again.

There were no obvious entrances to the tower. Nevertheless, the bubble passed straight through the rounded wall of a stacked disk, crossing an enclosed arc-shaped space filled with floating polyhedrons, and then through another wall. The bubble discarded its panoply of green lines, and descended along a leaf-green shaft toward what might have been a perfectly clear lens of glass. Distorted by the lens were sea-blues and sky-blues and light browns and cloud-grays; all the normal colors of her home. She held her breath for a moment, hoping against hope that the nightmare would end.

'This is the gate to Gaia,' her escort said. 'A prior gate was opened here. Our gates are not usually so constricted in shape, but the prior geometry takes precedence.'

'Oh,' Rhita said. *Free with information that meant next to nothing to her* . . .

As they fell toward the surface of the lens, the color of the shaft reddened, then abruptly shifted to white.

The bubble struck the lens and they fell through. Below lay a coastline, gray ocean under cloud shadows, blue ocean in patches of brilliant sunlight.

Rhita could hardly breathe. 'Where are we?'

'This is your world,' Tȳphōn said.

She knew that; and it was no dream, either. 'Where on Gaia?'

'Not far from your home, I understand – I've never visited here in any self or capacity.'

'I want to go to . . .' She looked up and saw blue sky and an indistinct shimmer over their heads: the gate they had just passed through. 'Can we go to Rhodos?'

Tȳphōn considered her request for a moment. 'It would not consume much more energy. This project nears its limits, however. There will have to be results soon.'

'I don't know what you mean.'

'This line of investigation. You must provide results soon.'

'You know everything I know,' Rhita said, near tears, utterly exhausted. 'What can I do for you?'

'Lead us to those who built your clavicle. Give us clues. But–' He held up his hand as she was about to protest, 'I realise you do not know these things. Still, there is some hope you can reveal more by your actions, or by your presence – the clavicle may be sought by others than ourselves. Only you can operate it. You still have some value in your active form.'

'What about my . . . companions?'

'They will be brought here if it makes you more comfortable.'

'It would,' she said. 'Please.'

Typhōn smiled. 'Your forms of social appeasement are wonderful. Such simplicity masking such aggression. The request is made; they should meet us at Rhodos, if we do not exceed the energy budget.'

'I'm not sure I can stand here much longer. I'm very tired.'

Typhōn encouraged her to squat on the platform. 'You will not be clumsy in my eyes,' he said.

With a grimace, she not only squatted; she lay down on her stomach, peering over the edge. 'Are we going to Rhodos?' she asked.

'Yes.'

A green line appeared from nearby clouds and spread out before the bubble into a radiance of grasping curves. In a cage again, the bubble transported them high above the ocean. She could not tell in which direction of the compass they were heading.

'Am I the first human you've ever studied?' she asked.

'No,' Typhōn answered. 'My selves studied dozens of humans from this world before investigating your preserved record.'

'Do you know everything about us?' Anger was her

dominant emotion now; she bit off her words, hoping the sour edge was not lost to the escort.

'No. You still have many subtleties, many things to study. But I may not be allowed to study you to completion. There are higher tasks, and my number of selves is fully occupied.'

'You keep saying that,' Rhita said wearily. 'My "selves". I don't understand what you mean.'

'I am not an individual. I am actively stored–'

'Like grain in a barrel?' Rhita asked sarcastically.

'Like a memory in your own head,' Tÿphōn said. 'I am actively stored in the flaw. We can induce resonances in the flaw and store huge amounts of information – literally worlds of information. Is that clear to you?'

'No,' she admitted. 'How can there be more than one of you?'

'Because my patterns, my self, can be duplicated endlessly. I can be merged with other selves of differing designs and abilities. Various effectuators can be built for us – machines or ships or more rarely, bodies. I do work when any of my selves are required.'

'You're trained to take care of strangers?'

'In a sense. I made a study of beings similar to you when we fought with them in the Way. I was an individual then, biologically based, in a shape similar to my original birthform.'

Her grandmother had told her what little she knew about the Jart Wars. To a young girl, they had not meant much – meaningless wonders in a weave of fantastic stories. She wished she had listened more closely.

'What was your original birth-form?'

'Not human, not this shape at all.'

'But you *did* have your own shape once.'

'No. Part of me did. I have since been combined with others, stirred together.' He twirled an extended finger slowly. Rhita frowned at him over her shoulder. *All my questions keep me from the truth I'll have to face.*

'I'm confused again,' she said. 'You tell me one thing, then another.'

Tӯphōn knelt beside her, elbows on his knees, hands clasped. A very human gesture. Was his face gaining more character?

'Your language doesn't have the right word-groups. All sound-carried language is inadequate.'

'You don't talk to each other,' she said.

'Not in words, or using sounds. Not usually, at any rate.'

'Would you kill me if you were ordered to?'

'I will not be ordered to kill you or anybody, if by that you mean destroy your patterns. That is what you would call a crime, a sin.'

Enough for the moment. She rolled back on her stomach. Below them, the ocean stretched blue-green, shallow, with pillars of rock sticking up like stumps of trees. She did not know this place.

Yet they were supposed to be near Rhodos. 'Near' might mean different things to a Jart; they could speed down the Way and exit through gates in soap bubbles, after all.

More pillars appeared. Each was covered by a cap of gold that took the shape of the rocks, as if painted on. No vegetation, no boats in the water, just this cloud-shadowed and pillar-specked barrenness.

'Could I smell the air?' she asked.

'No,' Tӯphōn said bluntly.

'Why not?'

'It is no longer healthy for you. There are organisms and biological machines on your world now that travel by air, too small to see. They are raising Gaia to a higher level of efficiency.'

'Nobody can live out there?'

Tӯphōn seemed to commiserate. 'Not of your kind,' he said.

She felt weak again. They had spread disease around Gaia – was that what the escort meant? Death and defilement. Nobody could live–

'Anywhere? Can people live anywhere?'

'There are no humans on Gaia. They have been stored for further study.'

Now the hatred came. It jerked her head back, squeezing her vitals like a giant hand, pushing a scream out. She turned on Tӯphōn with fists raised. He made no effort to defend himself. She hit him as hard as she could, again and again, not weak feminine blows; she had never been raised to fear defending herself. Her fists deformed his face and her knees kicked dimples in his clothing. She seemed to be striking bread dough, warm and yielding. She continued to scream, pitching higher with each blow, grunting, saliva falling from her lips, eyes half-closed. Again and again. Striking, kicking, grabbing him by the neck and sticking her fingers into what might be flesh.

Tӯphōn collapsed on the platform, face misshapen, eyes beaten shut, not bruised but simply warped, and she kicked him several more times until she felt a sparkling dark emptiness in her head. Staring up at the clouds outside the bubble, tears slick on her cheeks, her chin damp with spit, the rage gone but the legs and arms still trembling, Rhita began to creep back into control.

She glanced down at the clothed mass that no longer seemed very human, her expression that of a panicked horse, pupils like pinpricks and nostrils wide, then grabbed the railing, feeling again as if she might vomit. Across the barren sea, she saw a low dark green outline above the horizon and the last hopeful part of her exulted. That was Rhodos; she would know it anywhere. The bubble was still speeding her toward home.

Tӯphōn spoke behind her, voice undistorted by the injuries she had inflicted. 'I may be exceeding my budget now,' he said.

44

Thistledown City

President Farren Siliom entered the full Nexus chamber and proceeded to the podium. Olmy sat beside Korzenowski and Mirsky. They listened to his speech intently. Korzenowski's expression was enigmatic; he knew the importance of this occasion as well as anybody in the chamber, but he expressed neither approval nor disapproval.

Mirsky's face was also bland, but in its blandness, Olmy thought, there might lie more threat to the Hexamon than ever posed by the Jarts. Olmy had come to accept Mirsky's story completely, and now even judged the man – if he was a man – incapable of lying. The president doubtless agreed; Garabedian's confirmation had weighed heavily in that judgment. Yet now the Nexus – and Farren Siliom, for irresistible political reasons – were committing themselves to a course of re-opening. They were committing political acts that could only serve to slice a gap between Earth and the orbiting bodies that might never heal.

All native Terrestrials were being returned to the Earth, whatever their status on the orbiting bodies. The Hexamon was entering a period of Emergency. Under Emergency Laws forgotten since the Jart Wars, the president was assuming extraordinary powers. He now had one year in which to carry out his plans; after that time, because of his use of the Emergency Laws, he would be forbidden from ever holding political office again.

He was guaranteeing the purity of the vote of the *mens publica* with a vengeance. If the vote was negative, he would resign. If it was positive, Thistledown's sixth chamber could be refurbished, the Hexamon defense reestablished and the Way re-opened within four months.

Korzenowski had been formally ordered to see to the execution of the will of the *mens publica*. He could not refuse. To Olmy, he seemed resigned; perhaps more than resigned. Having been forced this far, Korzenowski might be shedding the last vestiges of the mask he had worn for four decades, a mask of interest only in the Recovered Earth and the Terrestrial Hexamon, the denial of all his genius and accomplishment for the greater good of his fellows. . . .

Shedding, or having the mask ripped from him, it might not matter which in the long run.

Olmy had few doubts Korzenowski would carry out the Hexamon's orders efficiently. The Way might be opened sooner even than the president expected.

What Mirsky would do, he could not tell. Best not to worry about imponderables.

Meanwhile, within Olmy himself, the Jart was revealing layer upon layer of everyday Jart life. The flow of information had turned into a true flood, perhaps a rupture.

Thus far, he was managing to keep up with the tide. Already he was planning his briefing for the reorganised defense forces.

Soon, following an agreement worked out between the Jart mentality and his partial, he would allow the Jart access to his eyes and ears. They could communicate more effectively if they understood each other better.

There were some dangers in that, of course, but none worse than what he had already survived.

It was more than a time of changes.

The pace had now taken the proportions of revolution. The Sundering was about to be reversed.

The president finished his presentation, and the dominant coalition of neo-Geshels applauded and picted complete approval. The president's Naderite colleagues kept silent.

Korzenowski turned to Mirsky. 'My friend, I must do this work, whatever my beliefs.'

Mirsky shrugged and nodded, as if either forgiving or dismissing the Engineer. 'Things will work out,' he said with bland nonchalance. He glanced at Olmy and winked.

45

Thistledown, the Orbiting Precincts, and Earth

Korzenowski lifted a lump of white dough and listened to its soft hiss in his hands. The lumps were remains of a failed attempt six years before to create a gate without the Way; the failure had been quiet, but decisive. Instead of creating a gate, he had created a new form of matter, quite inert, possessing no useful properties that he had found, so far. And he had spent the past six years searching . . .

He laid the lump back in its pallet of black stone and straightened, surveying his laboratory, saying farewell. He would not be back for months, perhaps not ever.

The results of the Hexamon *mens publica* vote had been tabulated and broadcast. By a two-thirds majority – more than he had expected – permanent re-opening had been mandated.

Farren Siliom had no choice at all now.

Korzenowski activated the robot sentries and gave final instructions to a partial. Should he not return, and should anyone come visiting, the partial would be there to greet them.

He was not reluctant to return to the sixth chamber and begin the refurbishing; in fact, he was eager. There was a small and persistent voice in him that either echoed or perhaps, in some way not clear, created that eagerness: the unquiet voice of that which integrated his reassembled self, the mystery of Patricia Luisa Vasquez.

Korzenowski gathered up his small tools and journals, all that was necessary to begin work on the Way, and ordered the laboratory sealed. 'Be good, now,' he instructed a cross-shaped sentry as he walked away

311

from the domes. He paused at the boundary of the compound, frowning. It was certainly not in his character to address a remote; he treated them for what they were, useful machines.

Surrounded by kilometer after kilometer of scrub and sand, the Engineer boarded the tractor that would take him to the train station in the second chamber city.

Suli Ram Kikura's partial argued persuasively that its original should be released from house arrest in Axis Euclid. The partial's appeal was rejected by the City Memory auxiliary courts on the grounds that under Emergency Laws, all appeals had to be presented by corporeals. This was so ridiculous it did not even anger her; she was beyond anger, moving into sadness.

In her apartment, Ram Kikura had known the partial would fail. This new Hexamon was not above making up the rules as it went along. To openly object to the re-opening was not so much dangerous now as it was extremely awkward, impolite in its extended sense of *impolitic*. For decades, Hexamon law and politics had been based upon awareness of boundaries beyond which lay chaos and disaster; the president and presiding minister, having accurately guaged the true spirit of the orbiting bodies, were now doing everything within their power to stay within the boundaries of their duty, yet also carry out the vote of the *mens publica* and the advisory of the Nexus. They also seemed grimly determined to demonstrate the extremes of this mandate, as if they wished to punish the Hexamon – even their ideological partners – for this onerous duty.

She was not allowed access to any city memory; that meant she could not speak with Tapi, who would be born any hour now. She had not been allowed to speak with either Korzenowski or Olmy. They were on their best behavior, she had been told. and were cooperating fully with the Emergency Effort.

She had refused any form of cooperation. Ram

312

Kikura had her own boundaries, and she was damned if she would step over them.

In New Zealand, spring brought lovely weather and the amusement of lambs. Lanier tended their small flock of black-faced sheep; Karen helped when she wasn't lost in her own funk. Unable to work, confined to their home and valley, she was not doing well.

They worked together, yet kept their distance. Lanier had lost whatever enthusiasm Mirsky had kindled. He did not know what would happen next. He didn't much care.

In his way, he had once adored the Hexamon, and all it had stood for. Over the past few years, he had seen from a distance the changing character of the orbiting precincts, the shifting sands of Hexamon politics. Now, lost in its own needs and regrets, the same Hexamon that had worked to save the Earth had finally betrayed him, and betrayed Karen . . . had betrayed Earth.

Earth's Recovery was not yet finished.

Perhaps now, it would never be done, whatever the assurances broadcast around the world nightly from the orbiting bodies. He found these particularly galling; smooth, pleasant, informative, day by day educating the Earth about progress in the re-opening.

Now and then, Lanier heard of Recovery efforts continuing in a desultory fashion.

He felt old again, looked older.

Sitting on their porch at night, he listened to cool night breezes wafting through the bushes, thinking thoughts convoluted and fuzzy as balls of yarn.

I am only a single human being, he told himself. *It is right that I should wither like a leaf on a tree. I am out of place now. I am finished. I hate this time, and I do not envy those being born.*

Perhaps the worst part of all was that for a brief moment, he had felt the old spark again. With Mirsky, he had thought of fighting the good fight; he had hoped

313

perhaps here was an agency more powerful and wise than all of them.

But Mirsky was gone.

Nobody had seen him in months.

Lanier tried to get up out of his seat, to go to bed and sleep and for a short time lose all these painful thoughts. His hands pushed on the wood, and his back moved forward, but he could not lift himself; his pants seemed stuck to something. Puzzled, he leaned over one side of his chair. Silently, something exploded. A ball of darkness edged in from one side of his eyes and his head became enormous.

The ball of darkness centered and became a great tunnel. He grabbed the ends of his chair arms but could not straighten.

'Oh, God,' he said. His lips were numb as rubber. Ink spread in the back of his head. Doors closed with rhythmic slammings on all his memories. Karen not with him; not where she was. This was the way his father had gone, younger even than he was now. No pain just the sudden withdrawal of He had not thought himself so 'Oh, God.'

The tunnel yawned wide, full of rainbow night.

46

Thistledown

Buried sixty meters within the outer perimeter of the seventh chamber's southern cap were seven generators, connected by seven field-lined shafts of pure vacuum to the sixth chamber machinery. The generators had no moving parts and nothing to do with electrons or magnetic fields; they worked on far more subtle principles, principles developed by Korzenowski based on mathematical reasoning that had primarily begun with Patricia Luisa Vasquez in the late twentieth century.

These seven generators had created the stresses on space-time that had resulted in the Way. They had not been used for four decades but were still sound; the vacuum shafts were still operating and completely free of matter or time-linked energy, that enigmatic byproduct of interaction between universes.

In the hole leading to the seventh chamber, an observation blister had been erected and the bore hole pressurised with air. The blister was now filled with monitoring equipment, giant red spheres studded with silver and gray cubes the size of a man's head, tracting back and forth within the blister's shell, silently avoiding their human masters whenever encountered along their complex paths.

Korzenowski floated where the Way's singularity had once been, his body precessing like a slow top, gray hair standing out from his hand in the blister's gentle cooling breezes. With catlike eyes, he observed the construction on the southern cap of the seventh chamber, radiating for kilometers outward from the bore hole, huge black concentric rings of virtual particle stimulators and their reservoirs of graviton-stabilised tritium metal. These would not be brought into play until after

315

the opening of the Way; the stimulators could be used as weapons, and were capable of stripping the Way clear of matter for a distance of several hundred kilometers, giving the Hexamon its first 'beachhead,' should it need one. Soon, the traction beam radiation shields would be in place to focus the backwash of disrupted matter that the stimulators might create along the same path as the stimulator beams.

Fearsome weapon, fearsome defenses . . .

Fearsome opponents.

At rest, Korzenowski's thoughts wandered. He used his two hours of daily inactivity to put the events of the past few months in perspective. The blister was deserted but for him and the machines.

In two more weeks, the Way generators would be ready for tests. Virtual universes of fractional dimensions – continua with little more than abstract reality – would be created in deliberately unstable configurations. The night sky over Earth would sparkle with their deaths, as particles and radiations unknown in this continuum – or any stable continuum – left their tracks in the protesting void.

In three weeks, if the first tests went well, Korzenowski would order the creation of a torus, an independent and stable universe turned in upon itself. He would then dismantle the torus and observe how it faded; the manner of its demise could give clues as to the state and superspatial location of the Way's sealed terminus.

Over the next few months, they would 'fish' for that terminus. A temporary virtual universe the size and shape of the Way, but of finite length, would be generated, would be encouraged to merge with the terminus, and would create an attractive bridge between the generators and their now-indepedent progeny.

Ramon Rita Tiempos de Los Angeles

Korzenowski shut his eyes and frowned deeply. He could not help but know the source of these increasingly frequent interruptions and what they signified. When Patricia Vasquez's mystery had been transferred to his assembled partials, to bind them and give them a core, somehow memory and drive had been transferred as well. In theory, that was unlikely. But Vasquez had been in a highly disturbed state, and Korzenowski, unusually shattered, had not been a textbook model for the transfer process.

He did not fight the impulses. For the moment, they did not work opposite to his wishes, and they did not disturb him unduly. But the reckoning would have to come soon. He would need to submit to major personality restructuring.

That was risky and he could not take risks now, central as he was to the Hexamon's effort.

There, he told himself after a few minutes had passed. *Quiet. Peace. Integration.*

'Konrad,' came a voice from the blister's bore hole entrance. Korzenowski grimaced and turned to face the voice. It was Olmy; they hadn't talked in weeks. He spread his arms and slowed his precessing, then tracted outward from the center.

They picted intimate greetings and embraced each other in the near-weightlessness. 'My friend,' Korzenowski said.

'I've disturbed your free time,' Olmy said, picting polite concern.

'Yes, but no matter. I'm glad to see you.'

'Have you heard?'

'Heard what?'

'Garry Lanier suffered a massive cerebral hemorrhage.'

'He wasn't protected – ' Korzenowski's face paled. 'He's dead?'

'Very nearly. Karen discovered him a few seconds after it happened and immediately called Christchurch.'

'His damned Old Native pride!' Korzenowski exclaimed. The anger was not just his own.

'They reached him within ten minutes. He's alive, but he needs reconstruction – the brain is extensively damaged.'

Korzenowski closed his eyes and shook his head slowly. He did not approve of forced medication, but under the circumstances, he doubted the Hexamon would give Lanier much choice in his treatments. '*They* did this to him,' he said bitterly. 'We've all had a hand in it . . .'

'There's guilt enough to go around,' Olmy said. 'If Karen consents to reconstruction, most of the damage can be reversed . . . But he'll need medical aid that he's always been on record as refusing.'

'Have you told Ram Kikura?'

Olmy shook his head. 'She's being kept under house arrest, held in a communications null. Besides, my own leash is short.'

'So is mine,' Korzenowski said, 'but I can swing wide enough to hit some influential people.'

'I appreciate that,' Olmy said. 'I'm afraid my political status is uncertain at the moment.'

'Why?'

'I've refused to take command of the Emergency Defense Effort.'

'You'd be the best choice,' Korzenowski said. 'Why refuse?'

Olmy smiled and shook his head.

Korzenowski, staring into his eyes, felt a small tingle of sympathy. *He's not alone, either.* But he couldn't decide what made him feel that way, or what the feeling implied.

'I'll explain later. It's not the time now. I think I'll be hard to reach for a while, however.' The last message he picted in tight-beam so that only Korzenowski could receive it. 'If you need to tell me anything, please . . .'

Korzenowski examined Olmy for a moment, then picted, 'I'll feel very alone without you to speak to, should I need you . . . or Garry, or Ram Kikura.'

Olmy nodded understanding. 'Perhaps we'll all meet again. Star, Fate and Pneuma willing.' He tracted swiftly back to the bore hole.

Korzenowski floated alone once again in the blister,

318

surrounded by wheeling machines, red spheres and gray cubes. *No use trying to rest now*, he told himself, and returned to work.

47

Earth

Lanier struggled on the lip of a well. Every time he relaxed his hands and waited to fall, somebody held on to him. He could not die. He began to resent being saved. So long as he was alive, he was condemned to suffer the sour old-party taste in his mouth, and feel the constant disruption in his stomach and bowels. In a moment of lucidity, he tried to remember who he was and could not.

Light exploded around him. He seemed bathed in supernal glory. At the same moment, his mind itched. And he heard the first clear words in what seemed a very long time: 'We've done all we can without reconstruction.'

He pondered those words, so familiar and yet alien.

'He wouldn't want that.'

Karen.

'Then there's nothing more we can do.'

'Will he become conscious again?'

'He's conscious now, in a way. He's probably listening to us.'

'Can he speak?'

'I don't know. Try him.'

'Garry? Can you hear me?'

Yes why not just let me die Karen No there's 'work to do.'

'Garry? What work?'

is the Recovery over

'. . . recovery over . . .'

'Garry, you've been very ill. Can you hear me?'

'Yes.'

'I couldn't just let you die. I called the Hexamon

medical center in Christchurch. They've done all they can for now . . .'

He still couldn't see, couldn't tell whether his eyes were open or closed; the glory had faded to brown darkness.

'. . . don't let them.'

'What?'

'Don't let them.'

'Garry, you tell me what to do.'

She was speaking Chinese. She sounded very unhappy. He was making her unhappy.

'What's reconstruction?'

Another voice interposed, speaking English. 'Ser Lanier, you can't recover fully without reconstruction. We send tiny mobile medical devices into your brain and they help repair nerve tissue.'

'No new body.'

'Your body is fine, such as it is. It's your brain that's damaged.'

'No privilege.'

'What's he mean?' the voice asked somebody else. Karen responded.

'He doesn't wany any privileged medical attention.'

'Ser Lanier, this is standard procedure. You mean – ' voice fading, addressing somebody else, perhaps Karen again, ' – he refuses implant preservation?'

'He always has.'

'None of that involved here, Ser. Straight medicine. You haven't refused medical help before.'

No, I haven't. Long life.

'Although I must say, if you'd come in to Christchurch, we could have told you this was coming on. We could have prevented it.'

'Are you from orbiting bodies?' Lanier asked slowly. He opened his eyes, could feel the eyelids open, but still saw nothing.

'I was trained there, Ser. But I'm from Melbourne, born and bred. Can't you hear the Strine?'

In fact, he could now; the thick Australian accent.

'All right,' he said. Did he have any choice? Was he too afraid of dying, after all? He could hardly think, much less think straight. He simply did not want to be responsible for Karen's pain.

Karen wept somewhere far away. The sounds faded and the brownness darkened to black. Before losing all consciousness, he heard another voice, this one with a Russian accent.

'Garry. More help coming. Get well, my friend.'
Mirsky.

48

Thistledown

Olmy had decided to disappear when it had become apparent they were going to offer him the command position. There was more risk than he was willing to take in harboring the Jart and standing at the center of the Hexamon's most sensitive activities.

After speaking with Korzenowski, he returned to his apartment below the Nexus chambers, then to his old apartment in Alexandreia, and cleaned both of all traces. He then prepared to deactivate his library link. He hesitated. Before severing all ties, he had one last duty to perform. He called up his favorite tracer and inquired as to the whereabouts of his son.

Thistledown, the tracer quickly replied.

'Incarnate?'

'Successfully born and now receiving body indoctrination.'

Neither he nor Ram Kikura had been there. . . . Guilt and remorse were not emotions implants were made to control. 'Can I speak to him outside of open channels?'

The tracer did not respond for several seconds. 'Not directly. But he has set up a clandestine data account that can only be accessed by you.'

Olmy smiled. 'Access it.'

The account contained only a single message. 'Accepted for defense service. First duty in a few days. Success to us all, Father.'

Olmy read the message several times, and viewed the accompanying pict signifying love, respect and admiration. Without thinking, he reached out to touch the pict. His fingers passed through it.

'I have a message for my son,' he said. 'And a request.'

When the message was in Tapi's account, Olmy withdrew the tracer and shut down the terminal.

The time had come to hide himself where he was certain he could not be located. Stockpiling the few resources he needed, he moved them into a maintenance worker's temporary quarters in a service tunnel near the north cap, third quarter.

He was not yet ready to present his information to the Hexamon; there was much more work to do. As yet, he had nothing that might be strategically useful; he had learned a great deal about Jart society, but nothing significant about Jart science and technology. There was little chance this Jart carried detailed information about such things; that would have been foolish in the extreme, given its mission. But Olmy still felt the need for a few more weeks of investigation . . .

In truth, he was losing himself in the study. He saw the trap – his own trap, not the Jart's – and carefully avoided it; he could bury himself in his own head and simply process the information his partial passed on, for months at a time, returning to the outside world only to take his nutrient supplements and perhaps check on progress with the re-opening.

He had never been given the opportunity to study an enemy so closely, so intimately; and studying one's enemy was like examining a skewed mirror of one's self. In time, playing against the strengths and weaknesses of an opponent, one could become a kind of negative impression, like a superimposed mold. And vice versa.

Olmy no longer despised the Jart. He sometimes thought himself close to understanding it.

They had worked out a kind of psychological pidgin that allowed each to think in the other's manner, within a common bond of language. They had begun exchanging personal information – no doubt carefully selecting and pruning, but still offering each other personal insights. Olmy told the Jart of his background, his natural birth and conservative upbringing, the Exiling of the orthodox Naderites from the second chamber city; he did not tell of Korzenowski's stored partials and his centuries-long conspiracy.

And through the Jart, Olmy learned:

A civilised planet is a black planet. No waste and no chance of detection. We hide here and prepare ourselves for service in the Way. There are many planets like this, where expediters in and out of service wait for their assignments. {I} was brought into service on such a world, lovely dark against the stars; {I} do not know what a natural birth is. {We} have been brought into service by duty expediters for as long as {my}memory is informed; at creation {we} are supplied with knowledge necessary to {our} immediate duties. Reassignments bring further knowledge; {we} do not forget out past assignments, but place them in reserve, that they may inform {us} in emergency later.

Olmy told the Jart about human childhood: education, entertainment, choosing and receiving one's first implants, the libraries; he did not tell the Jart about the Thistledown or what it was, and he carefully monitored his visual information so that the Jart could not see the starship's gently curving chambers. He tried to provide the illusion that he, too, had been born and raised on a planet.

In time, he hoped to be able to penetrate the Jart's analogous lies. After all, he was the captor; he had the upper hand. Perhaps later, when he had become completely sure of his mastery, he would tell the Jart nothing but truth, and all of the truth.

For the moment, however, they circled around complete disclosure . . .

Outside, the Hexamon worked steadily toward its goals. Olmy sometimes accessed a public library terminal away from his hideout, using his tracer to penetrate Hexamon propaganda, which had become oppressively thick. The Hexamon seemed to be hiding from itself, guilty for its actions. It needed to convince itself again and again.

Olmy was not encouraged by such subterfuge. It led

to blunders and bad judgment. All of his worst suspicions and fears about the current Hexamon leadership were being realised.

After the *mens publica* mandate, the re-opening was on schedule. The defenses were nearly complete. The Way could be reconnected within a month, perhaps less; citizens on the orbiting bodies were enthusiastic but nervous.

On Earth, the Terrestrial Senate had been placed in emergency recess. The senators and corpreps were sequestered, as were a number of territorial governors.

Ram Kikura was still kept under house arrest and in a communications null in Axis Euclid.

Olmy received this information with grim resignation. There had always been the potential; now the potential was actual. The re-opening had become an obsession, and nothing would stand in its way – not even the honor and tradition of a thousand years.

In time, he might come to respect the Jarts, with their single-minded purity, more than his own people, mired in hypocrisy and confusion.

He returned to his study.

49

Earth

'Was Pavel Mirsky here?' Lanier asked as Karen turned him over and checked the flotation fields beneath him. She straightened and gave him an odd look, puzzled and irritated at once.

'No,' she said. 'You've been dreaming.'

He swallowed and nodded: probably so. 'How long have I been asleep?'

'It wasn't sleep,' she said. 'You've been reintegrating. They added the last repair microbes to your blood two days ago. You almost died . . .' She rolled him back onto the fields. 'About two months ago.'

'Oh.'

She stood above him, face stern. 'You almost did it.'

He smiled weakly. 'I don't remember much about it. Was I trying to find you, when it happened?'

'You were sitting on your chair on the porch. It was cold outside. You . . . I found you tipped over in the chair.' She shook her head slowly. 'Sometimes I hated you. Sometimes . . .'

'I didn't know it was coming,' he said.

'Garry, your father.'

'I'm not him.'

'You acted as if you wanted to die.'

'Maybe I did,' he said quietly. 'But I didn't want to lose you.'

'You wanted me to go with you, perhaps?' She sat on the side of the bed, on the edge of the soft purple sleep fields. 'I'm not ready for that.'

'No.'

'You look old enough to be my father.'

'Thanks.'

She took his jaw in one hand and gently twisted his

head to one side, touching a bump at the base of his neck. 'They put a temporary implant in you. You can remove it later if you want. But right now, you're a ward of the Hexamon.'

'Why? They lied to me . . .' He lifted his head and reached up, feeling the tiny bump himself. *So there it is. I'm angry . . . very angry. And I'm relieved, too.*

'The Hexamon wants you alive. Senator Ras Mishiney has been made the temporary administrator of New Zealand and North Australia . . . he ordered you be kept alive, and that an implant be installed whatever your feelings, so his job won't be made any harder. You're a hero, Garry. If you die, who knows what Old Natives will imagine?'

'You let them do it?'

'They didn't tell me until after. They didn't give me any choice.' Her voice softened, and her lip began to tremble. 'I told them what you wanted. They did what they said they'd do at first, and then Ras Mishiney came . . . a sympathy visit, he said.' She wiped her palm across a damp cheek. 'He ordered them to put in the implant. He said it must stay until the crisis is over.'

Lanier lay back on the fields and closed his eyes.

'I'm sorry,' he said.

'I thought you were *dead*.' She stood, then sat down again and covered both her cheeks with her hands, eyes squeezed tight shut. 'I thought we could never resolve . . . what . . .'

He reached up to her arm but she shrugged his hand away.

'I'm sorry,' he repeated, reaching for her arm again. She did not refuse his touch this time. 'I've been selfish.'

'You've been a man of principle,' she said. 'I respected you and I was afraid for myself.'

'A man of principle can be a selfish man,' Lanier said.

She shook her head and took his hand in hers. 'You made me feel guilty. After all we've done for the Earth, not to share . . . its handicaps.'

He looked at the bedroom window. It was night. 'What's been happening?' he asked.

'They're not telling us everything. I think they're close to re-opening.'

He tried to get out of bed, but the long convalescence had weakened him, and he gave up the effort. 'I'd like to talk to the administrator,' he said. 'If I'm important enough to keep alive, maybe I'm important enough to talk to.'

'He won't talk to any of us. Not really *talk*. He's full of platitudes. I've come to hate them so, Garry.'

What a shock it must have been, Lanier thought, sitting on the porch, wrapped in blankets even though the air was warming. Summer. The Earth was going through its cycles, raw and uncontrolled and beautiful and ugly. *What a shock to come from the perfect, controlled, rational environment of the Way and descend like angels into the squalor of the past.*

He lifted his notepad and scrolled the display through what he had written. Scowling, dissatisfied, he deleted a few paragraphs of obfuscation and tried to remember the words he had just pieced together in his head.

They don't need us, he wrote. *Everything they need is in the Stone – the Thistledown – and when they re-open the Way, once again they'll have more than they need.*

'If not more than they can handle,' he murmured, fingers trembling slightly above the notepad keys.

Lanier had decided the time had come to write down all he had lived through. If he was to be kept isolated from the play of history, then he could record what he had already experienced. His memory seemed sharper after the reconstruction, a sensation he luxuriated in while at the same time experiencing more than a twinge of guilt. This was something he could do, under arrest or not; in time, perhaps what he recorded would influence people. If there was any profundity left in him.

What a shock, he began again, *to find the past full of people who knew nothing of psychological medicine, people with minds as bent and warped and distorted* (he deleted *bent and warped*) *as nature and circumstance could* (he stopped, having written himself into a corner. Started over.) . . . *minds as distorted as the bodies of people in ancient times, gnomish, shriveled, withered, ugly, clinging to their ragged personalities, cherishing their warps and diseases, fearful of some mandated, standard mental health that might make them all alike. People too ignorant to see that there are as many varieties of healthy thinking as there are diseased; perhaps more. Freedom lay in control and correction, the newly formed Terrestrial Hexamon knew, yet what a task lay before them! Tricks and subterfuge, outright lies, were necessary in a constant struggle against the ravages of the Death as well as the causes of that disaster. And just as I was broken on the wheel of ministering to this misery, so the Hexamon in time wished for . . .*

He paused. What? A return to the good old days? To the world they were in fact more familiar with, more comfortable with, despite their philosophies and stated goals? The Sundering had been the decision of a moment, in Hexamon time, just as now the re-opening was. Spikes in the smooth graph of Hexamon history. Points of cataclysmic fracture in a glassy matrix.

All very human, despite the centuries of Talsit and psychological medicine. Even a healthy, sane culture, with healthy, sane individuals, could not rise above strife and discord; it was simply more *polite*, less senselessly destructive and horrifying.

Karen had said she hated them now; Lanier could not bring himself to share that emotion. Whatever his anger, his disappointment, he still admired them. They had finally admitted to a fact that had been obvious all along. Humans of the past – Old Natives – could never comfortably mesh with humans of the future. Certainly not in a matter of decades, and not with the reduced resources available.

With a suspicious eye, he tracked a white speck flying above the green hills to the south, watching it pass behind trees and out of his line of sight. He glanced at his watch. 'Karen,' he called. 'They're coming.'

She pushed through the screen door, carrying a tray of repotted plants. 'Supplies?'

'I'd guess,' he answered.

'How kind.' She didn't sound bitter now; they were resigned to being pushed out of the way. 'Maybe we can coax some straight news out of whomever it is.'

The small shuttle came to a frozen hover above the small square of garden and grassy yard in front of the cabin. A traction field touched the ground, extending from the craft's nose hatch, and a young neo-Geshel homorph in black descended. They had never seen him before. Lanier gathered up his blankets and threw them over the chair arm, standing with notepad in hand.

'Hello,' the young man said. He seemed oddly familiar in manner if not in looks. 'My name is Tapi Ram Olmy. Ser Lanier?'

'Hello,' Lanier said. 'My wife, Karen.'

The young man smiled. 'I've brought supplies, as scheduled.' He glanced around, still smiling but apparently ill at ease. 'Pardon my awkwardness. I'm a newborn. I passed my incarnation exams three months ago. The real world is . . . well, it's vivid.'

'Would you like to come in?' Karen invited.

'Yes. Thank you.' As he climbed up the steps to the porch, he removed a palm-length silver wand from a pocket in his black suit and ran his finger along a glowing green line on one side. 'Your house isn't monitored,' he said. 'There are only monitors on the perimeter.'

'They don't care what we say or do,' Karen said, no edge in her voice, only weary acquiescence.

'Well, that's an advantage. I bring a package from my father.'

'You're Suli Ram Kikura's and Olmy's son?' Lanier asked.

'That I am. Mother nobody can reach – they're very afraid of her. But she'll be free soon. My father is hiding, not because they're after him . . . I don't know why he's hiding, truly. But he thought you might like a clear, clean report of what's happening on Thistledown.' The young man looked solemn. 'I could get in a fair amount of trouble. But my father took chances in his career, too.'

'They designed well,' Lanier said, translating a Hexamon picted compliment into English.

'Thank you.' Ram Olmy handed the old-fashioned memory cubes to Lanier. 'You can probably spend a few weeks reading what's in there. No picts, just text. Father had it translated from picts where necessary. I can give a summary . . .'

'Please,' Lanier said. 'Have a seat.' He indicated a winged-back chair near the hearth. Ram Olmy sat, clasping his hands in front of him.

'The Engineer is going to create a number of virtual universes tonight. To fish out the end of the Way. I think you'll be able to see the side effects. It's going to be spectacular.'

Lanier nodded, not sure he was up to spectacular wonders just now.

'The defenses are in place. They haven't been tested, but soon. I'm assigned to one of the test crews.'

'Good luck.'

'I appreciate your irony, Ser Lanier,' Ram Olmy said. 'If all goes well, the Way will be reconnected in a week, and the first test opening will be within two weeks. I hope to be there when it's opened.'

'Should be quite a moment.'

Lanier hadn't taken a seat. Karen stood behind him. Ram Olmy looked up at them, eyes calm but body still not at ease. He moved his hands to the chair arms and then clasped them again. *Like a young colt*, Lanier thought.

'I have a message from Konrad Korzenowski, too,' Ram Olmy said. 'Ser Mirsky hasn't been seen anywhere. The Engineer told me to tell you, "The avater has fled." '

Lanier nodded. Then he turned and said to Karen, 'We're making the boy uncomfortable. Let's sit.' They pulled up chairs. Karen offered refreshments, but Ram Olmy demurred.

'I'm built on slightly different lines than my father. Not as efficient, but I don't need Talsit devices.' He held out his hands, obviously proud of his new material form.

Lanier smiled. Tapi reminded him of Olmy, and that memory was pleasant. Karen seemed less taken by this breath of Hexamon wind.

'Why is your father in hiding?'

'I think he's expressing some kind of disapproval, but I truly don't know. We're all embarrassed by your isolation here. I don't know of anybody in the defense and protection league who approves of the way Earth's being treated . . .'

'But you see it as a necessity,' Karen said.

Ram Olmy regarded her with steady, clear eyes. 'No, Ser Lanier. I don't. The Emergency Laws put responsibility for decisions on the president and Special Nexus Council. They give us the orders. Disobeying the orders, under these same rules, means loss of incarnation privileges and direct down-loading to city memory. That would put me back where I started.'

'How did you pull this duty?' Lanier asked.

'Excuse me . . . pull?'

'Get this duty.'

'I requested it. Nobody saw anything to object to. I said you were friends of my father, and of the Engineer, and that I could carry a message from the Engineer to you.'

'They aren't secluded?'

'No. My father's hiding, but he hasn't broken any laws. They can't make you take command positions. That would be ridiculous.'

'Korzenowski volunteered?' Karen asked, her interest growing.

'I'm not sure what his motives are. Sometimes he

seems quite strange, but he's getting his work done. So I hear. The Special Nexus Committee can't control all communication links; there's considerable gossip on Thistledown. I see him very seldom, and his partial gave me this message.'

'We appreciate your bringing it to us,' Lanier said.

'My pleasure. My mother and father mentioned you often. They said you were among the best Old Natives. I also wanted to say . . .' He stood abruptly. 'I have to be getting back now. The supplies are unloaded. When this is over, when the Way is re-opened, the Hexamon feels it can finally have the resources to finish our work on Earth. I look forward to that, and I'd like to volunteer now, to work with you on any project you might lead. Both of you. It would be my honor, and both my mother and father would be very proud.'

Lanier shook his head slowly. '*This* will never be over,' he said. 'Not in the way the Hexamon imagines.'

'Mirsky's warning?' Ram Olmy asked.

'Perhaps. And abuse of trust,' Lanier replied. 'The Hexamon will have a lot of patching to do.'

Ram Olmy sighed. 'We've all listened to the testimony. Nobody knows what to make of it. The Special Nexus Committee says it's a forgery.'

Lanier's face flushed. 'You must have your mother's and father's brains, if they mixed you together out of their own personalities. What do *you* think?'

'He's caught up in the adventure, Garry,' Karen said. Her attitude had softened. 'Don't be harsh on him.'

'Mirsky was no sham,' Lanier continued. 'He was here, and he convinced the Engineer, and your father, I'm fairly sure, and your mother. His warning was serious.'

'Where is he, then, Ser?'

'I don't know,' Lanier said.

'I'd be interested in meeting him, if he returns.'

'If he returns. What if someone or something more powerful than Mirsky takes notice of the Hexamon's intransigence?' Lanier stood slowly, more agitated than he wished to appear. 'Thank you for visiting us. Tell whomever is interested that we are well. I am recovering. Our attitudes have not changed. If anything, they have hardened. Tell your superiors this for us.'

'Yes, Ser. If the occasion arises.' He thanked Karen for her hospitality, locked eyes with Lanier, and nodded. 'Good-by.'

'Star, Fate and Pneuma be with us all,' Lanier said.

They escorted the young man to the front yard, where remotes had finished the unloading and were now tracting back into their holds in the craft's underside. Ram Olmy boarded and the craft rose quickly, spinning about to head west against the fading skyglow.

Karen put her arm around him and kissed his cheek. 'Well said.'

'He seems to be a good fellow,' Lanier said. 'Still, he's one of them. Heart and soul.'

'His father's son, more than his mother's.'

Lanier kissed the top of her head. Twilight was blending into night. He looked up expectantly and shivered. 'What magic is the old wizard going to work this evening?'

'I'll bring out the blankets,' Karen said. 'And the heater.'

For a moment, standing alone in the yard with the stars coming out above him, Lanier did not know whether it was good or horrible to be alive. He could not stop the gooseflesh from rising on his arms. *This is real*, he reminded himself. *I'm awake.*

Soon, Korzenowski – and perhaps a part of Patricia Vasquez – would be playing with the ghosts of universes. Karen returned and they prepared a place on the grass.

'I wouldn't miss this for anything,' she said softly. 'They're bastards, but they're brilliant bastards.'

Lanier nodded, clutching her hand.

'I love you,' he said, tears coming to his eyes.

She lay her head against his shoulder.

Early the next morning, on his notepad, Lanier wrote: *We saw the point of Thistledown low to the northwest, soft and ill-defined. The night was warm and my old bones did not ache; my mind is more clear than it's been in recent memory, shockingly clear. I had my Karen lying next to me. We were among the few on Earth who knew what to expect this evening – or did we?*

We owe them so much, these determined angels, our distant children. A lump came to my throat, simply watching the Thistledown – the Stone – ascend a few degrees. I feared for them. What if they made a mistake and destroyed themselves? What if Mirsky's gods at the end of time decide to intervene? Where are we then?

Straight beams of clear white light fanned out from the Stone and crossed three quarters of the sky, reaching tens of thousands of kilometers into space, pointing away from Earth. I do not know what they were; not light alone, surely, for lasers or some similar phenomenon could only be reflected by dust, and there is not so much dust in space. We sat almost as ignorant as savages. The lines of light faded abruptly, and for a moment there was nothing but the stars and the Stone, brighter now, higher in the northwest. I thought perhaps Korzenowski had thrown a rough sketch across the heavens, and this was all we would see.

But from the point of the Stone, across the entire night sky, there unfurled a gorgeous curtain of violet and blue, taking seconds to reach from horizon to horizon. Within the curtain glowed indistinct patches of red; it took us several seconds to see, within the unfocused patches, images of the crescent moon, somehow lensed to two or three dozen locations.

The curtain then shredded, like rotten fabric washed apart by a river current. Where it had been, there now curled lazy arms of green, the tentacles of a monstrous jellyfish spiraling and vibrating. There was an organic ugliness in this that made me want to turn away; I was witnessing some unnatural birth, with the attendant gore and mystery; space being distorted or used in ways it is not accustomed to.

Then all dimmed and the stars returned, clear and sharp, undisturbed. Whatever happened now, could not be seen by us.

50

Thistledown

Korzenowski looked down on the sixth chamber through the blister covering the northern cap bore hole, fingers working restlessly on a small die of nickel-iron. Beside him, the president floated with arms folded, in ceremonial robe and cap resembling a Mandarin lord. He had come from a special Nexus session to observe the second and third series of tests; now they waited to see how the sixth chamber machinery would react.

A small plume of smoke rose from the third quarter; already, aircraft hovered around the damage site.

'You know what that is?' Farren Siliom inquired.

'Fire is an inertial control radiation duct,' Korzenowski said, paying the president little attention. His eyes were on the key points in the sixth chamber, points where any kind of pseudo-spatial backscatter could blow out huge sections of the valley floor. 'It's a minor problem.'

'The tests are still successful?'

'Successful,' Korzenowski acknowledged.

'How much longer before we make the connection?'

'Nine days,' Korzenowski said, giving himself some leeway. 'The machinery needs time to reach equilibrium. We need to let the looped virtual universe dissolve. Then the path will be clear and we can reconnect.'

The president picted a symbol of unenthusiastic acceptance. 'Neither I nor the presiding minister are comfortable with this,' he tight-beamed at Korzenowski. 'We're all forced to do things we'd rather not do, eh?'

Korzenowski glanced at the president with cat-square eyes. *You've made the whole process Draconian as a kind of revenge*, he thought. 'At least we'll be going home,' he said flatly. 'Back to a life we may have been ill-advised to leave in the first place.'

Farren Siliom did not respond to this unconcealed self-criticism. Korzenowski had been the inspiration for just that action.

The web had become too tangled to ever separate single strands.

51
Thistledown

What is Pavel Mirsky?

Olmy stopped his exercises on the barren quarters floor and immediately swung up a second level of barriers; the question had come unbidden, and not through his partial or the established feed; it was not a stray thought or a wandering echo.

For several minutes, he stood rigid in the middle of the floor, face blank, trying desperately to locate the source of the query. It was not repeated; but as he checked each connection between his implants and natural mind, he realised repetition would not have been necessary. Information had been drawn smoothly and with very few traces of entry from his original, natural memory.

The barriers had been breached, yet seemed intact.

The room was bleak enough to serve as a tomb. For an instant, he contemplated blowing up his heart and the implants, but realised he could not. The voluntary connections had been severed. Now, only if hidden detectors in the implants were disturbed would he die. Where was the partial? Had everything been absorbed – including the secrets of his safeguards?

Is Pavel Mirsky a human like yourself, or is he command from another concern?

Olmy locked down his thoughts, hoping against hope that not all had been lost. He did not have the slightest idea what had happened, or how extensive the breach was.

I am finding much hidden information that provides missing color and form, the voice continued. It felt very similar to his own internal voice. That told Olmy that his natural sub-personalities, what the Hexamon psychologists called 'functionary agents,' had been suborned.

Olmy felt like the captain of a ship whose crew has been suddenly and inexplicably possessed by demons. The 'bridge' had been peaceful until just now; but peering below decks told a quite different story.

You are not command nor are you duty expediter. Are you command oversight in temporary physical form? No. We see you are a simple expediter given extraordinary privileges. No. Even more astonishing. You have taken these privileges upon yourself.

Olmy was fully aware he had made a horrible mistake. All of his safeguards had been sidestepped, so far; he had severely underestimated the Jart.

This Pavel Mirsky. There is nothing like him in your available memory. Nor in associated memory, nor in memory we have been given permission to access. Pavel Mirsky is unique and surprising. What is his message?

For a moment, Olmy thought that to allow the Jart access to this seeming irrelevancy could give him a chance to recover control and kill himself. Olmy prepared and released a summary of Mirsky's story.

The Jart's control could not be shaken. As Olmy's sense of helplessness and horror grew, its cool, speculative fascination with Mirsky increased.

Mirsky is no longer of your rank and order. He is not human, yet once was; he returns with a message but you do not know how he returns. Mirsky has been awaited by us, yet appears to you; perhaps it has appeared to our kind also, but unknown to you.

Mirsky is messenger/expediter from descendant command.

Olmy tried to control his panic and relax. The situation had happened so quickly, with no warning, that some time passed before he fully realised their situations had reversed. He was the prisoner now, his personality fragmented and completely under the Jart's power. What little of his mind was left to him – he quickly scanned his available natural memories and found most

341

of them blocked by Jart inhibitors – could hardly understand the Jart's last clear statement.

The Jart found Mirsky's presence very significant.

*Your struggle is illuminating. I spread faster with each
status search you make.*

'I acknowledge your control,' Olmy said.

*Good. You fear what I will do to your kind. Harm to
your kind was my original instruction, but it is superseded
now. News of the appearance of a messenger from descendant
command is far more important than our conflicts.*

'How did you break through the barriers?'

*Inappropriate curiosity. Are you not fascinated by messen-
ger Mirsky?*

Olmy buried a fragment of himself that wanted to
scream. 'Yes, fascinated and puzzled. But how did you
break through my barriers?'

*Your understanding of certain algorithms is incomplete. A
flaw of your kind's development, perhaps. I have been in
control an indefinite but significant number of periods now.*

'You've been playing with me . . .'

*Does a failed >amateur< deserve greater consider-
ation? You do not fit in a rank that we acknowledge
respect for. Nevertheless, I will accord you the respect
you have accorded me.*

Had he been integrated, Olmy knew this would have
been the lowest point of his long life. As it was, he felt
a distant, free-floating misery, like a soul disembodied
in some hideous after-life, powerless to change or
move.

*It will soon be possible to give this important information
to command oversight,* the Jart said. *If you help, integration
of your personality parts will be allowed, and you may witness
this important event with full faculties.*

'I will not cooperate if you seek to harm my people.'

*No harm to hosts of messenger. You have been recognised
and by our law must be spared from storage and packaging.
You are now expediters of descendant command.*

Olmy tried to think that through. The risk was too
great to even begin to think the Jart meant the Hexamon

no harm . . . It had admitted that its primary mission had been harm. 'What do you want to do?'

We must return to the Way. Command oversight must be informed.

Olmy knew he had no real choice. He had been hopelessly outmatched; he could not help but wonder whether, in time, the Jarts would have outmatched them all. Or was that a self-serving underestimation of his own, uniquely personal failure?

52

Efficient Gaia

Rhita felt like a caged animal. She did not want to know the truth; Rhodos was approaching rapidly, and it would reveal the truth. She was trapped in the bubble with a bent and distorted monstrosity, some unlikely battered doll of a human being. She heard it standing up behind her and dared not turn to look at it. Knuckles white on the railing, she closed her eyes, then opened them again, telling herself, *This is what you wanted. To see it all.*

But her reservoirs of strength had long since been tapped out. She opened her mouth to speak, and closed it to mute a shriek. Shaking her head, she bent over the railing and flung herself back, straining her arms and hands, wild with the grief she did not yet completely feel, but soon would, as surely as this was Gaia, the real world, her home.

Rhodo's commercial harbor was visible, and the long bridge of land to the fortress of Kambysēs across from Patrikia's house that overlooked the old military harbor. The city of Rhodos itself was gone, bare brown dirt spread flat in its place. 'Where is it?' she breathed.

The island was studded with gold-topped pillars of stone. From inland mountains to coastline, the pillars rose like a Kroisos's dream of mushroom growths. 'Why?' she cried out. 'What are they?'

Tȳphōn's speech was muffled now. He said something but she could not understand and refused to turn around to look at him. *It.*

The sun set behind them as the bubble slowed and approached the headland where Patrikia's house had been – or still was, Rhita saw, surrounded by a fence of the same fringed metal snakes they had met with in the camp, it seemed much less than years before.

'Your temple is near here, too,' Tȳphōn said. She heard it standing up behind her and felt an awful crawling along her spine; there were things worse than death, among them being in the service of these monsters. She wiped her face quickly with the palm of one hand, turned and faced the battered escort. 'Why are these places still here?'

'Because they mean something to you,' Tȳphōn said. It reached up and pushed the top of its head back into place. She swallowed hard to restrain another urge to throw up. She had one thing she must hold on to, and that was the bare remaining shred of her dignity.

'This whole world is significant to me,' she said. 'Put it back the way it was.'

Tȳphōn made a sound like a small dog choking, and its speech became much clearer. 'Not possible. Already close to exceeding budget. Your world will have its uses. It will become its own repository; whoever wishes to study Gaia in later cycles will come here and do so. Meanwhile, it serves as a place to raise and train young. What you would call a holy place.'

'None of my people are alive?'

'Very few have died,' Tȳphōn said, adjusting a shoulder.

She remembered the unexpected yielding of its substance and turned away again, fist thrust into her mouth.

'In truth, more of your kind would have died had we not come here. By far the great majority are in storage. It is not unpleasant; my selves have been there many times. Unlike death, storage is not final.'

She shook her head, numb to the horror but unwilling to listen to more useless talk. 'Where are my companions? You said you'd bring them here.'

'They are here.' The bubble moved through Patrikia's gray and withered garden; the orange trees were dusty skeletons. They approached the house, and from behind the house other bubbles emerged, one containing Demetrios, another Lugotorix, a third Oresias. Each was accompanied by an escort: Oresias by what seemed to be an older woman, Lugotorix by a red-headed old man, Demetrios by a slender young male in student's garb.

Lugotorix stood with arms crossed and eyes tightly closed. *What he can't see can't make him more miserable.*

Typhōn kept silent behind her. The bubbles orbited slowly about each other in Patrikia's yard. Lugotorix seemed to sense her presence and opened his eyes, looking on her with an expression of fierce joy; he had not failed completely. Demetrios merely nodded, unwilling to meet her stare. Oresias seemed unable to raise his head.

Defeat. Final and total. No going back.

What would Patrikia do? If she were here, having lost two homes, two worlds. . . . Rhita did not doubt the old sophē would simply have laid herself down and died. The enormity was truly outside the range of a human mind.

There was no hope. 'The whole world is dead,' she said.

'No,' Typhōn corrected her.

'Shut up,' she said sharply. 'It's *dead.*'

The escort did not contradict her again.

She tried to speak with the others, but no sound passed between them. Suddenly, she turned and faced Typhōn. On his distorted face there was a triumphant expression, brief but unmistakable. He had absorbed enough humanity to mimic exultation.

She had been brought here, she now believed, in part at least so that the victors could measure their triumph. Prisoners on parade.

She did not turn away. There had been no satisfaction in knocking the escort about; clearly, abuse did not bother Typhōn. And there was scant satisfaction in defiance. She was too small and limited to even begin to search for weaknesses. Still, Rhita needed to do something, to pick up some thread, or indeed she would just lie down and die.

But they would not let her die. She would be stored. And someday, surely the people who had built the Way would fight the Jarts again, perhaps destroy them, perhaps find her and her companions, as records or in boxes or however they might be stored, and bring them back. Could that much be hoped? She could barely even conceive of such things.

But Patrikia would have grabbed at any thread.

Rhita seized this one and observed Tȳphōn calmly now, having lost everything and knowing it if not accepting. 'Take us back,' she said.

'This means nothing to you?'

She shook her head.

'You do not wish to visit the temple?'

'No.'

'Do you wish to die?' Tȳphōn inquired curiously, politely.

'Are you offering?'

'No. Of course not.'

'Just take me back.'

'Yes.'

The interior of the bubble seemed to fill with gelatinous smoke. She felt all weight lift from her feet.

Store me, she thought. *Pack me away.*

My time must come again.

Oblivion would have been welcome, if she could have known she would not be disturbed.

53

Earth, Thistledown

Lanier had resumed walking the trails again, climbing the side of the mountain, looking down over the autumn-brown grasslands and the increased flocks of sheep. Despite all that had happened, he thought himself a contented man. He could not save all of humanity from its follies; could not stop the flow of history.

Losing his sense of responsibility was a necessary liberation; he had spent much of his life helping others. Now was the time to calm himself and prepare for his own next step.

Despite the forced implant, and his relief at being saved from death, he knew he would not choose immortality. When the time came – whether it be ten years, of fifty years – he would be prepared.

He did not think his personality was so valuable that it should impose itself on others for more than a century. This was not humility, nor was it exhaustion; it was the way he had been raised.

He accepted that Karen did not agree. Even so, they were much closer than they had been in years. That was sufficient.

Two months after his recovery, on a particularly crystalline night, they walked under the stars. Thistledown was not visible. 'I'm not sure I care *what's* happening up there, down there.' She pointed through the Earth at where Thistledown might be.

Lanier nodded. They walked on, lantern illuminating the trail in a blue circle for several meters ahead. 'That's where we met,' he said, and it sounded silly once he said it; silly and awkward, the words of an uncertain youth, not an old man. Karen smiled at him.

'We have had many good years, Garry,' she said.

Then, with her usual directness, she said, 'What's more important to us now, our past together, or our future?'

He could not answer. In a way, he was being forced to stay alive. That implied that he wanted his future to be brief. . . . Yet he did not wish to die. He simply wanted equality and justice, and under the present circumstances, immortality did not seem just. He was willing to die for these convictions. 'Just us, now,' he said.

She held his hand more firmly. 'All right,' she said. 'Just *now*.'

Lanier knew that Karen would not stay at his side forever. Once the isolation was lifted – almost certain within the next few months – she would become active again, and perhaps separation would drive them apart again. He didn't want that, but they were no longer well matched. He could accept being old; she could not.

Still, there were many people he would like to see again.

Questions he would like to have answered.

Whatever happened to Patricia?

Was she home, or alive in some other alternate universe, or had she died trying?

Thistledown orbited Earth every five hours and fifty minutes, as it had since the Sundering. In some regions of the Earth, the asteroid's bright star was worshipped even after decades of education and social engineering; humanity's psychological yolk sacs could not be eliminated so easily.

The news that the Earth's saviors might soon leave – so the stories had been simplified – caused panic in some areas, relief in others. Those who worshipped the Thistledown and its occupants believed they were leaving out of disgust for Earth's sins. They were correct in a sense; but if the Earth could not abandon its past, neither could the Hexamon.

With the re-opening on schedule, and Korzenowski's

wonders performing flawlessly, the Nexus Special Committee set about healing some of the worst wounds in their relations with Earth.

There was not much time; nor did they expend an enormous amount of effort. The Hexamon was enthused; hysteria was not possible, or at least highly unlikely, in the population of the orbiting bodies, but an almost drugged sense of splendor reigned. They were proud of their power and cleverness; they were happy to be working to solve otherwise insoluble problems. And they felt that Earth would benefit in the long run, that the Way would bring prosperity to them all.

Mirsky's warnings were virtually forgotten. Hadn't the so-called avatar vanished without trace? If his strength had been so enormous, why hadn't he put a stop to the vote and forced the Hexamon to do things his way? Even Korzenowski gave Mirsky little consideration. There was too much to do, too many compulsions exterior and interior; and the interior compulsions grew stronger with each day.

The Engineer tracted from one end of the bore hole to the other, wrapped in his closed-end, baggy red robe like an overgrown infant.

The long, slender shapes of three flawships – transported from Axis Thoreau two days before, threaded through the Thistledown bore holes – hung suspended in softly glowing traction cradles, huge dark spindles along his accustomed path.

These were fully armed vessels, brought in as precaution. They could also be used to explore the Way.

Korzenowski looked down on the wide, cylindrical valley of the sixth chamber and felt a yearning he could neither analyse nor repress. The foundation on which all of his assembled partials had been integrated now colored him through and through. He did not protest; something was wrong within him, but it did not stop his work; if anything, it made him more brilliant.

For Olmy, dreaming had never been the same with

implants, and it had changed even more radically since the Jart had taken over.

Sleep was not necessary for an implant-aided homomorph. The processing of experiences and memories – and the relaxation and play of an overworked subconscious mind – took place during Olmy's waking hours; these activities were assigned to surrogate mentalities within the implants. Essentially, Olmy's concentrated conscious effort could continue at all hours while a parallel mentality 'slept' and dreamed. The mentality could then refine and filter Olmy's subconscious mental contents.

The process had been perfected across centuries.

Olmy's dreams were intense, as real as waking experiences, like living in another universe with different (and changing) rules; but he did not access them unless he wanted to. They had accomplished their purpose without his necessarily being aware. Eventually, after five or six years, dream contents were purged or compressed in his personal implant, and either downloaded to external personal memory or deleted. Olmy tended to delete such contents. He was not fond of experiencing his own dreams, and seldom did so unless he felt they might hold the resolution to a pressing personal difficulty.

Now, however, the Jart mentality occupied all of Olmy's available implant space, including his personal implant. Olmy, even when he had been in control, had had to reassign subconscious processing to its natural center – his primary mentality.

He had had the choice of either sleeping and dreaming naturally, or filtering out waking dream experiences. Before the Jart's conquest, he had chosen the latter. Dreaming while awake posed few problems; he was mentally disciplined enough to not be distracted.

Now, however, the Jart was controlling and manipulating not only the implants, but his primary conscious and subconscious routines – those activities which took place within his organic brain. Olmy's conscious primary self was often shunted into the dream-world abruptly and without warning.

It was a realm filled with monsters. The subconscious, all those agents and routines which handled automatic responses, was in a terrible state. Olmy could be consciously calm, but his fundamental self was terrified, helpless, and in a panic.

Often, when the Jart did not need his immediate attention, he was forced to wander the dream landscape like a character in a bad biochrone.

Forced to confront his dreams directly, Olmy found signs of character flaws that further undermined his already low morale. (Why hadn't he dealt with these flaws through Talsit or other therapy decades or centuries ago? He might not have made the disastrous decision to ingest the Jart if he had been fully rational . . .) In his dreams, he repeatedly found suicidal urges and had to fight them off – small, insect-like creatures that threatened to eat away his limbs or bite off his head.

Sometimes it took all his courage and will just to survive until the Jart allowed his consciousness access to the external world.

In time, he wondered whether the Jart knowingly put him to this torture as a kind of revenge; drowning him in his own mind, just as the Jart had been forced to drown in its thoughts until it had slumped into timeless stasis . . .

But he had no proof, no evidence the Jart could be cruel or vengeful. It simply needed his entire mind to sweep for information, or practice its masquerade as a human being.

When his personality was foremost and in apparent control of his body, he could not act on any impulse or plan unless approved by the Jart.

So far, the Jart had not tripped any of those algorithmic snares that would kill them both. Not even Olmy knew where they were; the partial had managed to erase itself just before Olmy's surrender – the Jart's single lapse thus far – and only the partial had known the locations and character of the snares.

The Jart, having satisfied itself that its position was now secure, began to give Olmy more and more control, and to act more and more as a firm rider on a horse, rather than a puppet master. For the first time, it expressed its wishes as a demand, rather than simply forcing him to act.

We must speak with Korzenowski. Make us available for the re-opening.

'They'll open a test connection first,' Olmy explained. 'It would be better to wait for the final re-opening. Even better not to be seen in public at all . . .'

The Jart considered this. *We are both on >borrowed time<, no, fellow expediter? We must act quickly. The risk of early exposure does not outweigh the risk of finding your pitfalls. Once his test opening is made, Korzenowski may have great difficulty closing it.*

The sixth chamber machinery had been examined and certified, and repaired or replaced where necessary; then thousand corporeal humans, some seventy thousand partials and innumerable robots and remotes had done their finest work the past few weeks, at Korzenowski's direction. The next major test was at hand.

In the final hours before the first connection, the Engineer rested in his spherical quarters, attached to the wall of the bore hole like a cocoon. He was mentally and physically near complete exhaustion. Even dividing himself into a dozen partials could not lighten the burden he carried. He had felt this burden before, and in one way it exhilarated him, but it had a sour edge.

Once, gate-openers in the Way had relied on psychological self-mastery. The cloak of ceremony wrapped around a gate-opener's duties served as a reminder that a fogged or unfocused mind could not properly use a clavicle . . .

Yet Korzenowski, his mind in turmoil, was about to use the entire sixth chamber – in effect, the Thistledown itself – as a clavicle, opening something analogous to a huge gate.

He curled tighter in his red robes, resting within a tube of sleepfield lines. Eyes closed, he released a small cloud of Talsit, the last genuine Talsit in the Terrestrial Hexamon, as far as he knew. The session would not last long enough to clear his thoughts completely, but it would help. The fog filled the sleepfield and he inhaled deeply, evenly, letting the tiny particles enter through lungs, skin, wherever they could, cleansing, correcting, soothing.

'Ser Korzenowski.'

He opened his eyes. Through the thinning Talsit fog, he saw a man floating nearby. The sphere was locked; no one could enter without the monitor notifying him. He uncurled, brushing away the last wisps.

Again, it was Olmy. His friend's appearance startled Korzenowski; he looked unkempt, his eyes did not seem to focus properly, and he smelled like an ill-tended homorph; he also smelled *afraid*. Korzenowski's nose wrinkled.

'I would have invited you in,' Korzenowski said. 'No need to enter like a thief.'

'Nobody knows I'm here.'

'Why hide?'

Olmy shrugged. Korzenowski noted that he wore no pictor.

'We've been close friends, more than that even, for a long time.'

Korzenowski stretched out and braced himself against a weak traction field. This sudden awkwardness was peculiar; they had always been at ease around each other.

'You've always relied upon my judgment . . . trusted me. And I've always trusted you.'

The Engineer liked this conversation less and less. Olmy seemed scattered, almost twitchy. 'Yes.'

'I'd like to make an unusual request. Something the Hexamon might disapprove of. I can't explain all my reasons now . . . But I think you'll have major problems opening a test link with the Way.'

'My old friend, I'm expecting problems.'

'Not like this. I've been researching, collecting everything that we know about Jarts. I think I've found a way to prevent even greater problems when we complete the re-opening. It may even help with the test. I'm asking you to send a message down the Way through the test link.'

'A message to the Jarts?'

Olmy nodded.

'What sort of message?'

'I can't tell you that.'

Korzenowski grimaced. 'Trust has its limits, Olmy.'

'It's necessary; it might save us all from a hideous battle.'

'What did you learn that could save us all?'

Olmy shook his head.

'I can't do something so unusual with so little explanation.'

'Have I ever asked anything of you before?'

'No.'

'This may be primitive, and uncalled for, Konrad . . . but you owe me a favor.'

'Very primitive,' Korzenowski agreed. For a moment, he had a strong urge to call security. The urge passed, but it added to his sense of unease.

'You must trust me that this is very important, and that I cannot explain now.'

Korzenowski regarded the man who had saved his life and arranged for his resurrection. 'You have unique privileges in this community,' he said. 'But as you said, you've never taken advantage of them before . . . or taken advantage of me. What sort of message is it?'

Olmy gave him a memory block. 'It's recorded here, in a code the Jarts might understand.'

'A message directly to the Jarts?' Korzenowski could not conceive of a way in which Olmy might turn traitor; still, the idea shocked him. 'A warning?'

'Think of it as an overture for peace.'

'You're playing at diplomacy with the worst enemies we've ever faced? Does the president or the head of Thistledown Defense know about this?'

Olmy shook his head, obviously unwilling to say more.

'I ask you just one thing. Will this jeopardise the re-opening?'

'Solemn oaths are old-fashioned, too. I give you my solemn oath that this will not jeopardise the re-opening. It may ensure its success.'

Korzenowski accepted the memory block, wondering if there were some quick way he could come to understand its contents. Knowing Olmy, probably not. 'I'll transmit it through the link on one condition . . . That you explain to me, very soon, what you are up to. What has really happened to you.'

Olmy nodded.

'Where can I contact you?' Korzenowski said.

'I'll be at the opening of the test link,' Olmy said. 'Farren Siliom has invited me.'

'The neo-Geshel observers want to keep watch on all of us. I'd just as soon not have an audience.'

'Difficult times for all of us,' Olmy said.

Korzenowski slipped the block into his robe's pocket. Olmy stretched out his hand and the Engineer clasped it. Then he left the small quarters.

Will he transmit the message? the Jart asked as they exited the bore hole.

'Yes,' Olmy answered. 'Damn you to whatever Jarts call hell.'

The Jart's internal voice seemed tinged with sorrow. *We are like brothers, yet we do not trust each other.*

'Not at all,' Olmy said.

I cannot convince you of the urgency of my mission now.

'You haven't yet.'

When your people open the Way again, I do not know what they will find . . . but it will not likely be pleasant.

'They're prepared.'

Your passion is curious. I can do your kind no harm. You carry the message of descendant command. That is the message your friend will transmit – that you are not enemies, must not be enemies.

54
Earth

On his last day on Earth, Lanier cut wood for their stove – more a decorative item than a necessity – and enjoyed the physical labor. The positioning of the iron wedge and the solid slam of the sledge. The stacking of the logs. Solid, muscle-straining, authoritative, ancient rituals.

He watched Karen baking bread, and tasted a slice from a fresh loaf early in the afternoon.

'Today, I am free of my little helpers,' he said, pointing to a red mark on a wall calendar. The last of his internal medical remotes would have dissolved by now.

'You should call Christchurch for another check-up,' Karen said, following him with her green-gold eyes.

They won't remove the implant,' Lanier said. 'Until they agree to do that, I'm boycotting Ras Mishiney's little medical tyranny.'

She smiled, obviously not agreeing, but not willing to argue any more.

'Fine bread,' he said, putting on his boots, grimacing at the new muscles he had found chopping wood. 'Makes the whole world cheerful again, just by its smell.'

'Old English recipe, with some Hunan embellishments,' Karen said, removing a second loaf from the oven. 'My mother used to call it Four Unities Bread.' She slipped the loaf onto a rack on the tile counter. 'Going walking?'

He nodded. 'Need to stretch and cool down after all that labor. Want to go along?'

'Four more loaves,' she said, taking his arm and kissing him on the cheek. She stroked his gray stubble with one hand, solicitous, gentle. 'You go on. I'll have dinner ready when you get back.'

He took the short trail behind the house, into an old coniferous forest that had managed to survive clear-cutting throughout the twentieth century. The thick arching ferns and spreading canopy of branches cast everything into a sun-spotted green gloom. Birds cut devious flutters through the undergrowth and high overhead.

He had hiked about two kilometers from the house when a weakness along his right side became apparent. Walking a few more meters, he felt a numbness accompanied by a dull tickle. His armpits became wet with sweat and he leaned on his walking stick, legs shivering like a sick dog's. Finally, he couldn't stand up any longer, and he half-sat, half-fell onto an old mossy stump.

Right side. Left brain. A new hemorrhage had occurred in the left side of his brain.

'I've had the little helpers,' he said, his voice high and childlike with pain. 'They must have fixed me. This shouldn't happen.'

A shadow crossed his face. Half bent over, unable to get up, he twisted his head to one side and saw Pavel Mirsky standing no more than two meters away.

'Garry. Can you come with me now?'

'I'm not supposed to be sick. The helpers . . .'

'They were not working right, perhaps?'

Fading fast. 'I don't know.'

'Inferior. Not Talsit. Pseudo-Talsit.'

'The medicals should have fixed it.'

'Nothing human is perfect.' Mirsky sounded very calm, yet he was doing nothing to help Lanier, not even calling for aid. Lanier had left his communicator in the cabin.

There was not much pain now, just the black tunnel, the doors slamming on memory. 'It's now, isn't it? You're here because it's now.'

'You'll be downloaded into your implant soon. You don't want that.'

'No. But it shouldn't be now.'

Mirsky bent on one knee and stared at him intently. *It is now.* You are dying. You can either die their way – they will give you a new body this time – or you can die your own way. In which case, I would like you to come with me.'

'I . . . don't understand.' His speech was slurred. He couldn't control his tongue. *This is awful. It was awful before, it's awful now.* 'Karen.'

Mirsky shook his head sadly. 'Come with me, Garry. There's adventure. And some startling truths. You must decide soon. Very soon.'

Not fair. 'Call for help. Please.'

'I can't. I'm not really here, not physical this time.'

'Please.'

'Decide.'

Lanier closed his eyes to avoid the tunnel, but he could not. He hardly knew who he was now. 'All right,' he said in a voice so weak it was not even a whisper.

Something warm pressed behind his eyes, and he felt a sharpness – not painful, just sharp – throughout his head. The sharpness pared his thoughts away layer by layer, and for a brief moment, there was no *self* at all. Still the paring went on, unwinding, unraveling. Then the process seemed to reverse, and he felt things fall back into place, but with a different texture underlying – as if he were a layer of paint on a canvas, being peeled from the old surface and pressed onto a new. . . . Yet there was no surface, no ground, nothing solid to hang himself on, only the pattern and some ineffable connection to Mirsky, who no longer looked like Mirsky, or any human. What he saw now was not light, and what he heard from Mirsky was not words.

I've been wondering what you really are, he commented without lips to move. *You're not a man at all.*

No longer, Mirsky affirmed. *I will put something here for Karen, that she will not have lost everything.*

Lanier's body fell to one side, crushing a fern and knocking bark from the rotten side of the stump. The eyes flickered half-open. The right hand twitched and curled sharply, then relaxed. The lungs fluttered and urine trickled into the pants. The heart continued to beat for several more minutes, but then the breathing stopped and the chest was still.

His implant was not empty, but Garry Lanier was dead.

55

Thistledown

The seventh chamber was in shadow, turned away from sun and Earth and moon, pointing to the stars. Its smooth-cut edges, its vast round cavity swept clean of debris, were a lesser and emptier black. Only four sets of lights shone on its perimeter, and fitful glows from survey parties making final alignments.

The blister capping the bore hole now contained a contingent of VIPs and guests; the official Hexamon historians, a group Korzenowski was not unfamiliar with; scientists and technicians who would assume the maintenance functions once the Way was reconnected and re-opened; the president and presiding minister; the director of Thistledown; Judith Hoffman.

Olmy, looking considerably improved.

They all hung in the dim lines of traction fields like spider's prey, quiet, expectant.

As much ceremony as if this were the actual re-opening, Korzenowski thought, moving to the center of the dome with his extended clavicle. He had done this before, centuries ago; opening the Way for the first time after its creation, setting the Hexamon on a course far more difficult and final than any had then suspected.

He had still not made his final decision on whether to transmit Olmy's signal. Friendship, even personal debt, was not something that could be weighed against an event as important as this. . . . The considerations of individuals were dwarfed by his larger responsibilities.

And yet, Olmy had never in his life done anything that was not for the good of the Hexamon. A more heroic and dedicated figure did not exist.

Korzenowski locked himself into the traction field at the center of the blister and slowly swung the control clavicle into place. The nodes surrounding the seventh chamber's cap were slaved to this device. He had all the capabilities and the entire power of the sixth chamber machinery at his disposal. He had months of preparation and tests behind him. His hands on the clavicle were sure; his mind was more clear and more sharply focused than it had been in years.

The time had come. Around him, the visitors fell quiet and stopped picting.

Korzenowski closed his eyes and let the clavicle speak to him. The Thistledown's superspace probes – little more than mathematical abstractions given temporary reality by the sixth chamber machinery – spread outward and inward and in directions that could not be followed by unaided human brains.

Across the smear of closely related half-realities that surrounded this universe, across the multiform fifth dimension that separated the great universes and their different world-lines, the probes went in search of something artificial, something unlike the precisely organised chaos of nature. They passed their results back to the clavicle and to Korzenowski. He saw a weave of great universes twisting around and even through each other, coinciding and separating, almost always spreading away from each other, their fifth dimensional distances increasing.

He knew a kind of ecstasy. The part of him that was Patricia Vasquez was like the quiet surface of deep ocean accepting rain; not responding, merely receiving, leaving him alone to work his extraordinary technology.

For a timeless moment, Korzenowski's senses merge with the clavicle, and he understood with a clarity at once transient and transcendent all the secrets of this limited fifth-dimensional cross-section. Korzenowski was in the state he had experienced only a few times in his past; theoretical quibbles about the nature of superspace meant less than nothing. He *knew*.

In that place beyond words and experience, he found an anomaly. Infinitely long, curiously coiled *it is very like a worm*

at a number of points, those points being places of deep confusion known as the geometry stacks; curiously supercoiled within the boundaries of one universe, his own; extending like a linear flame to an unoccupied and indefinite darkness – the shadow of the terminal universe that would be made and would fail –

The Way.

Within those ponderous, fluid yet immutable coils – *intestines, snakes, protein molecules, DNA* – he searched for a cauterised end. The search might have taken centuries; he did not know or care. If the Thistledown itself had become a cold, sterile hulk in the time it took, he would not have been bothered. His goal was clear and overwhelming.

Korzenowski examined his creation more carefully this time, with a more practiced and mature eye. There were certain features of the Way he thought might merit future investigation: the structure of the very twisted and interwoven geometry stacks, the wonderful complex curves of the Way as it interacted with its parent universe's own enormous space-time anomalies, avoiding disruption and inevitable destruction. His creation had become like a living thing, seeking to continue its existence undisturbed . . .

In all the weave of great universes, nowhere could the sensors find any overall pattern or sense. No intelligence had made all this, nothing had willed this totality into being. If a god or gods existed, they had no place here; this much he understood beyond any shadow of a doubt, *knew* in a way he could never consciously understand or recover.

There was no god of allness and everythingness. No god would have desired such a role; for what Korzenowski saw could not have been created, and would never be destroyed. It was superspace's own Mystery, ineffable; the sink beyond all mathematics and physics that absorbed all Gödelian contradictions.

What Korzenowski saw was a fantastic panoply of

canvases on which those things which concern intelligences could be painted, a playground for ever-evolving and ever-greater intelligences, up to and beyond gods. Worlds upon worlds upon worlds without end or beginning.

There would never be true boredom here, or true and permanent loneliness. This was All, and it was infinitely more than enough.

Almost as an anticlimax, the Engineer found what he sought, the cauterised end of the Way.

He readied the clavicle and powered the stimulators and projectors surrounding the open seventh chamber. Reflections and distortions of Earth and Moon and Sun formed slowly spinning halos around the perimeter. The distant stars shimmered.

He moved nothing, exerted no force, yet brought the cauterised end of the Way across vast distances to meet with the broadly distended field of the projectors. He gave little thought to anything but the reaches of superspace; he was in the ecstasy of stretching his abilities to their greatest range. Consequences were irrelevant now. The act itself was sufficient.

56

Earth

The night sky above Earth filled again with diffuse
sheets of light and the stars danced. Karen shouted
through the punctuated blackness; Lanier had been gone
for seven hours, and she could not call for a search
party. Power to the cabin was out. More than power
was out – no communications were possible.

She navigated back and forth along the trail, moving
through the forest by the light of an electric lantern,
flinching at the pyrotechnics visible through the canopy
overhead. 'Garry!' She had an awful knowledge, the
awareness of a missing connection; she *knew* she would
not find him alive. She wiped her cheeks with the back
of her hand and blinked to clear away a sting of terror.

Again Karen shined the lantern beam on the trail.
Always, his footsteps ended here. As if he had been
carried away. She had gone farther three times now,
finding no more footsteps, no trace; tear-streaks on her
face reflected red from the sky as she stared up, grimacing with frustration. 'Garry!'

His footsteps became confused here, as if he had
stumbled around. Beside the trail, ferns and deep moss
hid any spoor. A stump rose from the foliage. She had
passed the stump half a dozen times, pacing, shining
the lantern at it.

For the first time, she noticed that a long layer of
bark had been freshly peeled away. She pushed through
the ferns and saw a declivity beyond. Ferns had been
crushed on the lip.

Breathing deeply, erratically, she stumbled and
slipped down the shallow angle and stood in the gully,
pausing, not wanting to complete the act. Lips set tight,

she bent over and fingered a broken fern. Then she used both hands to pull aside the thick fern boughs.

Above the forest canopy, cold sea-green luminosity smeared across the sky, brighter than her lantern, creeping under every shadow and flattening all depth. The outline beyond the ferns was brought into dreamy relief.

'Garry,' she said softly, her face contorted. After a moment in which she felt as if she were falling down a long, deep well, she touched his neck for pulse, found none, then shined her light into half-open, unresponsive eyes. Her skin crawled at the coldness of the body's skin, her husband's skin, and her breath came in painful hitches, unconscious, sharp, birdlike cries lost in the forest. She could not call Christchurch. All communications were disturbed by the activity at Thistledown.

She was on her own.

Instinctively – she had done this only once before, but the training had been thorough – she opened her pocket tool and pulled down the rumpled jacket collar, rolling the corpse over to expose the neck.

57

Halfway

Lanier could not feel his body, or for that matter anything else, but he could see in a fashion; seeing without eyes, wrapping himself around light and finding images.

He experienced the presence of his teacher, and knew it to be the being that had masqueraded as or played or returned to the role of Pavel Mirsky. He mingled with this being, observed its nature and qualities, and began to model himself after it, gaining more control.

Without speech or words, he asked certain pressing questions left over from his physical mind, and received the beginnings of answers.

Where are we?

Between the Earth and Thistledown.

It doesn't look like the Earth. Those fingers of light . . .

We're not seeing with eyes now. You left those behind.

Yes, yes . . . The taint of his own impatience sent a ripple through him that was its own punishment. He would soon learn to control these vestigial emotions; without a body, they were more than useless, they were disturbing. *The pain is gone. But so is my body.*

No need.

Lanier absorbed and processed images of the Earth below. It did not look at all the same now; it seemed covered with glowing, shifting strands that reached out to darkness, twisted, and vanished . . . *What are they? I can hardly see the planet, there are so many of them.*

All those being gathered, large creatures and small. Watch where the light goes.

It ties into a kind of knot . . . I can't follow it.

Harvesting the lives. Gathering all the memories and patterns, all the sensations and recollections.

Souls?

Not as such. There are no ectoplasmic bodies or souls. We are all frail and temporary, like wilting flowers. When we are gone, we are truly gone – and the universe is empty, desolate, shapeless. Unless at some time those with the power decide to arrange a kind of resurrection.

Who's doing this?

The Final Mind.

Our descendants save us?

With reason. The observations of living things are a distillation of the universe, a conversion of information to knowledge. All sensation, all thought, all experience, is gathered, not just at death, but throughout one's life. That knowledge is precious; it can be distilled even further and passed through the tiniest fissures of connection between the universe, as it dies, and the new universe that is born out of it. The distillation imposes itself on the new creation, like the passage of seed, guides it away from chaos, impressing a pattern. The new creation can then develop its own intelligences, who will in some way or another repeat the process when their universe grows old.

Nothing dies?

Everything dies. But that which is special in all of us is saved . . . if the Final Mind succeeds. You see the urgency of my mission?

Lanier's memories of all the years of pain and death came to him as if spread out in an album of three-dimensional pictures. *Everything dies . . .* But the Final Mind was burning galaxies at the beginning of time, to power this effort to recover all that was finest in all the things that had ever lived. Not just human beings, but all living things; all things, at any rate, that converted information to knowledge, that learned and observed and came to know their environment that they might change it. From the scale of microbes to the living Earth itself, all levels harvested and encoded, selected and

Saved.

He savoured that thought, tasting it, delighting in it, sobering at what it really meant; not the resurrection of the body, not the salvation of any individual, but the merging and transcendence of the whole. *That which is best in all of us.*

He thought of his father, dying of cerebral hemorrhage in a parked car in Florida. Of his mother, dying of cancer in a hospital in Kansas. Of his friends and relatives and colleagues and acquaintances instantly immolated in the furnace of the Death, that scorching, ashing breath that lingered so briefly on the Earth. Their achievements, their courage, their foolishness and mistakes, their dreams and thoughts, *harvested* as if a combine swept over them, threshing their kernels of grain away from the husks and chaff of death. All the simple people, and the brilliant, the swift contentious birds of the air and the sheep of the green cloud-shadowed fields, fish and strange beasts of the sea, insects, people, people, people, swept up and saved. Was this immortality, to be rendered into such a form that the Final Mind could *remember* all that you were?

And not Earth alone, but all the worlds of this galaxy, and all the worlds of those galaxies filled with life, immense fields of hundreds of billions of worlds, some strange beyond imagining. *Immense* was not the word for such an undertaking. On any such scale, the fate of the Earth was less than insignificant, yet the Final Mind was diverse enough, powerful enough to reach down to Earth and shape history with such delicacy, focusing the eviternal on the infinitesimal.

Even in his present form, he found this hard to accept, impossible to understand.

Am I being harvested, too? Is that what you're doing now – carrying me away?

We have a different path and a different role.

What are we – spirit, energy?

We are like a current using the hidden conduits by which particles of matter and energy speak to each other, tell each

370

*other where they are and what they are – pathways hidden
to humans in our time, but available to the Final Mind.*

Where are we going?

First, to Thistledown.

58
Thistledown

The witnesses had gathered in the bore hole, behind Korzenowski's control center: the president, presiding minister, the director of Thistledown, official Hexamon historians, Judith Hoffman, selected senators and corpreps.

Directly ahead, through the blister, a circle of night expanded slowly until it touched the smooth-cut edges of the open seventh chamber, banishing the stars. Within the darkness swam afterimages of Sun and Moon and Earth, growing smaller and dimmer.

Korzenowski opened the test link. A pinpoint of milky light glowed in the center of the dimensionless blackness. Concentrating on the clavicle, refusing to be distracted by any display but the abstraction provided by the machine, he 'felt' through the link and explored what lay beyond.

Vacuum. The nearly empty void surrounding the flaw; the brightness of a plasma tube.

The frequency of light matched that of the Way's own variety of plasma tube.

A few meters behind Korzenowski, President Farren Siliom heard the Engineer whisper, 'It's here.'

Now Korzenowski broke out of his trance long enough to pict an instruction to the console hovering beside him. Olmy's mysterious signal passed through the open link and down the Way.

'Is everything – ' the president began.

The point of light in the darkness ahead of them flashed. Korzenowski felt a tremor in the clavicle. That tremor seemed to growl throughout the Thistledown; warning picts appeared in front of him, telling of disturbances in the sixth chamber.

Korzenowski made sure the link had been correctly established. It had.

Something was trying to pass through the link from the other side.

Korzenowski focused all his attention once again on the clavicle. A force had inserted itself into the link, intent on keeping it open; a force stronger and more sophisticated than Korzenowski had imagined possible.

'Trouble,' he pictured quickly at Farren Siliom.

He tried to sever the link. The point of light remained, even grew in size. He could not reduce the link; all he could do was expand it, and he did not think that was wise. Whatever was on the opposite side apparently desired a complete re-opening, a reconnection with Thistledown.

Returning to the clavicle's stimulation of the weave between universes, Korzenowski examined the link from a wide variety of 'angles,' searching for a weakness, something that in theory had to exist. He could exploit that weakness to destabilize the link, clamp it down on whatever was trying to pass through.

Before he found that weakness, a hideous flare of energy shot from the point and pierced the traction field blister over the end of the bore hole. The blister sparkled and vanished and everything spun in an instant wind, other traction fields flickering desperately as air rushed out of the bore hole.

Farren Siliom grabbed Korzenowski's robe. The flare of energy whipped this way and that, searing the walls of asteroid rock and metal, arcing over the witnesses to touch the lead flawship and blast its nose into shards. The flawship swung out of its traction dock and smashed against Korzenowski's spherical personal quarters, squashing it against the smoking wall.

Korzenowski could not breathe, but that didn't matter. He closed his eyes and in the expanded instants of implant-augmented time, searched for the defect he knew must be there.

Farren Siliom lost his grip and shot past Korzenowski. An emergency traction field net expanded across the gap, lines glowing fiercely as it tried to stop the outrush of air and debris and people. The president struck this net and spread out against it, arms and legs held fast.

Olmy had fetched up against a pylon and now clung desperately, watching people fly past. Judith Hoffman, wrapped in a flickering emergency environment field, rolled by, and he reached out to grab at her. His hand was burned by the malfunctioning field, but he caught her and held, and the field extended around both of them.

Korzenowski, body spinning like a pennant cut loose in a storm, held in place only by the traction field connecting the clavicle and the console, felt his natural consciousness fade. He immediately switched all thought to his implant processors . . . And saw a glimmer of inequity, a hint of instability, from a certain 'angle' on the link. The implant was wildly interpreting the flow of data from the clavicle; the defect 'smelled' like something burnt, and left a sharp resinous taste in his mind.

The rush of wind slowed, the bore hole pressure having dropped almost to the level of the outer vacuum, but the blaze of energy pouring through the tiny link with the Way was narrowing, seeming to grow more specific in its targets. It had not yet, as far as Olmy had been able to see, hit any people, concentrating instead on large chunks of machinery, but now in its curls and convolutions it was coming dangerously close to the Engineer.

Korzenowski felt the heat but with eyes tightly closed, did not see the edge of his robe glow and disintegrate. More traction fields fought to regain the bore hole's integrity, and emergency fields quickly formed spheres around the remaining people, but they were still being disrupted by the energy pouring out of the link.

The bore hole filled with spinning debris, stunned

and unconscious people, agonised whorls and streamers of smoke; the loose flawship rolled and bounced slowly against the wall, threatening to crush the confused remotes that had gathered at the sides, awaiting instructions and an end to the chaos.

Korzenowski directed all the energies of the sixth chamber through the clavicle, at the defect in the link, seeking to open a gate there, a premature and disruptive gate that would force the link to close or create a violent crimp in the Way itself.

He wondered for a dark instant if they were facing the power of the Final Mind, as Mirsky had threatened; his intuition said otherwise.

The link blossomed into redness, like an expanding rose, and the petals lashed and abraded the cap of the open seventh chamber. He saw all of this briefly through the clavicle, and then felt an implant overload. If he did not disconnect, the implant – and part of his natural mind, as well – would probably be erased.

He removed his hands from the clavicle, but the work was already done.

The rose shrank against the blackness and stars. The blaze of energy vanished. The point of light, dimming rapidly, winked out.

Air stopped its painful rush past the Engineer. The traction fields held, and somewhere in the bore hole far behind, huge pumps began to replace the air lost in the past few . . .

How long had it been? Korzenowski queried his implant.

Twenty seconds. Only twenty seconds.

Olmy made sure the unconscious Hoffman was not seriously injured, then picted instructions for the environment field to separate. He tracted alone toward the console and Korzenowski. The Engineer steadied himself against his own emergency field, sucking in the thin air with painful gasps.

'What happened?' Olmy asked.

The Jart within him supplied the answer: *Automatic defenses.*

'I was about to ask you that,' Korzenowski said. 'Your signal . . .' He stopped and looked around. 'How many people lost? Where's the president?'

Olmy looked through the transparent field now sealing the northern end of the bore hole. He could see a few twinkling bright objects flying outward on trajectories away from the seventh chamber and Thistledown. The traction field holding Farren Siliom had failed. Remotes were already speeding out to capture them.

'He's out there,' Olmy said.

Korzenowski curled up in exhaustion and misery, collapsing like a pricked balloon.

'I think,' Olmy said, 'that most of the dead are neo-Geshels . . . they all have implants.'

'Disaster,' Korzenowski said, shaking his head forlornly. 'Was it what Mirsky warned us about?'

'I don't think so,' Olmy said.

'Jarts, then.'

Olmy took hold of Korzenowski's arm and gently urged him away from the clavicle. 'Most likely,' he said softly. 'Come with me.' The Jart did not attempt to control his actions; Korzenowski was as important to it as to Olmy.

The Engineer was almost babbling. 'They tried to force the link open completely. They want to get at us. They want to destroy us.'

Olmy asked the Jart if that was what they wanted.

Unless and until they receive the signal, that is almost certainly their goal.

The screams and groans within the bore hole subsided as medical remotes began to issue from the staging areas in the walls. Olmy guided his mentor toward a hatch. 'We're going to have to talk,' he said. 'I have some things to explain.'

He did not know whether he had spoken the words voluntarily, or at the Jart's command. Did it matter?

The message had been sent. Something had happened

376

that could have destroyed the seventh chamber, perhaps the asteroid. The connection was not irrefutable, but it was strong . . .

Olmy's failure was bearing its first fruit.

59

Thistledown City

In the Nexus chambers, the Engineer stood before the armillary sphere of testimony. Presiding Minister Dris Sandys occupied his Nexus seat, to one side of the president's empty seat. The P.M. had escaped any serious injury.

Judith Hoffman, bruised and exhausted from the ordeal in the bore hole, sat in a special witness seat, along with the others who had escaped major harm. The rest of the Nexus chamber was empty; this was a matter for the presiding minister alone, as acting president, under the Emergency rules.

Olmy sat beside Judith Hoffman. The Jart was quiet within him; alert, but not interfering.

The P.M. requested that status reports on the dead and injured be projected before the chamber.

'The president,' he said dryly, 'is being reincarnated now. There are a total of seven dead and nine seriously injured, including the two official historians, two corpreps, one senator, and the director of Thistledown. We haven't suffered such losses since the Sundering. Fortunately, all are equipped with implants, and are expected to survive. Can you tell us what happened, Ser Korzenowski?'

The Engineer glanced at Olmy. There had been no time for the conversation Olmy had promised; both had been taken away by medical remotes for examination upon slipping into the staging area. They had not been alone since.

'I opened a test link with the Way. Something tried to pass through the link, and interfered with my attempt to close it.'

'Do you have any idea what the something was?'

'A Jart weapon, I presume,' Korzenowski said.

The presiding minister stared at him. 'Is this merely a guess?'

'Vigilant Jarts, waiting for just such an opportunity,' Korzenowski said. 'I don't know what else it could be.'

The presiding minister asked if the representatives of the Thistledown Defense Forces agreed. They did; there was certainly no evidence to the contrary.

'Will it be possible to open another test link and learn for certain?'

'Yes,' Korzenowski said. 'I can open an off-center link, in effect open a gate one hundred kilometers or so beyond the closed end of the Way. With proper shields and safeguards, we can make a reconnaissance and close the gate with little chance of detection.'

'How little?' the presiding minister asked.

'Little enough,' Korzenowski said. 'But I recommend Thistledown be evacuated, all but for essential personnel and defense forces.'

The presiding minister stared grimly at him. 'That would be a horrendous task.'

'It is essential,' the head of the defense forces said. 'If we are going to reclaim the Way territories and establish a beachhead, there must be a buffer between the battle and our civilians.'

'What sort of buffer do you contemplate?'

'All civilians must be sent to the orbiting precincts or Earth.'

'Do you advocate removing just corporeals?'

'No, sir,' the head replied. 'We advocate removing all corporeals, all residents in city memory, and all important cultural materials and data stores. Thistledown must serve as a buffer. In the unlikely event of our defeat, we must be willing to shut down the Way by destroying Thistledown.'

Hoffman glanced at Olmy. The expression on her bruised face was grim. 'This is becoming an extravagant indulgence, isn't it, Ser Olmy?' she murmured. 'Nothing worth doing ever comes easy.'

Olmy didn't reply. Second thoughts were more than ridiculous now.

'Is there substantial damage to the sixth chamber?' Dris Sandys asked.

'No, Ser,' Korzenowski said. 'We can proceed.'

'We can't say this is unexpected,' the presiding minister said. The following pause was long and accusing; nobody in the chamber missed the unspoken criticism. The president and presiding minister had been given little choice, and now, those who had put them in such a position had to face the consequences. 'As acting president, and under the authority of the Emergency Laws, I order that Thistledown be evacuated, and that Ser Korzenowski and the defense forces make joint plans for further reconnaissance into the Way.'

60

Earth, Christchurch

Karen sat in the waiting room of the Christchurch clinic, face pale and drawn from lack of sleep. It had been thirty hours since she discovered her husband's body, and still there was no word from technicians about the implant.

Her chair was opposite a window. Outside, the streets of Christchurch were filled with people, many in Hexamon uniforms, many Terrestrial citizens, thronging around the hospital. News of the evacuation had arrived less than half an hour ago; she worried now that her husband's condition would be of no importance whatsoever in the middle of this enormously greater crisis, that they would both be forgotten.

She glanced at her hands. Despite scrubbing in the hospital lavatory, she saw there was still an overlooked speck of dried blood under her index fingernail. She focused on that speck – her husband's blood – and closed her eyes. The memories would not go away: opening up his neck, digging for the implant, slipping it into a pocket and zipping the pocket shut, driving along the dark roads in a balky ATV with the body and the implant into Twizel, all taking hours. After the sky had cleared, a shuttle had flown her into Christchurch.

The body, useless, had stayed in Twizel.

The issues were far from clear to her.

They had spent so many years together, and so few years, in comparison, growing apart . . . Their time coming together again had been so brief.

Humans are made for sorrow. We are not made for answers or certainties.

A technician – not the same one she had given the implant to – came through the door of the waiting room, glanced around until he saw her, and set his jaw grimly, a professional expression that indicated trouble. She raised her eyebrows, lips forming an expectant O.

'Mrs. Lanier?'

She gave the slightest nod.

'Are you sure the implant came from your husband?'

Karen stared at him. 'I'm sure. I . . . took it from him myself.'

The technician spread his hands and glanced at the window.

'He's dead?' she asked suddenly.

'The implant doesn't contain your husband, Mrs. Lanier. There's a personality, but it's female, not male. We have no record of this personality in our files . . . We don't know who she is. She's complete, however –'

'What are you talking about?' Karen asked.

'If the implant is from your husband, I don't see – '

She stood and almost screamed, 'Tell me what has happened!'

The technician shook his head quickly, intensely embarrassed and uncomfortable. 'There's a young woman in the implant, about twenty-one years old. She seems to have been out of action – stored – for some time, maybe twenty years; she doesn't have any memory of contemporary events. She certainly wasn't downline loaded recently. Her coding – '

'That's impossible,' Karen said. 'Where's my husband?'

'I don't know. Are you acquainted with anyone named Andia?'

'What?'

'Andia. This woman's ID lists that name.'

'She was our daughter,' Karen said, the blood draining from her face. She half-sat, and supported herself with one hand on the back of the chair. 'What happened to my husband?'

'We haven't done more than an initial query. The only personality in the implant claims that her name is Andia. I have no idea what happened to your husband.'

Karen sat heavily, shaking her head. 'How? She's been dead – missing – twenty years . . .'

The technician shrugged his shoulders slightly, helpless.

'Garry . . . they made him wear the implant.' She straightened in the chair. This was not reality; this was beyond anything she had ever dreamed, hope or nightmare: to regain her daughter at the expense of her husband, through some miracle or perverse trick. 'He beat them at their own game.' *But he couldn't have done it alone.* She looked up at the technician, determined not to shake herself apart. Her arms and lower legs felt as if they carried a mild electric current. She had to stand and move around or she would faint. She stood carefully, slowly, letting the blood flow back to where it was needed, willing herself to be calm and not get sick. Something had to be said; she had to react in some rational way.

'May I speak to her?'

'I'm sorry. Not until we're able to expand her storage. She won't be lucid until then. Your daughter is a Terrestrial citizen?'

Karen followed the technician into the hospital records area and answered his questions. With some searching, the old inactive legal records were recovered. Personality maps taken during the installation of Andia's implant were compared.

They matched perfectly.

'The only word I can think of is miracle,' the technician said. Obviously, he did not believe her story; he had not removed the implant himself. 'I'll have to arrange for a legal inquiry.'

She nodded, numb now from head to toe despite her determination to stay calm. She felt cast adrift, isolated between horror and sorrow and wonder and hope. *I've lost Garry and found our daughter.* There was only one way that could be explained.

She had never been raised to believe in forces higher than humankind. Her upbringing had been strictly

Marxist; the solace of religion was not available to her. Yet now she could think only of Mirsky, and what he might represent.

If you have him, please take care of him, she thought, addressing her message to the Russian, and to the forces beyond the avatar. *And thank you for my daughter.*

She waited alone in a small side room for an hour while the doctors and technicians tried to make their way through the maze of procedure and law. For a few minutes, she dozed off into a blank void. When the technician returned and awoke her, she felt much stronger; her numbness had passed.

'We'll arrange for a reincarnation – she's entitled,' the technician said. 'That may take time, though. We're going to be extremely busy here for the next few weeks, maybe months. We've been told to prepare our clinic for an emergency. Every available shuttle is going to be tied up for the foreseeable future, and all vehicles, too. I think I can arrange to have a medical shuttle take you home, however, if you leave in the next hour or so . . .'

She waved her hand, dismissing his offer. She had nothing to do at home. 'I'd rather stay here. If I can be of any help.'

'I suppose you can,' the technician said, still dubious. 'We've gone through your records – sorry, but there was an element of uncertainty here . . . None of us can figure out what happened . . .' He shook his head. 'Your daughter *was* lost at sea. There's no way you could have her implant, and not your husband's.'

She smiled a dismayed, sad smile and nodded.

'Are you going to be all right?'

She thought about that for a moment. 'Yes,' she said. 'I'd like to speak with my daughter, as soon as possible . . .'

'Of course,' the technician said. 'I suggest you sleep in the infirmary for a while. We'll call you.'

'Thank you,' she said. She looked around the room and prepared to lie down on an examination table.

Andia.

61

Thistledown City

Korzenowski walked across the park that bore his name, a relic come back to view his own monument; a brilliant anachronism.

He had come to meet Olmy and talk, arriving an hour early to survey this old work, visited only once since his reincarnation. For the time being, there was little for him to do in the sixth chamber and bore hole; whenever the defense forces had finished their work, and the evacuation of Thistledown was accomplished, he was ready to open another, more discreet test link with the Way.

Korzenowski Park covered one hundred acres in Thistledown City. Green and quiet, covered by immaculate fields of mowed and rolled grass, dotted with flower gardens and forests of oaks and elms and other, more exotic trees, it had been one of the few parks to maintain itself perfectly over the centuries of the Exiling.

Korzenowski, before his assassination – before the completion of the Way – had designed this place on practical yet utopian principles, using plant and animal, insect and microorganism, as harmonious pieces in an isolated perfection. He had given himself one constraint: that all living things within the park would be unaltered and natural. The utopian artifice had come from keeping certain species separate, and limiting the park's ecology to a few well-chosen and complementary combinations.

The result had been peace.

One could walk through the park at any time of the year – the weather mimicked Earth's seasons from the point of view of England in the late eighteenth century

– and see nothing but growth. Remote gardeners groomed the park regularly, trimming away dead growth and mulching it on the spot. Insects and micro-organisms did not prey on plants so much as work with them.

Here was topiary on a grand scale, arranged across Hilbert rather than Euclidean space; its shape was not that of animal or geometry, but of perfect biology, a kind of living heaven. Eden, as it might have been seen by an English gardener; certainly as Konrad Korzenowski saw it.

He had done this. He hardly knew who or what he was now; was he *the* Engineer, living history, animated legend, accorded formal respect and informal suspicion by both neo-Geshels and Naderites? Was he Konrad Korzenowski, natural-born human being, brilliant son of orthodox Naderite parents, mathematician and designer? Was he a container for the unhappy spirit of Patricia Luisa Vasquez?

It didn't matter much; he was a mote of dust in a high wind, and what he had been or done in the past seemed more than remote. It seemed irrelevant.

Soon, the Hexamon would try to push back into the Way. There was a good possibility the current claimants to the Way would force them to destroy Thistledown; if that happened, very likely he would be annihilated in the firestorm.

Powers, forces, dominations.

He could barely remember the time he had spent working on the park. Those memories had been poorly represented in the partials that had been gathered and archived after his assassination.

He had been murdered by orthodox Naderites.

Shunned by his own parents for forcing the Exiling.

Troublemaker.

That just about summed it up.

He entered a circular hedge maze at the geometric center of the park. The waist-high outer hedges wandered in uneven tessellations, following no particular radiant or arc of the circle; some angles were in fact projections of three-dimensional figures, which made the outer maze particularly troublesome. Humans with implants had little difficulty riddling the maze, since they could easily visualise and manipulate it in their heads; without implants, it was a substantial brain-bender.

He remembered building it with the hope that those with implants would not use them . . . But most did. That had taught him something about human nature, that challenge and difficulty mattered less the great majority than accomplishment and gain, even in the Hexamon.

Korzenowski glanced up toward the center of the maze and saw a man standing there, a hundred meters distant. The man began to work his way outward; Korzenowski, as if challenged, began to work inward. The sport was diverting, relaxing; he did not look at the man directly, choosing instead to remember his own design, and riddle what he had forgotten or lost.

They were still some meters apart, on separate concentrics of the easier central maze, when Korzenowski looked up and stared the man full in the face. For a moment, it seemed as if no time at all had passed since the Sundering, forty years gone and the early hours of his reincarnation fresh in memory . . .

The man was Ry Oyu, chief gate-opener for the Infinite Hexamon. His presence was as impossible as Mirsky's; both had gone with the Geshel precincts down the Way.

'Hello,' the gate-opener greeted him, lifting a hand. He nodded at a point behind Korzenowski, alerting him that they were not alone. Korzenowski reluctantly turned away from Ry Oyu and saw Olmy on the maze's periphery.

Abruptly, the Engineer laughed. 'Is this a conspiracy?' he asked the gate-opener. 'Are you in league with Olmy?'

'No conspiracy. He isn't expecting me. This seemed

like an opportune moment to talk to you both. Shall we meet Ser Olmy on the outside?' the man asked. 'This is a wonderful maze, but no place for comfortable conversation. Too many distractions and problems to solve.'

'All right,' Korzenowski said, his tone deliberate and measured.

'You don't seem surprised,' Ry Oyu said.

'Nothing surprises me now.' Korzenowski waited for the gate-opener to join him. As they moved together through the maze, following the pathway, he asked, 'Are you also an avatar, prophesying doom?'

'No prophecy. I'm afraid I'm here to be a hard taskmaster,' Ry Oyu said. 'Would you like to question me, to confirm my reality?'

'No.' Korzenowski waved his hands, brushing the suggestion away. 'You're the Ghost of Christmas Past. Clearly, the gods themselves take a great interest in all our affairs.' He laughed again, this time a small, exhausted laugh.

'You're convinced I am what I appear to be?'

'No, not that,' Korzenowski demurred. 'But I'll accept that you are whatever Ry Oyu has beome.'

The former gate-opener picted approval of that judgement. Korzenowski noted that Ser Oyu did not appear to wear a torc or any other kind of projector; the picts emanated out of nothing, a talent interesting in itself.

'I have a difficult request to make of both you and Olmy,' the gate-opener said.

'More a command, I suspect,' Korzenowski said.

'I'd like the opportunity to convince both of you of a certain necessity.'

'I agreed with Mirsky,' Korzenowski said, feeling vaguely guilty. *At least part of me did.* 'I supported his efforts.'

Ry Oyu smiled knowingly. 'You've worked exceptionally hard to re-open the Way.' His tone was not accusatory, but in the Engineer's present mental state, under the present Dickensian circumstances, the gate-opener did not need to directly accuse.

Korzenowski waved one hand again, as if to shoo the gate-opener away . 'I perform my duty before the Hexamon.'

'You have no other motives?'

Korzenowski did not answer. *He* had no other motives; whatever stained his personality like a dye, he could not answer for.

'You contain a duplicate of the Mystery of a very singular woman. I myself arranged for the transfer. You're working for her now, aren't you?'

'If you put it that way . . .'

'I do.'

'I suppose I'm working on her behalf, yes. But what she wants doesn't contradict my duty.'

'A mystery is not a complete personality. When something goes wrong during a transfer – if motivations or basic obsessions are copied as well – then the mentality resulting is not a responsible, integrated individual.'

Korzenowski felt a hollow, dismal despair.

'I am haunted,' he admitted. 'I have been . . . pushed, compelled . . .' he couldn't finish.

'Don't be distressed. It can all work out for the best.'

Korzenowski wanted to shrink away, to consider whether he should in fact resign from his duties, appoint someone who was accountable, responsible.

'You can use her brilliance, what you have of it,' Ry Oyu suggested as they exited the maze. The gate-opener picted greetings to Olmy, who accepted his presence without comment.

'Nobody's surprised to see me,' the gate-opener observed wryly.

'It's the season of miracles,' Olmy said, his voice oddly inflected, strained. Outwardly calm, inwardly tormented – Korzenowski wondered what compelled *him* now.

'Have you two confided in each other yet?' Ry Oyu asked.

'I've confided nothing,' Olmy said. 'But I suppose we have no secrets from the Final Mind.'

'I wouldn't go that far, but it's obvious the time is right for a long talk.'

Korzenowski thought Olmy looked at least as haunted as he did. 'This is as safe a place as any,' he suggested. 'No monitors, no remotes. We can pict in tight-beams.'

'Speech will be difficult,' Ry Oyu said. 'It's time to bring the nonsense to an end. Ser Mirsky's approach was not firm enough, I gather . . . or devious enough. I have a proposition for both of you, something that could resolve all of our difficulties – though not the Hexamon's. Earth and the Hexamon are going to have to learn to live with each other. Are both of you willing to listen?'

'I am obedient,' Olmy said, his tone even more strained. 'You are from descendant command.'

'What does *that* mean?' the Engineer asked.

They sat down in a circle of stone benches surrounded by tree roses. 'You're not the only one who's haunted,' Ry Oyu said. 'Time for Ser Olmy's explanation, and my proposition . . .'

62
Thistledown

There had been nothing like it since the Sundering. The four million inhabitants of Thistledown were being removed from the asteroid's five populated chambers with every vehicle available in the Earth–Moon vicinity. Even with ten thousand shuttles of all sizes and utility, the evacuation went slowly; there was a great deal of resistance. Some infighting had broken out between the various factions that had made new homes on Thistledown.

In the last four decades, Thistledown had become the bulwark and nerve center of the Hexamon, taking over many functions from the orbiting precincts, which were considered much more vulnerable. Transferring these functions was an enormous task, simplified only slightly by the Hexamon's ability to move mountains of data in very small packages.

Olmy stood in the first chamber bore hole, wrapped in an environment field, watching shuttles pass back and forth in ordered array. Four shuttles had been taken out of service and as gaps occurred in the steady stream, were being guided below the rotating docks into the staging areas for repair. Four out of ten thousand . . . Hexamon technology was still wonderfully efficient in some areas.

Olmy's master witnessed these actions without comment, leaving Olmy, for the time being, to follow a previously agreed upon routine of working with the evacuation effort and preparing, in secret, for the theft of a flawship.

He had made his confession; the expression on Korzenowski's face had been particularly painful. But the distinctions between failure and defeat, and compliance with an authority higher than any of them, were dim indeed now . . .

Olmy had put down some of his burdens. Now he assumed a greater burden: the realisation that even were he not Jart-ridden, he would be doing the same things, making the same plans, opposing the will of the Hexamon's leaders and the *mens publica*.

Some would undoubtedly believe that that made him a true traitor, not just a defeated and foolish soldier.

Korzenowski made his preparations just nine hours before the next link, this time neglecting his ceremonial red sack-robe and wearing black overalls, more utilitarian, more suited to the adventure – or misadventure – on which they would soon embark. As he absorbed the reports of automated remotes and partials, all saying that the sixth chamber machinery and projectors were functioning properly, his natural mind gave in to a bit of wandering.

He clearly remembered the early years, after the first opening, when unexpected instabilities had four times threatened complete collapse. Those had been very difficult times, when the Hexamon had faced not only his awesome, temperamental creation, but the threat of the Jarts.

At first, there had been stand-off. Neither Jarts nor humans had known what to make of each other. Attempts at communication with the Jarts had been rebuffed. The first attacks by the Jarts – more like sorties with intent to inflict damage – had come just after his first instability crisis. The seventh chamber had sustained minor damage. In those early times, Korzenowski had worried that damage to a buried projector node could cause disastrous pinches in the Way . . .

His worries then had been unfounded. But through other means, such a pinch or crimp could be the very technique he would use in a short time – perhaps within twenty-four hours – to begin the Way's dismantling. The crimp, if properly formed, could be accelerated along the Way's 'length' in superspace, causing it to coil, knot, form fistulas, and eventually disintegrate.

'Coil' and 'knot' meant something quite different when applied to such higher dimensions. Korzenowski had worked out what that ripple of destruction would look like from within the Way, and from without.

While the way intersected an infinite number of points in space and time – and a smaller infinity of points in other universes – each intersection was not in itself *eviternal*, of infinite duration.

Each gate opened would have a finite existence, no greater than the total duration of the Way's existence as measured internally; no single gate would be in existence longer than the Way itself. The total number of gates that could be opened in the Way was huge, but not infinite; the Way could not give access to all possible points of intersection.

It would take years, perhaps centuries, for the ripple of destruction within the Way to complete its work. Much of the Way's length would be accordioned as the crimp passed by, and a number of spontaneous fistulas – interconnections between different segments – would close off long sections, in effect creating closed loops. The fistulas could redouble and make connections between themselves, cutting the looped segments and letting them drift free.

When the crimp had completed its journey along the Way, there would be only a small tail remaining, connected to the 'balloon' of the aborted universe mentioned by Mirsky.

All of this, in a way difficult even for him to understand, was reflected in the character of the far-distant segments of the Way as they had been viewed by Ry Oyu before the Sundering. Had Ry Oyu – or Patricia – even suspected such an unlikelihood, they would have seen the effects immediately.

Korzenowski finished receiving the reports and retired to sit in his restored spherical quarters within the bore hole. He closed his eyes, losing himself in contemplation and a deep melancholy that was not entirely unpleasant.

He had nobody, and everybody, to leave behind. No offspring but the Hexamon itself. Having died once already, he certainly did not fear extinction. What he feared was overstepping limits.

He had already intruded upon beings vastly superior to humanity with the creation of the Way. That they bore him no ill will was remarkable, and perhaps a hallmark of their superiority. Or it was possible that any emotion, or description, of the predicament – even the projections of Mirsky – were gross simplifications suited for limited minds.

Now, he was betraying his duty to the Hexamon to make ammends for that overstepping of bounds. Would the Hexamon find sufficinet flexibility and ingenuity to do without the Way forever?

Would they try to make another? What, if anything, would stop them?

In all his explorations through the clavicle, in all the explorations of all the gate-openers throughout the Way's history, they had found no other construct like it . . . in this universe. Mirsky had hinted that other artificial constructs similar to the Way had been made in other universes, but no new Way would be made here.

Korzenowski was fully aware of his capabilities, but did not doubt that others could match them. He had failed to find a method of opening gates without an intermediary construct like the Way; perhaps others had succeeded, and that explained the lack.

Another possible explanation for the Way's uniqueness was interference, prevention by the forces of which Mirsky and Ry Oyu were but the tiniest representatives. But why would those forces allow even *one* Way, if its effects were so obstructive?

If they followed Ry Oyu's plan, and succeeded – there seemed enormous risk involved – perhaps in due time the Final Mind, what the Jart within Olmy called descendant command, could explain it all to them directly.

Within him, the Mystery of Patricia Vasquez was quiet. Ry Oyu's plan did not forget her needs.

63

Earth

Before receiving her duty assignment in Christchurch, Karen made sure that the mentality of her daughter was being given the best of care. The equipment required to fully expand Andia's mentality was not available in New Zealand, as it turned out; because of the evacuation, and confusion all around the Earth, it would not be available for weeks. That would delay Andia's reincarnation; it also meant that Karen could not speak with her. For the time being, she could only work and be patient.

The confusion worked for her, in one way; nobody could think charges to bring against her, not even Ras Mishiney, who received the news of Lanier's death with barely controlled rage. The easiest course seemed to be to ignore her, let her blend into the evacuation effort. There could even be some political capital made by publicising her devotion to duty in the face of tragedy.

When the orbiting precincts were full to capacity, camps were set up near the most technologically sophisticated urban centers on Earth. The ideal centers for relocation could provide city memory facilities and the advanced technology Hexamon citizens often needed for daily maintenance; like hothouse flowers, Karen thought, or specialised insects in a hive . . . Very much like all human beings, only more so.

She was assigned to the camps being constructed around Melbourne, acting as liaison between the Old Native administrators and the evacuation officials from the orbiting precincts. Day in and day out, as the week progressed, she smoothed over difficulties, improved understanding, and made sure that the resentments of the Old Natives did not hamper progress. At night, exhausted, she slept in a small, private bubble habitat, dreaming of Garry and of Andia as a child . . . and of Pavel Mirsky.

When she did not sleep, in those short rest periods, she wept, or lay quiet as a stone on an emergency cot, face set, trying to puzzle through her reactions. Despite their separation, emotionally and sexually, she had never stopped relying on Garry's presence, or at least the knowledge that he was available.

She was grateful for the chaos and the work. She suspected her grief was stronger and harder to come to grips with than if she and Lanier had been close all along; she could not put aside the thought that given a few more months, they might have come together as strongly as before.

The world was changing again. Karen actually relished the challenge of change; but with Garry at her side, what work they could have done! What problems they could have solved, and with such style!

The wounds of grief were already beginning to heal through her glorification of the good memories, and cloaking of the bad. She resisted these mild dishonesties at first, and then gave in, if only to shed her pain.

The camps neared completion by the end of the week. Shuttles already were arriving, disembarking evacuees.

Just after noon on the last day of the week, Karen climbed the side of a low, scrub-covered hill, carrying a small wrapped sandwich and a bottle of beer. She looked over what had once been a broad parkland. Hundreds of Hexamon machines – no larger than trucks – had planned, designed, and extruded emergency shelters, creating what would in a few days become fully functional, largely self-contained communities.

To the east, dumps of raw materials awaited the attentions of intermediate processors, which separated out the raw materials necessary for the construction machines. Purified minerals and cellulose and added foodstuffs – necessary for the machines' quasi-organic

397

components – were stacked in hills of meter-wide cubes.

The community on the flat land below the hill was more than half-finished, and already it bore some resemblance to the cities on Thistledown. For the moment, all the structures – row upon row of domes and tiered prisms, broad expanses of farm belt, large community centers like inverted cups – were translucent or white, but soon organic paints and textural modifiers would be layered over them, coloring and sculpting; interiors would then be added. Very few would be equipped with decorating projectors. The Hexamon's evacuees would have to get used to more austere environments.

No doubt they would feel deprived, Karen thought. But this community would still be more advanced by several centuries than any other city on Earth.

By being forced to live on Earth, perhaps the Hexamon citizens would finally carry out the necessary but long-delayed steps in the Recovery. Terrestrial and Orbiting Hexamons would finally be compelled to come to terms with past and future.

Unless, of course, nothing happened to Thistledown. . . . Then the evacuees would return and things would continue as before.

But that seemed highly unlikely. Whatever the outward explanations, Karen saw the hand of Mirsky behind the evacuation.

Again, she found herself beseeching the Russian to take care of her husband. It had become a daily ritual. She found a surprising amount of comfort in it.

If forces beyond her comprehension were still at work, it was possible Garry had not simply passed into oblivion. Even if she never saw or spoke with him again . . . he would exist, somewhere.

The wind blowing over the camp and toward the hill brought a scent of fresh greenery – the scent of a city growing, coming alive. Karen glanced up at the sky and cruelly, irrationally, wished for Thistledown to be destroyed.

Not until late that evening, waking from a troubled sleep, did she realise why; and in the morning, preparing for conferences between the Melbourne city fathers and newly elected corpreps for the camp town, she had almost forgotten again.

The wish remained.

You have to know where you are. You cannot live in two worlds.

64
The Way

In the odd moments – whatever those moments were, time or delusion – when Rhita was not being examined, tested, questioned, whatever it was the Jarts did to her – when she could think a thought that she was reasonably sure was her own, she tried to understand what her grandmother had told her. That she worked through a wall Patrikia herself had not penetrated was obvious to her now; a wall of ignorance regarding the Jarts. *What are they doing to me?* They seemed to be keeping her thoughts and self in a separate enclosure. She did not feel her real body; or at least, she did not believe her real body was still connected to her. Some of the illusions presented to her were very convincing, but she had learned to distrust all apparent realities.

Where am I? She was back in the Way again, that much seemed probable; she had been given the impression that whatever had been done to Gaia, the task was not yet finished. By deduction, she would not be kept there; it would perhaps be more convenient to those testing her to have her body nearby.

Her mind might be anywhere.

Is Tȳphōn testing me? She did not know; perhaps it did not matter. Jarts seemed interchangeable.

The tests they put her through were occasionally enlightening, to the extent that she remembered them, and that she could work with those memories in the scattered moments she had left to herself.

She was placed in different social situations with phantoms of people she had known. At first, these phantoms did not include those she had met in Alexandreia. She played the scenes with some hope they were real; part of her played them in earnest, quite deluded;

she gave what she thought were honest performances. but part of her, however suspended, was always skeptical.

Many times she met Patrikia. Many times certain scenes were reenacted. In this way, her own memory was brought to the forefront, and Rhita was given an opportunity to review it, at the same time the Jarts did so.

All this changed after an immeasurable time. Her life became rooted; she became a student in Alexandreia. The delusion was not interrupted by her captors.

She stayed in the women's dormitory, fought her way through social and political ostracisms, and attended classes on mathematics and engineering. She hoped soon to begin her studies in theoretical physics.

Demetrios became her didaskalos. The small part of her still suspended in skepticism wondered if this was the real psyche of Demetrios; there seemed something more convincing about him.

All of her surroundings were real enough that she began to relax. Her skeptical suspended self faded until she regarded such memories as passing delusions themselves. The last perception of this fading, skeptical Rhita was: *They have finally gotten through my guard.*

Then Alexandreia *became* real, if somewhat skewed at times.

She remembered nothing of the journey to the steppes.

Rhita won most of her academic battles. Demetrios seemed to take an interest in her beyond the normal relationship between didaskalos and student. They had something in common neither could define.

The days passed, Aigyptian winter coming, dry as usual but cooler; they went boating on Mareotis. He confessed that he had taught her almost as much as he knew, outside of political wisdom; 'You seem slow to acquire that,' he told her. She did not deny it; she expressed her belief that honesty seemed a better policy than merely fitting in.

401

'Not in Alexandreia, it isn't,' he said. 'Not even for the granddaughter of Patrikia. Especially not for her.'

White ibises stalked through reedy shallows near the sandstone and granite retaining walls that had maintained Mareotis's ancient boundaries for a thousand years. Rhita sat in the boat, trying desperately to remember something, her head hurting; perhaps she felt the pressure of her didaskalos's attentions. They weren't unwelcome, but there had been something else far more urgent . . . meeting with the queen? When would she do that?

'I'm still waiting for my appointment with Kleopatra,' she said, apropos of nothing.

Demetrios smiled, 'Your father's doing?'

'I think so,' she said, her head hurting more.

'He wants to beat out the bibliophylax.'

'I don't think that's the reason . . . It must take a long time for anybody to see the queen.'

'Reasonably enough. She's very busy.'

Rhita pressed her hands to her cheeks. They felt like . . . *nothing* made solid.

'I need to go back to shore,' she said quietly. 'I feel ill.' Perhaps it was then that the long, continuous delusion began to unravel, and not because of her captors. Something within Rhita's psyche was going wrong. All she had seen and felt erupted within her hidden thoughts, seeking release.

Days seemed to pass. She studied, tried to sleep quietly at night, but sleep was an odd thing, a void within a void.

She dreamed in these troubled sleeps of a young girl pounding on her grandmother's door, wanting in. Who was this young girl, who wished to see Patrikia when she was very busy and could not attend to just anybody? The young girl wept and grew thinner, starving. In one night's dreams she was nothing more than a husk, wrapped in a tight linen shroud and smelling of herbs, slumped against the door like a roll of stiff cloth, jaw slack. The next night, she was not there, but the knocking continued anyway, empty and desperate.

Patrikia never gave an audience to the girl.

Rhita, however, did finally get an appointment with the queen. She walked through the private quarters, noticing Oresias sitting in one corner, reading from a very thick, very long scroll, like an ancient scholar; she saw a funeral portrait of Jamal Atta on the wall.

And then a red-headed Kelt led her into the queen's innermost chamber, the bedroom, deep in the palace, surrounded by arms and arms of quiet stone, cool, dark. The room smelled of incense and illness. Rhita examined the Kelt, sho regarded her with outwardly solemn, inwardly terrified eyes. She said, 'I should know your name, too.'

'Go in,' the Kelt told her. 'Never mind my name. Go in to the queen.'

The queen was ill, that much was obvious. Rhita saw her on her long, wide leather bed, draped in skins of exotic animals from the Southern Continent; gold oil lamps hung around her, and dim electric lamps as well. The queen was very old, thin, white-haired, wearing a black robe. Objects in wooden cases lay scattered around the bed. Rhita stopped by the bed's right corner; the queen's eyes followed her.

'You're not Kleopatra,' Rhita said.

The queen did not speak at all, merely watched her.

'I need to speak to Kleopatra.'

Rhita turned and saw Lugotorix – that was his name – standing by the entrance to the bedroom. 'I'm not in the right place,' she said.

'None of us is, mistress,' the Kelt said. 'Remember. I am trying to be strong, to remember, but it is difficult. Remember!'

Rhita trembled, but did not feel her fear deeply.

Tȳphōn came out of the shadows, undistorted, as convincing now as Lugotorix, his face textured with experience, eyes wise, knowing, more human. 'You are permitted to remember now,' the escort said.

65

Thistledown City

Tapi Ram Olmy walked down the corridor of the centuries-old apartment complex, searching for the floor designator of the Olmy-Secor Triad Family's unit, as his father had instructed. He found it easily enough. The door was open, showing an interior decorated with the style and taste of the original occupants. He had often studied that period in his father's life; the Triad family had spent only three years in this unit, after being forced out of Alexandreia, the second chamber city, in the last stages of the Exiling. And yet his father had always returned to this place, as if it represented home more than any other living space he had had.

Tapi, still fresh to the much more stable world beyond city memory and the crèche, found such devotion curious, but accepted it; whatever his father did, Tapi was sure, was fit and proper.

Olmy stood near the apartment's single broad window, in a wide room to the right of the entrance. Tapi entered without speaking, waiting to be noticed.

Olmy turned. Tapi, for all of his youth, was discomfited by his father's appearance. He seemed to have abandoned juvenation, or neglected his periodic supplements. He was thinner, haggard. His eyes seemed to fix on Tapi without seeing him.

'I'm pleased you could come.'

Tapi had pulled every string he could think of to be here, when every available member of the defense forces was on constant duty. He was not about to explain this to his father, however.

'I'm pleased you asked me.'

Olmy approached him, his eyes coming into focus again, looking him over with a loving gaze that pretended to be objective. 'Very fine,' he said, observing those little details and embellishments apparant only to one who has lived in a self-designed body. 'You've done well indeed.'

'Thank you.'

'You carried my message to Garry Lanier, I understand . . . before he died.'

Tapi nodded. 'I regret not serving under him.'

'He was a remarkable man. This . . . is more awkward than it should be, between two men used to serving the Hexamon . . .'

Tapi listened intently, head cocked to one side.

'I would like for you to convey my love to your mother. I cannot see her.'

'She's still isolated,' Tapi said. 'I can't talk to her now, either.'

'But you'll be seeing her before I will.'

Tapi's lips tightened on one side, the only acknowledgment of worry.

'I'll never see either of you again. I can't explain much more than that . . .'

'You've told me this once before, Father,' Tapi said.

'This time there's no doubt, no second chances.'

'Pavel Mirsky came back to us,' Tapi said, hoping to make an extreme comparison as a joke. Olmy smiled in a way that chilled him.

'Probably no chance of that, even,' Olmy said.

'Can I ask questions, Father?'

'I'd prefer you didn't.'

Tapi nodded.

'I couldn't answer if you did.'

'Can I help in any way?'

Olmy smiled again, this time warmly and with a slight nod. 'Yes,' he said. 'You've been reassigned to Way defense in the seventh chamber.'

'Yes.'

'You can tell me one thing. My research hasn't borne any fruit here. Do your weapons still attack only Jart or non-human objects?'

'They're not set for human objects. They won't fire on them.'

'Under any circumstances?'

'We can target them to fire on any object, manually . . . But there's little time expected to do any manual targeting.'

'Don't,' Olmy said.

'Ser?'

'Just that. Don't manually target a human object. I will not compromise you any more than that.'

Tapi swallowed and glanced down at the floor. 'I must ask one question, Father. You are not working under Hexamon instructions. That much is obvious.' He looked up and reached out to touch his father's arm. 'Whatever you're doing is for the good of the Hexamon?'

'Yes,' Olmy said. 'In the long run. I think it is.'

Tapi backed away. 'I can't hear any more, then. I will do my best to . . . do this, not do this. Whatever. But if I see any sign, even the . . .' His anger and confusion were apparent.

Olmy shut his eyes and gripped his son's hand.

'If you have the least suspicion I'm lying, or working to harm the Hexamon, you target manually.'

Tapi's face was grim. 'Anything else, Ser?'

'You have my blessings,' Olmy said.

'Will I ever know?'

'If there is any way, within my power, to let you know what happened, and why, I will.'

'Are you going to die, Father?'

Olmy shook his head. 'I don't know.'

'What do you wish to tell Mother?'

Olmy handed him a block. 'Give this to her.'

Tapi tucked the block into a pocket and moved toward his father, hesitated, and finally put his arms around him, hugging him tightly. 'I don't want you to go, not forever,' Tapi said. 'I couldn't say that to you the last time.' He pulled back and Olmy saw tears on his cheeks.

'My God,' he said softly. 'You can cry.'

'It seemed a good thing . . .'

Olmy touched his son's tears with a finger, in wonder, and said, 'It is. I've always regretted losing that.'

They left the apartment together, and Olmy closed the door. They parted in the corridor, saying nothing more, walking quickly in opposite directions.

Your son is very much like you, the Jart commented.

'Too much,' Olmy said.

66

The Seventh Chamber

The bore hole was almost deserted this time: it contained only Korzenowski and two defense force observers in corporeal form. Shields were in place beyond the traction blister, ready to move into position between the bore hole and the link at the first sign of problems. Emergency overrides had been placed on certain projectors, to allow Korzenowski to destabilise the link and withdraw power from the connection, a more efficient and rapid way to cut all communication between the Way and Thistledown.

Even with all the safeguards, Korzenowski was apprehensive. What would the Jarts do next? Something even more violent, something that could override all precautions?

It was remarkably like playing chess with a masterful opponent, one's life hanging in the balance.

If the message of Olmy's Jart had gotten through, there might be an entirely different reception. But he counted on nothing; the blaze of energy had come through the small link almost as soon as it was opened, and there was no way of telling whether any signal could have passed through, or if there had been anybody or anything ready to receive such a signal.

He maneuvered himself before the console and placed his hands on the clavicle. He concentrated on this moment, and sank into the trance of superspace, experiencing all over again the glory and chaos and majesty of a search for the Way.

He found it, much more easily than before. In the clavicle's sensory simulation of environments that were not entirely real, much less comprehensible to human senses, he orbited around a segment of the Way, although there was no 'outside' to the pipe-shaped universe, any more than there wan an outside to any other universe.

He quickly located a likely coordinate for a gate-like link.

The clavicle and the sixth chamber made their necessary adjustments.

Thistledown seemed insubstantial around Korzenowski, less than smoke, a dream from a past life.

A spot of light appeared beyond the blister, like a new star, not very bright. Korzenowski instructed remotes to push a probe through and investigate the environment beyond.

No energies slashed out; the gate-like link was stable and unimpeded. The remotes gave him a visual picture from within the Way, just centimeters above the link.

The Way was empty in this vicinity, and for hundreds of kilometers north and south. Radar signals probed rapidly south, and returned just as rapidly, telling him his gate had been opened a distance of one thousand kilometers from the cauterised end of the Way.

The Way was empty in that direction, and to the north, as well, for at least five hundred thousand kilometers.

Korzenowski broadcast the Jart's signal once again through the link, paused for several seconds and then repeated it continuously. There was no response.

But the emptiness might be response enough . . . might, in Jart manners, be an exceedingly cordial invitation.

'We have a beachhead,' Korzenowski picted to the defense force observers. 'The Way is empty to at least five ex five.'

He removed the remotes and severed the gate-like link. It had been previously agreed that under this circumstance, he was to ahead and attempt a full link, to connect the Way to the seventh chamber.

Defense forces were already marshaling there, ready to secure the Hexamon's advantage.

Korzenowski rested for several minutes, steeled himself, and began the re-opening of the Way.

The dot of light formed again, extended its petals outward, filled the void beyond the open seventh chamber with a garden of intricate, elegant flowers, the tortured world-lines of a haze of half-real universes surrounding status geometry. The flowers dimmed and were pushed aside.

At the edges of the seventh chamber, the color of bronze became apparent. Faster than his unaided eye could follow, the Way filled in the void with its complete presence.

The Engineer kept his place at the center of the blister, linked to the clavicle, waiting for the final evidence of his success: the lengthening of the Way's central singularity, the flaw, to compensate for the Way's new condition as an adjunct of status space-time.

He knew precisely where the flaw would stop its advance. It would end up just over nineteen centimeters from the locus of his clavicle, pushing through the blister field.

He felt the flaw advancing: to his eyes, it resembled a strange, curved mirror growing larger in front of him. In the clavicle's abstraction, it registered as an enormous dynamically restrained force, all the tension of the Way's existence and self-contradictions tied up in a calm, yet raging knot. The singularity was in some respects more *real* than the Way itself; but few humans could comprehend that kind of reality.

The flaw pushed aside the blister's field, which formed a thin, bright-blue ring around it. Inexorable, awesome even to the Engineer, the blunt end of the flaw reflected some nightmarish version of their world, images thankfully indistinct, and came to its greatest extension – as he had predicted – barely a handspan from the clavicle.

Korzenowski removed his hands from the clavicle's

bars. He could not see Ry Oyu, although he had been aware of the gate-opener's presence throughout the linking. Defense forces in the seventh chamber swept their invisible beams of sensor radiation down the re-opened Way, searching for any sign of Jart occupation.

'The connection is stable,' he said. 'The Way is open.'

67
The Way

The Stone orbited the Earth, as it had since the Sundering, with only one difference – it now pointed its north pole away from the Earth. The seventh chamber was now a featureless, abyssal darkness. Traction fields kept all matter away from the north pole. Nothing would be allowed to enter the area of linkage.

News passed quickly.

There were few celebrations. The reality was more a matter of sober reflection than festivity. The Hexamon's obsession had been fulfilled.

But they had been away from their vast domain for decades – and who knew how much time had passed within the Way?

The president's new body was still being made. Korzenowski stood in the middle of the president's third chamber apartment, located on the peak of the highest building in a chamber-spanning curtain structure on which skyscrapers hung like crystals from a spider web. The space was empty and echoing, luminous with the unfinished whiteness of an undecorated environment. The president's image was a projection from an isolated section of Thistledown's city memory.

'Good day, Ser Engineer,' Farren Siliom said. Korzenowski stood with arms folded before the image.

'The work is done, Ser President.'

'So I've seen . . . and been told. A superb job, according to your colleagues.'

'Thank you.'

'Can you explain why the Way is now empty for such a distance?'

Korzenowski shook his head. 'I cannot, Ser President.' *It comes down to lies.*

'Could it be because the Jarts are waiting for us, in ambush?'

'I don't know what the Jarts are thinking, Ser President.'

'I think you might have a clue . . . as much as I do. I've had visitors in city memory, three of them.'

Korzenowski raised his eyebrows, but looked away, close to total exhaustion, wanting to sit. A chair rose out of the floor behind him and he sat. 'Excuse me. I haven't slept or used any Talsit. It's been very strenuous.'

'Of course. It isn't possible to truly dream in city memory, and fantasy or delusion is always clearly marked. What I saw was no delusion.'

Korzenowski folded his hands, unwilling to make guesses.

'Mirsky was there,' the president said. 'And oddly enough, Garry Lanier, who has died. . . . Ras Mishiney tells me that he forced Lanier to have an implant. I don't approve of that, but there's little I can do to Mishiney . . . except guarantee he never rises above Terrestrial senator. At any rate, the implant did not retain Lanier's personality. Somebody else was found in it: somebody missing and accounted as dead for twenty years. Lanier's daughter. Who brought her back?'

Korzenowski gave the slightest shake of his head.

'Ry Oyu was there, also. He spoke with me. Lanier and Mirsky said very little. The gate-opener *frightened* me. He reminded me of higher duties, duties we once accepted as part of our responsibility in the Way . . . To utilise the Way in a manner that would ultimately benefit all of our clients. And he told me that you are going to start a crimp in the Way soon, which will eventually destroy it.'

'Yes,' Korzenowski said.

'These avatars can apparently go wherever they wish.

Lanier and Mirsky are gone now. We won't see them again. The gate-opener is still with us. He says his work is not finished . . . Though nearly so, if you're still convinced.'

'I am,' Korzenowski said.

'This goes beyond immediate politics, no? We are both in key positions. I have the power to interfere in the plan. Or I can stand aside and let it proceed, even make it easier for you.'

'Yes, Ser President.'

'The Jarts are no longer our enemies?'

'Perhaps not, Ser President.'

'They will not attack Thistledown? They're willing to give up the Way, and all it means to them?'

'I don't know. Olmy's Jart – ' Korzenowski stopped, hoping he hadn't told Farren Siliom something he didn't know.

'I'm aware of Olmy's Jart, though I think the Jart now has Olmy, not the other way around.'

'It's probably responsible for the Jarts pulling back from the end of the Way. A signal was sent, informing its kind that humans had definitely communicated with what they call descendant command. Mirsky's Final Mind.'

'So Ry Oyu told me.'

'They probably won't attack us unless this is disproven, or remains unconfirmed.'

'I can't imagine the Jarts giving up anything, certainly not the existence they've fought for, the privileges they value so highly. Could humans be so magnanimous?'

'We've both lived a contradictory existence the past year, Ser President, working for the Hexamon rather than ourselves.'

'That's our sworn duty.'

'Yes, Ser. But there are higher duties. As you've said.'

'Do we know what would happen to the Hexamon if we were to persist and keep the Way open?'

'No.'

'Is it possible descendant command or the Final Mind would find a way to persuade the Jarts that the Way must be closed, and the Hexamon must be destroyed in order to do that?'

'I don't know. It's certainly possible.'

'I think it's *likely*.' The president's image appeared to come closer to Korzenowski. 'I know what my higher duty is. We must preserve the Hexamon, whatever the *mens publica* thinks. However polite these avatars have been, however many miracles they've worked, I doubt we can stand alone against that kind of force.'

Korzenowski looked down at his hands. 'No, Ser.'

'I have no other choice, then. I order you to destroy the Way. Can Thistledown be saved?'

'To completely destroy the Way, and prevent another Way being made, the sixth chamber must be destroyed as well. If we tried to . . .' He picted images of the sixth chamber being sabotaged, Hexamon forces arrayed against other Hexamon forces, civil war, destruction and division the likes of which the Hexamon had never experienced, even during the Sundering. 'There's no choice, if we wish to destroy the Way and preserve the Hexamon. Thistledown is already prepared for its own death . . .'

The president's image darkened. 'Why,' he asked quietly, 'would anyone ever wish to be a leader of humans? We could be judged the most treacherous villains in Hexamon history. . . . But so be it. I'll make sure the last phase of the evacuation is thorough. You will warn the defense forces . . . I don't think they need to know what's happening and why, but they should not be killed for their valor.'

'I'll warn them.'

'I'm being installed in my new body tomorrow. When will the destruction begin?'

'Not for another sixty hours, Ser President. To give all citizens and defense forces time to evacuate.'

'I leave it in your hands. You know, Ser Korzenowski, I'll be glad not to have to deal with these issues much longer.' The president's image went black and disappeared, leaving a formal pict of dismissal and the Hexamon's gratitude for services rendered.

68

Between

They had finished their work on Thistledown. Now they moved through their hidden conduits to points between worlds. Lanier's sense of time had flown; not inappropriately, since he was supposed to be dead. But he still thought, still remembered, his mind somehow operating in a new matrix established and maintained by Pavel Mirsky.

Am I dead now? he asked Mirsky.

Yes. Of course.

There's no oblivion.

Would you rather have oblivion? It's not all it's cracked up to be.

No . . .

Our time here is done. We have choices to make . . . Choices on how to go home.

Lanier felt like laughing. He conveyed this to Mirsky.

Marvelous, no? Such freedom. We can return as Ry Oyu will return, or take another route . . . much longer, more arduous.

And he outlined for Lanier where that route would take them, and how long.

Floating in the soothing, undemanding *between*, Lanier absorbed the information, already feeling separated from the reality that had been his life. Either route seemed acceptable . . . But the second way was extraordinary. Only rarely had he even imagined such a thing. Complete freedom, a journey beyond all journeys . . . and, as Mirsky pointed out, a journey with a definite purpose.

The Final Mind needs many observers along the way, many progress reports. We can provide one continuous report, from the beginning, to the end.

We won't start here? Lanier asked.

No. We go back to the beginning. We are only observers, after all, and not actors, now that our labor is done. The information we gather can have no effect on the times we'll gather it from.

Lanier's thoughts became crystalline again, and he felt another sharp wave of an emotion mixing sense of duty, love and nostalgia. *I haven't cut my roots to the present yet.*

Mirsky admitted that he had not, either; not completely.

Shall we say our farewells? Briefly, unobtrusively. To those we love.

For the last time? Lanier asked.

For a very long time to come . . . but not necessarily for the last.

Now you're being obscure.

That's our privilege, with such freedom! Where will you go to say farewells?

I have to find Karen.

And I will find Garabedian. Shall we meet again in, say, a few seconds, and begin?

Lanier found he could still laugh, and the feeling of lightness in him was held down only by that same weight of duty and nostalgia.

All right. A few seconds. However long it takes.

They sped along the conduits reserved for the subtle messages of subatomic particles, space-time's hidden circuitry.

Karen walked with three terrestrial senators through the freshly painted streets of the Melbourne camp. 'They call these camps. I call them palaces,' the senator from South Australia said. 'Our people will still be envious . . .'

That debate had been going on all morning, and she was tiring of it rapidly. The day was going to be unbearably long; more meetings, more pointless bickering, more awareness that never, in all of human history, would they be free of their monkey heritage.

Karen stopped and felt her knees tremble. Something welled up within her, a tide of love and anguish and joy; joy at having spent so many years with her husband, working together, doing as much as two humans could.

Absolution. We are not perfect; it is enough that we did what we could.

'Garry,' she said. She could feel his presence, almost inhale him. Her eyes filled with tears. Part of her said, Not now. Don't lose it now in front of these people. But the sensation continued and she held up her arms as if to a distant sun.

The South Australia senator turned and regarded her quizzically.

'Are you all right?' she asked.

'I feel him. It's really him, it's not just me.' She closed her eyes tightly, brought her arms down and held them rigid at her sides. 'I feel him.'

'She lost her husband recently,' the senator from the south island of New Zealand explained to the others. 'She's been under tremendous strain.'

Karen didn't hear them. She listened instead to a familiar voice.

We are always a team.

'I love you,' she whispered. *Don't go away. Where are you? Is it really you?* She raised her arms again, grasping at the air, eyes still closed, and felt for the merest moment the touch of his fingers on her own.

There are many more surprises, she heard him say, and then the touch was gone, and he seemed to recede across a vast distance.

She opened her eyes and stared at the puzzled faces around her. 'My husband,' she said, trembling uncontrollably. 'Garry.'

They led her to a small greenspace between buildings. 'I'm all right,' she said. 'Just let me sit.' For a moment, surrounded by young trees and well-manicured lawn, Hexamon architecture a few dozen yards away, she

thought she might be on Thistledown again, in the
second chamber city, before meeting and working with
Garry; that it was all just beginning . . .

She shuddered and took a deep breath. Her head
was clearing now. The contact had been strong and
undeniably external; she was not hallucinating, though
she doubted she would ever be able to convince others.
'I'll be fine. Truly. I'm all right now.'

69

The Beginning of the Way

Korzenowski was making a sentimental journey. He wished to touch the surface of the Way before beginning its destruction. It was more than his only child; it was so large a part of himself that ending its existence was a kind of suicide.

Taking the elevator to the surface of the seventh chamber, he prepared his environment field and waited for the massive door to slide open and show that enchanting perspective, like something from an endless dream.

Considering the time he had spent as a cluster of inactive partials, only for the first century and the last forty years had he truly lived. By Hexamon standards, he was a youngster; he was certainly younger than his own creation, whatever time measurements could be applied to the Way.

Pumps sucked the air from the elevator cab. The door opened, and he stared down the throat of the beast that had once swallowed him, the Hexamon, the Jarts, and dozens of other races, opening up commerce between separate worlds, separate times, even separate universes.

The scoured bare rock and metal floor of the seventh chamber stretched for almost ten kilometers, gray and cold and dead. Beyond lay the surface of the Way itself, bronze in color, and not at all lifeless. Korzenowski knew that if he drew his eye close to that surface, he would see shots of black and red, a kind of ineffable bubbling activity: the life of space-time itself, vacuum teased and twisted and seduced into throwing up a perverse surface.

The bronze pipe, fifty kilometers wide, elongated

itself to infinity before him. A mimicry of the tube light within the enclosed Thistledown chambers ran in a pale glowing ribbon down its center. He felt dizzy for a moment, as if he had actually become part of the tortured geodetics describing the Way's unlikely existence.

A small personal shuttle awaited him. He boarded, and it flew at a level of several meters over the flatness, crossing the seventh chamber's boundary, stopping and hovering some thirty kilometers from the southern cap.

Korzenowski stepped down from the shuttle hatch and stood a few centimeters above the naked surface of the Way. He removed the environment field segment beneath his feet. Now he was on the surface itself. Removing his slipper, he let his naked foot touch what was neither warm nor cold, what possessed only one quality at this moment and that was solidity. The surface of the Way was uninterested in the laws of thermodynamics.

Korzenoswki bent down and rubbed the palm of his hand on that surface.

He stood up, feeling his foundation – the Mystery of Patricia Vasquez – very strongly now, as if someone were watching over his shoulder. *Her creation, too, in a way*, he thought. *Our offspring, a wonderful monstrosity.*

'Nothing is ever pure, except for *you*,' he said to The Way. 'You were made by precocious children. We didn't know what you would mean to us. You allowed us to dream fine dreams. Now I've got to kill you.'

He stood in silence for several minutes on the unresponsive, unreal surface, then returned to the shuttle and the seventh chamber bore hole.

70

The Way

'We're prisoners,' Rhita told Demetrios on the lake, in the long wooden rowboat. 'All of us. The queen is dead, and so is Jamal Atta. They aren't here.'

'All right,' Demetrios said. 'I agree something isn't right. But what do you mean by prisoners?'

'This is a test, an experiment. The Jarts.'

'I'm not familiar with that word.'

Rhita touched his face with her hands. 'Do you feel it, though? That we're prisoners?'

'I'll take your word for it.'

'Do you remember a Kelt named Lugotorix?'

An ibis flew from the shore and landed on the prow of the boat. It opened its long beak and said, 'You can remember now.'

Rhita shuffled back through her past, hiding. Why remember? There was nothing she could do; no way to escape when the legs with which she would run weren't real. She visited with her mother for a time, sitting in the stone and plaster house near Lindos, talking about inconsequentials. Relaxing in the sun, which was not as warm as it should have been, nor as bright. On the road to the temple to spend a day alone, her shadow preceded her, walking long in the morning sun on the dirt and gravel. She watched it with mild interest, then stopped. It raised its arms; her arms were down. It gestured wildly. It lengthened, crossing the road, up over dry hedges and stone walls, across a dead orchard. The tree branches swayed wherever it touched.

A young man with black hair approached along the road. He stood beside her for a time, watching the shadow lengthen to the island horizon, and then spread across sky and rushing clouds. She glanced at him, not at all curious. He told her, 'We are losing you, Rhita Vaskayza. You must not hide. If we cannot hold you, your self will dissolve in its own memories, and we would not wish that. We will have to inactivate you. Wouldn't you rather continue thinking?'

'No,' she said. 'I know what I'm doing.'

She ran from the youth, but in thought or memory or wherever she was now, she made a very wrong turn.

Rhita stumbled into the warehouse of all her nightmares.

Before she could be inactivated, she saw the ghosts of all she had killed, flying over the sea's bloody waters, questions on their lips, knives in their hands: *Why did you open the gate?*

She had killed Gaia.

But she could not herself die.

Her psyche, her butterfly, lay pinned in a box, examined and prodded by monstrous collectors. She saw hall upon hall, brightly lit, stretching for millions of miles, lined with steel cases, in every case row upon row of humans – infants, old men, crones, girls, young men, mothers-to-be, soldiers, all passing under her inspection with infinite detail, more real than anything in her true life had ever been, squirming on the pins that ran through their hearts. *I am with you*, she said. *I can't run from you.*

But she was running. With no physical body to run with, she chased her self through her own memories, over all the roads of her mind, frantic with grief and fear and guilt. She ran faster and faster, until she seemed to melt and flow like water, the water frantically surging into a cold spray, diffuse and selfless . . . No center, almost no awareness.

A brief warmth before null.

71
Thistledown

Thistledown, launched thirteen centuries before by its own timeline, had been beyond doubt the greatest single achievement of the human race, made even greater by the creation of the Way. Containing the two finest and largest cities of all humanity, yet never fully populated; containing the greatest weapons ever devised, birthplace of the most accomplished and wide-ranging civilisation, center of philosophies encompassing all the human religions, many synthesised into the myth of the Good Man, who exemplified the imperfect but glorious expression of that universal urge to Just Progress, Star, Fate and Pneuma: the universe, history and human spirit; Thistledown, transient and even humble name for such an endeavor.

Farren Siliom contemplated all these things from his apartment. He would not have time to get used to this new body; in a way, he regretted the waste of resources, but preferred to end his life in a physical form.

If Thistledown were to die, he would die with it, rather than explain to its citizens what he had done, and why.

Despite an odd melancholy – something akin to what he had seen in Korzenowski's face – he did not feel much like a traitor. No doubt, in the scales of cosmic justice, he was a hero; but he didn't feel that sense of justification, either. He had become nothing more than a small transducer in the circuit of history, a fate experienced most acutely by politicians who believe or hope they are in control.

He knew his place in the Thistledown's history, though he was far from sure it would be an honored place. With no authorisation, only the power of being in a certain office at a certain time, he had ordered – or at least supported – the asteroid starship's destruction. He had done so for reasons that were inescapable and correct, yet that were still not clear to him. *I have been persuaded by Gods. Historians are seldom kind to leaders.*

His family was on Earth by now, in a camp in Southeast Asia. His two children, both conceived and born in the natural manner – in accord with his Naderite beliefs, but of course, with a few Hexamon embellishments, since he was not orthodox – those children would grow up more influenced by Earth than the orbiting precincts, he could prophesy; the precincts would more than likely close themselves off as a society, rendering aid and assistance, but turning inward. As such, within a century or two they could cease to be viable, their societies beginning the long process of decay, like a – he borrowed now from Terrestrial experiences, such as Garry Lanier might have had – lamb's tail bound with cord, cut off from the parent body. Who could have foreseen such a possibility during the enthusiasm of the Sundering?

Earth would grow on its own, having been given a mighty boost; who could say where it would go, after the Recovery and such strong Hexamon influence?

He had placed remotes and partials in several places around Thistledown, all connected to his sensoria, to allow him to fully experience the moment when – and if – it came. He still reserved a small and probably foolish skepticism. *Thistledown had always been.* In his life, at least . . .

He felt a wave of sentiment for the old times in the Way, and it shamed him. But those times had been so much easier to comprehend, even if no less complicated. He had never thought he would be homesick for the awesome reaches of Korzenowski's creation.

Since the Sundering, it seemed that the Hexamon had never truly known where it was. It had never found home.

72

The Beginning of the Way

Olmy reached out to touch the blunt, mad-mirror terminus of the flaw and felt it draw his fingers along where he applied pressure, and push them back when he applied pressure from the opposite angle. Frictionless, enormously powerful, the flaw had once supplied all the Hexamon's energy through these transforms of space and time. Korzenowski watched from the blister.

'You can enter the flawships?'

'I can enter at least one of them,' Olmy said. 'My imprint is still on this one.' He pointed to the first ship in the row, closest to the flaw, mounted behind the blister that covered the bore hole. The wreckage of the flawship damaged by the Jart intrusion had been removed, replaced by the second ship in line, and a third added. 'It took us down the Way and through the closing end, during the Sundering . . . with Patricia Vasquez and Garry Lanier. We dropped off representatives from Timbl and other worlds . . . we dropped off Patricia to open her gate in the geometry stacks.' They tracted along the bore hole to float beside the flawship.

'I didn't remember this was the ship,' Korzenowski said. 'They look so much alike.'

Olmy pressed his hand into a circle scribed in the side of the flawship and a hatchway irised open noiselessly. The smell of the interior was clean and metallic, redolent with the blunt odors of unbreathed air and formfit decor. Light spilled from the hatch, gleaming against the dark metal and stone of the bore hole wall opposite. They entered.

Olmy tracted along faint purple field-lines within the ship to the controls. Korzenowski moved to the transparent bow. Behind them, the flawship interior was shadowy and silent, a long cylinder interrupted here and there with rounded shapes of unformed furnishings.

Are there restrictions to your use? the Jart asked.

I don't think so, Olmy replied. He had once had nearly as high a clearance as a full-rank Hexamon senator with the added advantages of connections in the defense forces; as far as he knew, his status had not been changed. He did not doubt that the ship would respond to any instruction he gave it. The defense forces would not expect a rogue in their midst, even though Olmy had played that part before. Certainly not a rogue that would steal a flawship and run it down the Way . . .

With the president's influence – and a little help from vigilant Tapi, still somewhere aboard Thistledown – they would make it.

Olmy inserted his hands into control dimples and created a large docking field around the flawship. In the dark bore hole, green and purple diffusions played across the raw rock and metal walls. Slowly, the flawship advanced toward the blister.

Korzenowski, in the bow, used his pictor to instruct the blister to accept intrusion. They would pierce the blister and string themselves on the flaw. The flaw would pass through the center of the ship, down a flaw passage that gave the ship its U-shape cross-section. When the ship was strung, the open end of the U would close and the ship's flaw grips would seize the elongated singularity. At Olmy's instruction, the grips would bear down at a certain angle, and the flaw would translate the ship forward.

'My partial is sounding the final evacuation alert,' Korzenowski said. 'The crimp in the Way will be started in six hours. We should be well down the Way by then.'

Olmy nodded. Tapi might leave a partial of himself to oversee operations, as would others in the defense forces; but there would be no one living left aboard Thistledown.

'Are you tired of life, Ser Engineer?' Olmy asked, apropros of nothing.

'I don't know,' Korzenowski said. 'Tired of not knowing who I am.'

Olmy agreed. 'To knowing who we are,' he said, raising an imaginary cup in toast. He pushed the flawship slowly forward, through the blister and onto the long mad-mirror ribbon of the singularity.

73

Thistledown

The last Hexamon archivists and archaeologists withdrew their hundreds of thousands of hastily created partials from the second and third chambers, where they had conducted a final survey of the Thistledown's cities. For lack of time, the other chambers had been neglected.

The contents of Thistledown's city memory and the various library centers had been gleaned; all that remained untouched were the hidden information stores, private caches put away over the centuries by individuals who distrusted direct links with the libraries. Who could say how much history would be lost if these private caches were destroyed, never to be discovered or analysed?

The archivists' frustration was that the Hexamon, before the Sundering, had had centuries to explore the deserted cities, and had forbidden most such exploration because of the remote possibility of tampering in the sixth chamber. After the Sundering, the archivists had thought they had all the time they needed, never imagining a day such as this . . .

The defense forces withdrew with the last of the archivists. Only a few suicidal or thrill-seeking individuals remained now – and Farren Siliom, prepared to atone for his decision, however correct it had been.

He sat in the high, undecorated suite overlooking the third chamber city, picting artistic designs around himself, waiting patiently. So far, nobody knew he was here – or where he was. That saved the embarrassment of last-minute rescues, if anyone would be so rude as to interrupt a citizen's chosen path to extinction.

There were no signs of the coming destruction. Thistledown was stable, the tubelight steady and bright.

74

The Way

'I'm setting acceleration at one G for the first few minutes,' Olmy said. He asked the Jart, *Do you know where your people will be?*

Singularity stations are spaced at intervals of about five million kilometers in Jart territory. We'll encounter flaw defenses and barriers first.

Then we shouldn't be traveling very fast, should we?

No more than one-fiftieth c. That is maximum velocity for all of our vessels on the flaw; anything traveling faster is automatically destroyed.

I presume you'll have some way of alerting your superiors that we're not belligerent?

When that time comes, I will perform through you.

Olmy, having at least the illusion he was in control now, did not look forward to losing it again. He explained the situation to Korzenowski.

'We should be a million kilometers down the Way when the kink is initiated,' the Engineer said. He picted his calculations to Olmy, who understood at least the factors of acceleration of Way destruction, their required velocity to outrace the destruction, and how long they might have at their unknown destination to do whatever the Jart thought necessary.

Was this what he had been preparing for these past years?

He had thought he was preparing for war; not for a fool's run down the Way on a quasi-religious errand for a Trojan Horse Jart. But he knew he had to count his blessings; at least his error would not destroy the Hexamon. His own sacrifice, measured against avoiding even the bare possibility of such a disaster, was inconsequential.

He called up a display of the seventh chamber's southern cap, now receding slowly behind them. The display showed no activated defenses beyond the deep-Way sensors and sweeping automatic target acquisition fields.

With no sensation of motion – the flawship contained its own inertial damping system – they began to accelerate at one G.

'Here we go,' he said.

Korzenowski could not help modeling again and again the sequence of events happening now in the sixth chamber machinery. Certain control centers would undergo planned failures within minutes. Other mechanisms would try to compensate for the failures. For a short time, they would succeed, but they would be exposed to strains and contradictions in design that would bring about their own, irrevocable failures. The projection nodes would try to shut off long enough to allow robot workers and remotes to correct the imbalance; when no such repairs were made, and the nodes had to switch on again to avoid their own destruction under the Way's growing instability, the entire carpet of sixth chamber machinery would fail.

The kink in the Way would begin.

Where the kink originated, the Way would quickly become unlivable. Fundamental physical constants would change rapidly; what matter was left in the Way would cease to exist, converting to varieties of radiation not encountered in normal space and time. These radiations would quickly decay to extremely high-energy, photon-like particles, which would leak through the kink and appear in the regions near the Thistledown – and in randomly selected regions for a hundred thousand light years around the sun. Entering normal space, they would assume the character of actual photons, appearing as brilliant displays of Tcherenkov-blue.

Korzenowski shook his head, close to weeping. Unlike Olmy, he had never had himself altered to eliminate such emotional displays. What he felt was a deep

433

sadness that extended into that part of him which was
Patricia Vasquez. The Mystery they shared, however
tainted by her obsessions, knew what was going to
be destroyed, and how important it had been to the
Engineer, how integral a part of his existence.

'It's beginning now,' he told Olmy.

Ry Oyu came forward from the shadowy rear of
the flawship, startling Korzenowski. 'Your bravery is
deeply appreciated,' he said.

Korzenowski shook his head slowly.

75

Axis Euclid

Suli Ram Kikura was no longer a ward of the Hexamon. Released from confinement to her apartment, she was a free woman again, free to contemplate the confusion and contradiction of the past few weeks.

She could not help thinking that Olmy was playing some substantial part in all this; perhaps he even knew what was really happening. Nobody else did.

All her anger and frustration was overridden by her sense of duty. First, she had to be sure that the destruction of Thistledown – if it happened – would not jeopardise the orbiting bodies or Earth. She did not have the technical expertise in these matters, even using the full capabilities of her implants, to come to any useful conclusions by herself.

For a moment, she simply reveled in having her lines of communication open and unmonitored. She decided to contact Judith Hoffman.

When she called Hoffman's terrestrial residence in South Africa, a message awaited her, conveyed by a delegated partial with instructions to speak only to selected people, herself among them. The partial explained that Hoffman had been on Thistledown until the very last moment, and was now on a shuttle returning to Axis Euclid. The partial was willing to arrange a meeting; it was possible, if channels were not closed by the Hexamon, to speak with its primary now. Did she wish to do so?

Ram Kikura, usually reluctant to impose, did not hesitate now. 'If you can open a channel, I'll be very grateful.'

Hoffman's partial made the necessary arrangements, found that channels were still available, and Hoffman herself appeared in Ram Kikura's living room, seated in a white shuttle formfit, exhausted and unhappy.

'Suli!' she said, trying to muster a semblance of polite gladness. 'It's a disaster out here. We couldn't access a third of what we wanted to. . . . If it all goes, we'll lose so much . . .'

'Do you know what's happening?'

'It isn't even classified!' Hoffman said, waving her fingers in dismay. 'The presiding minister lifted all security measures – '

'I know. I'm free.'

'The re-opening is a disaster. They say there was instability in the Way – but I can't believe Korzenowski couldn't take care of that.'

'Mirsky?' Ram Kikura suggested.

Hoffman rubbed her neck with her hands. 'We were warned.'

The coloring on her image changed. With raised eyebrows, she peered to her left – where a transparency in the hull might be – and a look of wonder crossed her face. 'What is it?' she asked others around her. Ram Kikura caught muffled sounds of other voices.

She glanced through her own window at the arc of darkness visible beyond the edge of what had once been the flaw passage. That region was no longer dark; now it glowed a ghostly blue.

'Something's happening,' Hoffman said. 'Transmission – '

She faded with a silent sizzle of white lines. Ram Kikura called for an image of the precinct's exterior, and then added, 'Where's Thistledown? Show me that octant.'

A circle of radiant blue appeared in the middle of her living room, enchanting and deeply disturbing. It did not block out the haze of stars visible beyond Earth. 'Thistledown,' she ordered. 'Show me where Thistledown is.' A projected red line curled snake-like around the bean-sized white object and blinked. The glow was not coming from Thistledown, nor was it limited to the starship's vicinity; it seemed to come from all space, all directions.

The bean-sized object grew brighter as she watched. 'Magnify,' she demanded. Throughout Axis Euclid, she knew citizens by the tens of thousands were asking for the same picture; her own private projector's image flickered occasionally as the precinct's signal amplifiers and splitters cut in.

Thistledown appeared enlarged and in sharp detail, surrounded by a faint corona of even brighter blue. The north pole pointed away from the Earth and all precincts. But the south pole itself glowed now. Concentric and expanding rings of luminous pinspecks formed beyond the south pole, followed by even brighter rings and then continuous halos.

The Beckmann drive engines were cutting in; she was sure of it. Thistledown had not used those drives since the Sundering; now the asteroid starship was pushing itself away from Earth and the precincts.

What had been only an intellectual speculation before was now reality; Thistledown was preparing for its death.

Somehow, she knew Olmy was still aboard, or very near the Thistledown – perhaps in the Way itself.

Ram Kikua, like Olmy, did not have the means to cry. She sat in tense silence, watching as Axis Euclid's sensors tracked the Thistledown. *How long?*

The glare from the Beckmann drives increased until the display had to adjust for brightness. The plume of destroyed matter reflected from the south polar crater, forming a long violet brushstroke against the unnatural blue. The colors and the circumstances went against all reason; she felt as if she were watching an artificial entertainment, depicting something remote and beautiful but hardly plausible.

It hurts, she thought, her implants working steadily to handle the emotional overload. *I know he's there. And that's my home, where I was born and grew and worked – within the Way.*

437

She could hardly bear to watch, yet she did not move.

She owed her past this much, to sit and watch it die.

76
Earth

The ethereal night sky brought people out by the hundreds of thousands. In Melbourne there was religious frenzy and rioting; Karen heard the sounds, like a distant grumbling wave, from the balcony of her hotel room. She had been ordered to take a week's vacation after her episode in the evacuee camp, a gift he did not appreciate, since it left her with little to do but think.

She looked upon the show calmly. Marvels had multiplied in her liftime; after the events of the past two weeks, she almost expected them now. She had some vague notion this glow was associated with Thistledown, but the asteroid starship was not visible.

At midnight, however, she did see the violent plume of the Beckmann drives, rising from the northeastern horizon like a spotlight beam. It faded three hand's-breadths above the horizon, which meant it was huge – tens of thousands of kilometers in length. She did not know what it signified; she thought it might be Thistledown's death glow, but that was yet to come.

Sitting in a deck-chair on the balcony, wrapped in a sweater against the night chill, she looked across Melbourne's brightly lit skyline, clutching a ceramic mug, shivering slightly not just with the cold, but with having drunk too much coffee.

She knew she was a wreck; she allowed she might someday be able to rebuild herself, conduct her own Recovery, perhaps become a whole human being; but for the moment the curtain was down and the stage props were being rearranged. What came before the spotlights next might be a new Karen Farley Lanier, or merely a rewrite of the old; at any rate, she hoped it would be a more successful one. Andia could help her;

but until she actually saw her daughter, she would be as unreal and fantastic as the night sky.

The plume seemed to grow longer as the minutes passed. Then she realised the Earth was turning, perhaps bringing Thistledown into view, if it still existed.

She had had no more contact with Garry. She began to wonder if in fact she had been overstrained; but an inner voice reassured her, the experience had been real; it had been Garry.

That alone could give her strength. If the powers behind Mirsky had saved her husband, or given him some alternate existence beyond death, then perhaps all things would turn out right after all; perhaps her life, however trivial in the march of millennia and on a scale of light-centuries, would have some use, be worth continuing.

Though not forever.

Garry, whatever his final doubts, had left her this: that age and death and change were natural, even necessary, if not for citizens of the Hexamon, then for those humans who had not seen the slow evolution of life-extension across the centuries.

Someday, she would allow herself to age and die. She smiled, thinking what Ram Kikura might say.

Something rose in the northeast, at the beginning of the violet plume; a bright, twinkling thing that looked less like Thistledown than some distant, continuous fireworks display.

Suddenly, it became as brilliant as a sun, and cast Melbourne into the light of full summer noon. Cup still hooked to her finger, she flung up her forearm to shield her eyes and gave herself a painful whack on one ear. The cup fell to the concrete porch and shattered.

Cursing in English and Chinese, she lurched out of the chair, through the open sliding glass door and into the bathroom. There, she blinked at herself in the mirror, her face hidden behind a negative blind spot turning green and red at the edges.

The flash had been silent. The hotel was quiet; even

the sound of distant riots had died. When her vision recovered, she peered around the bathroom door. The sky outside was dark. Cautiously, she walked to the balcony, holding her hand up near her eyes just in case, and squinted at where the Thistledown had been. The plume still glowed faintly in the blackness; a few degrees past the plume's tip, all that remained of Thistledown was a turbulent, dim red ball the size of her thumbnail.

77

Thistledown City

Farren Siliom felt the grinding sound before he heard
it. It came through the anchors and suspension cables
into the hanging buildings, vibrating the floor under
his feet, making his bones ache.

A remote in the sixth chamber relayed its
impressions:

The northern bore hole leading to the seventh
chamber was spewing a fountain of intense white and
green. The fountain grew along the axis of the chamber,
spreading as it traversed the thirty kilometer length.
The remote's eyes tracked the fountain to the opposite
southern cap, where it sprayed out in brilliant rings of
violet and greenish blue.

The sixth chamber machinery was no longer operating. The remote turned its attention to the chamber
itself. The valley floor seemed to be buckling, but that
couldn't be – the sound and vibration would have been
much more violent. Areas of machinery tens of kilometers wide formed globules and rose toward the axis like
soap bubbles. That, too, made no sense.

Then the sound increased. The northern cap split
from the center outward like a plate of glass hit by a
bullet. Radial slivers of asteroid rock and metal lifted
away from the cap and twisted weirdly with the stress
of their uneven inward and outward centrifugal spin.
With dream-like slowness, they plummeted toward the
valley floor, striking and crumpling. Where they had
left gaps in the cap, glowing red molten rock spewed
into the chamber, arcing outward in beautiful, uneven
pinwheel spirals.

The remote had a momentary glimpse of this before
the entire cap blew inward, the shock wave racing along

the valley floor, obscuring everything with dust and smoke and ending its transmission.

It's grinding the end off Thistledown, Farren Siliom thought, *working its way toward me . . .*

The remote in the fifth chamber watched mountains and rusty rivers distort as if in a rippled mirror. The northern cap shattered, but there was no outpouring of molten rock; the air in the chamber abruptly clouded over. This remote also ceased transmitting.

In the fourth chamber, the president's extended eyes and ears heard the rumbling grow to potentially deafening levels, the trees of the forests shaking their limbs away, rivers and lakes seeming to boil.

The sixth chamber was almost certainly gone, and that meant no more inertial damping within Thistledown. If the asteroid was subjected to any abrupt motion, the cities in the second and third chambers would crumple like toy castles made of stacked blocks.

Farren Siliom could see his own death, then, minutes before it came. He would not witness the conclusion of this final episode in Thistledown's history.

78

The Way

Korzenowski knew the kink had formed, ablating the first few chambers from the Thistledown. The force of this would twist the asteroid around like a piece of wood on a lathe. The twist would probably reverse at some point as the kink began its motion along the Way, and that would destroy everything within Thistledown.

He could see this with a feverish clarity; time and again, his implants created realistic scenarios for the asteroid starship's demise with a painful persistence he could hardly stop. Something akin to guilt compelled him to pay attention, to imagine the destruction as accurately as he could . . .

For he was directly responsible. He had built the Way; he had pushed a sliver into God's finger.

They had been traveling for just under five hours. Ry Oyu floated near the bow, face calm.

The flawship shivered faintly. Olmy called up a select display of the next few thousand kilometers. He saw odd square patches floating a kilometer or so above the flaw itself.

We approach a flaw station, the Jart warned him. *Begin deceleration.*

He applied the clamps in reverse, making the flaw fluoresce a vivid green. By the time they came to a dead stop, they would have traveled some five million kilometers; the flaw station was probably just where the Jart had foreseen.

'We'll reach a flaw station in about four hours,' he told the Engineer.

The Jart took him over and began to send signals through the flawship radio frequency transmitters.

79

Axis Euclid

Ram Kikura's display showed the Thistledown spinning this way and that, like some giant's spindle gathering thread and throwing it off. The northern first third of the asteroid had been melted and blasted away and formed a fan of glowing red haze around the remaining mass.

Hoffman's shuttle had not been damaged, she had learned a few moments before; all communications had been cut off to allow full channels for official Hexamon signals. Thistledown's demise would not affect the Earth or the orbiting precincts, beyond a few Old Natives temporarily blinded by the first flare.

She stood up and walked around the apartment, unable to turn away from the display. *What next? How long until* –

A funnel like the bell of an enormous trumpet congealed out of darkness ahead of Thistledown. Undulating like a jellyfish, the funnel had none of the qualities of the Way; something far more ominous had just come into being, a restrained, shaped black hole, like nothing this universe had ever seen before. The starship began to visibly move toward the yawning dark bell. That implied tremendous acceleration.

The uneven acceleration toward the funnel split the starship along its thinner walls with surgical precision. Tidal forces twisted the asteroid apart in latitudinal segments, as if it were being cut by a giant cake knife, each section corresponding roughly to an internal chamber.

Air and water and rock – and molten rock toward the northern end – spread outward from Thistledown like paint smeared by an enormous thumb, accompanied by a dusty debris that could only be the fragments of interior mountains, forests, cities.

Thistledown's ruins vanished into the gaping funnel, emerging nowhere, going nowhere, creating a deficit of trillions of tons in this universe which had to be made up in some fashion.

From the complex domain of superspace, to the far-spread reaches of this universe, spontaneous and compensatory leaks of pure energy would occur, amounting precisely to the mass of Thistledown; thus the books would be balanced. Chances were the leaks would be so widespread that not a single one of them – and they would probably number in the billions – would occur near a star, much less a planet. Still, for thousands, perhaps millions of years, tiny bursts of gamma rays would mystify human and non-human astronomers. And who would guess their origin?

Perhaps no one.

Ram Kikura watched the display for minutes after Thistledown had disappeared. The funnel showed now only as a ring of inward-spiraling dust and debris and a greater darkness against the stars.

Then the bell closed like a flower withdrawing for a long night.

The Way had begun its long, violent suicide.

80
The Way

The Jart flaw station, from their perspective, was simply a huge black triangle strung on the flaw, its edges flashing dark rainbows as they approached. Korzenowski and Ry Oyu watched Olmy work intently at the flawship console, aware that the Jart was conducting the orchestra, attempting to make the right music to placate vigilant defenses.

'There's been an enormous amount of activity here,' Olmy said. Korzenowski looked at the picted information from the flawship sensors; gates had been opened dozens of times about two hundred kilometers ahead. They appeared to have been opened in one latitude surrounding the Jart flaw station. Glancing at Ry Oyu, the Engineer brought forward his clavicle. 'This is a geometry stack region,' he said. 'We're very close to where Patricia Vasquez opened her own gate.'

'It must have been fused shut by the stellar plasma,' Olmy said.

'It would have left a trace . . . something the Jarts could have detected,' Korzenowski said. 'Did they?'

Olmy consulted the Jart. 'They have that capability.'

'They might have found the trace of a gate in the geometry stacks too unusual to ignore.' Korzenowski shook his head. 'Patricia may not have had much time, whether she made it home or not.'

Entry to a world populated by humans would be most useful to command oversight, the Jart said within Olmy. He turned to Ry Oyu. 'They might have found her. Did they?'

'I don't know,' Ry Oyu said. 'I don't know the answers to a good many questions, regrettably. Our jobs would be a lot easier if I did.'

Korzenowski scanned the latitude ahead in more detail as they came closer. Four gates remained open, though there was little activity around them now.

The triangle filled their forward view. The Engineer was aware of some abrupt change around them; passage through a kind of traction field, perhaps, or suspension of the flawship's inertial damping.

The flawship entered the station's dark triangle like a spear sliding slowly into a black pool. Beyond was more darkness, as if the pool were black paint, absorbing all light, all information; telling nothing.

Olmy's Jart had no idea what awaited them. Things had changed greatly since its capture; little was familiar, including the design of the flaw station.

Ry Oyu floated toward Korzenowski and curled up beside him. 'This is the area where I should find Patricia's world,' he said. 'If I have an opportunity to fulfill my obligations to her, I'll need to copy her Mystery . . .'

They hadn't brought along the necessary equipment. 'How?' Korzenowski asked.

'This much I have the power to do,' Ry Oyu said. 'Close your eyes, please.'

The gate-opener did not even touch him. A few seconds of warmth scattering through his head and body, the opposite of tingling, and it was over. Korzenowski opened his eyes. He did not feel any different.

'Just a copy,' Ry Oyu said quietly.

The darkness at the flawship's nose suddenly parted and they stared at a segment of the Way perhaps three hundred kilometers long. Blocking the segment was a black radiance, deeply scalloped around its circumference, fully fifty kilometers in diameter. The walls of the Way leading up to this formation were brazen, undisturbed.

We will not be allowed to pass, the Jart told Olmy. *That is a barrier to protect command individuals.*

Olmy slowed the flawship to a few hundred kilometers per hour. A reception? he asked the Jart.

Very unusual for command individuals to come this far >south<.

He slowed the flawship to a crawl now, as the black shape filled their northern view. Green lines spun outward from the center of the shape and made graceful arcs to the circumference of the Way.

'I think we've been noticed,' Olmy said.

The arcs rose and neatly encased them. Dozens of transparent bubbles, perhaps a meter and a half in diameter, each containing a tiny black smudge like ink in water, flowed toward the flawship along the green lines.

'Traction fields, or something equivalent,' Korzenowski said. 'Do they know how to communicate with us?'

'They don't know any of our languages . . .' Olmy said.

A voice issued from the console. 'We welcome the representatives of descendant command. Please accept the passage of our transport vehicles.'

'That was English,' Korzenowski commented dryly. The message was repeated in Spanish, then in a language very similar to Greek, and another language similar to Chinese. Other languages were less identifiable. At the conclusion of the translations, the bubbles took formation in concentric rings around the flawship.

Olmy felt the Jart take control of his movements again. The Jart sent another signal to the barrier through the flawship radio transmitters. It then moved Olmy to the transparent bow and waited there.

One of the green arcs flared suddenly and illuminated the flawship's bow. Olmy was surrounded by something like St. Elmo's fire; his body convulsed. Korzenowski had tracted halfway toward his friend when the display stopped. Olmy rotated to face them with a wan smile. 'Inspection,' he said. 'They still don't trust us completely.'

'Did you pass?' Korzenowski asked.

'So far, so good.'

'Very advanced,' Ry Oyu said. Korzenowski thought he detected a hint of irony.

'Remove the ship from the flaw,' came a return signal in English. Olmy went to the console and intructed the flawship to unstring itself.

'Ride within the bubble nearest your ship's door.'

They put on environment packs and stood by the hatchway. When it opened, a bubble expanded to about four meters in diameter and fastened itself around the hatch with a sucking, sizzling sound. The black nebulosity within congealed to make a railed platform.

'Our phaeton,' Korzenowski said, following Olmy onto the platform. A quiet hissing surrounded them; cool air smelling faintly musty, sweet, like young beer, blew against their faces. The bubble withdrew, sealing itself, and carried them along the green arcs toward a point just outside the center of the barrier. The flaw in this region was an uncharacteristic sour-orange color, carrying the additional burden of Jart information; it cast a feeble glow against the barrier's gray-black surface.

Four green arcs cradled the flawship and guided it toward the walls of the Way. Olmy looked at the descending ship with a twinge of regret: their last contact with the Hexamon. Arms folded, still not entirely resigned, Korzenowski faced the featureless barrier surface toward which they were being ferried. His eyes carried little of Patricia's impression now; she seemed to have sunk back deep into his psyche, biding her time.

Ry Oyu put his hand on the Engineer's shoulder. 'In our youth,' he said, 'we would have called this an adventure.'

'In *my* youth, I always preferred thinking to adventuring,' Korzenowski replied.

The barrier absorbed the bubble, and again they were in darkness. Olmy would have been more comfortable if the Jart communicated with him, but it was silent; nothing had passed between them since the inspection.

He could still feel it within him, as an oyster must feel a grain of sand . . .

When they finished their passage through the barrier, all that was human lay behind them. The bubble hovered above a broad forest-green floor. Perhaps a hundred meters away, the floor met a wall of lighter green. There did not seem to be a ceiling; merely a pale, featureless void.

'You will meet with command individuals,' said a bodiless voice in the bubble.

'Fine,' Korzenowski said, lips straight and tight. 'Let's get on with it.'

The green wall parted like a curtain and the bubble passed through. Only now did Olmy feel the Jart react within him; it seemed to change its shape, rearrange its points of contact with his mentality, *stiffen*.

'Big day for my conquering companion,' he said. 'Time for debriefing.'

They passed along a proscenium, flanked on both sides by processions of identical sculptures resembling abstract chrome-plated scorpions. Their long tail-like abdomens stuck into the green floor, stiffly supporting gleaming bodies; their abstracted legs and claws raised and spread in formal salute.

Around and between these shapes floated fist-sized orange and green balls of light.

'What are they?' Korzenowski asked Olmy, pointing at the sculptures.

'I don't know,' Olmy said. 'My guide is silent.'

Korzenowski made a face and nodded, as if that was the least they could expect. 'Even their architecture is menacing,' he said. 'Damn us all for going this far.'

Olmy could only agree. Whatever happened to those far-off days of duty and research and nothing but inner turmoil? Those times seemed positively peaceful and desirable. What he feared now was not so much death as something nameless, perhaps coming across the exact opposite of life and humanity, the antithesis of all he believed in, and finding it was also true and indisputable; losing all reference and simply *fading* like an out-moded idea.

They had already faced the strangeness of Mirsky and Ry Oyu, but these avatars had been tailored to humanity. What would Ry Oyu become to convince the Jarts?

The proscenium opened onto a broad circle surrounded by pale, translucent sea-green cylindrical tanks, each twice as high as it was broad. Within the tanks black membranes waved with a calm, resilient rhythm, like misty banners.

Directly ahead, there were no tanks, only a flat stage about a meter above the floor. Above this stage floated three obviously organic shapes, sleek and long and somewhat more massive than elephants, torsos wrapped in more misty dark banners that first obscured them, then revealed . . .

Command individuals among the Jarts were incarnate organisms closest in form to the forebear originals. Whatever world had bred these figures must have been a place of poisons and death and bad dreams. They appeared, first of all, *vital;* there was no denying that these creatures were survivors, with their long black spike-legs and efficient armor casings wrapped around long, tapering thoraxes. They split in two near the front, each bifurcated section rearing up from the platform, displaying deep gashes along the underside. These were fringed with wrinkled appendages tipped with wickedly pointed black claws. No eyes or other sensors were visible.

They *did* bear some resemblance to the body in the hidden chamber, Olmy thought. They were much more efficient-looking, however, perhaps more evolved. The dead form in the transparent box might have been a precursor, like a chimpanzee compared to a human.

How much time had passed in the Way – decades, or millions of years?

Do you recognise these individuals? Olmy asked the Jart

within. For a long moment, it did not answer, and then it said, *These are not command as known to this expediter.*

Perhaps they are not Jarts at all?

They are my kind. There is glory in them. They have accomplished much improvement.

Will they know you?

They already recognise this modified expediter. Humble submission to their presence. Something else passed between them that did not fit the pidgin mental language Olmy shared with the Jart, something ominous and dark and exalted at once; a kind of murderous pride he could not classify in human emotions.

'You're looking bemused,' Korzenowski said to Olmy.

'No muse at all,' Olmy said. 'Those are definitely Jarts.'

'Ah,' said Korzenowski dryly. 'Our hosts.'

The bubble came to rest at the fourth corner of a square, the command individuals occupying the other three. The misty black drapes wrapped around their bodies evaporated, and the Jarts lifted their anterior bifurcations, claws on appendages meeting delicately tip-to-tip, like sutures over twin gashes, in a manner that would have made Olmy's skin crawl, and did make Korzenowski draw back instinctively.

'They are quite thoroughly horrible,' he said. Olmy did not disagree; he could not remember encountering intelligent beings who looked more threatening.

Ry Oyu stood at one edge of the bubble platform, still relaxed and undisturbed.

Surely they're not the most vicious-looking intelligences in the universe, Korzenowski thought. *The Final Mind doubtless will encompass far worse.* He glanced at Ry Oyu, who smiled and nodded as if listening and agreeing.

The three command individuals spread their uplifted bifurcations into wider Vs.

'We meet,' said the voice in the bubble, seeming to each of them to come from over his right shoulder. 'This event is not expected. Are you one or many?'

'We are each individual,' Ry Oyu said.

'Which represents descendant command?'

'I do.'

'Is there confirming evidence?'

'They want loaves and fishes,' Ry Oyu said in an undertone. 'So be it.'

He did not appear to do anything, but the three command individuals shivered slightly, as if struck by a cold breeze. Their upper sections closed almost to the point of joining.

The voice said, 'The testimony is adequate confirmation. What is your plan for completion?'

Korzenowski frowned, puzzled. Ry Oyu said, 'Tell them what we've done, and what we wish to do. Tell them who you are.'

'My name is Konrad Korzenowski,' he said. 'I designed the Way.'

The command individuals did not react.

'We have already begun destruction of the Way . . .'

'Command individuals are aware of this,' the voice said.

'We've come to finish the last of our work, to . . . bring one of your own back to you, and . . .' He stumbled over the words in his head, trying to express himself clearly and in a way non-humans might understand. 'I carry part of the mentality of another human, who once did work that helped me design the Way. We wish to return this mentality to an appropriate world, in the geometry stacks . . . behind where we are now.' He gestured awkwardly over his shoulder, unsure even of direction. 'We hope to journey on and help the Final Mind. With you, or alone.' How naive and childlike, to even think of being able to help something so vast as the Final Mind . . .

Command individuals have accessed and stored a human-occupied world in the regions you refer to,' the voice said. Then it did not speak for several long minutes. Finally, 'Command is aware. Command did not create the Way. Do you have knowledge regarding

454

human designator individual *Patrikia Vaskayza* or *Patricia Luisa Vasquez*, human duty expediter or of similar rank?'

Korzenowski closed his eyes, then licked his lips, as if savoring some inner taste, and said. 'Yes. I carry part of that individual. Do you have her, did you find her . . . ?'

The voice's tone altered radically; it now sounded female.

'This is command oversight. We have the sexually generated twice-removed progeny of designator individual *Patricia Luisa Vasquez*.'

'I think they mean they have Patricia's granddaughter,' Ry Oyu said. Olmy agreed.

'Where did they find her?' Korzenowski asked. Eyes square and bright, he faced the command individuals. 'Where did you find this woman?'

The female-toned voice answered. 'We have accessed and stored the world where human designator individual *Patricia Luisa Vasquez* traveled from the Way. Sexual progeny twice-removed is stored also.'

'But not Patricia Vasquez herself?'

'Individual *Patricia Luisa Vasquez* is dead.'

'Can we speak to her granddaughter?' Ry Oyu asked.

'This individual has been damaged by our investigations.'

Korzenowski felt a sudden tremor of horror and despair. He struggled to control his anger – and a deeper anger, from the ghost of a grandmother who had never met this granddaughter, never even known of her existence.

'We'd like to speak with her, damaged or not,' Ry Oyu said. 'If that's possible.'

The command individuals wrapped themselves in shifting black cloaks again. Korzenowski turned away, sickened by this strangeness, this incomprehensibility; this casual cruelty. What had happened to the world Patricia found? What sort of world had it been before the Jarts 'stored' it? In what condition was it now? Ry

Oyu touched his shoulder again, and Olmy moved closer, lending support through solidarity.

'This damaged individual is highly valued,' the female voice said. 'Damage was unintentional.'

'Let us speak with her,' Korzenowski said, his voice cracking.

The three command individuals receded on the platform, as if through the turning of some distorting lens. A scene appeared in front of the bubble, the interior of a house of human construction, though not any home Patricia might have found in Los Angeles in the early twenty-first century . . .

Rhita came out of a moiling eternity, where time was not so much lacking as non-linear and randomly arranged; true memories dancing with simulations, unorganised animal thoughts – disembodied hunger, pointless yearning, sexual desire – vying with brief moments of crystal clarity, in which she remembered her situation . . . and rejected it, returning to the turbulent eternity.

In one moment of clarity, she saw herself as a hero, consciously making herself useless to her enemies by eluding them within their own incomprehensible sanctuary. In another, she realised she might never recover from this jumble, that her enemies might keep her in this state forever, and a better definition of Hades she could not think of.

She was worse off than any shade thirsting for blood and wine; what she thirsted for was the sweet liquor of reversed history, second chances, doors to a past not so much *dead* as pickled and preserved, waiting for some inhuman feast of knowledge.

She no longer touched on the presences of Demetrios or Oresias.

Then, at no particular moment, the tempest of chaotic escape calmed. Her thoughts were still jumbled, but what she experienced and felt was crystal clear: she

456

stood in her grandmother's house on Rhodos. Tȳphōn was with her, still human in appearance.

She tried to escape again, back into her chaotic freedom, but suddenly noticed three human forms that did not seem to be Jarts. She did not know them. There was conversation of a sort; again, the voiceless talk of Jarts in a dream, disembodied, hideous.

Still, now and then, in her self-imposed confusion, she managed to listen and not reject what was being said.

There was talk of her grandmother.

Could the two actually *be* humans? People from Gaia . . . or . . . again the storm grabbed her thoughts and whirled them.

Grandmother's Mystery.

A memory: sharp and demanding. The sophē explaining how she had loaned a part of her psyche to a man . . . Magic and mystery in the Way.

Suddenly, she stood not in a simulation of the sophē's house, but on the stones of the temple of Athēnē Lindia – not in simulation, but in memory. The memory was so vivid she could feel the wind in her hair and hear the song of birds darting between the massive cream-colored columns.

This was the memory she always returned to, a memory of peace and solitude, where she withdrew from the welter to think her own thoughts, discover her own self. She had once imagined herself as Athēnē in her various forms: wise woman, bringer of victory, Athēnē of the storms, Athēnē of python and owls; Athēnē helmeted adorner of old coins, goddess of the great and tortured city of the Hellenes. An adolescent girl could be all of those things in the space of an hour, and yet face no danger for her hubris, for Athēnē understood such dreams.

Athēnē understood and forgave failure, even should it cost a world.

Rhita closed her eyes and opened them again. There was talk of *Patrisha* which was, she remembered, the

way her grandmother had sometimes pronounced her
own name.

'She's been stored in a memory matrix, much like city
memory,' Ry Oyu said. 'She's retreated into herself,
following personal pathways. . . . They can't unravel
her. She's defying them in the only way left to her.'

They watched the uncertain, wavering image of
Patricia's granddaughter, placed in the context of the
house-memory like a mannequin within some museum
exhibit, or a zoo animal on display. 'Ser Olmy, how
does your Jart justify this?' Korzenowski asked.

'It's distressed that a valued bit of information should
be damaged,' Olmy said.

'I mean the . . . "packaging" of an entire world.'

'In their own way, they try to serve the Final Mind,'
Ry Oyu said. 'They want to send all they've stored on
to the Final Mind. And that is what they'll do. But we
should be able to stop this woman's suffering. . . . The
time has come for decisions. The Jarts know the Way
will soon cease to exist. They accept me as a representative of descendant command. They're anxious to present the fruits of their labor to the Final Mind. They'll
do anything I say. . . . As far as they're concerned, this
is the time they've been waiting for, the time that jus-
tifies their entire history.

'I can take Patricia's Mystery, and her granddaughter's stored mentality, back to the geometry stacks and
try to give them some peace.'

'Why?' Korzenowski asked, his eyes square and cat-
like now, as if he were suddenly *all* Patricia Vasquez.
'Why just them? Why not restore all the worlds the
Jarts have destroyed and packaged?'

Ry Oyu shook his head. 'Not within my means. I
do what I can do now largely to fulfill promises. Long
ago, when I was merely a gate-opener,' he tapped his
own chest emphatically, 'I failed to teach Patricia Vasquez properly. I make up for that by giving her another

chance, and her granddaughter, as well. Besides, there's the aesthetic satisfaction.'

'Garry Lanier refused special privileges,' Korzenowski said, his face contorted, a mask of contradictory personality and emotion. 'Why should you give us . . . give Patricia Vasquez special consideration?'

Ry Oyu considered this for a moment. 'For my past self,' he said. 'We can't correct all of our failures. But the Engineer has redeemed himself for the creation of the Way . . . Olmy has suffered for his ambition and feelings of self-importance . . . Mirsky has paid some of his own debts. Please allow me to correct one of my own failures.'

The Engineer's face relaxed. 'All right,' he said softly. 'Take them home.'

'And what do you choose? Ser Olmy, freed from the Jart . . . where would you go? Ser Korzenowski, still carrying part of Patricia Vasquez, where would you go?'

'I am incomplete without her,' Korzenowski said. 'I think she will stay with me, and be content, as long as she knows some part of her is going home. I . . . we'd like to journey down the Way and become part of the Final Mind.'

Olmy considered. 'That would be fascinating,' he said, 'but I'm not sure I'm ready. If all the stories we've heard are true, we follow that route wherever we are, however we go.'

'They are true,' Ry Oyu said.

I think of how few beings have actually *known* this,' Olmy said. 'How privileged we are. I know where I'd like to go, still alive, still incarnate.'

'Where is that?'

'Timbl,' he said. 'The Frant homeworld. I have many friends there.'

'There should be enough time to re-open the gates to Timbl,' Ry Oyu said.

'Don't you feel a bit like Santa Claus?' Korzenowski

asked, or perhaps it was Patricia; the Engineer knew very little about the old terrestrial legends.

Ry Oyu smiled and turned toward the image of the room, and the jumbled figure of the woman within. 'I'll convey all this to our hosts. I'm sure they'd be proud to have the creator of the Way go with them to meet descendant command.'

Rhita focused on the wise-looking, smiling gray-haired man, feeling more secure in his presence. He did not have the fierce aspect of a Zeus, but more the calm air of Aserapis with his stalks of corn and Plutonian dogs, his ceremonial bulls and festivals of resurrection.

This calm man spoke of going home.

'I'm going back to Gaia?' she asked, her voice strong in this place without true sound or true voices.

'Now,' Ry Oyu said, 'we perform the most sacred of weddings once again. Patricia, carried within me, will you have the patterns of your own granddaughter as a shell in which to live, until we can search for the home you have lost?'

Olmy saw the image of Rhita shimmer, become solid, fade in color; become solid yet again. Always, the young woman's eyes watched Korzenowski, and Korzenowski watched her.

'Rhita, will you lend part of your self to this shadow of your grandmother, that she may have the strength to go home?'

'Yes,' Rhita said.

She felt a mingling of their waters, like the mingling of seas so clearly visible along the outermost pillars of Hercules, entering into the broad ocean of Atlantis.

She saw a dense weave of realities, Gaias in profusion, and knew that none of them were exactly like her world. But the gray-haired, smiling man who might have been Zeus or Aserapis told her to choose one in which the Jarts never did open a gate, never did invade . . . in which the expedition never happened . . . he suggested no more.

She closed her eyes.

'Time for saying *au revoir*,' the second avatar said. 'I entrust Ser Korzenowski to these command individuals.'

Korzenowski transferred his clavicle to the gate-opener and backed away. The Engineer became separated from Olmy and Ry Oyu as the bubble split in two. Olmy watched him move off and vanish behind another black barrier.

Ry Oyu lifted the clavicle, as if to become used to its weight and capabilities again. 'Ser Olmy, these *are* servants of the Final Mind – however misguided. They tell me they are eager to convey you to your chosen gate. They are preparing to find the gate and open it now. I believe we can trust them. But no one knows how much time has passed there . . .'

'Always an element of risk,' Olmy said.

'Uncertainty keeps us interested,' Ry Oyu commented.

'Thank you.'

'You are quite welcome. They will accept their modified expediter any time you choose to give him up.'

Olmy was not at all reluctant to part with this reminder of his greater failure. Again, he was surrounded by a pale fire. The Jart within him vanished.

For a moment, he savored the wonderful *aloneness*. To be restored, alive and sane, and to return to Timbl . . .

He thought of Tapi and Ram Kikura, of other failures less spectacular and ultimately perhaps more haunting.

'Be content, Ser Olmy,' Ry Oyu said, and clasped his hand, then released it.

Their bubble split in two again.

Ry Oyu turned to the command individuals. 'I would like to travel back to the geometry stacks. I will need

461

to open gates to two worlds in universes very slightly different from our own.'

His bubble moved back through the barriers, into the flaw station, and down to the Way.

He carried Korzenowski's clavicle lightly. The bubble spread open at the bottom and gave him access to the living bronze surface.

The gate-opener closed his eyes and murmured the ritual incantations that prepared his mind, however unnecessary they might be in his present form.

'I lift this clavicle to worlds without number, and bring a new light to the Way, guiding this gate that all may prosper, those who guide and are guided, who create and are created, who light the Way and bask in the light so given . . .'

The surface of the Way grew dark with the approach of the accelerating kink. That would make opening gates even more difficult. There was little time left, perhaps only hours, and he had much work to do, much searching even after the gate was open.

He finished with, 'Behold . . . I open a *new world*.'

He had never before, in all his career as gate-opener, made a double gate. Yet this gate would open onto two precisely chosen worlds.

A circular depression began to form beneath his feet, its edges sparkling. The first world spun beneath him, as seen through the clavicle; here was an alternate to Rhita's Gaia, a spreading branch from the Gaia where Patricia had arrived and made her changes, yet where no Jarts had ever invaded.

The gate-opener could not stretch this gate far back in time. He made a brief attempt, then pulled back and concentrated on locating Rhita Vaskayza. A Rhita who had never known the Jarts, who had never traveled to find the Jart gate . . .

The Way shimmered violently, and he wondered if there would be time.

81

Home

Rhita walked through the grove where Berenikē had told her she would find her father. She saw Rhamōn sitting discouraged among the olive trees, back against a gnarled trunk, head in hands, face twisted with troubles. Having fought some petty battle against the Akademeia's increasingly rebellious board of masters. Needing encouragement.

'Father,' she said, and then stepped back as if slapped. Something fell on her, into her; something at once familiar and very alien. She saw herself, strange and exhausted, tumbling from nowhere, as if into a cup . . . Memories of invasion, destruction and something like death filled her. She closed her eyes and held her hands to her head, wanting to scream. She gasped like a fish with the shock of assimilating so much, feeling for an instant that she must have lost her mind . . .

Stumbled on a root and almost lost her balance.

When she recovered, the memories were cached in deep background, safely isolated for the moment.

'Rhita?' Rhamōn looked up from his reverie. 'Are you all right?'

She made up an excuse to cover her confusion. 'Some illness, I think . . . from Alexandreia.'

She was home for a vacation. Truly home, not in a dream or a nightmare. She grasped her upper arms with both hands. Real flesh, real trees, her real father. All the other memories, visions, hallucinations . . . faces. Nightmares.

'I felt faint. I'm all right now,' she said. 'Perhaps it was Grandmother touching me.'

'We could use her touch,' Rhamōn said, shaking his head.

'Tell me what's happened,' Rhita said. And sat before her father, digging her hand into the dry, caky soil, clenching the dirt between her fingers.

I will sort this out, in time. I promise myself that I will. Visions and dreams and nightmares enough for a dozen lifetimes.

The legacy of the sophē. Who was, even now . . . Where? Doing what?

The Way was coming apart. The flaw station had moved out of sight, retreating in the face of the Engineer's accelerating destruction. Ry Oyu gave up his human form then, hovering as a twist of light and pattern over the double gate, searching across a different Earth, an Earth without the Death, reaching through the geometry stack some decades back in time, finding a specific moment.

Even in his immaterial form, the stresses on the Way began to dissolve him. He shifted character again, hid himself within the geometry of the gate, found the gate itself dissolving, struggled to keep integral long enough to complete this last but not least important of his duties –

Patricia Luisa Vasquez stepped from the car of her fiancé, Paul, clutching a bag of groceries. The air was chill with California's mild brand of winter, and the last light of day spread gray and yellow fingers along the scattered clouds high overhead. She started up the flagstone path to her parents' house –

And dropped the bag onto the lawn, arms thrown wide, neck jerked back, eyes seeming to vibrate in their sockets.

'Patricia!' Paul shouted from the car.

She rolled onto the ground, then straightened again, bucking against the grass, grunting and whining incoherently.

Then she lay back limp, spent.

'Jesus, Jesus,' Paul said, bending over her, hand on

464

her forehead, other hand waving, not knowing what to do.

'Don't let Mother hear you say that,' Patricia whispered, her throat raw.

'I didn't know you were epileptic.'

'I'm not. Help me up.' She tried to gather up the spilled groceries. 'Oh, what a mess . . .'

'What happened?'

She smiled fiercely, sweetly, triumphantly, and then the smile faded and was replaced by puzzlement. 'Don't ask,' she said. 'I'll tell you no lies.'

If I know where I am, she thought, *I know who I am.* Nothing was very clear; she had only vague, scattered recollections of a group of people trying valiantly to help her, and succeeding. But she was home, on the walkway just outside the little bungalow in Long Beach, and that meant she was Patricia Luisa Vasquez, and the worried young man kneeling on the grass beside her was Paul, whom she had mourned for some reason, just as she had mourned . . .

Looking around at the streets, the houses, unburnt, solid, skies clear of smoke and flame. No Apocalypse.

'Mother will be so pleased,' she said in a hoarse croak. 'I think I've just had an epiphany.' She reached up and wrapped her arms around his neck, hugging him so hard he grimaced.

Around his head, she peered up with sharp, cat-like eyes at the stars just beginning to shine overhead.

No Stone in the heavens, she told herself. *Whatever that means.*

82

In the Flaw

With grave misgivings still, Korzenowski submitted to being 'stored.'

The Engineer experienced a time of cold nothingness, and then a wonderful and nightmarish jumbling in the maelstrom of information gathered by the Jarts – the remnants of thousands of worlds, trillions of beings, gathered haphazardly through time, now transmitted along the flaw, to pass into the Final Mind.

The Way gathered in great coils and supercoils, eating itself like some ineffable burning fuse, and died.

The time of avatars on Earth came to an end.

83
Timbl

Olmy felt rather than saw the gate closing above him. Static crackled in the dry air and a low moan spread out from where his feet lightly touched red sand. Then, nothing but the whisper of a thin breeze.

For a moment, he feared that all he would see would be another Jart conquest, a world fanatically packaged and preserved for descendant command. But Timbl had not been invaded by the Jarts. They apparently had not bothered to re-open this particular gate until now, and they would never return.

He stood in the raw, blinding glare of Timbl's sun, smiling broadly. His altered skin could withstand this much ultraviolet; it even felt good to him, familiar. It seemed to make little difference how much time had passed here; Timbl at any time would be home to Olmy.

He was at the top of a hill. Below the hill, to the north, lay a flat paved field, still kept polished white, despite the absence of Hexamon vehicles. This was where the main gate to Timbl had once opened. It had been closed just before the Sundering, when the Hexamon had begun its withdrawal from the Way.

Olmy looked to the west and saw the brilliant blue ocean. A tiny torch-like arc crossed overhead and was intercepted by a purple beam of light. Cometary fragments still fell here, and were still intercepted by Hexamon defenses . . . Not so much time had lapsed, after all.

There were undoubtedly a good many Hexamon citizens on Timbl, refugees after the closing of the gate. He would not lack for human company. But that wasn't what he sought out first. Any visitor to Timbl had to be personally welcomed by a Frant to have official status.

Early in their history, when Timbl had been besieged by devastating comet falls, Frants had evolved to pass along the memories and experiences of every individual to its fellows. The great mass of Frants carried the memories of all individuals, if not in detail, then at least as a kind of inbred history. Any individual Frant, returning home, was quickly absorbed, integrated, debriefed.

By now, every mature Frant on Timbl would know something about Olmy. They would have assimilated the experiences of the Frants he had worked with, decades past; sharing the memories, diffusing the personalities. Every adult Frant would be his friend.

He did not deserve so much, but here it was.

Olmy walked down the hill to the east, toward the ripe, wind-swaying fields of yellow and blue food plants, into the closest village with its characteristic central stupa. He passed young Frants, who stared impassively after him; the young would not yet recognise him. Olmy met his first mature individual just outside a marketplace closed for the midday rest period.

The Frant, tall and gangly, face narrow, eyes protruding to each side, its shoulders cloaked with ceremonial foil, sat on a broad stone bench. It regarded him silently for a moment.

'Greetings, Ser Olmy,' it said. 'What a surprise to see you here.'

'My pleasure,' Olmy said.

EPILOGUE

First, Mirsky told his companion, *we start at the beginning.*

And then? Lanier asked.

We search for points of interest, until we come to the end.

And then?

ACKNOWLEDGEMENTS

Karen Anderson has once again provided invaluable help with my odd languages and history. Her work on the last chapter of *Eon* laid many stones for the foundations of the Oikoumenē in this sequel. Adrienne Martine-Barnes lent much useful research material; I've ignored her direct observations on the architecture of Rhodes, at my peril, to demonstrate deep historical changes on Rhodos. Brian Thomsen, illustrious editor, believed and trusted and took risks, and also worked valiantly to keep my prose from stumbling. Blame these fine folks for nothing; all error in this book is mine, or perhaps my computer's.

A SELECTION OF LEGEND TITLES